Feb 8, 2008

Dear R.

This is the se...
C Hyjealis. I hop...
enjoy them both; and that
they inspire you for a more
peaceful life.

Clemence Hunn

01753 - 648 - 187

ARYA

by

Clemence Massaad Musa

authorHOUSE™

1663 LIBERTY DRIVE, SUITE 200
BLOOMINGTON, INDIANA 47403
(800) 839-8640
WWW.AUTHORHOUSE.COM

First published by AuthorHouse 9/4/2006

ISBN: 1-4184-9214-0 (sc)
ISBN: 1-4184-9213-2 (dj)

Printed in the United States of America
Bloomington, Indiana

This book is printed on acid-free paper.

Cover painting by Marie Mouawad Smith

Acknowledgments

Books are amalgamations of years of accumulated knowledge, experiences and insights. They are made of the culmination of impressions gathered from other people. To those people involved in the making of Arya, I offer sincere thanks. I have to mention a few by name here. His Excellency Fouad El Turk, Dr. Georges El Turk, Henri Zheib, Nadim Shehadi, Terry and Marie Smith, Hadleigh Measham, Henri Forget, Paul Burt, and my family, Indee, Abie, Sandra and my beloved Samir. Lastly, but not least, to all my human family, those who are working diligently at pushing humanity forward into an age of clarity and evolved living, thank you.

For Nicholas and Laurice Massaad, and my beloved Celine.

ONE
WIDOWER MOURNS HIS BRIDE

The balcony sat over an expanse of virgin Mountain forest. The absence of machines afforded nature a chance at keeping its tranquil serenity; as a result of which it blew a pure breeze, in sheer gratitude. What with the ministering toil of scores of spruce and pine needles, the oxygen made people giddy, giddy with the soft air. A personable sky dipped low overhead making clouds of cotton candy jump playfully around the orange sun. The Creator awoke joyous and playful that day to paint away on a canvas of blue, a myriad of amazing shapes in colour. They, the designs, stood as symbols of joy, not pain. The colours He chose shone with much hope, a language onto their own: the pink for hope, the lilac of dreams, and the most startling white of love, His love. That, the widowed youth missed; his heart sat like a boulder inside his chest with sorrow, as his blood boiled with black fumes which rose to his skull to wrench faith away. For what Creator was He that managed this world, the young man thought; that He should pluck an angel of purity and golden soul? The widower wore a black tie, navy trousers, a white shirt, and stared dreamily over the impasse. His bride of six weeks had died a horrible death down there inside the valley killing for good his love for his cherished vista.

The man stared stony-faced at nature's lack of sensitivity. Birds blew overhead singing joyfully their lack of suffering, their good fortune at having to do nothing but sing. Whereas their songs brought a lifting to his heart, he now felt like flying among them to break each and every pretty neck.

"Despair will be mine for evermore," the man thought.

His brain chattered useless negativity steering him astray onto a path of hate and loss where no viable solution could ever be found.

His parents had not planned the murder, but rather executed it on a whim- having known the conditioned state of his mind'- that he would never believe them capable of committing the heinous crime; this had emboldened them to surrender to the venomous hatred they had harboured for the young bride. They were not murderers in the classic sense, never. They were good parents who had worked hard to raise their children. They, however, not thinking of their son's wishes and rights as a separate entity from their own, had believed thoroughly to have acted in his best interest, in the long run. Never having cared for his choice of a wife from the onset, they had tolerated her to please him. Once the city girl had come to stay with them, they grew assured as to the wrongness of his choice. So, when an opportunity presented itself to them, purely by chance, they acted upon it swiftly and with amazing accuracy. The murder proved, not only ingeniously executed, but creative as well as faultless.

That is the state of hate; the function that runs amok to fuel the body with emotions so as to make all thinking obsolete had taken them over. Before any thinking could ever happen, Alaya, their son's bride, was dead with a multitude of bee stings.

"It is just as well," his mother had told her husband. "It is an accident, you know."

It was not an accident at all. The old woman had opened the lid of the beehive, smeared Alaya's body with honey knowing the bees would find the young bride to reclaim their elixir.

Because the motive was based on a pure emotion; family love and unity, and as the parents believed that the bride threatened their nucleus, they felt little if any remorse at having killed her; justifiable homicide to their mind offered prompt relief. After all, it was parents' duty to protect their children, surely.

Their village, ancient and untouched by time, had upheld these "norms" as to mystify time and science. So ingrained had the love for parents and siblings been implanted, that the children grew up believing in its sanctity above all other teachings, above God, their Maker; the fact that ensured ample opportunities for earthly clutches to take hold. They went away to far off universities, to come back and buy still into the fallacy of family love above deity.

The love, Alaya the bride had quickly figured out, was one of deep conditioning designed to enslave rather than free and uphold these children.

They saw the knowledge in her eyes, as she stared their way intently, saw the danger her knowing could hail on their family plans, and vowed to act promptly at cancelling her as a danger.

Although present to the spirit, the bride was nevertheless not self-realized. Had she been conscious of her greater powers, she would have been selflessly meek; allowing the frightened people, ones she would have known to have been lost manifestations of the divine she upheld, to grab her garments had they chosen so as to save the divine frustrated within them. For, it is through such acts of meek surrendering that all God's children were saved from the clutches of desire and earthly bondage. As such, the two camps vying for supremacy over the man Alaya had married, were equally lost to their respective legacy of pure heritage of love, had surrendered to the loss of self-appropriation, so as to suffer and learn; as only through suffering would the fire seer accumulated dross attached to the flesh, that transient manipulator, the abode of loss, the dwelling of evil.

"What!" his mother told her that first week. "You want to take him away from me?"

"Where would I take him?" Alaya had answered baffled.

"You think you could just pluck him away from his mother's love, you think?"

Alaya thought the fear madness, as extreme, unjustifiable fear invariably was. Further, the different members of the family were aware of the horrible scheme set-up in the aim of undermining newcomers. For, she reasoned, why else keep it hidden? It was a definite covert operation. Try as she did to dredge clarifications from her groom, he would not explain the reason his parents attacked his wife, and attacked him when he defended her. The husband figured he could find a way to appease his parents without his wife's ever finding out.

That sort of duplicity made his bride's sense of the honest rebel; for on that score, she felt doubly duped. Also, because honesty stood at the foundation of any alliance, marriage failed from the onset with pre-deliberated schemes. The single most threatening factor of all, however, remained singly the fact that, when her husband hid from her as he schemed with others in secret, he weakened her position, her standing as his valued mate; further weakening their bond.

It made her feel suckered, less intelligent than they were, less valued somehow, and definitely less aware.

Her most endangering aspect became the fact that when his sister stared her way like a mystic trying to reach her inner eye, Alaya read her mind. They told the young bride that she was a fool to believe herself anywhere near important in the great hierarchy concocted to devalue and use all those who entered the family. Also obvious, when the old mother softened her attitude slightly towards the bride, the sister invariably jumped in to salvage the plan of abuse that had just been dropped.

As such, the new bride was afforded not a chance, not even a chink of manoeuvre inside the insurmountable fortress they had steadfastly erected to keep all outsiders out. Her bridegroom inside, she felt beached, all alone out there. He could neither remain with her out there, nor pull her inside. The Amazonians forbade it by the power of a contract written long ago with the agent of the night.

He could abdicate, sure, but at what risk? It was obvious from his actions that bespoke of conditioned control, sustained over long durations that he had been totally enslaved by manipulation. He truly believed in his lack of viability without these people, to never, ever consider his own rights concerning the treatment of his bride inside the laws that fritted her out.

It was truly a mad scheme devised by mad people. That would be the body. That was the second clue. When all their speech revolved around the body's survival, its sustenance, sheltering, paying the bills, sheltering their pooled assets, she received and filed the second clue. They feared for their bodies in a way only mad people could. Their collective energies had so catered to the fear of hunger, have mushroomed into the anchored belief that they were the body that needed to be sheltered at all costs. As Alaya threatened their deepest fears by needing a separate life with her husband, not that she was ever afforded the chance to voice her wishes, more that they simply knew by watching her knowing eyes, she became expandable. She stood like a beacon of light, a lighthouse inside a raging, dark sea during a heist of jewels, screaming to be cancelled.

Although they spoke of love, and how only mothers could love their boys, and how a sister was forever while a wife was for a bit of time, going as far as repeating a saying handed down with their breast milk, "My wife is for now while my sister is forever. If my wife goes, I can surely get me another. Where would I get a sister and my mother is old; unable to get me another?"

These furnished clues the girl analysed to further deduce. Through hearing such archaic sayings, Alaya found the modus of victimization they used: Brainwashing.

An accomplished scholar, she had studied all that was written of important works of literature, in several languages. The fact afforded her tools of in-depth analysis with which she could figure their scheme from the start; not knowing guile, however, made her gifts of uncovering and assimilation work against her.

"They fear me taking him away. Where would I take him to, though?" she reasoned.

Then, she got that one as well.

It was their fear over losing that unity they so enjoyed sharing.

"But," the young bride thought. "They could not possibly have their unity if we are to be afforded a family."

As such, she felt that her recent union with her groom stood as good as doomed by their mad resolve to remain glued together.

As such, all the children were doomed, never having an original idea of their own, as their spouses and mates were doomed; for people to live they had to separate from their families. That oneness the primary family shared could not be extended to mates; it created a havoc of allegiances. That lack of separating was not detachment but deeper respect. Love grown sick affirmed the loss from the onset of all the children. These, thinking themselves normal and beloved by a family that protected them, had not noticed that the very love fashioned a noose around their necks; shackling them in servitude, forever barring the possibility to ever separate to make their own families, conduct their own lives.

"Perfumed bitches do not belong in our region," his mother had continuously screamed for the country to hear.

Alaya had understood that his mother spoke directly about her. The young woman, having never known or seen want, felt abused, never allocating for their point of view. Even if her husband were to explain to his young bride the state of poverty they had endured as a family, she would have neither believed, nor understood the magnitude and dimension of their shared state. Also, as her family knew nothing of the type of life that existed on the other side of the spectrum of social strata, he feared losing her.

It was this second omission of the truth that formed the nuclei of all the troubles to come. Each time his mother ranted about the stupidity of city girls, Alaya of the pure soul jumped.

"Is she speaking of me?" she asked her husband, who laughed delighting in her difference.

He loved the lady. She, his wife, exemplified all his dreams of the perfect woman. Not only was Alaya soft, and sweet of speech, and comportment, but also intelligent and spiritual, tender and giving, and extremely correct. Above all her other attributes, he loved her voice. She had a soft, raspy, low voice, which told volumes of mellow tenderness. He had fallen in love with the voice before having seen the girl.

Alaya understood just then the reason her voice could enthral him; women around his village grew hard with the heavy toil; resentful of husbands who made them work, that they sounded harsh, hoarse and bitter.

"Do not worry about her," he giggled lovingly.

Alaya did worry. Having been raised to please, and offer older people respect, the fact that her mother-in-law hated her so openly pained the young woman. It was as though the girl, who failed at nothing, had finally managed to encounter failure. The bride loved her husband and found the hate from his family unreasonable. They knew of her desire to please them and rallied wickedly about to scheme ways to secure her failure.

She thought long that night vowing to do her best to please the mother whom her husband worshipped beyond deities. She vowed to put forth great efforts to show the woman her love. The older woman, sprightly and funny, a good cook, was pleasing to the eye, and loads of fun. Alaya adored her already, and wanted to be loved by her in return. For how else could they strive as a couple with so much resistance around? The young bride thought.

"Good morning," the bride greeted joyfully that next morning of their stay.

"Good morning to you," the old mother, with the white hair-bun, shrieked mockingly.

Alaya's husband, his sister, and his second brother exploded in mirth at the insider joke.

"They are making fun of me." It pained her to hear her husband join in with the ridiculing.

She bent her form to kiss the woman's cheek, only to receive another jolt of humiliation; the woman moved her face away quickly.

"Go away, go away," she shrieked hurtfully. "Do not ever kiss me. I do not allow my own children to kiss me. What are these stupid city habits? We are peasants who work hard, and have no time for these stupid city habits of yours."

The children ran indoors laughing. Peals of laughter returned muted to the young woman on the terrace out there with the brooding old woman, with the foreboding small, piercing black eyes and the strange expanse of unfamiliar vista.

"What have I ever done to you? Why do you hate me so much?" Alaya needed to know.

"Listen," she shook a fat index in the woman's face. "My son has never, ever, disrespected me in his entire life. He is the most dutiful of the four children I have birthed. He only went against my wishes to marry you. I do not know what you did to him or how you did things. But for that, I shall never forgive you. If you are sixty years old, and have birthed him six sets of twins, I shall do my best to divorce you away from him. That is a solemn oath," she swore.

Alaya heard the words failing to grasp the distinct meanings. What have you done to him? She could not decipher this one. How could she have done anything to him? Like what? So many questions abounded with no answers to them.

"I did not want to marry anyone. Not that I was dying to get married. Your son pursued me for over three and one half years. In all that time, I have never called your home once. What are you talking about? If he wanted to marry me, it is because, obviously, he loved me. There is nothing ominous about that. Is there?"

The best discoveries Alaya stumbled over were accidental. She developed a knack for investigations with these people. With a word such as *love* the old woman lost her temper to sing some demented truth. Casting her in the throes of accidental jealousy where logic is no more able to save her; she sang some decent truth, shed some viable light. As the ultimate success of their plan depended largely on their ability to hide it totally, they felt screwed, clamoured for a remedy; admonishing their mother to exercise caution lest she place her son in the path of dire destruction so as to get the entire village gossiping behind their back.

"Love you? Love you, harlot. What kind of a woman are you to speak of the love of a man regarding you before his mother?" she frothed dangerously at the mouth.

Giggles from within the ancient home with the gables, reverberated distorted, wickedly frightening, to reach Alaya.

"I raised him with the tears of these eyes." She hit her eyes with both palms to shock the soft girl who grew with a woman that spoke sparingly, and even then, as little as possible.

Alaya knew that something had grown askew in the household. All mothers loved their children deeply. Why did this woman think she accomplished a rare feat for which compensations of love and life were due her in return?

"All mothers love their children like that." Alaya committed the cardinal sin.

"Not like this woman, not like this miserable woman, not like this shattered woman." The beating moved from the eyes to the chest, where a cracking of ribs sounded.

Being embarrassed by this crass show and form of communication, one never allowed at her parents' home, Alaya shook with fear. The bride shook indignantly; she shook her way out of the terrace, leaving the cup of coffee untouched on the tray before the maniacal old woman.

As the bride's back turned away from the old woman, as her tiny frame stood wedged inside the ugly green, wrought-iron door, her legs nearly buckling to collapse under her, the older woman screamed.

"Stop, woman, stop; I am not finished speaking to you."

Alaya froze in her place. Her eyes darted nervously vying to spot her husband's form inside the house hoping for a rescue before she fell and dishonoured herself before the hateful woman; she heard another roll of laughter. That came from his sister's mouth.

His sister, two years her senior, seemed to get the most thrills from her abuse. They laughed hysterically to make her demented with anger. Had she been able to move, Alaya would have run to break their necks. She, blissfully, felt a general paralysis brought about by shock, and fear.

"I hate this woman. I am going to break her head one day," the bride vowed solemnly.

Alaya with the mark of God gathered a huge clump of hate just then. Hate, never having featured inside her make-up, came rushing to ally itself with another entity, anger. Together, the two evil attributes culminated to form that hideous entity, fear. Fear of all sorts assailed her once pure being, and as a result, a mass of feathers flew from her back to bring tears of the saddest kind. Alaya with the mark of the universe was initiated into evil to survive. A counter metamorphosis of the most horrendous happened just then.

"May God deal with you promptly," she turned her eyes to the skies to pray.

No sooner had the words left her mouth than a commotion happened indoors, inside the bedrooms where young groom, his older brother, and their sister giggled mercilessly over her plight.

Their fight forgotten, the young bride ran instinctively to find the source of the commotion, only to witness husband's sister sprawled on her back, holding her hip joint, unable to move. Both brothers laboured to pick their sisters up the concrete floor as tears of pain streamed a river down her cheeks.

"What happened?" Alaya asked having never connected her curse with that accident.

"It is so strange," Alaya's husband, whose eyes watered still with so much shared laughter, said. "She was getting off the bed, when she just stumbled and fell."

"It felt like someone pushed me," his sister added confused.

"Nobody pushed you," both her brothers refuted vehemently.

"It felt like a push." She stared their way suspiciously.

Hatred for husband and his family drove deep inside Alaya's spirit at such times.

And so it was that a butterfly, born to make changes inside the earth, had moved camp, making the world suffer a great loss. People such as Alaya took thousands of years, scores of births, and deaths, and a multitude of good deeds to be formed. When the earth loses a human of such quality, it awaits years, upon years, for the forming of another. As such, the universe mourned the loss of its child, deeply.

That day of her corruption, Alaya heard shrieks of pain inside the valley. Coyotes howled backwards their grief, the owls in the pine tree to her right sent forth heart-wrenching sounds of the most disturbing, while the birds stopped singing. A pack of dogs got together in the lane beneath the balcony to howl, and howl. All the occupants came outside to check on the source and reason for the unusual commotion, only to have the donkeys bray, bray, and the horses join in to deafen the region. The neighbours came to the balcony to speak of a strange emergence of snakes from all their hiding places from under the rocks. They spoke of having already killed four snakes in the village that morning alone. Scorpions moved out from inside their hiding places within the cracked rocks of the ancient homes.

Unable to sustain the hatefulness, as ugliness did not feature in her character, the sister and mother beat her at the game to madden her. Alaya's heart was a soft flower of pure white where ugliness could not easily strive. If it were to alight, it died swiftly, for lack of sustenance.

Still, her husband acted as though deaf and blind to the entire drama. It irked Alaya deeply that her husband, supposedly educated at the best university in the capital, found such mirth in her abuse.

Two
A MOST BAFFLING POSITION

The young bride went into her allocated room for a respite and a solitary thought. She remembered reading that some Sufi sage had spoken about peace and the need to cultivate it. His words had eluded her then, only to come back and reclaim her mind. He said that peace was a quality of a strong, powerful spirit that is always fair in its relating to humans and life as one. That, he said, had nothing to do with knowledge or education. That peace comes when the spirit of God asserts itself on the body as to reclaim that which is his right on earth; by offering fairness to all.

Seeing no relief in sight, Alaya decided to find a quick solution to her miserable plight. So, when the solution presented itself, with the murder, she simply surrendered without the slightest resistance.

In an ironic way, to kill her and have to live with her murder stood as her way of punishing them. She wanted them tortured by her death, as surely as they managed to torture her with her life among them, all of them. Yet her having taken punishment in her hands angered the universe. Karma stood as a punishment by the universe that cared nothing for vendettas, but as a gentle learning tool to those who erred. These invariably were erred against, the tormentors tasting thus the bitterness of their actions onto others. This way, everyone secured his own salvation, and was afforded a choice.

The sun shone warmly, tenderly, caressing his hurt face, lapping the unshed tears that rolled down his cheeks, and held him, held him, as he blamed it. The sun, having seen him grow, understood, knew the state of the crude body, and cruder brains, which constantly chattered, shielding them from that truth, the real truth.

She was dead, the bride, and her groom had remained, to pay with grief and confusion, the price of blind attachment and guilt. Mostly, however, the bridegroom felt deep remorse for the way he never took a stand where right was concerned. Those who kill are murderers, the Holy Koran says, and those who watch, without intervention, the violence done onto others are horrid entities, worse than the killers; they are silent murderers.

Gone for good were the days when the man could draw, in times of trouble, solace from this land. It had been eternally marred by the death of his bride. The river, which has flowed since the early times of the region, had seen the tragedy and bubbled mournfully, hiccupping in grief; muted, sorrowful spasms, shattering. That river cried for the loss of humanity, mourned the sleeping state of humans. The rocks, polished into magenta by its caressing and years of patient tenderness, the incessant kissing by the sun, the bathing of the rain, grew shiny, smooth, and so tender, also cried, but nobody could see the tears that ran with the rushing waters. They, the rocks, had also seen the angel die at the hands of hateful, jealous in-laws.

The birds that nestled in the willows, and the pine trees, the shrubs that drank from the river, their branches stretching in constant worship towards the skies and the Maker, the squirrels that jumped from branch to branch munching on hickory nuts, the chickens in their coops, and the foxes that awaited to eat their young, the flowers by the riverbed, and the thyme, the parsley, and the mint, all saw what happened. They could do nothing but cry, cry silently over the comatose, sooty state of Man's machine.

"Come eat," the old woman in black summoned her son.

"I am not hungry," the widower answered.

"You need to eat, son," the white-haired woman cajoled. "Starving yourself will not bring your wife back."

He had changed, somehow, the trusting man: He could not understand the reason he resented his parents. They were good folk, his people, who had been shattered by numerous tragedies. Still, his spirit ached in solitude, longed for detachment.

"I would like to leave this land," he announced that day.

"Why do you need to leave? This is a good land. A man never feels whole except in his homeland," his father said, as he ate.

"I know. I just need to leave. There are better opportunities for me in the west."

"Right, right then, you leave," his father answered, anticipating gold.

"Not before you remarry," his mother laughed jovially. "You marry first, a woman from the village, and leave."

The man looked his mother's way resentfully. Her dismissal of his marriage and his grieving annoyed him.

"I do not want to marry, mother. I have just lost a woman I loved, tragically."

"Well," she painted a frown of the most compassionate between her closed-set eyes, "to be sure, to be sure, but, life goes on, and my grandchildren await their birth." It was always about her needs.

"Life is for the living," his father sermonised.

He left them to their naps, and decided to go for a walk; the big house was closing in on him. As his wife was buried in the cemetery close to where she had died, on the hill facing the willow tree, he decided to take her flowers.

"She loved pink roses," he thought.

The only florist in the region, situated in the next village by the hill that faced their own, sold yellow roses; there were no pink ones; the florist apologised sincerely.

It had barely been a month since his bride's accident and already, his parents spoke of another marriage, he thought, as he walked down to the cemetery with the superb view of the town.

People picked their crops of olives for pickling. Those olives to be pressed for oil needed six additional weeks to mature. Everyone spoke of the bumper crop they had due to that rain the month before, and the man, who walked stooped by grief, wished his wife could have been there to share this joyous season with everyone.

"She is gone, though. That is a fact," he thought.

Having had to tell her giant father of her death proved the most difficult task of his life's duties. He fretted over the possibility her family blaming him for her death. He blamed himself as well. People spoke of planned homicide. Villagers grew antsy when life took a young person, he understood. He had to admit that the events surrounding her untimely death were strange.

He had returned to the house from the meat market to find it empty. Even the servant girl had run away that day. The police looked for her still, a month after his wife's accident.

"The young servant is involved somehow," he believed.

The police could not eliminate her from their list of suspects until they spoke to her; her absence grew more damning by the day.

His father, who had gone with him that day, had left him to ride down in a car from the village, as the husband met a childhood friend, and decided to walk with him.

"I should have ridden back in the car." The man blamed himself for the accident. "I would have saved her."

The spirit of the wife groaned in pain at the innocence of the man she loved beyond death.

"You had no way of knowing," she whispered to him. "She loved you deeply."

"Did she really love me?" the man answered what he assumed was his mind chattering. "It was never clear to me, her love."

"Oh, great, thanks," his wife answered back.

"I don't mean it that way." He felt guilty about doubting her.

13

"How else did you mean it, then?" The dead young woman did not leave all her ego on earth.

"Well, she was a brooder, one never knew for certain."

"You should not have married a spoiled, city girl, knowing how fierce your parents were," she told him.

"That is true. She was probably shocked by the change of life. They do nag, I admit, they are naggers."

"They are more than naggers," the woman corrected.

Now that she was dead, the woman vowed to know the enigma of the intelligent man she married, who, despite the clarity of things, had refused to see his people for what they were.

"Well, they are controlling. These people have known deep poverty. Their children are assets for an easy life in old age." He offered more pacifications and excuses.

"Is that not using their children for their own furthering? Is that love?" The woman countered.

"Not really; more like fear of life. This land is made this way. One could never change these millennia-old traditions," he explained.

"He is such a good man," the woman groaned.

"Oh, well, what do you do? Should we throw them in the bin when they get old?" he asked.

"Of course not; if parents needed help, their children are obliged to care for them. These people are wealthy, though. What would the need for control be in their case?"

"When I went away to university, my father handed me his last three-thousand dollars, broke down and cried. He said, 'Here, take it, and go become a man.'"

"You have since returned them many times over, though. He is wealthier than all his children combined. The need is no longer valid. I think, it is more about loneliness, than security," Alaya told him.

He placed the roses on her fresh grave, bent down to kiss the marble slab where her name had no time to be dirtied by the weather.

"I will always love you, Alaya of the pure heart," he told her.

"I will always love you," the woman answered in his head.

He turned around to see if anyone watched him.

"I feel you here beside me," he said fearfully. "Am I going mad?"

"I am here beside you. The heavens are before your face, all you have to do is plug in the spirit," Alaya told him.

He turned around fearing someone watched him and reported his madness.

The man had heard stories about the cemetery being haunted.

"Of course, it is haunted," the wife said. "Where would we go in the meantime? Did you think the dead go to a dormitory school in some faraway destination in the skies?"

"I have no idea where they go," he thought.

"What lovely roses. Thank you." Alaya loved the roses.

"I am glad you like them," he said aloud.

He turned to leave, having become spooked by the lively grave, when he noticed, a little to his left, another fresh grave. The young man turned, picked a rose from his wife's grave, and carried it slowly to the man with whom he had grown, and placed it gingerly, if quizzically on his tomb.

"What happened to you? Why did you kill yourself?" he asked.

The man of the bulging eyes, having watched his beehive swarm and kill the girl, had hanged himself in his cabin. He had seen the man's parents scale the mountain, had greeted them, and had gone inside to fetch water for the old woman that sweated dangerously. When he handed her the water, he'd noticed the lid off his beehive wide open.

"You are not thinking of being a child in their home, are you?" the man of the honey asked the dead woman beside him.

"Yes. I need to go back; I managed to thwart my destiny, cutting it short," Alaya told the man.

"You are mad, woman. You agree to go back to him?" the man protested.

"I probably am, but challenges entice me. This time, I am not an in-law, however, but their child, so my status will be considerably higher." She delighted at the prospect of torturing them as their child.

"Stop it, Alaya," her master and friend admonished. "You have carried bad habits with you."

Alaya ignored her. Having changed her thought patterns to match the prowess of the people of the dark, she felt corrupt, even in the spirit form.

"You sound excited," bee-man said, sounding resentful.

"I missed him so. Seeing him dejected kills me deeper than death. The wound of the soul is eternal. Killing the flesh is nothing in comparison," the woman informed the honey man who loved her.

"What about you, what are your plans?" she asked.

"Me? I don't know. I am not as lucky as you are. Nobody awaits me down there. Maybe, I should be born to your neighbour Fatima, and become your neighbour, fall in love with you again, and marry you."

"Better study hard, as I tend to like intellectuals," she said.

"Good luck to you, beautiful eyes of the desert," he laughed merrily.

Some ancestral soul nearby, the woman could not place, as during time memorial, and countless births, and rebirths, she had lost count of her relatives, had influence on the young woman's choice of father and husband.

"Your husband mourns his loss. Find an already married person whose wife is already expecting," the entity said.

"I want this man back. It is bad enough the way things are. Not only do I have to watch him love another woman, you begrudge me returning as his daughter?" Alaya proclaimed.

"Do not go arranging his second marriage," that entity admonished, "that should gather bad karma for your next life."

"Bad karma it is." Alaya ignored that cloud.

"What is wrong with her?" her grandfather asked Sycamore.

"She has brought along a great deal of sorrow, and resentment. We need to work on her before she returns back to earth," Sycamore told and Alaya heard.

"What do I do?" Alaya asked her Sycamore.

"Try to soften your heart, Alaya, my love," the tree directed.

"How do I make my heart soft again? It feels like rock inside me," she divulged.

"That is the first step, Alaya: awareness. Be aware of your hardened emotions. The next step is to wish everyone well, pray for their well-being, be happy for their joys, and cry over their woes."

"I am doing just the opposite, master. I am so jealous that they are with him, and I am here alone," the bride admitted.

"Be joyous for them, your enemies, Alaya. Remember the law of karma that states: Whomever you hold in hatred will stick to you like a second skin until you learn to love him?"

"Yes, I do." Alaya did remember.

"Do you want his mother and sister, his brother, to stick to you like glue?"

"No, I surely do not," the bride replied.

"Love them, then," Sycamore directed. "Be rid of them."

"You cannot order love to enter your heart. Bad memories stand in the way of love," she said.

"Then, stop the bad memories," Sycamore told her.

"How do you do that?" Alaya asked.

"By stopping your breathing, or stopping your eyes, or watching your body quake with the hatred, any of these methods works," Sycamore taught.

"I don't have eyes in this form, though," she stated in consternation.

"Sure you do, Alaya, you have your third eye. Make it stop, turn it towards your heart," the tree clarified.

"I don't have that either." The tree forgot the girl was dead.

"The heart is with you; it is in your mind's centre, make it soft," she directed.

"How do I soften my non-existent heart centre?"

"By truly wishing everyone well. That is the way." Then, she was gone.

Wishing everyone well was the very last desire in the bride's designs; she needed to go back to reclaim that which was hers by law, by the creed of the church, and the words of the man of peace who stood witness over the altar, beyond the sacristy during the marriage ceremony. He had said that no person was to break asunder two people he united. She was united to the man who stood besides her looking like love incarnated and purity embodied, selfless giving unconditional. That was whom God in heaven united and blessed, regardless of how his sister sent stabs of hatred in her back, and how loudly his selfish mother wailed during the ceremony, of the hateful looks his brother darted her way laced with poisonous arrows, regardless. Omniscient God, who willed this union, had sanctified their union; the universe had made him her half, she was to stick by him and flourish.

"You see what went wrong, child?" Sycamore checked with her charge.

"No, master, I do not rightly see," Alaya replied testily.

"You tried to appropriate the man as surely as they had done, in the worst manner," she explained.

"How so, was I not entrusted to love the man with all my might? They stood against our love. That was evil, Sycamore. How could you compare my fighting badness to their fighting to disrupt that which God had ordained as our covenant? That is not right," Alaya objected vehemently.

"Seeing it from their perspective, they fought for their son's love also. You were judged the disrupter of love in their view. How is that different?"

"It is different," Alaya said flustered.

"How is it different, Alaya? Is a wife controlling the spirit of love in her husband different from a mother trying to control her son's spirit of love to his wife? Explain it to me," she asked.

"It is different because a son loves his mother unconditionally; it is the stranger that feels the need of her husband's assurances of love. That is the way things differed," she announced pleased with herself.

"It is control. There are to be no gradations in the potency and quality of control. To venture into the realm of directing the harmonizing of any spirit, to change, affect, or redirect its tendencies of innate love to anyone is the body's way of evil intent," Sycamore explained saddened.

"Why have you not explained this law to me while in the body, then? As my master you have also failed," Alaya accused.

"Free will forbade me from giving lengthy explanations."

"My powers were holy. The blessed Virgin came to help me."

"The heavens cry for their wayward beloved," Sycamore engulfed the cloud of her charge with her own tenderly to explain. "You were afforded a great deal of assistance from the higher realms, Alaya, true. You lost everything because you grew arrogant; believing yourself better than people."

"Is that what I did?" Alaya got the picture. "How did that happen?"

"Easily," Sycamore said, "the more powerful the light entity, the more watchful the dark entities that need to destroy it. That is the reason good people need to be that much more diligent at never swaying. Their fall is as steep as the height they have painstakingly scaled, very painful," she concluded.

"How do I keep that focus going?"

"First thing to do is to know that you are nothing, not a thing, but for the grace of God, your Maker," Sycamore explained.

"That is not possible for the body," Alaya proclaimed resentfully.

"That is the ultimate way," she replied.

"Is there no other way?" Alaya needed to find a loophole.

"No other way."

"Oh, that is too tough," Alaya exclaimed annoyed.

It is tough because you are controlling," Sycamore said. "That needs to change."

"Otherwise?" the woman asked.

"You will be tested more severely until, on your knees, you relent, and relinquish all powers of self to the Almighty Creator, Father of all creations, you included, you especially, Alaya," Sycamore said.

THREE
WIDOWER DESPAIRS
MYSTERIOUS DEATH

The widower's cousin braved the steep hill, the dead wife saw. Watching the smile of smug pleasure painted over her mouth made fumes of displeasure rise inside the bride's cloud. She bore great news to the family that day. She told her aunt, as Alaya watched from above her hair, that Alaya's husband's old sweetheart, married and sent to the Americas with her rich husband, had come back, a widower. Giggles of mirth exploded wickedly all their intentions at having been so blessed; not only with killing the city intruder, but their good fortune at getting the man's childhood love back, a widow to boot. What great omens these events hailed. Never, as far as the dead bride could ascertain, had one person among the greedy group given a thought to the widower's feelings in the matter. Why should they? The poor soul in the cloud form concluded, to them, the poor man was never a free entity replete with private thoughts, feelings, or emotions. Considered a property of the household, and parents, the comrade stood in the way of being fixed. The anomaly of his last marriage needed to be righted, and they were about to right it.

There grew a general stirring at the house atop the hill and the village in general. The family agreed that the widower would definitely bite the bait, marry his old sweetheart from the village, inheriting the money left by her dead husband, ensuring happiness reigned all around.

"It is always about money in the planet of doom," Alaya, of the spirit, thought.

The man had told his wife early in their courtship about his first love. Her beloved had said that his first love was the most beautiful girl in the village. Sally was her name. He said that he had willingly offered to fill water in the heavy jugs for anyone who needed it so as to pass by Sally's house near the fountain to get a glimpse and a smile.

"I loved seeing that girl. She had the most amazing purple eyes," he'd said.

"Go on," she said, feigning lack of interest, as her insides tore to shreds.

"Well, we were children, mind you; she was fifteen, and I fourteen. One cursed day, my friends decided to go shooting in the mountains. We shot wild game and cooked on wood fires, and generally thrilled in the fact that we were grown up, and free. We came back to a great fanfare in the village. That was years ago. Nothing ever happened in this village. People, who milled about the square, threw anxious looks my way, then, my best mate asked about the great uproar. Sally had gotten engaged, and her wedding had just taken place, an hour earlier at the Greek Orthodox Church, by the spring, they'd said."

"It is strange about people's lives. How extreme joy always trails behind it extreme sadness," she'd said.

"Could you stop interrupting me? I am trying to share something deep, divine here," he snapped.

"Yes, sorry. Go on, then." Alaya chattered always, when anxious.

"Well, I ran towards the house, halfway through the ascent, my friend huffing behind me, we encountered the motorcade. Sally, just fifteen, sat in a white Cadillac, with an old man the age of her father." He sounded pained.

"What did you do?" Alaya had asked.

"I stared her down pitifully, impotently, lost as to a course of action. I thought of stopping them to ask her what she thought she was doing, of throwing my body under the wheels of the car that took her away. I did nothing of the sort; instead, I stared her down like a demented bull."

"What did she do?"

"She turned her face away towards the old man she'd married."

"What happened?"

"Could you not imagine the rest?"

"Yes. Great despair, and walks in the wood, and visits to her house."

"Correct."

"Honestly now; did you expect her to wait for you to finish high school, your freshman year and five years of university abroad as she sits in this village?"

"I know that now," he said.

"So, you marry me on the rebound?"

"No. I thank her now for having gotten married."

"Sure, sour grapes," she said.

"I swear on your life," he vowed.

So, as the woman who professed to be born again, ambled with heavy calves up the hill, the dead wife waited, knowing the evil plan. Had he lied to her then, if he were to even consider flirting with this old girlfriend, Alaya thought, so soon after her death, she was not coming back as his child, period.

"People in spirits have hatred?" she wondered.

"Not hatred," her grandfather replied, "attachments. Love does not change up here. We carry it through. We carry everything. If you were to die angry, then you remained angry. It is very simple, really."

Disgusted with a corroding feeling that gnawed at her insides, the woman of the spirit decided to amble down to check on her parents. It would be a couple of days she knew, before they would get together with the widow in the village.

"You know," she told no one in particular and everyone in existence that cared to hear, "before these people, prior to my fall in hatred, I never knew this horrible feeling called jealousy."

"This is grace. Not knowing hate is grace," Sycamore said.

"They changed me. The people of the dark managed to ruin me," Alaya stated mournful.

"No Alaya, you had the control inside you; that changed you," her granddad corrected.

Alaya cried dry spasms of the most shattering; as soulful crying shakes the moon, and causes huge storms on earth, such is the depth of its nature. A storm system raised the Mediterranean Sea level to wreck havoc with the region. She cried for the loss of wisdom, and the obnoxious state of the body that had stealthily managed to corrupt her.

"So they were merely the igniting spark," she thought.

"Stop it, Alaya. Stop it. There is nothing you could do now. Go back, go back and learn to control the beastly nature within you. Instead of teaching them goodness, you managed to learn hatred," her Sycamore directed.

"It is so difficult to be good in the face of evil in the body. It, the body, wants revenge. It is very difficult," honey-man interjected.

"Oh just shut up," Alaya shrieked red. "If it were not for your stupid bees, none of this would have taken place."

"These two are wild," Alaya's grandfather complained. "Do something Sycamore, about your charge."

Watching the scenes unfold in the village by the hill so disturbed the dead bride that she finally dropped on her father's house. Her parents lived in the new house still, and had suffered father's heart attack after her death. He, father, polished his Colt 27, his eyes crossed in deep anger. Father never liked mysteries; he needed conclusive evidence. The children ate their afternoon tea, as they worked different school assignments in various rooms of the house. Alaya of the dead fluttered lovingly over the baldhead, kissing, kissing, the baldness, as an ache, a gash in her entity seared with the pain of longing to touch the eyes, truly touch his beloved eyes.

"Hey, Dad," Alaya greeted the giant with the heart of the sun. "How are you, my love?"

"Hey, babe," he said, and wiped a hot tear that felt salty.

"I miss you, Daddy," she whispered inside his spirit.

"I miss you, Alaya of the desert eyes. I miss your spirit, your laughter, your naughtiness and your life. I should have never married you off. You should have gone to university, stayed until my old age, became a burden."

"No, no no, listen Pappy, listen to me."

The man stopped moving, and looked behind him seriously.

"Who is there?"

"It is I, Father, Alaya." Having had to scream exhausted the girl.

"What do you mean it was not like that?" he asked.

"Daddy, listen to me. Life and death are not separate occurrences, but one. It is like a line of continuity, we come and go, come to go, come and go. Do you understand?"

"No. That is not true. My daughter is gone."

Alaya laughed at the futility of helping these people with the bodies; they could not be helped as they had set for themselves beliefs cast in iron and concrete slab. Frustrations of the girl's entire life gathered to make her cloud navy blue in colour.

"No listen Dad," she begged, but he cried.

Alaya went to check on her mother.

She cooked with an elderly lady. They made a feast for Sunday. They cooked the Kibbe; a difficult dish which took hours to prepare, and broke backs.

"Good," Alaya thought, mother has her cooking, and feeding the many children to distract her from death in general.

"Good for mother," Alaya admired her then.

She visited each of her siblings, talked to her sisters in their heart; finding them grieving over her fate.

Jezebel slept over her book. Alaya laughed at the incongruity of the matter; how they could be so alike and yet so different from one another.

"I love you, Jeez," Alaya said.

Groggy with sleep, her eyes reddened by disrupted slumber, Jezebel awoke dazed to look over her bed.

"Mom," she ran out shrieking. "She is on the wall in my room."

Jezebel slept in her parents' bed trying to still her sister's voice in her head. She, the dead woman, had a plan, and needed to talk to her sister.

"How is school?" she came into her dream where defences were weak, to ask.

"Fine, Alaya, fine," she said.

"My husband is free, and he might want to ask you to marry him. Accept, darling, accept, for me. Accept him if you loved me. I carry a huge burden of having abandoned him. Besides, he would love you, as you are more like me than you think. You are like me minus the huge mental centre. He needs that now."

"Oh! Okay," Jezebel agreed.

"Good," Alaya thought. "The bug is planted."

"What do you think you are doing?" her master asked, irritated.

"If they could plan his life so can I, dear Sycamore. It is only fair. Fair is good, no?"

"How did you get so lost, child? Evil must work speedily."

"It must. It is more fun," Alaya sounded flippant.

"Stop it. What you do is controlling. And to answer your earlier question, no, fair is not good when it plays alongside evil."

"What is good then?" Alaya asked, rattled by the Cosmic Laws.

"Good is good. Nothing else is good. Explaining bad away is never good, Alaya."

"Listen master darling. I have been brutally killed by these people who arrange a swift wedding for my husband. Do you expect me to remain good?"

"Yes," Sycamore replied quickly.

"I can't. It is simply impossible." Alaya wanted to cry but no tears were allowed in that form of gas she inhabited.

"Well then, learn." Sycamore grew angrier.

"What do I need to learn?" Alaya was starting to hate the people in that foggy realm.

"Learn that good stands on its own volition. It is never connected to other people's behaviour. Your good is that which concerns you, nobody else."

"Why is that? So, they think me stupid?"

"It does not matter what people think, child. They are not up here paying for the results of your reactions to their bad deeds, are they?"

"No," Alaya responded weakly.

"They are down there enjoying the rest of their natural lives, while you are dead and confused about a way to proceed, paying the price of bad reactions."

"I am paying for the reaction to their actions," Alaya answered confused with the unfair law.

"Here you go," Sycamore said with finality.

"That is most unfair," Alaya proclaimed self-righteously.

"These are the laws Alaya," the master declared.

"They are not fair laws," the bride objected.

"They are our universal laws. They make sense to a much higher intelligence than you could grasp; either you follow them, or you perish by disobeying them."

"Is it fair for them to have gotten out free of blame?" the bride asked.

"Everyone pays the price of their sins, everyone," the Sycamore announced.

FOUR
PERFECT MURDER BEYOND SOLVING

Feeling hurt and dejected, with even her mild master showing lack of solidarity with her as a charge, and a dead charge at that, the bride decided to rebel and resume her earlier escapades.

"What do you think you are doing?" Some spirit marvelled at the woman's loss.

"I am going to fix things," she responded angrily.

"That also is control. What makes you think you are better than they are then?"

She ignored everyone. Hate grew to engulf her being forbidding higher thought. Negativity of thought cancelled her former goodness, making the woman's heart hard, harder than stone.

"If you thought them bad," Sycamore screamed at her charge's blindness of state, "why convince your sister to join them and suffer your former plight? That is so wicked, Alaya."

The charge, maddened by fears of landing anew at the frightful house and needing to secure one loving entity in her future, ignored all. She marched adamantly towards a future she alone needed to plan.

At the big house by the river near where the woman died, she found her husband's sister getting herself ready for the day.

Leaving her house in such a mess, the daughter of the old woman who prophesied cleanliness like a religion, was a closet dirt-bag. Nothing was made, not a thing. The woman gathered her skirt around her ankles quickly to visit her self-appointed missionary cousin above. In reality, the entire world stood above these people, only the river remained below their vision.

She clamoured quickly, her mind chattering, chattering, and making plans. She heard her brother's sweetheart had returned to the village after years of absence, following the widow's husband's death of leukaemia overseas.

"He will go for it," she had told her cousin over the phone. "He married his wife on the rebound."

The cloud that was Alaya hurt deeper than jealousy.

The cousin opened her door and shrieked in delight.

They sat down to drink coffee on the balcony by the airless kitchen, overlooking the cemetery, and the lower hills below.

"Did you see her?" the cousin asked.

"No. I plan to pay them a visit today. They say she looks old, and worn out," his sister replied.

"What do you expect when you marry for money at fourteen?"

"She was actually seventeen, because my brother was fifteen," sister dearest replied.

"What does that make her, thirty-two, three?" her cousin needed to figure out.

"Something like thirty-seven," the sister replied, suddenly unsure.

"Would she be able to bear him children?"

"She has four grown children. I honestly would not know. It all depended on her state of health, would it not?" his sister said.

"How could we possibly save him, Granddad?" Alaya ran back to ask.

"You could never save him from these people, Alaya, never. Go down there, and make him happy."

"But, Granddad, Why should I have to go back down, otherwise?"

"Sycamore, I had initially thought my destiny involved saving the sweet angel I married."

"What do you mean?" Sycamore grew confused in the ether. "Save him from what?"

"Save him from his people who want him perished, needing to control him, usurp his freedom of choice, of course," Alaya proclaimed vehemently.

"Now now, child, that is not true, surely; it is a matter of perspective," her grandfather corrected. "Besides, he knows, he knows about the women. The man is not stupid. He does not need you to introduce his people to him. He does not want you to know, fair and simple. So as such, give up the crusade. Go down for your own salvation to learn compassion in the face of adversity; as it is easy to be compassionate around goodness and transparent people, come back triumphant and free."

"Is this the way it goes?" Alaya fumed with anger.

"Yes Alaya, that is precisely the way it goes," her grandfather replied.

"Fine, then. Just do not plan on my being nice to this aunt of mine, his sister, I mean," she announced for good measure.

"She is your most difficult challenge. If you cannot conquer your deep hatred of her, she will have finally won, Alaya. Be very cautious with this woman. The way you feel about her could retard your growth, cancel your development, return you to the realm of pain and suffering numerous times," he said.

"No. Listen, all of you. I draw the line of compassion around this one. There is no way."

"Then do not go to these people," the old man ordained.

"She makes me feel stupid," Alaya complained. "I hate her."

"Like she insults your intelligence?" some man interjected.

"Precisely," she admitted.

"This horrendous tragedy has been about mutual control?" Sycamore asked.

"Yes." Alaya felt sheepish before her master.

"Oh my, Alaya, when did you care for earthly games?" Sycamore inquired. "Enough, to die for it, and leave this beautiful man to suffer like that?"

"Since she started wanting to play. Ever since she started fighting me and making plans to destroy me. I decided that she would get nothing, not one thing from him or me."

"Damnation always ends up being about control, does it not?"

"And money," Grandpa added.

"It is more than that," Alaya refuted hotly.

"It is about that; always about money. That is the curse of the world. Your ego grew beyond redemption." Sycamore mourned her charge's loss of grace.

"Sycamore, you know that is not true." Alaya needed an ally.

"It did not use to be true, dear child. The Chrysalis I knew understood the song of the birds as a child to cry the death of Camomile on the fence in the fall. Whatever happened to change my child butterfly?" Sycamore bemoaned.

"The wicked woman could always die young, and spare us all," Alaya thought.

The clouds around the woman shrank in consternation and objection to her thoughts.

"You know. I am sorry. Looks as though my wings are to remain forever clipped," Alaya apologised.

"Once a butterfly dies, there is no way to return her to her former state of purity for a second chance," all their beings declared. "She has to undergo usual birth, and metamorphosis."

Then, Alaya understood the need to be reborn, suffer all the stages of her metamorphosis. That would be her just punishment.

"We were raised on pride. My father thought pride a good trait to instil inside us, drilling holes inside our tender shoots to plant it within.

Everything about that region pivoted about the pride to be part of this land. He sang the songs: We are your people, O Zhil. We die to never still. Our river distributes strength and honour to all. Basil smiles our way and the brave fears our sway. The state is mighty, the day the swords appear; as stabbing for us a feast and we proclaim: May God add onto us; the swords get weary but our hands never get weary. Oh, you whose house sits by the timeless river, to have shared infinite glories together, we were gone to war an entire month, to return your way, check on you. I knock on your front door the night, my sword dripping woes. 'Who might you be?' you say. 'The tamer of wild mare is me,' I say. She exclaims assured of the identity, 'my brother, in my bosom slither.' "

"What does it mean?" Sycamore asked.

Alaya's grandfather chuckled knowingly. He shook his head from side to side distressed.

"Zahle, Zahle, our Zahle, the drinking of Arak, our custom, Al Birdawni our waters. It gives pleasure and cools, O, abode of peace, in your lion's den we sleep. In the face of defeat, the Lord our witness, we will never slumber. Our death happens in the eye of the barrel," Grandfather sang.

"What is that Zahle?" the lady that spoke of pride asked.

"It is a legendary town in the Bekaa valley in the region of our birth. Its people are gentleman farmers, singers, poets, and brave fighters. This is the legacy that taught us national pride." Alaya explained the source.

"Pride is not a bad thing. It becomes bad when a person believes himself the beholder; better than others," Sycamore explained.

"That is what happened in my case, surely." Alaya could see where things went wrong. "How does one shelter from such an easy pitfall?"

"By keeping all praises unto God we are safe as humans."

"I understand what went wrong." Alaya felt the depth of despair.

"You need to let him go," Sycamore dictated.

"I cannot. How do I separate from that which has become my entity?" she cried bitterly.

"Pray," all the souls in that realm shrieked towards her form, "pray for purity of heart. The love you feel for him is sick. That is not love. It is self-absorption. That is ownership. He does not own himself, how do you suggest you can own that which does not belong to itself? Everyone belongs to God. He alone is the sole owner and dispatcher of all created things. Pray for forgiveness. Pray for meek return to him that which you believed was your property. Of all things created, the grace of the Beloved Creator lent us for our pleasure: our parents, siblings, lands, country, children through all times, graces, gifts, everything. Return to the Lord what belongs to the Lord alone. Ask His forgiveness for the theft. Pray for all His children created on His earth," they said.

"O Lord, I pray for all injuries propagated by my person while in the body. How numerous they were, and how blind to them I was in that state of utter dream. Now that I see what damage my words had done, my deeds had created, I shrink in utter embarrassment. The absence of Your light depresses my energies, and how I long to catch a glimpse of Your great love. I am not worthy, my Lord. I will ask for Your forgiveness for as long as it takes, now that I understand who I am, that time is not, that space is solely the illusion made by the body for its own appeasement. My praying will eventually straighten that which was made crooked by mundane influences on that planet of material existence. It will take time, my Lord, but please allow me the opportunity to reverse what has become totally corrupted. I will endeavour to abide by all Your beloved laws so as to never suffer the dejection I feel with Your absence."

FIVE
FAMILY PLANS ANOTHER WEDDING

The cousin duo decided to walk up the steep hill to pay a visit to the woman who had come back to the village, thirty years after her marriage. Watching them, Alaya felt a deep aversion to the pair waddling up. That hill had frightened Alaya to death when among them; such was the state of her thumping heart upon braving its sharp angle.

"We could go and have lunch at my mother's house afterwards," sister panted inviting her cousin.

"Yes," the cousin accepted, delirious with the joy of stirring trouble.

It was washday at the big house with the green shutters. An old woman was hired to replace the urchin that had run away. Ritualistic, repetitive orders, and replies had never changed.

"What robots," Alaya thought.

"Stop your negative thinking," her grandfather snapped.

"I know, Grandfather, I know. Their negative auras have followed me here," she blamed them.

"Stop blaming other people for your failings. You give people too much power by allocating blame like that."

"Yes, Granddad," Alaya promised to shed awareness on her own failings.

When she started to think positive thoughts about these sentient beings' suffering and release from pain and confusion, a wall rose inside her cloud, thick and tall, and hatefully forbidding. The hate had grown into a thick, brick wall.

"I can't pray for them. How do I pray for the people who have killed me?" she groaned resentfully.

"Exactly the way Jesus prayed for those who killed him; by knowing that they do not understand," he directed. "It starts by going into the motions. Pray as though you mean it, then soon, you will mean it."

"I do not want them to be released of pain and suffering, though. I feel hypocritical."

"No. It is magnanimous. Jesus of the cross prayed for the people who crucified him."

"He is the great Man of Peace. I am Alaya of the soul. There is a huge difference."

"Pray, Alaya, pray for them. Pray for the universe is one, and people are really all one. If you were raised with their parents, under the same conditions, you would be exactly like them."

When next she looked, she saw the group of women, her husband's mother and his sister, his cousin and his former beloved. They sat facing the valley, sipping at the black coffee, contentedly.

Looking at the woman now, for the first time, created deep sorrow within Alaya; for the widow, who related nothing to the idea and myth the family had built about her in the aim to torture the new bride they hated, was nothing like the bride was made to believe.

"She is actually extremely sweet and proper." Alaya liked the woman.

Gentle in tone if browbeaten by life and disappointment, she spoke about the gentleness of the man she had married without knowing, and his kindness as a husband and father, genuinely.

"Did you ever grow to love him?" the cousin grilled her.

"Of course I loved him. Why would I not love the man? He'd become my life. He was extremely loveable. If I did not love him, I would not have had children, four of them, with him, would I now?" Sally the widow, explained.

"Good for you," Alaya cheered the woman.

She did look battered by life.

"My husband would never go for this. She looks sixty-five if a day," Alaya thought.

Her eyes, the legendary purple eyes, Alaya had so heard about, were truly a shade of purple, large, soft, and soulful. She really liked the woman. Liking her had surprised Alaya, for some reason.

"You are supposed to love everyone beyond self-love." Sycamore had become annoying in this new realm.

"Sycamore, now that is absolute bull. Excuse the earthly expression."

Sycamore nearly choked herself to death laughing, but she did not care much for she knew about rebirth, and that death was an illusion created by the mind that so feared for its own continuity.

"You are too much." Peels of laughter shook the earth, creating a storm in Nicaragua. "There was a time when you loved those who hurt you, as I remember vividly. That, Alaya, was your mark of greatness. You were the child of love, and compassion, Christ-like and magnanimous."

"Yes. And do you remember that my father beat me up each time I returned home bloody?"

"Yes, I do," Sycamore agreed.

"Until one day, I straddled the boy and broke his two front teeth with a rock, went home to great jubilations by all."

"Yes. I remember." Sycamore felt sadness over parents teaching children violence.

"I learned that lesson then. I learnt that compassion did not help you survive in their world. It got you killed. The very reason I am in this realm at twenty. That is something to consider, dear Syca. Don't you think?"

"In the long run, however, opting to get even has made you lose your powers, your greatness."

"No. I want to go back to these very people to teach them a lesson," Alaya vowed.

"You intend to go back as their grandchild to make them suffer and avenge your death?" Sycamore knew her charge too well.

Alaya grew confused. She, in reality, was not very sure as to the exact reasons for her wanting to return to them.

"I do not know. I know that I miss him. That is all I know, Sycamore."

"Do not change the subject." Her granddad despaired over finding a way to correct the girl's bad habits. Sycamore is attempting to teach you that which is divine wisdom."

"Sorry, Granddad," Alaya said, fearing to think as he read her mind.

"You do not have a mind, Alaya, up here." He read it anyway.

"Fine, Granddad, whatever I have up here feels like a mind."

"You must learn to think differently, more silently, less impulsively, with equanimity," he said.

"Yes, thank you, Grandfather. Are you not planning on leaving soon yourself?"

He smiled. When Grandfather smiled, Alaya thought, the sun shone in England. It is brief, but so noted, so appreciated, so brilliant, so difficult to explain.

She switched back to the women at the morning coffee in the mountain village. They were dispersing. The two cousins remained.

"Well, we hope you pay us a visit soon," scheming sister invited.

She put on smiles, frowns, and nothing was ever genuine with this creature.

"Could you possibly hold the psychoanalysis and leave the woman alone?" her grandfather ordered.

"Why don't you visit Mother? All your sons are over our house today for a feast of Kibbe," Alaya told him.

He giggled happily.

"See, Grandpa? Attachments never cease. We do love them so." Tears of the desolate kind poured over mother's conservatory.

"Yes," Sycamore needed to finish her lecture.

"Wait," Alaya asked. "Please darling, Syca, let me hear what they say."

"Of course, I heard he has lost his bride, just a month ago. How tragic," Sally said genuinely touched. "I will go see them this afternoon. Pity, really. I heard she was a beauty."

"Here you go," Alaya cheered. "Oh God, my vanity will banish me to suffer through many lifetimes."

"Fine, now you can continue, Syca. I am sorry."

"No problem. Where is the young man with the eyes?" Sycamore suddenly realised he'd been missing.

"He jumped into our birthing neighbour. She just had a boy. He is so sweet," Alaya told her.

"Oh, bless him with silence," Sycamore prayed.

"So? You were saying about loving people and wanting their happiness more than your own; please try to explain how this works," Alaya sounded cynical.

"The bad habits you have accumulated, Alaya," Sycamore mourned her charge. "They are serious charges that carry alongside them scores of debts for they involve the suffering of many lives. That is not acceptable."

"Sorry. I shall endeavour to wrench them by their roots, somehow."

"Yes, that you need to work on doing with focused concentration."

"I see. What are you talking about? Have you gone daft up here?" Alaya giggled.

"No, you do not see, and no, I have not gone daft," Sycamore replied.

"So, I pray for their health and happiness, as they kill me, and where does it get me?"

"It is not like that. If each person prayed for all people, then they would pray for you too. Good will and great karma ensues, and happiness, for all sentient beings, would reign on earth."

"You are delirious, Syca, baby. How old are you now?" Alaya grew assured.

They laughed together as they had always done, happy, happy to feel the roots of gentleness returning to the girl of the heart.

"I love you, Alaya," Sycamore told her charge. "It was not easy, I know."

"I love you, dear Mother."

"You do have an ego problem, dear, natural with such a huge intellect; work on that and the ether is yours eternally," Sycamore promised.

"I will," the woman, whose centre contracted in pain, promised.

She turned her head to watch the scene unfolding to her vision, on that other line, the line of the world.

She feared knowing, seeing his love to the woman of his childhood who left him in true disdain to the pain she knew he would undoubtedly feel, as she followed her dreams of gold in the far-away land.

"If he still loves her," the bride thought, "I shall simply die."

"You are dead, Alaya, get used to it," the sun said, laughing.

His colour rose ominously, and his palms sweated, as his voice sounded as shrill as that of his father's, sitting on the ugly green plastic rope rocker by the side of the river smiling at his fortune secretly; the one he got from conspiring to kill her, the wife of his son.

"Is that not evil?" she asked a star that happened by.

"Evil," the star shone its agreement.

"Should evil not be punished, then?" she asked excited.

"No. Punishment is evil. Praying for evil to become good, working at changing evil is virtue." The star shot away from her cloud.

"I cannot," she mourned. "Not yet, not yet."

The husband spoke with a hypertensive tone of anxiety. Alaya jumped into his heart to find out whether the bodily change was due to love or some other reason.

"He loves her. He has never loved me. I was just a rebound. His sister was right." She felt totally suckered.

She turned her face away from the scene resentfully, only to return and stare, stare at his demeanour.

The widow, knowing the two levels of discourse that took place among the people who sat around the balcony witnessing that reunion, acted calm.

"That woman has self-control." Alaya envied that.

The man reminisced about their shared childhood, time in school; dishing out the names of people who were no longer in the village. The widow answered his questions innocently, and calmly.

"I am sorry about your loss," she finally said.

"Thank you. I am sorry about your husband's death," he responded in kind.

Silence, an uncomfortable silence, reigned over the balcony, as each person roamed respective miseries of personal loss. Alaya waited to hear the end of this tragic comedy of humans, who spoke what they knew were lies, and hid that which society told them was hurtful truth.

Nothing happened. Village people could sit in silence if they chose. That was accepted, even encouraged by everyone. They kept certain purity stolen from the time spent tilling the earth.

"Coffee?" shrieked his mother, too uncomfortable inside the sad, deep silence.

"No, thank you. We have just had some," answered the widow. "Please, sit down. Do not worry about keeping us entertained."

"Oh no, you are like a daughter to me. I loved you dearly as a child, and befriended your mother like a sister for years. May God rest her soul."

"Oh, brother, give me a break." Alaya abhorred lies.

"Watch in silence; no judging, no judging. If you were so perfect, you would not be in the holding station," Alaya's grandfather commanded.

"Don't you have anything else to do, Granddad but snoop on me? Like, grind some coffee, water the mint or something?" Alaya hated the lack of privacy.

"I just had a hysterectomy," the widow confided then.

Alaya had missed the preceding statement that led to this crude revelation, as she argued with her grandfather.

"See? You made me miss this," she complained.

"Your busy body sister-in-law asked her the reason she stopped having children." Granddad filled in the gap.

"Oh! Good," Alaya said.

"She won't do," sister stared the statement into her cousin's eyes.

The cousin nodded signalling her agreement.

Having lost interest in the widow, the pair stood up, made their excuses and left.

Alaya hovered over her husband's head stupidly.

"Stop it," she told him.

He turned towards her cloud in shocked recognition.

"I miss her deeply. She was so interesting, and funny," he said just then.

"Here you go," Alaya cheered her man along.

"I will go visit her parents tomorrow," he announced to jerk his mother's neck painfully back. "I need to see them before leaving this country."

"You need to get married," the widow suggested, "before you leave to final immigration."

"Who said it is final?" His mother feared the final loss of control.

"Once they leave and stay, they can never live here again," the widow answered wisely.

"I will not think of marriage for at least two years, if ever," he informed them.

"That is my boy." Alaya encouraged his resolve.

"Does she have a sister?" the widow asked.

Alaya grew to admire the woman's keen intuition.

"That is the reason he loved her," Alaya concluded.

"Yes, she does. She has a younger sister who looks exactly like her," he told her.

His eyes took on a dreamy look, his mother noted. She saw the return of her nightmare and shrieked hysterically.

"Why, her sister, dear friend? Why are there no more women left but these people? Why, right here in this village we raise the best women. I never understood his fascination with these people. They were very bad people. I never really cared for any of them. Chanel this, and perfume that, and they are good for nothing with their French speaking, and thinking themselves better than us simple folk. They were devout Catholics to boot. And that father of theirs! He acts as though his daughters are regular princesses; he sent them off to the best schools, and dressed them as though they were royalty. Give me a break. I would rather have a peasant any day."

"It is my in-laws you speak badly about, mother," Alaya's husband rose to defend.

The sweet widow rounded her eyes frightfully as though catching a freakish thought, which she believed wholeheartedly. Her energies egged to leave as fast as possible.

The widow got up to leave, and husband decided to go for a walk.

"Where are you going?" his father asked. "I will walk with you."

"No. I would like to walk down to the willow tree by the river alone," he said.

"Suit yourself, then." He turned back to the ugly green rocker to stare at the river, the cemetery, counting the money he had managed to weasel from everyone.

"Leeching sod," Alaya caught herself thinking.

Not one spirit noticed her ugly thought.

"If only you knew how to spend the money you so adore accumulating," she shrieked hoping he would hear.

"You know," the old man's wife announced, in a rare discourse with her husband, whom she generally totally ignored, "I think these people have written something dire for your son. I have heard about these voodoo customs in the Caribbean islands. If you were to write for a man to become eternally enthralled by you, it works. He could never leave you, regardless."

"Give it up, woman," he commanded. "Otherwise, so help me God."

"I hate the way he addresses her so generically, disdainfully," Alaya thought.

"If he married her sister, I would kill myself," she announced.

"That would be a miracle and about time, also. I shall encourage him then," he spat disdainfully.

"Bastard," she spat back.

He took off after her tiny, square form at a run, grabbed her arm and twisted it roughly.

Alaya enjoyed watching them fight. The woman had always suspected his sadistic, latent violent nature, and the fact that he abused her. She revelled at the realisation that her doubts were founded in reality.

"Let go, you stupid man. I hate you. I have always hated you," she shrieked.

"I know. I know you have. You made it plain to see, haven't you?"

He slapped her hard on the face and walked out of the house from the back door.

She started cussing, raving and ranting in his back.

Alaya felt surprising sympathy for the woman.

She would never like this man, regardless. Hate must reside inside her for this human.

She vowed to remember, for as he would become her grandfather in the next life, she needed to know his true nature, as to be saved by the knowledge of the hurtful human who disdained women.

The woman of the soul watched the old man amble like a goat down the hill, buy a Coca Cola, drink it standing before the shop, throw it inside a bin; his neatness his only virtue, and return to the house in time for lunch.

The wife finalised the noon meal. Alaya knew that the smells would be appetising, as her mother-in-law's ability in cooking transcended all her other qualities. She was an amazing homemaker as well as a skilled seamstress. The okra stew looked scrumptious in a red sauce of tomatoes, coriander, garlic, and spices, lamb meat shank. The pilaf boiled in a saucepan nearby, as the woman busied herself with cooking, so as to act as though she did not hear the mountain goat return.

The servant they had hired from the village snipped herbs from the garden in the back courtyard for the salad she prepared.

They all awaited the arrival of sister and her cousin to serve.

"Has he returned?" he asked as though nothing had transpired.

The wife ignored him.

"I am talking to you, blasted," he raved.

She ignored his second outburst as though she stood deaf to any sounds.

"Your killing his wife has made your son confused and miserable."

She served the pilaf in a shallow dish of white pottery, decorated with a rim of blue petals.

"Selfish creature, you are an animal." He spat venomously at her.

Alaya's heart went out to the old woman in compassion. She, the dead bride, suddenly understood the reason her husband's mother became such a resentful woman.

She came close and caught the shock of white hair wrapped in a doughnut, and decorated by two white combs of mother of pearls and fake diamonds, to hug the neck that throbbed.

"She is so proud and feminine." Alaya surprised herself with the love for the tiny woman who adored her children enough to stay with the hateful man.

Her husband, raging with fury, came close, too close to her body, and screamed.

"Have you gone deaf?"

She did not flinch.

Alaya felt as though she would strike him a deadly blow. The poor woman felt the same way.

Instead, she advanced towards a kitchen cabinet laden with platters, reached for a deep serving bowl, took it out slowly, and walking back to the stove, she uncovered the lid of the stew pot. The woman poured the thick stew inside the bowl carefully with focused concentration. She then turned back to the cabinet where huge crockery jars held the precious olives they pickled the last season, got a ladle in one to come out with the shiny, green olives. She placed them into a small bowl. As she served, her servant carried the platters into the dining room nearby all the while having to bump into the body of the old man who stood staring his wife down wickedly, intimidating, an arm planted firmly on one hip, his legs apart ready to attack.

"He is an animal," some spirit watching, announced.

"How could that be?" Alaya marvelled at the wicked state of the man.

"Humans are of varying degrees of beings," that entity explained.

SIX
BRIDE WATCHES AND INTERVENES

Alaya could read anybody's mind; as thoughts are nothing but energy, and as dead peoples' spirits are composed of the same form of energy, the two could easily exchange places. Dead entities could easily go in and out of sentient beings' minds to read thoughts, stage scenarios as these dreamt so as to impart and help, or else disturb and blame. Similarly, live people could as easily access the death realm, as that stands inches before their noses if they were to keep the body and its spokesman hushed. As the diseased brain grew increasingly more astute, people in the body neglected their spirit that could read and find solutions from the ether and its inhabitants.

"Are you happy, woman? Is your control assuaged finally?"

"He will get over it. Do not give me grief. You could have stopped it, but did not." They were alone in their room by then, everyone having eaten and gone to their respective rooms for a rest. Husband had never showed up for lunch.

"May the devil take your soul," he cursed.

"He already has it. He took my soul the day I married you," she mumbled softly.

Alaya ran away from their hatred. She joined her husband on his walk, talked to him in his head, over his thoughts, of their wedding; the way he spoke to her mother about her purity, and their amazing stay in the city of the prophets.

He smiled tenderly, while tears streamed unnoticed over his face.

"I wish I knew of our short time together. I would have said that I loved you more often," he said.

"You never, ever spoke," Alaya cried over the loss.

"No. I never have. I thought you would never stay if I were to tell you the extent of my love, or use it, or abuse it. Now..."

"Well, it does not matter. I knew. I never felt as loved as by the touch of your hand on my shoulders, never."

"Really?" the poor husband asked.

"Absolutely," she confirmed.

"I love you, Alaya, breath of the wind, spirit of the fog, scent of all the flowers, transparency of all the summer skies, purity of all the white clouds, and springs, and wild boar, and African rain, and sunsets of India, and seagulls over Madras, and fairies of the fairytales, and essence of magic," he enumerated.

"My," Alaya melted.

"I wish I could find some pink roses in this cursed place," he told her.

"I like wild lilies," she whispered in his ear.

"You will have to settle for some wildflowers, I guess," he said. "I never gave you a diamond ring or a fur stole, a white lace negligee, a Valentine card with a box of candy, never shopped for Christmas, and saw your expressions of joy. I never had time to even have a child with you."

So shocked had Alaya grown by the romantic nature of the husband whom she had considered dead emotionally, that she could not answer.

A cloud opened just over the man's head, and poured rose water.

"Strange," the man wiping his hair said, "one lone cloud."

"Do you smell roses?" he asked a man passing by on his donkey.

"No sir, I smell horse dung," the old man replied.

Under the willow, a cluster of white lilies and butterflies mingled in shared harmony.

"Strange this," the wise old man pointed to the flowers, "lilies in fall. I have never seen that."

Alaya's tears dropped diamonds on the lilies, and the husband bent down to pick one.

"And dew, and dew at dusk," he murmured confused. "I am going mad."

The energy rode the setting sun to plant a tender kiss on his forehead.

"I will see you soon, beloved. Go marry my sister now. Do marry Jezebel of the spirit with the soft heart that was never hardened by so many words and books. My sister is so close, so close to full awareness. She will remind you of me, and I shall help her awaken you," his bride said.

He felt better understanding somehow that his moods were attributed to his visiting the site of her demise.

"Your mother is cooking grape leaves, your favourite meal."

"It is not grape leaf season." He argued with the realist in himself.

"She has pickled some for winter," Alaya informed him.

"She was cooking okra when I left the house," he remembered.

"She made a small pot of stuffed grape leaves just for you," she told him.

He refused lunch feigning tiredness. The women sulked disappointed.

He slept with the cover halfway up his mouth, as his elbow curled to shield his eyes from light. His mind buzzed with confused possibilities as to the murderers, none-of which came close to the real scenario.

Alaya pirouetted over his head, in the dance of the spirit. That is some feat to see.

He thought he dreamed that his wife was over his bed, dancing, dancing her love to him, expressing sorrows for his sadness. She fluttered about like an angel, wings flapping, touching his face, his mouth, his eyes, and his heart.

He awoke to hear noises coming from the side of the main balcony. The widower greeted the visitors, apologized to them, also feigning weariness.

The man went inside the room he had shared with his bride, only a month before, and started to pack his bag.

His mother stormed in unannounced demanding to know the reason for his packing.

"I am going to see my wife's parents tomorrow," he answered simply.

"What did you say?" the woman's shrieks shook the mountains.

The man stood transfixed in his spot, shocked by the fury of the woman.

Shocked, and humiliated by her reaction, he resumed his packing. A muscle in his back throbbed visibly, and a hot shaft like fire shot down his leg to stop behind his knee.

"Please leave my room," he asked unusually angry.

"You are shutting me out of my own home?" she wailed to bring her husband on the run inside the room. "See, your son, mister? See the man you spent your last penny on educating? He is kicking me out."

The father ushered his wife with a hand on her waist, as he stared his son down threateningly.

"No. Leave me alone. I need to know about his fascination with those people."

"Do not call them 'those people'. My in-laws are good and kind people. They are also extremely polite."

"Are you implying we are peasants, boy?" she raved and ranted.

The man understood how his wife could have grown distraught by such fury. He envied her passing just then.

"Answer me." She hit her face with both her palms.

"You really are a drama queen. My wife was right." No sooner had the words escaped his mouth than Alaya groaned pityingly.

"Your wife what?" Now the neighbours ran to the house.

"My wife nothing, Mother, she is dead. Can we not leave her alone in death?"

"Even in death she controls you." She banged shut the door.

"No problem. I am used to being controlled."

She came back.

"I heard that," she screamed.

He held the door shut holding his entire body against it.

"Leave him be," his father droned.

She left.

He left town the next morning. They barely talked. He kissed his parents dutifully, as his mother cried a torrent.

"Go, go, go, do not look back," Alaya egged him along.

The man's trudged up the hill tiredly.

The driver started the car as to leave fast before anyone ran up the hill to delay departure.

The car sped down the hill, forked left then took off before the man could breathe.

From the hill, they could both see the cemetery.

"Oh dear God, I am leaving her in this strange place alone." Her groom brushed away a tear of the most tender that fell off his face.

Alaya kissed the place where the dew fell. Tenderness and longing to alleviate his pain seared her being, making her wish she fought the entire universe to remain with him. She did not know. The girl bride never knew of his depth, his love and his unbelievable dedication.

"You are an angel," she whispered to him.

He smiled not knowing she spoke. The groom believed himself dreaming of what had been.

"That used to be my wife's cooing," he thought. "The woman child was skilful at expressing her love. She made me feel like a king."

"You are a king," Alaya said.

She sat on his lapel, the butterfly whose wings returned upon death, and watched the roads she missed, and the hills she loved, and listened to the man whose life she briefly shared to enrich her, enrich her forever.

"No man will ever come close to your gentleness," she said to him.

She had loved the blond man instantly. Theirs was a love of great depth. It bloomed beyond the usual pull of the body, went deeper than looks, desires, crassness, and attachment. They were the same sort of people: Children of light; they were bound to the earth and committed to ethics, and their duties.

Theirs was a soulful connection, a rare happening; a deep union, where together they ceased to be, together they ceased to be two people, but two zeros that amounted to not a thing. One with nature, the stars, the sea, the sun, and the rocks, they were in silence together.

It would take maturity to understand the man of few words, much more maturity and cunning than she was afforded at that time. As it turned out, with the silence of the man, and the naïve outlook of the girl, the jungle caught up with the butterfly; how could a butterfly possibly survive the jungle for long?

All that the woman figured in the spirit; things clarified vastly to people in the souls, she found out. If only she had had the same clarity of thoughts down there, she could have possibly survived.

SEVEN
WIDOW VISITS IN-LAWS

The travelling pair finally arrived at the building in the city where the girl's parents lived. The driver pulled the ancient car under the awning, to ask the widower whether he should wait. He told him to leave, that he would ask for a ride from his late wife's sister. He had not seen her parents since the wedding three months before. A tension tightened his muscles to elicit a nervous cough. He narrowed his eyes, took a deep breath, and went down the stairs.

Her parents had not attended her funeral; the region where the bride died settled resentfully under the siege imposed by the conquerors, as they needed a pass to cross the separating wall. That was not granted.

They had celebrated Mass in her memory at the church by the ravine where they were married, and where also their first child was baptized. They had a wake at their home where she was born.

The father was ill, and had taken to his bed in grief and anger.

A maid in a black apron answered the doorbell, ushering the man into the living room.

Their once-lively house felt dead; each member stayed in his room silently. He noted the difference in the silence level at his wife's parents' home sadly; riddled by guilt because he believed himself to have caused it. Whereas once their house sizzled with jubilant activities and joyous sounds, it hovered now under an unspoken cloud of silent doom brimming with despair.

"Welcome." Alaya's mother took him in her arms crying silently on his shoulders.

"How is Dad?" he asked.

"He is not well, as expected. How are you?"

"Not too good," he answered, guilt painting a streak of blue in his eyes. "Can I see him?"

"He sleeps. The medication, you know."

The girls came in wearing black dresses, and white stockings. They hugged him and cried, then sat across from his chair to stare in their shock.

Silence shrieked shriller than screams, laden, laden with lead. The man understood their blame of him, also the depth of their kindness to receive him still with open arms.

"How are your folks?" her mother asked politely.

47

"They are fine," the man replied as he looked at his shoes. "They sent their best regards and deepest sympathy."

Things were not flowing; each person relived the last moments of seeing their sister alive at her wedding, their goodbyes through the decorated car, silence deepened to madden everyone with the black energy emanating from their bodies and thoughts.

"What exactly happened?" second sister summoned enough courage to finally ask. "We really don't have much detail of my sister's final days, hours."

"Well," he struggled for words, admonishing care. "We are not sure, yet. The inquisition is still ongoing."

His eardrums burned badly; something inside him knew; knew the lie he had just told, the likelihood of a homicide, instead of an accident, as he had initially announced their daughter's death, unnerved him.

"Does Jezebel not look exactly like me at her age?" the dead bride asked her husband.

"You look so much like your sister at that age," her groom told her sister.

She blushed crimson, straightening the thick tresses that crawled down her back.

"They look nothing alike," the mother interjected. "Jezebel's eyes are larger."

"Thank you, Mother." Alaya thought that her mother stuck staunchly to her guns concerning her confusion as to her first daughter.

"You will lunch with us," Mother ordered the widower.

"I would like that. Are you sure Dad would not mind?" the poor man asked.

"Of course not," came in a chorus.

"They love him so." His bride delighted. "They are a good-hearted bunch."

She also noted, the secret looks, sister Jezebel threw the blond man's way.

"She likes him. Good," Alaya thought.

"Are you sure you want this union?" Sycamore asked surprised.

"Yes. I'd love to be their daughter," the woman announced delighted. "It would be good being their first daughter."

"Do you not fear for her?" Sycamore asked surprised.

"No. I shall be there to help her throughout," Alaya promised. "Besides, Jezebel, unlike me is not a snob."

"And the months in the womb, does that not worry you?" Sycamore needed clarification lest her charge met with a fate far worse than the one she had just escaped.

"What is the alternative, can I remain in this realm of suspension?"

"No," Sycamore looked pained. "I fear this place is only a way station for unfinished works."

"How many other stations are there?" Alaya wanted to know.

"There are several planes as well as several stations," Sycamore replied.

"How about the earth?" the child bride asked.

"That is the lowest plane of existence," Sycamore stated.

"So, as long as we have impurities, earth is our dwelling?" Alaya sounded surprised.

"True enough, Alaya," her master agreed.

"What is the reason humans hate leaving planet earth then?"

"They get used to it and hate the unknown," she explained.

"What happens after they have paid all their Karmic debts?" she wanted to understand.

"They come back to this way station to get assigned a higher realm of learning and self-purifying."

Mother noted the interest the pair showed in one the other, saw her newfound opportunity to grab the man with the future and marry yet another one of her daughters.

"Excuse me as I oversee the meal," she announced and got up walking towards the kitchen.

She gave orders for the noon meal, and went into her husband's room, not before she signalled to the second and third daughters to follow her.

The son-in-law was left staring at the blaring television, with Jezebel watching him tenderly. His grief broke her heart. She thought the man extremely decent to suffer so deeply concerning her sister's fate.

"So Jezebel, how is your school going?"

"That is the only line of conversation he knows, the poor dear," the dead woman thought wistfully.

"I am not the scholar, brother, dear," she replied as she giggled, showing a perfect set of white teeth.

"What do you mean?" he asked startled by her honesty.

"I will finish my freshman year, and find a job; schools have never held great interest for me."

"Not like your sister."

"No. Nobody was like my sister when it came to school." She smiled mournfully remembering her sister.

"Yes, I know," he said.

"So who are the scholars in this family then?" he flirted openly now smiling broadly.

"Your late wife definitely, then comes second sister, and finally second boy," Jezebel laughed joyously, as she told him.

"In this manner of succession?" he wanted to know honestly.

"Absolutely," Jezebel affirmed.

Father showed up to interrupt the sweet interlude jolting his son-in-law badly. He looked haggard in a brown robe, and matching pyjamas. His face looked ghastly with his grief and disease.

"Poor Daddy," the bride thought.

"Dad," her husband stood up to greet her father.

They hugged and cried tears of the most shattering. Jezebel sobbed as she watched the men mourn her sister's untimely death.

"Thank you for coming." The father patted the younger man gently on the back.

"Of course, of course, I am so sorry Dad. There was nothing anyone could have done. I promised to watch over her, I know, but fate intervened." He brushed a wayward tear, as he babbled guiltily.

"Her fate," Dad answered sweetly. "I miss her so much. Hers was a spirit of the rarest kind."

"Yes. She was a rare human being," her husband approved, nodding.

"What exactly happened, son? I need you to tell the minute details of that time you two spent together, especially her last hours."

The groom looked towards Jezebel, pleading. He found speaking to his wife's father of that honeymoon they shared, the weeks together, shattering to recount, as it is horrendous to hear. The miserable widower shook with the gamut of confusing emotions; there were the guilty ones at having never stood up in his wife's defence, and the blissful private times. Neither tale should please the father, the man understood.

Jezebel got up and summoned her mother to assist the man with the father.

The groom recounted snippets of their time together, omitting, omitting, the phone calls on their honeymoon night, their spats, her refusing to bow to his ancient ways of deep control, and issues, and issues of stupid learning she had resented. He told them of how his village people loved her, and the way she loved their countryside, her walks in the wild, and attachment to that river by the castle. He recounted their journey into the holiest of all Lands, and how she loved seeing things, and eating the food, and talking, walking about the shrines and historical places.

Father gobbled up the stuff as though he was starving for news about his poor daughter.

"Do you think she suffered?" he asked begging the man to lie.

"Of course I suffered," the woman screamed over their heads soundlessly.

"I am sure it was very quick, Dad." Jezebel came to the rescue of the man who knew not a thing about lies, just the internal ones he grew accustomed to accepting.

"Tell him, tell him, dear, about how your mother tortured both of us, every chance she got. Tell them how she called me a French, perfumed whore, how she cussed me every morning as she separated the twin beds, tell him, dearest. That would free you; just once own the purity of truth; one time will free you," Alaya prayed.

"No," that would hurt him.

"Yes? And you are worried about him, of course," Alaya giggled hysterically.

"Excuse me?" Father asked thinking that he had missed a part of the conversation. "You were saying, son?"

"Nothing Dad, no, she did not suffer. Of this fact I am sure," the groom affirmed.

"If I helped you to marry my sister you would have to wake up, do you hear?" She lost energy screeching hysterically inside his ear.

"Next time around, things will be very different," he told her in his mind.

"How so?" She needed to hear specific plans not empty promises.

"I shall run away to the New World never to return," he affirmed to appease her.

"Good man. That is more like it. I had told you about how your parents helped seal my fate. Do you remember?" she asked.

"No. I do not want to know." He dropped the veil on hearing her.

"You do have to know," she insisted straight into his cranium.

"Why do I need to suffer?" he asked.

"Because, if they were to kill my sister, I shall commit patricide myself by killing you," she vowed.

"You think they killed her?" he asked not knowing who talked in his head.

"I know they did. I was there." He probably thought her God or some other spirit.

"How did they kill her?" He wanted proof.

"No," Sycamore realising the plan shouted. "Do not tell him. That is evil."

"No, Sycamore. They will not get to kill my sister as well. He needs to know."

"Not now, maybe later. Let him have a respite of solace, a measure of peace. He has lost so much; to lose both his parents could neither be kind nor good." The tree feared for the groom.

"Fine, I shall help the inquisition then," Alaya vowed.

"How do you expect to achieve such a momentous feat?" her Sycamore needed to know.

"I will find a way," Alaya vowed.

"I wish you would let things go, Alaya."

Lunch went as brilliantly as it always has at the house of culinary delights, with the mood jumping from deeply morose, to hysterically humorous.

"They jumped both poles desperately." The bride wished she could have some of her mother's spiced fish with the Tahini sauce, and the hot peppers.

"The Tajeen looks amazingly good." Grandpa joined the woman to drool.

"What? We keep our palates after death?" she asked.

"Of course; if we liked foods down there, we still remember them up here." Her grandfather drooled.

"What are your plans, son?" The father sounded hoarse.

"I am leaving in two weeks to find work in the New World."

"Would you come back?" Mother asked fearing his fleeing for good.

"I shall come every summer to see you, and check on my parents," he promised.

"It is all right, then." Father genuinely loved the man.

"You take care of yourself for me." He got up to leave.

"It is early yet." Mother needed an opening.

"I need to trek back. It is a long journey."

"Sleep here," both parents asked.

"Thank you," he responded. "I will come to see you before I leave the country."

"Make sure to do that," the father said.

"I will come back," he promised, waved and was gone.

Eight
EVERYONE FEELS ALYA'S PRESENCE

His visiting Alaya's house disturbed him deeply. He had come back to his village for the last time to finalise his affairs and leave.

People left the balcony in droves, until only he remained with the moon, and the stars, under the clear dark skies of his beloved village.

"Remember how you loved the nights here?" he asked his late wife.

"Of course I do."

"Do you feel things now?"

"More acutely," she cried frustrated.

"Would you hug me?"

She engulfed him totally within her wings. The man closed his eyes, and drank the love of the woman who now was nothing but love. He flew with her to the top of the nearby mountain, and together they drank from the elixir of flowers, fluttered over gurgling fountains, and visited the surface of the moon. So lovely was their flight, so innocent, and pure, so crisp, so tender, that he knew that death was truly not the end.

"Thank you, darling. Now I can go on living," he said to her.

In the dream, upon his sleep, Alaya placed him in a field of white daisies. The vista, an immense expanse of fields, brimmed with nothing but white flowers and their green leaves. The daisies hugged the man like lovers. The spirit of his wife, able to project on the husband's mind any picture she chose, had chosen the daisies, to please and comfort him.

He awoke refreshed and disturbed at once: The daisies had rejuvenated a deep sense of the aesthetic that made his spirit soar, soar in delight.

"Did you sleep well?" his mother spoke to rattle his nerves.

"Yes, yes, fine, fine," he answered.

The woman narrowed a pair of already tiny hawk-like-eyes towards his form. She feared he suspected her in his wife's murder. His attitude of late stood clearly arrogant, clearly out-of-character for him. He had never taken a stand against any of their actions.

"So, when do you leave?" she asked.

"Tomorrow," he said.

"You look crumbled of late, confused." She opted for an offensive, as one did in such cases.

"Ah, yes, maybe because I feel crumbled of late."

53

"How are your in-laws?" she asked. "You told nothing of your visit."

"They are superb. How do you expect them to be, Mother?" he said, his tone biting.

Sensing the futility of communicating with him, she got up slowly, made a giant effort to straighten her back, raise her neck, tighten her eyes, to walk away from him looking straight at the door, never turning, ever.

"Where are you going?" he shrieked.

"I am leaving. I cannot talk to you," she replied.

"You never could talk to anyone. You have always issued orders," he accused angrily.

The bride resented his last statement to no end. Finding he understood his flawed people hurt her beyond comprehension. That made him as evil as they were to her mind. To know of evil and terror and turn away from it is the epitome of all terrorising abuse. She died because her husband could not face the evil nature of his family. That made him a partner in crime of the first degree.

"So, leave. What do you wait for?" his mother returned to announce.

"I will leave. First, I need to see the constable. Someone needs to solve this mystery. I need to find out the reason murders never get solved in this village. Why is there a score of deaths, and not one conviction? My wife's death will get solved. On that, I swear to you, mother dear."

"Do you threaten me, boy?" she shrieked loudly enough to awaken the snakes in the valley below. "Do what you can. That is nothing to me."

"You two better not have anything to do with her murder now," he shrieked right back, and just as loudly.

He impressed Alaya. That was a facet of his nature she had never witnessed during the brief stay with them. She had initially thought him weak, and deluded. Finding out differently, the bride delighted in this newfound prowess of her beloved.

Her husband walked the hill, down to the shops, farther down to the cemetery, and farther still to the tree under which she had died. Seeing him dejected and injured brought the only bout of compassion to her heart, or whatever it was that felt in that cloud form, to make her turn pink.

"She loves him," Sycamore told the big cloud.

"She will be with him very soon." The cloud sounded sad.

Alaya fluttered around his head, planting kisses on the balding spot around his forehead, his eyes, the tears that ran down his cheeks for her, his neck where the tears fell, his chest. There, on his heart, she settled and stayed.

He hugged his chest tenderly, sensing her presence. She snuggled inside his arms and together they slept, lulled by the whooshing sounds of the limbs of that willow that cried, cried the young butterfly that had recently died under her limbs.

"Jezebel looks so much like you," he told Alaya. "Were it not for your memory, I would have taken her out to lunch to feel as if you're around. She also laughs like you; sounds of the most joyous giggling roll, roll, and chuckles like a spring shower tumbling in the stream. I felt like crying. Funny, I had never noticed it before."

"She is the only child that reminds me of myself. We do have a great deal in common," she said.

"If only she were not so young," her husband said.

"She is very mature for her age. Go and ask her to marry you. I would like to know that you two are together."

"Would that not upset you?"

"No. It would upset me if you succumbed to their plans of marriage for you."

"Do not be ridiculous. Had I wanted to marry a woman from this village, I would have. I humour them Alaya, but know, my darling, that you are my true love through all eternity and yes, I should have stood up to them, I just thought maybe you would not notice; stupid, ha?"

"No. It is fine now. Stop fretting."

"Let it go, Alaya, let it go." The big cloud finally intervened.

"No Sir, it is about justice. He needs to know the truth. You said justice is divine."

"No. I said justice is mine. Leave them to the universe to deal with."

"With respect Sir I do not see the universe dealing with anyone but the victims."

"What happened to you? You were the best woman I have ever created. Whatever happened to you, Alaya? You, the hope of women, have grown fangs worthy of the worst woman ever created."

"It is the studies she did," Grandpa interjected. "That grew her centre. She started using her brain instead of her heart."

"Yes. The heart centre breaks easily. I got tired of being so broken," Alaya agreed.

"Alaya, you once knew the reality of things. How could you have forgotten so totally?"

The big Cloud cried for the first time since the butterfly that had shed her wings showed up. He, the Cloud, shirked, shirked, under the futility of His Creation. That even those who remembered their destinies could get so muddled saddened him deeply.

"I am sorry," Alaya said deeply embarrassed.

"Do as you please, Alaya of My Heart. You are adamant at self-destructing. I had giving you free will out of respect to your divinity. Do with the knowledge that which pleases you."

"Thank you, Father. I shall weigh things carefully."

Then, he was gone. With that information, Alaya of the skies, and the shattered wings, sat still, motionless almost as to consider her options.

In her spirit a storm of fury and anger rose. So acute that rage grew that it shook her being like a leaf. The woman understood about the corroding nature of hate, but also the deep pleasure of getting even. It was not easy; she realised now, to get rid of hate for those who so deeply hurt her to death. To forgive them contradicted her very being. It was as though she needed to side with the evil enemy against her own energies. That, the woman found, was more unbearable than death.

"This compassion Law is beyond human endurance," she announced to nobody in particular, her cloud shaking, shaking in anger.

"That is the very reason humans had never found their own divinity," Sycamore said, coming to her rescue again.

"It does not make sense, Sycamore. To forgive those who intend us injury, hurting our parents, our souls, our goodness into this state of utter destruction, is wrong, surely," Alaya proclaimed onto the entire realm.

"Do not fear for good people. Those who never hate would never be shattered by the hatred. The very nature of evil shatters itself from within. Hate is its own enemy. As death is not, then only evil is the punishment," she explained.

"What do you think I should do?" Alaya needed help.

"Like our Master said, you must do what you want to do. That is the only law of the universe, free will and incurring the consequences, Alaya. There is no other law."

"I shall weigh my options carefully. To go back to the very people that shattered my former life, so as to save them and myself seems horrendous to me. I am not that good," Alaya admitted honestly.

"To go back to them as their own child, love them, and teach them pure love will cut off many of your lives, shielding you from scores of suffering and pain. They are the shortcut for your ultimate flowering," Sycamore tried to clarify.

"I will think seriously and fairly on these things." Alaya felt confused.

"It is not about justice, but growth; the growth of the soul to love without limit, even those who hurt it," her grandfather explained.

"The reason for such self-deprecation is what?" Alaya suffered the intricacy of the plan.

"The ultimate purity of that soul is the aim. The purity that ensured that spirit could forever rest within the entity of the Godhead that allows no pollution of thought or action."

"Yes." Alaya had initially understood this fact before her wings were destroyed by the hatred of greed and control. "Yes."

Nine
A MOST INGENIOUS MURDER

Husband sat in a shabby office, on a tattered sofa of the ugliest green possible. He had walked the few miles up the hill towards the constable office. The latter leafed quickly through the notes made by his police officers during the inquiry of the death of the woman by the river, under the famous castle.

"No witnesses. Is this possible?" Her groom inquired suspiciously.

"It says right here that no witnesses were found," the man said, resenting the implication. "Do you doubt our work, sir?"

The groom shook his head in desperation. He failed to answer. The chief constable, not expecting an answer, had gone back to his reading.

He read avidly the account, turned the finished paper upside down to reach for the next one, his eyes darting, his mouth mumbling disbelief, but otherwise saying nothing aloud.

"So?" the nervous groom asked.

"So, nothing of any substance is new. Things stand as we had left them. What do you expect us to do? Are we expected to produce a miracle for you, sir? Why was your bride wandering along the bank of the river? Where were you?"

Upon hearing this attack, Alaya feared for her husband's involvement. She made the green shutters in his office slam violently.

The chief jumped, startled. He then proceeded to scream for his aide to secure the shutters.

"You should have been a prime suspect." He was not distracted. "I see here, you had a firm alibi with several witnesses. Still, has anybody asked the reason your young lady was allowed to roam the countryside? It is unseemly. Females of status are not allowed to roam unaccompanied."

"That is true." The constable had finally exposed a raw nerve of deep guilt the poor man had been feeling. "That is beside the point. Making a mistake of comportment should not assure a young lady's death, however," he stated.

"Our region is filled with armed foreigners. There are the spies who spy for the other side. And we have the army of the spies that run this region on behalf of our enemies. Then, you have the few legitimate police that belong to our land. Then you have the guerrillas that fight inside the hills against the spies, the enemy army, and the mercenaries the enemies have hired and had placed on their payroll. Sir, surely having been raised in this place from birth, you should have explained the dangerous state of affairs to your young bride. As such, you are solely to blame for her untimely demise."

Husband hung his head in guilt, knowing the man to be correct on all scores. The region had not been secure for many years, and the countryside grew treacherous with the many fighting factions.

"Well, if you were to stumble on some new lead, please let me know." He got up to leave.

"Will you be at the same address?"

"For a short while, otherwise, my parents will be for the next three months."

"The olive picking season," the official stated.

"Precisely," the widower agreed.

He got up slowly, like an old man, broken by life before even having had a chance to live it, extended his right hand towards the huge man who towered over him, shook it firmly and left without so much as looking back.

"I would not, if I were you, hold much hope on this investigation."

"Excuse me?" the educated man blushed crimson at the boldness of the statement.

"Even if we knew the culprits, we might not be able to divulge their names."

"Reason being?" the man turned at the door to ask.

"The lawless state of the region, the power of certain individuals in hiding that which they deem fit to hide. Let it go. Go on with your life. You are still very young. Sometimes it is better not to know."

Husband stood by the office door, jaw hanging, trying desperately to gather and assimilate all that he heard.

"Is there something you know that you hide to protect me?"

"Not yet. There exists a little discrepancy in the report that implicates your..."

He stopped to pick up the ringing telephone. Alaya feared the revelations he planned to divulge. She made a sudden decision, and was not willing to go back to grandparents in jail, a family with a scandal.

She whispered in the constable's ear.

"It is not conclusive evidence. You should not divulge it as it is a basis for a possible lawsuit."

He stood up, shook the man's hand anew.

"Excuse me. An urgent and private phone call," he told the man.

The man left, having forgotten the last statement that had so intrigued him, and only seconds before, concerning the murder of his beloved, departed wife.

Alaya had made up her mind. Based on the laws of forgiveness, she decided to come down as their grandchild, and forgive, forgive, forgive. That was the only way.

"Not only forgive, but love," Sycamore said.

"To love as well," she promised.

On the hill, the groom placed the last touches for the trip to the New World. Alaya stood by his head, as his mother and sister gave directions as to its content.

"Take this pair of trousers, son. Leave that one to your father."

He did precisely as asked.

Finally done, they all went to lunch.

Lunch was a tray of kibbe prepared by both women when the man went to talk to the constable.

"I shall pack some kibbe balls for your journey," his sister commanded.

"Thank you," he said gratefully.

"Routine," Alaya, thought perplexed.

She placed the balls of kibbe about twenty of them in a supermarket bag, twisted the top to secure it, and handed it to him like a precious trophy.

"Here. Think of us poor women when you eat them."

He brushed an expected tear from his cheek, as his voice quivered with the love.

She dipped inside his heart to find it still; excited even about that leaving. She then proceeded to invade his thoughts, finding them quiet, jubilant at the prospect of travel and far-away lands, and freedom.

"What is he doing?" Alaya grew confused by the mixed messages.

"He is acting," Sycamore announced. "He knows that the women expect him to tear up, so he does."

"He can tear right on cue?" Alaya inquired amazed.

"On cue," Sycamore confirmed.

"That is so dishonest." Alaya hated this revelation about her former husband.

"No. That is kind," Sycamore corrected. "He is touched by their sadness, hating to cause any pain."

"Does he at least suspect their self-interest in the actions?" Alaya needed to understand.

"Of course he does. He is a very intelligent man," Sycamore confirmed.

"Why does he do it, then? Why does he not tell them to get off his back instead, Sycamore? This is horrendous for me," Alaya announced angrily.

"Because he is kind; he does what he wants while making them happy. It is called not making waves, Alaya. Maybe you should learn that. It is also called Diplomacy."

"You want me to learn Diplomacy? That is a polite form of lying."

"True. It also ensures people lived full lives," she said.

"That hurts," Alaya said.

They were kissing at the door now. The women cried and wiped tragic faces, and the father carried the son's heavy luggage up the hill. There was also a carton box secured with a green plastic rope.

"Some food for your trip overseas," his father patted the box proudly.

"Thank you. I will carry it."

"No. Leave it. I am fine. You have the suitcase to carry. Take care, son. Never fail to write us or call," he directed.

They hugged tenderly. The old man sweated his lack of expression as the groom suffered a jolt to his heart from having been taught never to express.

"Let us go," the groom directed the driver of the old Buick.

The neighbours had congregated before the doors of their houses that lined the length of the street, all the way down the hill. The groom waved dutifully to each occupant with a tender smile.

Then, he was gone. They turned the hill that overlooked the village. The groom turned and brushed a tear of sadness upon seeing Alaya's grave.

"I never thought I would leave you here to roam this world alone," he told his wife.

"I am fine." She kissed his eyes. "Do not cry for me anymore. Go see my parents before you leave."

"Of course I will."

She sat on his shoulder, the butterfly of the skies, whose spirit remained attached to her earth mate, a sin, a deadly sin to annihilate her next life, she knew. Sycamore, her ever-present angel, whose destiny remained fixedly bound to that of her charge, watched the drama unfold, making little headway in the matter of the young bride's love for the husband, one that even death could not break.

"I wish I could cry," Alaya thought.

"You cried so much. I never want you to cry again," her husband thought back.

"He can read my thoughts," the bride said thrilled.

"He thinks himself thinking. Humans do not understand about their abilities to catch souls," Sycamore explained.

"It is good. It is very good, though. Even if he misunderstood his abilities, I know differently, and knowing appeases my distress."

Ten
HUSBAND PURSUES FORTUNE IN THE WEST

The woman's mind whirled like a loose rocket after the clarification of her Master. She looked to find her husband paying his driver before the house of his parents. She remembered this street well, and something like a heart within ached from longing to that physical world she so missed.

"God, please help me forget so I could make a decision to go back to them, and finish my karma of tolerance," she prayed out of habit.

He stripped down to his jockey shorts; such was the stifling heat in October. They had married in late August, the hottest day of her entire existence, maybe of all her existences. It was only eight weeks since the wedding ceremony. He sweated as he strolled to the kitchen for a drink of water, came back to sit on the rickety sofa. The man switched the television on and tried to find the news. He thought of calling Jezebel to find out whether she passed her make-up tests; he feared her flunking them anew. The news managed to distract him from making the call.

The phone rang at this moment, and his anxiety rose with the noise it made. His sister needed to check on his safety and whether he ate. He assured her as to both, his safety, as well as his lack of hunger.

"Guess what? It is pouring rain." He smiled at the relief from the heat.

"Raining in early fall? It is impossible," his sister exclaimed, surprised.

Water ran in clogged drainage pipes, long stuffed by dust and soot, jumped over the waste, ran over the roads, the people, the merchants' carts on the streets, the vegetable wares, the fake watches from China, the sellers of watermelon, the umbrellas on the beach, over naked bodies in bikinis where she herself swam two months prior, on the vendors of ice cream, on all the region. Not a drop was seen in the adjoining region.

The dead bride threw her form about, ran to the clouds, in the blue sky above, shook them and shook them, and willed them to pour, but they had no more water left.

She ran back to the upper realm where Sycamore and her grandpa sat about watching her goings and comings, shaking their clouds in desperate sadness for her plight.

"You must stop visiting the body realm," Someone said.

The bride's cloud shook, shook, and shook with disgust.

"You are going to be his child," Sycamore said.

"He is a child. I shall never trust him to love me like a dad should. He will probably look to me for protection, when he loses his mother," Alaya announced.

"Help him. Try to talk to him now, in this realm," Sycamore said. "You still have some time before he marries, has a child."

"Are you joking? Nobody could reach this soul. They do not allow him thinking time. If they were not physically with him, they install the cues, or telephone, and his father writes him all the time telling him what to do. I have got no chance. The man is doomed."

"What is the solution?" her grandpa needed to know.

"No solution," the bride screamed.

"Stop overreacting." Sycamore grew harsh with her charge. "If it were not for your dramatic penchant, we would not have been in this predicament."

"Listen to her," her grandfather pointed. "She ignores your clarifications of empowerment and runs to blame the sister for her demise and destruction."

"But listen, Grandfather, let me explain." Alaya felt horrible.

"No," the old man ordered. "You listen," he said furiously. "Every time an earthling defends his actions with a, 'but listen, let me explain,' phrase, I shrink in horror. It points straight to the trouble. There is a dire need for you to understand, that which stood as the basis of all your problems on earth so you could remedy your next life. Pending this awareness, you are landing back here for the same conversation, down there with them. Next time around, however, your fate could be worse."

"Thank you, Grandfather." Alaya began to get an inkling of the trouble.

"It is your ego; that false, self-important fake self you have developed. That is all the trouble. It is that which makes you always perfect, always right, while other people are always mistaken."

"What is that?" Alaya experienced a problem holding on to that false identity.

"It is 'the branch that has cut itself from the vine'. Jesus told us to watch for it in ourselves."

"That was his cautioning to remain within the church," Alaya objected.

"What church, Alaya? Jesus knew nothing of a church," Sycamore interjected.

"What is it then?" the bride started to hear.

"The ego, the false ego, my child," her grandfather told her.

"If it is in us," Alaya reasoned, "how could it be false?"

"It is not in us," Sycamore said, "it grows. We grow it. Little babies have no pride; they never care about what they wear or how their houses look when people visit, or what model car their parents drive, none of that. Therefore, that is a false personality that we grow, like a branch by our authentic vine."

"I see." Alaya did see.

Sycamore shook like a cloud in a storm. Alaya understood the problem. She knew that she missed some deep point, and that unless she focused totally, her next life would start badly, end up more tragically than the one that had preceded it.

"Fine, what did I miss?" Alaya asked her master.

"Possession; you wanted to possess him," Sycamore clarified.

"It is difficult to twist one's thinking this way. They have also caused me great grief; to shoulder all the blame is, to my mind, unthinkably unfair," Alaya argued.

"She is incorrigible," her grandfather returned to despair over his grandchild's corruption. "Once corrupted, always corrupted, even after death."

"I will work on righting things. I need time," Alaya promised.

"Good," Sycamore delighted in her charge's wakefulness, "Keep watching for signs of that false pride you have nurtured and grown. Pride and greatness belong to the Divine Lord and Creator of all things."

"I will work hard at wrenching that branch off its roots," Alaya said.

"It is not easy, Alaya. In the body, the false self hides like a chameleon inside the divine, mimicking, beguiling and convincing you of its viability, of its rightness. It, the self, wants to survive at all costs. It is deeply focused on its survival. You have to remain more focused as to catch it always, and uproot it," Sycamore said.

They decided that Alaya should spend her entire time waiting for her husband to make his decision to remarry, without interfering in his choice. Sycamore instructed her charge to stop thinking of the past, and to clear her mind from the shackles of time, and space; a habit carried through death by all those who are recently deceased. Ultimately, however, Sycamore needed Alaya to purify her soul with devotional thought, and feeling love to all creatures.

"First, you give loving devotion to the Head Master in the realm above in the seventh plane in His Kingdom, the head of all things, who is in everything. Then, you pray for all saints, and prophets. Thirdly, you pray for the entire universe on earth, all the entities in all the other planes of existence. You pray for your enemies first, and then people you did not know, then you pray for your beloved ones."

Eleven
ALAYA ARRANGES HER FUTURE LIFE

Alaya left her devotional session, and went down to check on her husband. He prepared to go visit her parents once more to bid them farewell before he took off towards his future in the West. The process of dressing up wrought an emotion of acute tenderness that baffled her; such was the state of its humanity. How could she possibly dream of the way he smelled; that tangy, spicy Habit Rouge de Guerlain, in the red bottle that had melted her heart? Such potency scents encompassed that imagining the beloved smell made it waft enticingly around her. She wondered what smelled in the absence of a nose.

"Your soul smells," Sycamore answered from above the clouds.

"How could a spirit smell things?" Alaya knew so little.

"The nose is the body's instrument of sending the scent to the soul. Without the body, your soul needs no instrument to smell," she explained.

"How little do we know about that which we are in the body," Alaya told her master.

The man, they saw, wore a pair of flannel trousers, a camel-coloured silk shirt, and no tie. A twinge of leftover jealousy tweaked her being as she watched him dress with care for her sister, the beautiful, raven-haired Jezebel with the doe eyes.

"I need to pray about detachment. How could love be detached? Ultimate love and total detachment sound like a sadistic formula." Alaya knew that should prove quite an arduous hurdle to overcome.

She rode on his shoulder down the lift, where he had given her a kiss so long ago during her first visit to his home.

She played over his blond curls, by his ears. Thinking her a fly, he flicked his ear roughly.

"Hey," she complained.

His eyes moistened and glistened with unshed tears. Not understanding her to be near him, her husband thought that he generated the memories. Those pained him.

"Hey," she repeated with more energy, which exhausted her little form.

His mind rambled with constant memories of their brief life together, and their long engagement.

Instead of being with her in the moment, truly being by silencing the ticker tape up his forehead, he continually reviewed the past; here blaming himself, there blaming her. Alaya found no feasible entrance to penetrate the thick in flux of constant rehashing of dead memories.

"I am here. Stop thinking so I can speak to you," she wasted energy to infiltrate and tell him.

"Oh, my God, I am going crazy. I am hearing her inside my mind," he thought.

Distraught by such destructive mechanism as his brain, and destroyed by the effort to speak to him, the woman felt like melting away with no energy to pursue this conversation.

"Their bodies are so crude, so crass, so controlling," she thought.

"Your mind worked as busily, my beloved child. Do you see now where your fight happened? Your soul that understood things of the divine got drowned by your body and its demands," Sycamore said.

"Yes. I can see that," Alaya answered, grieved.

Alaya tagged alongside him down to the garage, into the little Simca, onto the boulevard towards the casino by the hill which straddled her beloved sea that hugged the shore, by the rocks that stood guard over the beloved majesty. They made a right turn, climbed the seven-hundred-foot ascent, to the prestigious residential region, to make a left turn, and pass all the familiar and beloved villas, which sheltered the pine trees. Under the building with the many Roman-style colonnades, under which cars sheltered, she smelled her mother's food wafting enticingly.

"This is torture. She is making a hot spiced fish," Alaya thought.

Husband smelled it too, and smiled.

"Wish Alaya was here. She loved that," he thought.

"I am here, and I still love that," she screamed.

"If anyone could come back from the dead, it would be you," he thought.

"It is me. We all come back from the dead."

"Where are you?" he asked.

"Right here on your shoulder."

They buzzed him in and he pushed the gate, walked down the flight of stairs. The door stood ajar for him to enter. There, dressed to perfection, stood little sister Jezebel.

His eyes twinkled brightly at her. She bent down to plant a kiss on his cheeks. Alaya tried hard not to think.

"Keep the tape flat, flat, flat, flat," she chanted to herself.

Her mother greeted him with a sweet smile. Dad came by shortly afterwards to offer him a drink.

"Déjà vu," Alaya thought.

"There will be no commenting on your part," Sycamore came on her wave to say.

"Why can't I think? Surely, they could not hear me. Where is the damage in that?"

"All actions are intentions in motion. Whatever we think, we can make happen. If you sent them jealousy now, their lives would be ruled by it to make you all suffer the consequence."

"Do you know how tough it is to watch this?"

"Yes. If you cannot handle it, go away. It is more merciful all around."

"No. I shall have to get used to things sooner than later."

"Fine, then. Keep a lid on the thought process."

"Yes. Thank you, Sycamore."

"There is a way to get around it: Meditate on selfless love. You love them both and they will soon love you in the body as their child. Think on that."

Alaya hovered over the bald head; smelling his clean scent of soap and after-shave. Father was a pure soul of great potential whose pure heart raced for all humanity alike.

"I love you, dad," she said.

He wiped a tear, knowing that Alaya was there. Contrary to all the others, her father had the ability to hear the universe.

"You can hear me," she checked.

He shook his head affirmatively. They had always shared something deeper than kinship.

"Is there joy in the beyond?" Father ventured to ask his firstborn of love.

"If there were to be joy, I have yet to find it. So far, I hover in a realm beyond earth, suspended over the earth like a bird, a bit beyond the realm of humans, not yet able to cross to the reality of pure spirits," she told honestly.

Hearing her speak of death and its finality distressed his body, making his already weakened heart race frightfully. The group having wolfed a scrumptious meal, stood up gently, straightening chairs, and garments.

"Honey?" her mother called for her husband.

"Coming," he answered.

"Dead or alive, you remain the most interesting," he told Alaya.

She dared not answer; for that was pride and should incur her next life much karma. Nevertheless, inside her form coursed an involuntary thrill.

"Thanks Dad. You must not say things like that, though," she said.

"Why can't a father be proud?" he needed to know.

"No, Father; pride is a terrible thing. It is the body's way of enslaving the spirit," she told him.

"Ah, what rubbish. Pride is to love like fathers are to their children," he told her.

"No, dear father: Pride is to the devil what humility is to God," she corrected him.

"Dad, come on," Jezebel screamed for help entertaining the confused man.

"Coming, Jezebel." The man resented the interruption of his visit.

He stared at the corner of the large living room, as though dazed, dazed, drunk by the new information, feeling anger rise like a fog inside his chest cavity to engulf all the empty spaces around his vital organs. The news his daughter shared had distressed him.

"You will come back as my grandchild?" he asked, confused. "Who will his wife be?" he sounded sad.

"Hopefully, my sister Jezebel will agree to marry him."

"He is seventeen years her senior."

"You are that much older than my mother. That does not mean anything. Time and space, food and drink, Father are the concerns of the body, never the soul."

"She will make her own choices like you did," he dictated.

"Yes Father, she will. I am not allowed to interfere."

"I will be delighted. Oh well, you have given me reasons for living. I respect your husband and am assured that you will have a wonderful father, and a tender mother."

"That is my only break. To have you back in my life will be amazing."

"Yes. I shall look for that twinkle of mischief in your eyes as an infant."

"Yes. And I will know you immediately."

"How could you be sure of that?"

"You were the last longing of my last breath."

Tears rolled over his cheeks, over his shirt, over his trousers, and he reached toward thin air in an attempt to catch her.

"I am above you, baldy."

"It is you, rascal. Now, I know it is you. Not one human has ever dared call me baldy beside you."

"Remember on your fifty-fourth birthday I gave you a huge comb?"

"I was so offended. I thought you made light of my baldness. I have never dealt well with that horrendous shock of losing my beautiful head of curly, jet-black hair."

"I had never known that until that day. I was fourteen years old, and could not have loved a human being more completely."

When he ducked his head down in misery, she kissed the bald head to leave. There before her vision, sat her former husband on the same recliner of the same balcony of that long-ago failed proposal, speaking to sister Jezebel. "So, Jezebel," he faltered badly. "How do you feel about marrying me and moving with me to the west?"

"We will see when you come back," she said. "Who knows what could happen in two years?"

"Nothing could happen. I will go find a job, save some money to return and marry you. I need to know if you have any objections."

"I don't have an objection. We need to speak to my parents. They will probably ask you for a formal engagement, though."

"That is not good enough for me." He sounded angry.

"What do you want me to say in the matter? That I love you, you are my late sister's husband. I don't know whether I could ever see you otherwise," she stated wisely.

"You can't think of me like that. It is not a healthy way to look at your future husband," he said.

"Maybe with time and some separation, we both shall forget, maybe Alaya's shadow will retreat and stop haunting us both. You need time to heal, figure things out. We must not rush the matter," Jezebel told him.

"I will speak to your father to get your parents' approval, and leave. Two years later, I will return."

"In two years things would clarify either way," she said.

He promised to leave immediately, find a job and come back to visit her each summer until such a time they could get married. The plan pleased Jezebel, who had always liked the man with the golden looks, and heart of the sun. He was easy to love, and easier to like. She knew that her parents loved him enough to approve of his plan.

"It would be good if you were to study some English so as to facilitate your life there," he suggested.

"I would have to either live in the capital, or else commute there. Father would not approve," she said.

"Do not worry about anything. I will try to dispatch your papers so as to get married as soon as possible. This way you could attend university there. You do need to study the language. Try to find a way to prepare for that eventuality," he explained.

"Could I attend university after we get married?" She became excited.

"Of course you could. You could do anything you wanted to do." Her excitement surprised him. "I thought you were not one for studies?"

"I did not think I was. Honestly, my sisters and I were deeply troubled when our father refused Alaya permission to resume her higher studies, so we figured, why bother. The prospect of higher learning is sounding more enthralling. It would be interesting to get a degree than waiting around the house until you returned from work," she explained excited.

"Nothing pleases me more than to have a wife I could speak to about things of importance. That would be good. Good, so it is settled. I will try to get a job, apply for your residency papers, return, and get married," he said.

He felt happy. The absence of the feeling suddenly returning thrilled him; he had not noted its absence. He had become morose of late, deeply dejected by the escalations of sadness and grief. It pleased him to see how soft and gentle Jezebel was. In a way, she proved even more practical than his late Alaya.

"Should we get engaged," she asked, "before you leave?"

"Is that what you want?" he asked.

"That is what my parents would want for us. Being engaged affords me a certain status in the eyes of the people, you understand. We could start preparing for the wedding," she suggested.

"I have no problem with that. It does have to be a private affair. Just your parents, siblings, you and I, is that okay?"

"Sure, we are still in mourning."

"Our wedding will also have to be somewhat private," he added.

"Sure," she agreed.

"Seeing that it is my second marriage, it is not seemly. We will have a church wedding, some trimmings, a small reception, but nothing elaborate. It is not proper."

"I understand," Jezebel said.

With that, they went and announced their intention to the parents who looked moved, shook hands, kissed all around.

"When do you leave?" the father asked.

"In two weeks," the young man answered. "We will buy the engagement rings together next week, come here to wear them before the family, with your permission, of course."

"God bless you both," the father prayed.

Alaya's mother cried softly in the corner of the room as she hugged her child.

"This good man is destined to be our son," she said, as she cried.

Twelve
JEZEBEL WEDS FORMER BROTHER-IN-LAW

Jezebel looked beautiful in her grandmother's gown. Alaya stared at the innocence showcased to perfection in the organza gown, yellowed by age to a seasoned honey-coloured gold. She noted the Chantilly lace Mantilla framing the oval of the bride's stunning head where black silky hair cascaded enticingly to create a contrast of sheer mystery. The stream of black hair scattered in ringlets over the olive skin of her shoulders, flowed all the way down to her waist creating a vision of the most startling beauty. In her ears, Jezebel wore a pair of old diamond studs, yellowed by age, and around her thin neck, a string of small diamonds anchored the magic.

Already, the woman thought, her sister showed a keener sense of maturity than herself; Alaya had been offered the dress and had refused it, opting for a modern simple one, an A-line dress, decorated with a relief of flowers woven on the outside of the material.

There were people fixing the bride's hair in their mother's room, with the three-sided mirror, others fussing over her make up of simple pinks and soft beiges. Her big black eyes showed nothing; her calm amazed Alaya, whose nerves shattered her last days of maidenhood, to send waves of electrical vibes as to madden Mars.

Sisters buzzed through the house generating an electrical charge, which coursed alongside their movements.

Their mother assisted their father in dressing up. He wore a deep grey tuxedo, with tails, and looked withdrawn and pale.

Mother fastened the silk, black and grey tie, as she cooed assurances to him.

Alaya watched keeping her emotions steady. She did not know about the innocence of souls, and the purity of their intentions.

Now that her masters and helpers had clarified the need for her to resume past-life karmic payments; especially those involving control and jealousy over her former husband, her energies stood perfectly aligned for redemption and the absence of attachment.

"But I do love them, Sycamore," her intelligent self, proclaimed guiltily.

"You need to love them, child. Love is all there is of goodness in any realm," Sycamore answered sweetly.

"I thought..." Alaya was baffled at that science of purity.

"No. Lack of attachment is widely different from detachment," her master replied.

"There is no difference. Detachment is the lack of attachment," the poor woman corrected.

"There is a big difference between the two notions, my child. To love is divine. We must love the entire universe, and each person in it. It is impossible to forfeit the love to those we grew attached to in the realm of the body, Alaya. We must not feel deep attachment, in the form of appropriation; should never feel that another human is our property. That is what God disdains beyond all else."

"Love knows no logic, Sycamore," Alaya moaned pitifully.

"Love should know no bounds when it comes to our ultimate goal: The crazy love for our God, the ultimate attainment to him."

"Yes. I got that. It is not as easy as it sounds, though." Alaya felt an annihilation melt her form.

"You must not have this memory of love. How could you deal with being your sister's child and your husband's daughter if you were to remember them as being your beloved sister, and husband; untold heartache and problems would arise from that attachment," Sycamore admonished.

"How could I possibly cope?" Alaya feared for her sanity in the next body.

"You will not remember, not on any conscious level," Sycamore assured the woman.

There rose a cacophony of car honking, and cheers from the neighbours. Both spirits rushed to witness the jubilation, only to find that the wedding party was already settled in different vehicles lining the long, dipping driveway, as the well wishers shouted the bride's name, throwing a shower of rice and flower petals over her head; wishing her good luck and much prosperity.

"Bye, bye, bye, Jezebel. We shall miss you," her friends cheered.

Jezebel lowered her gaze shyly as she smiled and threw her arms around in waves of goodbye and thank you.

The couple headed towards the Maronite Church nearby where Alaya had graduated from high school, and where the sisters attended still. The church was a mere mile away from the house by the cabbage patch, over the main road, over the railway tracks, just two bends away from the Souk.

The entire school showed up to watch Jezebel get married. There were the invitees inside, seated by ushers, and loudspeakers for those who showed up uninvited.

A fresh burst of cheers greeted the long, black Mercedes Benz, decorated with a lovely wreath of white and lilac roses.

Alaya hovered over the sacristy, right over Father Paul's shoulder, the man who gave her First Communion. She was dressed then like Jezebel now; a bride with a dress of organza decorated with silk ribbons.

Husband came around and raised the veil over sister's head, fussing with it nervously, fixing it neatly behind her back. She raised her oval face, and received the body of our Lord in his memory.

"How quickly do I leave this realm, you think?" Alaya wanted to go down already.

"It all depends on your sister now, does it not?"

"Let us figure some things out before you leave me." Alaya sounded fearful.

"I am your acorn, and one of your masters, Alaya. I shall be bound with you whichever destiny you choose."

"Why do you always make the choice an option which exercising I hold steadfastly in my hand?"

"You do."

"I could choose not to go back to that lot again?"

"Sure, you could. You could roam around this realm for a long time, Alaya. Eventually, however, you need to resume making your karmic payments."

"Right," Alaya agreed. "What do we do now?"

"We wait. And let us give them their privacy, shall we, Alaya?"

"Sure." Alaya sounded disappointed.

She was sorely tempted to drop in on the newlywed couple, who travelled through the countryside towards a seaside hotel, awaiting a sailing ship to the Mediterranean basin the next morning.

She took a quick glance inside their car, to see husband take Jezebel's hand inside his.

"Are you okay?" he asked.

Alaya could not bear to watch any more of this.

She flew away towards her realm heavily.

The bridal party stood by a pier she saw the next time she checked. She stood in the face of Jezebel, who shone in luminosity and fear. She was thrilled to embark on her journey, eager to surrender to the new life with the gentle man, yet, there was the matter of going so far away from her parents. Alaya felt sorrow for her state. Seeing the pride in her father's eyes made things easier for everyone. The sisters cried wiping joyous tears with dainty kerchiefs, as the mother swooned ready to collapse, only to brace herself and smile. Alaya noted that her former husband's parents were nowhere around. They must have again boycotted the poor man. Renewed grit showed on the groom's face.

A huge cruiser sounded its shattering horn to signal time for embarking. He placed his hand on his bride's waist, to apply gentle pressure.

"Let us say our good-byes," he said.

Jezebel jumped perceptibly, looked to the gathered crowds around her, as the entire bridal party had come to see her off.

"Should we kiss everyone?" she asked confused.

Kiss your parents and siblings, and wave to everyone else," he directed.

The man stood silently beside his bride, holding her as though she would fall if he let go, cooing gently, gently that everything was going to be fine.

On the deck, the newlywed couple waved incessantly to the group on the pier until the boat disappeared inside the waves to gobble everyone up.

"Should we see our room?" he asked finally.

"Yes," she said and took his arm.

They sailed towards the new land in a luxury cruiser. Husband afforded the time as he held no job, and the prospect of holding one fast stood as remote as the moon that shone full and jubilant over the ship.

Sister Jezebel wore a suite of pink linen, all pink, that managed to set off her silky, black hair and her dark eyes, whose brows arched, perfectly shaped, and long.

Alaya watched husband place a hand around her waist, and noted the sudden gleam in sister's eyes.

"She already loves him. He is so sweet, and gentle," she noted with a measure of detachment that thrilled her.

"I am actually happy for the pair of them." Her thoughts delighted her.

"Womanhood needs to uphold its gender. Life for women is difficult enough without the cattiness they harbour for one another," Sycamore said.

"It was my cattiness that killed me," Alaya announced sadly.

"You went dancing with the devil," Sycamore corrected.

"Here you go. Learn, Alaya that the world is created with Love, for love, and is all about love. Nothing else is real. All else grows inside the body's unreality. Like a dream, like a dream, the body's life is perceived, only love matters."

"There are certain people one could not possibly love," Alaya resumed her pattern of blame allocating that had ensured her undoing.

"These people that are difficult to love are there to challenge our sainthood, Alaya. Surely, a saint would never pick and choose what people to love. He would love everyone, regardless."

Alaya could not grasp this concept. "How could one love the unlovable?"

"Easily; one loves because one is love," Sycamore said. "One that has love in the heart does not see a bad person. All God's creatures are worthy of being loved, regardless of their state, especially if their state is one of malevolence. They are more in need of care than the good ones. Knowing that God is in every creature, one looks at every human as though he or she is God Himself. Can't you see that?"

"No," Alaya told her the truth.

"It is not easy. If it were easy, the world would be in Light. The entire world would instantly be saved. All the world needs to save itself is this understanding: That everyone is God in the flesh, regardless. As it stands muddled, things are in a state of utter destruction."

"Because, I did not love totally." Alaya felt such guilt.

"No. You loved selectively. Because you abused your powers, and fell from grace."

"But, they killed me, remember?"

"No. They were allowed to succeed in killing you. There are no victims, only people who accept the victimizations. You had grown beyond help. You gave away your positive powers. You needed to return."

"Ah, so, what can I do now?" Alaya needed to understand.

"Now, we wait until they decide to have a child. In the interim, you, child, reflect on love."

"How do I regain my heart? I feel as though, I have lost that centre of tenderness. I just cannot remember when it happened. Awareness of the time I lost it has not registered."

"You start by praying for his sister and mother. Pray for their safety, and deliverance from pain and suffering." Sycamore directed.

"No. I could never do that. The best I could possibly do is to pray for my own deliverance from sin for having allowed the hate."

"No. You did not get anything," Sycamore laughed frustrated.

"It is tough, Sycamore. Memories are difficult to wipe out completely."

"Sure, it is tough, Alaya, Soul of the Universe, the reason there are so few saints."

"And the world thinks good is dumb, Syca, dumb," Alaya muddled in her ego.

"You are so stuck on your image, Alaya. It does not matter what people think. Your greatest quality had been that strict disregard of the general norm. You only heard your own authority. See, darling, the world enslaves those poor people who need to please. It enslaves them by catering to their insecurities. The syndrome is called the mob complex. To capitalize on their weaknesses, huge corporations install departments that analyse their mass needs, create commercial campaigns targeting their syndrome of crowd pleasing, so as to sell them their products. That is a very dangerous thing," Sycamore explained the dangers of needing to please.

Thirteen
HONEYMOONERS REACH THE NEW WORLD

In New York, things bustled noisily; sounds of joy, of much love, of much rejoicing exploded everywhere. The big boat blared its horns signalling its arrival. Well-wishers gathered around the deck to greet loved ones. People kissed, and cheered one another happily, Alaya saw from above the sails; nobody welcomed the newlywed couple.

An acute sense of loneliness invaded Jezebel's heart. A dark cloud, like a jab of pain, pierced her chest, squeezing her breath holding it siege. Husband, sensing her fear, wrapped her tiny waist with a loving arm.

Alaya flew down to speak to her sister inside her heart. She told her that things were going to be fine. Jezebel longed for home, the sights and smells of the homeland, silently. Her mind, an expanse filled with thoughts of all sorts of fears, missed her oldest sister's cooing encouragements.

"This place is so big." She shook nervously.

"It is the most thrilling place. Ask him to take you to Radio City Music Hall and the malls," Alaya told her.

"Could we go sightseeing?" Jezebel asked.

"I only have five dollars in my pocket," her husband replied with a chuckle.

Typical of husband, Alaya thought, trying to figure out the reason he never carried cash around.

"Are you serious?" Jezebel marvelled fearfully.

"Do not worry. We will be fine," he appeased her. "The banks will open soon. What do you need?"

"I need nothing; just for fun."

"You people do shopping for fun?"

"Who are we people?" she asked to impress Alaya. "Why do you refer to us as though we are of a different species from you?"

"Do I do that?" Her remark startled him.

Alaya discovered that her sister Jezebel possessed an innate sense of calm retorting; she heard the things people said, and answered simply. Obviously, the dimension was lacking in her. Although astutely analytical, Alaya's mind could not fathom the reason he frustrated her. Jezebel zeroed in immediately, honed in on the problem, asked for its clarification to shed awareness on the other, to drop it.

"I was a horrible listener," she deduced. "I need to work on that."

"You lived up in your own head," Sycamore remarked.

"It is more that I could read their minds most of the time as a child; nothing they said was news to me. My lack of listening stemmed from that ability, until I lost my powers. I am impressed by her."

"They are more attuned to one another," Sycamore announced jubilant. "I am sorry."

"It is fine. No reason to feel sorry," Alaya replied.

"So, who are we?" Jezebel would not let it slide.

"I guess it is about your family," he admitted, shamed.

"She brought awareness to him," Sycamore commented, "he feels a limitation."

"He was taught to see himself apart from the world and its people. His mother spoke of other people as though they were from another planet. She once told her children before me, 'where in the world did I get these strange people from?' which wrought peals of laughter from everyone."

"You would think grown people analysed their parents' words," Sycamore bemoaned.

"I did," Alaya announced proudly.

"You sure did," Sycamore laughed. "Look where it got you."

"Yes, now I shop from over people's heads." Alaya watched her sister shop for a nightgown.

He sat on a stuffed chair watching his wife flip through a stack of pastel-coloured under-garments.

"Is there anything you like?" he asked her.

"No, I have things." Jezebel looked delighted with her adventure.

"Let us go get some money and buy a meal," he suggested.

She smiled, and slipped her hand inside his tenderly. He squeezed his elbow to secure her clutch. On the long stairs, he held her tightly by the waist so as to shield her from a fall.

Sycamore and Alaya followed them through the streets, watched them go inside the bank, and followed their progress through breakfast.

"This is such fun." Alaya's mood lifted. "They are good together."

"They are going to have a good marriage. She is not too proud to ask for what she wants."

He hailed a cab, and went to a café, where a belligerent New York waiter asked them gruffly what they wanted.

Jezebel shook from the lack of courtesy, and seemed to shrink inside her chair fearfully.

"A cuppa coffee?" he spat gruffly, condescendingly.

"Yes," the groom replied.

"Something to eat for you two?" he spat disdainfully.

"No, thank you, just the coffee," the man answered sensing the waiter's disdain.

"Does she not talk?" he motioned Jezebel's way.

Her husband ignored him. The waiter turned around aiming to leave scarcely caring as to a reply.

"Let us leave." He picked his coat.

"Why?" She did not understand the discourse.

"I will tell you outside," he said.

Outside, they walked the perfectly planned city with the diagonal streets. They asked a man for directions to a Lebanese restaurant.

"Yes," the young man replied. "There is Hanbali."

They were feet away from their native food.

"I missed our foods," she said.

He laughed saddened by the strange surroundings that distressed her; guilty as to the predicament he imposed on her.

"It will be fine. Once in Michigan, you will eat and live as though you are home," he promised.

The place featured a huge hall where tables dressed in white linen shone in cleanliness, and old country reserve. Smells of familiar dishes wafted their way to please Jezebel.

"I feel like we are home," she said, tearing.

"You are not going to cry," he said fearfully.

"I am not going to cry," she assured him.

"When my oldest brother left home to sail to the Americas, my middle brother having gone to the city to university, I was the only one there to hear my mother cry the nights away over their absences. The sounds were so shatteringly distressing that I could no longer bear to hear a woman cry," he confided.

"That bad?" Jezebel munched on a hot pita loaf from the basket.

"It was the worst thing imaginable." He looked upset by the memory.

They ordered an entire meal, a bottle of white wine, and settled to a relaxed meal.

"You have never asked me about my marriage to your sister," he said.

"I will never do that," Jezebel replied. "That was your life; it had nothing to do with me."

Hearing this, Alaya knew beyond a doubt that this woman was, by far, the sanest one of all the children, herself included.

"I would have badgered him for details," she told Sycamore.

"She is sane like your mother," Sycamore replied.

"Thank you. Does that mean I was mad like my father?"

"You had your qualities. Jezebel lives in the moment. She has a great deal of peace in her," Sycamore said.

"They look happy enough," Alaya told her.

"Yours was a sizzling marriage. Each type has its definite advantages. She will suit his temperament for he is an easy person to live with. He enjoys life without needing to analyse it. Theirs will be a comfortable place of little arguing, if any," Sycamore tried to project.

"It would be good to be in their home." Alaya delighted at the prospect.

"They will offer you a great deal of support as a child."

"It would be good to be accepted for a change," Alaya said.

They finished their meal, linked hands, and resumed their walk towards the Empire State building.

"I used to see this in the movies," Jezebel squealed.

"Should we go to the top?" he suggested.

"I would love to see the city from the top of this building," Jezebel told him.

They took the lift and went up to the roof where telescopes sat fixed on the banister to accommodate the many visitors that cared to get a closer glimpse. He took two quarters from his trouser pocket and slid them inside a slot, yanked a lever down, and directed her to place her eye on the binoculars.

"This is beautiful." She sounded like a child.

"What do you see?" he asked.

She moved away to afford him a glimpse of the glorious skyline.

"Is that not something to behold?" he asked, pleased.

"That sure is." Jezebel sounded proud; as though he had built the city.

Watching the innocent delight, Alaya remembered their trip to the holy places in Palestine. She had shown the same wonderment, and he had reacted the same way; so pleased to give pleasure.

"Don't look back, Alaya. That is a bad habit," Sycamore suggested.

"How could trying to figure out what one did wrong be a bad habit?" Alaya needed to know.

"For one thing it cancels the present," Sycamore said, "for another, it cannot correct the past. Do not dwell on either the past or the future. Always live the present in sheer focused stillness; there, all the secrets of the universe, all life, and all of eternity reside," Sycamore told her.

"How does one still the mind? You speak of mind-stilling and I have no idea how this is done," she admitted honestly.

"To still the mind takes focused, serious work," Sycamore said. "It is not easy. There are techniques. If you were to make your eyes as hard as rocks, your brain cannot function. As long as the eyes are moving, thinking is present. Another way is to stare fixedly an object's way without blinking; your eyes might tear at first. A third way is to tell your brain to send all speech to the tongue."

"It will do it?" Alaya was surprised how little she knew.

"Of course it would do it. Go ahead, try it."

"I don't have eyes, remember?"

They shared a laugh, came out to realise that the newlyweds were speaking on the phone to their parents from their hotel room.

"Let us leave them alone," Sycamore directed.

"No. I want to watch them," Alaya refused.

"You must let them be," Sycamore insisted.

"Go then, I will follow you," Alaya beseeched her master.

"This could not be good for you." The tree commiserated over her charge's lot.

"It will be fine. Is there a law against watching earthlings copulate?" she asked.

"Not really a written law. It is just good manners," Sycamore related.

"I want to watch," she insisted.

"So you could compare?" Sycamore guessed.

"Yes," she sounded ever so sad.

"It is masochistic. Why would you want to hurt yourself like that?" Sycamore asked.

"I just do," Alaya insisted.

He opened the small fridge in their room, opened the curtains to look at the view.

Watching Jezebel come out of the bath distressed Alaya; such was the physical resemblance between the two sisters.

"You look stunning," he looked up from his newspaper to say.

"Thank you," she smiled his way.

He patted the space by his side. She came and cradled herself inside his arms. He read as he rubbed her back. Jezebel dozed while she smiled.

"That is too much bliss for me." Alaya left promptly.

"What happened?" Sycamore was surprised to see Alaya in the realm so fast.

"Nothing happened," Alaya laughed. "They fell asleep in each other's arms again. With these two, it could be years before I get a rebirth."

Fourteen
NEWLYWEDS IN THE UNITED STATES

The bus rolled over miles upon miles of dry, arid land, with humidity ranging in the nineties. The land stretched seemingly endlessly to startle the woman whose entire country could fit inside New York State with a bit leftover for Manhattan. It felt as though one should happen suddenly on the end of the earth, the last stop on the planet.

Jezebel slept soundly, her handbag clutched between long, lean fingers, with the nails painted pink. She looked a child in her ivory suit. Alaya noted that husband insisted on suits for all his brides; the memory made her smile. Remembering how stupid she felt in her first suit with the pumps wrought deep sorrow over lost chances.

He stared from the window seeing nothing. The man's mind never stopped; it chattered incessantly. The fact that Alaya could hear his mind explained many things about their brief life together. His mind chattered about the fears of never finding a job, and the viability of supporting a wife, renting a house, buying a car.

That explained the reason behind her confusion around him. When her active soul picked on the negative vibes he then negated the feelings with statements of the most positive.

"He was not a sharer, that one," Alaya thought.

She had asked him once, close to the time she left, at the reasons his father spoke not a word, especially about feelings. He laughed and told her that he felt that if he were to share people would invariably hurt him. The answer baffled the girl whose father spoke to the wind and the birds, sharing his innermost thoughts with the tide, and the moon.

Once as a toddler, he built her a sandcastle under the balcony that jutted out over the sea from her bedroom. She heard him tell a crab he caught in his hands with a handful of sand. "'Hey little one, are you lost? Where is your mommy? Do not be afraid, I shall dig you a hole and place you right where I fished you from, so as not to cause you pain and distress. When your mom comes to get you, she will be so pleased that you have not moved.'"

Alaya thought him mad, as he returned the crab placing it gingerly inside the warm sand, he ran to the sea to scoop a bucket full of water to carry back and dump it inside the hole where the baby crab huddled awaiting his mother's return. Only then, did her father move to another mound to fashion her castle.

"But Dad, crabs do not have parents," she had said to help the madman.

"Of course they do, Alaya, of course they do, my love. You must never disturb the creatures of God, lest some mad soul come and disturb your security with your parents," he answered seriously.

"Is that how things work?" she asked him.

"That is the only way things could work, Alaya. What we send forth inside the universe of deeds we get right back on the wind."

He was mad, Father, truly mad.

"God has more important things to do, Father, than watch over a little crab which has lost his mom," Alaya, only four years old, had said.

"No. God sees everything in the world. He sees all creatures big and small the same way."

His madness aroused a feeling of joy within her, as her spirit rose, rose with the unusual talk, and some energy got separated from within her, melted her heart with its heat on its way out, to swell, swell, and swell, hug the entire sea, rise as to meet the setting sun, kiss it, kiss it, kiss it, and get kissed right back. She came back to feel a bit outside her body.

"You talk such nonsense, Father," she giggled hugging his neck.

He gathered her small form to his body, and she felt the warmth of the sun all over again.

"You are magic," she said.

"So are you, Alaya, so are you, soul of the world, child of my heart."

"Not to speak is miserly, a miserly form of spirit. Not to be able to share one's life and thoughts with one's children bespoke of a small spirit that harbours evil intentions, and selfishness beyond bounds."

"Must not think along these lines of people even if it were true," Sycamore admonished inside her being.

"Why, if it is true?" Alaya had a problem in the realm with lack of privacy.

"That increases the negative vibrations in the world," Sycamore said.

"Please," Alaya begged. "Give me a little break."

"It is so true, my darling. Intentions are forms of energy that pollute the world to poison people if they were to be negative. It is black magic. Good intentions create white magic."

Dazed to her environment Jezebel awoke startled. She looked straight at her husband without recognition. Fear roamed in her eyes as she clamoured frightfully to place things in her mind.

"Where are we?" she asked. "I just had a dream of Alaya. It was so vivid that it disoriented me," she said.

"I did too," he admitted.

"You do love her still."

"I shall always love her, Jezebel. There will not be another Alaya in this world."

Tears streamed over her face. The loss of her sister grew to profoundly affect all their lives.

"Dad will be inconsolable. She was the light of his eyes." A bout of homesickness took over.

"All losses grow, except death; that is the loss that diminishes with time. He will be fine." He prayed it would be true for all their sakes.

"Do you think?"

"I know. Get ready to go down and freshen up. There will be a supermarket if you need a drink or a sandwich."

"Do you still have money?" she giggled.

"Yes. We have enough for a sandwich for you and two drinks."

"How about you, are you not hungry?" she asked.

"No. A drink will be fine for me."

Alaya grew so fond of the man. He always gave to others things he needed the most. She had thought the divine trait idiotic, weak somehow, to feel a deep shame now for having so misjudged his greatness.

They arrived well after midnight. Old uncle Howard opened the door groggy with sleep and worry.

"What took you so long?" He sounded cross.

"I took Jezebel on a sightseeing tour of New York," he said.

"You are in your home. This is your room. Ask for whatever you need. You know where the food is," the kindly man said.

"Thanks, uncle. Go back to sleep," her husband replied.

"We will have coffee tomorrow," the uncle said, as he disappeared.

"I have an interview with a chemical plant in Dearborn," he announced the next day over coffee. "Do you want to come along, Jezebel?"

"Jezebel will go with Iris to the airport. Your cousin is arriving at noon from the old country," uncle intercepted. "Do not worry. Go find yourself a job. That is top priority."

"Thanks, Uncle," he said.

"No problem," he said.

Uncle Howard dipped his hand in his pocket to hand the groom a wad of hundred-dollar bills. "Go buy your princess a gift from us. We did not know what to get you."

Howard stuck the money inside the pocket of the man's jacket, turning his back to kiss his wife's cheek. With a rattling of keys inside his pocket, the door banged behind him, as he shouted for all to have a good day.

Husband fumbled inside a black briefcase, found and opened a map of the area, unfolded the newspaper to the place where he had marked in some addresses, and proceeded to map his route for the day.

"You go with Iris and get my cousin," he asked Jezebel.

"Fine," she said.

Iris called after him.

"Should you not kiss your wife, dear?" she hollered.

Husband ignored the woman at her front door, got in a rented car, and sped away, waving goodbye to the women who stood by the door.

"He will come around. These people are like that when they come from the old country," Iris said.

Jezebel nodded gently, trying not to show resentment, as her heart brimmed with fear of the vista of aridity her life would encompass.

"My father, my uncles, nobody we know is like that." She resented the woman's statement.

"Oh, well. Do not worry about it now. How could he possibly not bend before such loveliness?"

"He is such a good man." Jezebel felt compelled to defend him.

"That he is," Iris agreed. "We are very fond of him. The airport is a good forty minutes away, we better get moving."

The women dressed fast and got out into the garage to fetch Iris's car. It was a huge pink Cadillac. Jezebel felt a definite unease clutch her entire body. The woman who was dressed in a hot-pink pantsuit, a pink hat with matching pink gloves, pink shoes, got behind the wheel of her huge pink vehicle, to place pink hands on a white fur steering-wheel covering, reached to her dashboard, took a gadget and pointed behind her towards the door. She pushed on a button and the doors creaked into motion to open the heavy metal door.

Jezebel felt a giggling fit seize her body, if unleashed to brand her forever rude in all their eyes. She quickly swallowed the craziness; thoughts of her sister's shocking murder calmed the fit of hysteria. She could hardly believe the way people dressed, and the way they lived. She wore a beige linen suit with matching pumps, a tan handbag.

"They think that we are the peasants," she thought.

They crossed the length of the street where Howard lived with his wife, crossed two similar streets, then onto a highway. Huge roads buzzing with fast-moving cars of all sorts unnerved the young bride.

"Are you afraid?" Iris asked.

"Our entire country can fit on this highway," Jezebel giggled.

The woman could not fathom the vastness of the country, which was one of fifty such places.

"It is huge," she told Iris.

"This is the United States," Iris replied proudly.

Jezebel noted the pride these foreigners felt for their adoptive land with curiosity. Attached to the homeland, as they called it, they nevertheless offered passionate allegiance to their new country that superseded any love the bride had ever felt. Their allegiance to their new homeland loomed in the realm of passionate fervours, one, she wished her country could instil in the population that made hatred a feverish pastime over which ridiculing the culture stood, that premise that united them in hate towards their government.

Fifteen
COUSIN DEAR HISSES ALONG

The bride sat in the arrival lounge sipping coffee with the woman she had met just that day, who, despite their recent history, grew to encompass her entire life. She looked about her, dazed by the size of things, and ease of life. As she stared to the coffee shops brimming with their clients, and the passengers that arrived from different destinations, her heart ached the miserable lot of her people. She would have given anything to afford her father a glimpse of this new world he adored through the movie screens.

Iris sipped her coffee as she periodically darted anxious looks towards the monitors, overhead. Finally, the screen announcing the arrival of their awaited flight appeased them.

The cousin arrived ashen with fear and nerves. Cousin jumped on her aunt's neck, hugging tenderly to her breast the frail woman then she approached Jezebel to peck her cheek.

They walked back through the many people toward the parking area where they had left Iris's huge, pink Cadillac.

"Here, let me help." Jezebel offered to pick the massive suitcase the woman had carried across two continents.

"No," she shooed her away, "I am not invalid. I shall die fighting."

"Who is talking about dying? I merely wanted to lend a hand," Jezebel answered gruffly.

"Thanks, but no, thanks."

"Fine, suit yourself," Jezebel muttered under her breath as she walked to her seat to settle in.

"She is a better fighter than you were," Sycamore commented chuckling.

The pair flew over the many cars on the rushing motorway, now eavesdropping on the silly conversations that all these villagers repeated without fail.

"Okay?" Iris asked.

"Fine, thank you Auntie," Jezebel replied with a brave smile.

"When do I go down there?" Alaya ached to rejoin her family.

"You jump inside her at the second of conception," Sycamore said.

"I stay there for the duration? I can't possibly; I am claustrophobic."

They chuckled enjoying the joke; mates, made closer by the tragic death.

"You look fat," cousin spat at tiny sister, who smiled.

"Thank you," Jezebel replied sweetly. "I have never been able to put weight on these bones. So, thanks."

"She wanted to insult her," Sycamore noted.

"No. They work at destroying one's self-confidence. They shatter you from within," Alaya corrected.

They drove the twenty miles in relative silence that brimmed with unease, dotted by questions about the villagers the cousin answered. Iris sounded concerned about everyone back home. They arrived home with the pair still visiting with one another in the front seat.

Having not succeeded at shattering Jezebel's calm, cousin stared dreamily towards the chattering box where, a young bubbling youth with a great deal of golden hair ticked a list of misfortunes that had befallen the city and the country during that day. Jezebel looked at the pictures understanding none of the words, as she spoke not that language of her host country.

"Do you understand anything?" the cousin smirked.

"Some things," Jezebel, who needed no speech, answered cryptically.

That put cousin on the defensive: One cannot shatter the silent, and the secure. Like a fisherman whose tasty bait a snobbish fish turned down, the cousin looked unnerved.

"See, I needed speech, and thirsted for approval. These were my two major pitfalls. They knew it, and played with my emotions," Alaya said.

"What did you do?" Sycamore needed to remember.

"I went into my room to plan my exit from the family. I thought that as soon as we reached the new world, I would disappear somewhere inside the bowels of the place," Alaya said.

"And husband?"

"That was a desperate matter altogether. He thought he protected them by lying constantly to me."

Iris yawned, stretched, and got up.

"I will go to bed now. Make yourselves comfortable, you two," she bid them goodnight.

Cousin glared her pleasure; a tiger left with a lamb, she looked towards Jezebel in sheer anticipation.

"I will follow you, Auntie. It has been a busy day." Jezebel got up, and marched behind Iris. Cousin's face crumbled.

"When does your husband come back?" she asked, needing her own kind to survive the stay.

"Early tomorrow," Jezebel said and yawned as well.

No sooner had the women entered their respective, allocated rooms than the doorbell rang startling everyone. Jezebel ran to greet her husband, delighted at having him return sooner. He looked jubilant, as he kissed and greeted his cousin.

"I got a job," he told Jezebel.

"Why did you not say anything about coming to the US when we saw you?" he asked dubiously, suspecting machinations.

"I did not know two days ago," she said.

"Come on. You must have boarded the second we left you to arrive that quickly," he argued.

"Well," she darted a look towards Jezebel, "I have had a medical emergency."

"Hope nothing serious," he asked, concerned.

"Nothing I cannot deal with, thank you." She closed the subject.

He visited with his cousin for a little while, begged off swiftly to run to his wife's bedside.

"Is that not great?" he asked her.

"Sure, great," she squealed.

"I am so relieved," he said.

"Is it good?" she asked delighted. "Does it pay well?"

"It pays the usual engineering rate," he said. "I feel relieved, though. Don't you?"

"Of course," she said. "Where is it?"

"In Chicago, Illinois," he grinned, fearing her reaction.

"How far is that from here?" She was praying for a warm place like California.

"Not too far, about eight hours away by car."

The mere idea of riding on the freakish motorways for an entire day unnerved the woman whose country of ten-thousand kilometres could be crossed six times over for that amount of time; she found the scale of space intimidating. Being with him, however, filled her with a sense of security to appease all concerns.

"I will have loving parents," Alaya, watching the scene unfold, thought.

They visited for a little while, depleted, as everyone slept.

"Sure," he said. "Soon, very soon, things will be fine."

"They have been fine all along," she said.

"For you sure, not for me; I have been going mad with the fear of having to find a job," he said.

His announcement shocked his bride. In her family, fear was not allowed. Their father had admonished against the manifestation and surrender to fear calling it the tool of the devil, the killer of faith. Even when fear happened, they never spoke of its manifestation in their circle. Her husband thought of fear as though it was a good quality, something to be proud of having, a badge of responsibility.

"Fear is not necessary," she said. "It is a sin."

"How is fear a sin, Jezebel?" He giggled, thinking her soft in the head.

"It does not accomplish anything. It is an emotion that sticks people in an illusionary space that does not exist."

"How does she know that?" Alaya asked her master.

"Some people are more intuitive then others," Sycamore replied.

"How so?" She had gotten his attention.

"Well, nothing can happen in the future. How could it? It is not here. To fear for the future is to waste emotional energy. It is a useless exercise."

"So, we live like animals, for our present now?"

"If we were able to live like animals with our intellect we would be all saints," she said.

"What are you talking about?" he raised his voice startled by her opinions.

"If you feared for your future, would it change?" she asked him.

"No, but I could plan for it to be good."

"Sure plan, but don't fear. That fear is useless work; plan as you keep the fear at bay. You can never live in the future anyway; when it comes it is the present."

"That is true," he agreed.

"We forget our past also?"

"Sure," she agreed. "Not forget, but not dwell. The only real moment is this moment. Live it at its fullest in awareness, and you have touched eternity."

"I like my sister," Alaya proclaimed onto all her realm.

Clouds of spirit groups gathered around her just at that moment. They agreed that her sister was a woman of substance and clear thought. They exchanged information about that place called Chicago. There was a man from Chicago Heights who was killed, he told everyone, when the house of a gangster was stormed. It was an interesting place to be. They called it the Windy City because wind travelled there at such high speed to wrench huge trees from their roots. He spoke to them about the swinging era with the music, jazz, bands, and dancing.

Her husband was kissing her sister passionately on the bed. She held to his form tenderly. Waiting to feel a jolt of jealousy, Alaya realised that only love for them was there inside her.

"There is a rumour that you might be going down," Sycamore ran to Alaya's side to inform her.

"Sure," Alaya answered distracted.

"No now Alaya, not later," Sycamore said.

Everyone grew excited around her. Alaya was not sure how ready she was to go down and spend nine months inside a cramped space totally submerged in water.

"Are you sure?" she asked Sycamore.

"Yes, sure," the tree sounded anxious.

"Are you coming along?" Alaya needed assurance.

"I am coming along, also your angel," she said.

"Is he ready?" Alaya did not see angels in that realm.

"He is ready. He will meet us in the womb," she assured her charge.

"That is sudden." The bride felt a bit rushed.

"The powers like the timing," Sycamore said. "As Alaya, you were born a Leo, in July. If you were to be conceived in September; that should place your birth at around the latter part of June; making you a Cancerian."

"That is not right, though. As far as the horoscope law is concerned, I should be born after my own sign, I need to be reborn at least one sign after mine on the Zodiac so as to receive the attributes of advancement. I need to be at least a Virgo," Alaya suggested.

"In all honesty, yes. Seeing however, how you have impetuously planned your own exit from earth at whim, the decision is to return you to a lesser sign, not take you forward," she sounded guilty explaining.

"I have been demoted? What cheek!" she objected hotly. "What is that for, a demotion for God's sake?"

"A Cancer woman would be soft, attached to parents, and servicing, if on the insecure side of the world. That should serve you in humility," Sycamore clarified the sign.

"As a Leo, I enjoyed great literary prowess, and prestige. How could I possibly regress?"

"Count yourself lucky, Alaya, some people are returned to much lesser states of being," the tree explained.

"What would be my birth date, then?" she needed to know.

"You did not lose much in the numbers, only one day. From July 25th to June 24th, you lost about a month's time. These are good numbers. They should prove quite lucky. Besides, the Cancer sign is a truly creative sign. These people are highly active and generally creative. You might enjoy the rest from literary prowess."

Husband celebrated his new life along with the finding of the job, they saw. He looked as though filled with tenderness and care. It hurt

Alaya's heart to see how different he was with her sister, who, in return showed a great zeal to the things of the body; the fact which thrilled him.

Numerous soul groups watched other scenes unfolding, to look around and check Alaya's progress. They came to her side to say goodbye, when suddenly, the girl started feeling a loss of energy.

"She is getting ready to leave," she heard someone say. "She is turning pale."

Alaya felt a weakness descend upon her, coupled with a sense of loss, a faint confusion, as though already in two different realms.

"Are we leaving already?" she asked her Sycamore.

"We are leaving," she answered.

"Would I remember this realm, the lessons, and legends?" Alaya sounded faint, faint, to herself.

"I will remind you," Sycamore assured her.

"What is my legend this time around?" Alaya had not asked.

"It is to live in acceptance of those lesser than you," Sycamore said.

"I needed to write a book in that first life," Alaya despaired. "I would like to write that book."

"It all depends on you. The main things to remember are these: You are not better than anyone, regardless, and you need to live in true Cancerian mode of service and patience. Mostly, however, try not to kill yourself again."

"I did not kill myself," she proclaimed.

"Just try not to hurt people enough to get them to kill you."

Suddenly, however, at the point of formulating an answer, Alaya's cloud faded, faded, to such a point where consciousness evaporated, in all realms.

She flew with such a horrendous speed to slam inside a thick wall of flesh, go into a tightly confining spot, and pass out.

Her mind worked furtively; the flight having dazed her, she felt dizziness, and confusion, which made her forget everything. There, in that wet, dark atmosphere, she felt like a fish, so she went on swimming, swimming up a channel. Other little fishes pushed her about; some elbowed her to get to the end of the tight tunnel. She had no idea why she swam except for the need to find a space inside which she could breathe. Then, something happened and everyone else lost the race. Another wall blocked her exiting. She tried to wriggle her way out only to pierce the ball of soft flesh, and lose consciousness again.

"Hey," someone called for her. "Are you okay?"

"Who are you?" she spoke without words.

"I am your guardian angel," the soft entity introduced himself.

"David? Thank God you are here. What happened?"

"You were conceived by your sister," he said.

"Sycamore?" she asked, her wits having returned.

"She prepares the womb for you. It will be fine."

"How long do we stay in these cramped spaces?" she asked.

"A couple of days; you will be so busy dividing that you will not feel a thing. It should fly by. In there, there is more space, food, a bit of light, and sounds. It is more fun for you and Sycamore. I will soon join you also."

"What a freakish thing that flight," Alaya announced. "I will work so hard this lifetime so as to never have to go through this procedure again."

"Although we are in the physical realm of the earth now, we do not have to stay cramped inside the womb; we will go in and out using our ethereal bodies. You have the capacity to roam outside the womb as though you are still in the realm of the spirit," David assured her. "If there were to be a need for you to be present, only the body would need to be here."

"Thank goodness for the power of our spirits. To sit cramped inside this tiny womb is a prospect of dire stress." Alaya felt a distinct relief wash over her. "What happens, though, if we are needed back here for some reason?"

"We would be called upon to return promptly, at which time we would fly in faster than the speed of light. From the look of things, your sister is healthy enough to have an uncomplicated confinement. You will have nine months to roam so as to figure things out for your next life on earth. Lean to understand where things went wrong while in that former body," he directed.

It pleased Alaya to know that her life outside the earth's realm was extended for a short while. That she could go in and out of her mother's body stood as a bonus and a gift.

"From now on we travel together," he said.

"Who travels?" Alaya asked.

"You, I, Sycamore and your guide," her angel explained.

"Fine," she agreed.

"In nine months, when you are reborn, things will be different," he resumed.

"Different?" Alaya needed more information.

"You could still fly out at night to gather information, and exercise some freedom for your spirit entity. To remain inside the tabernacle of the body is deeply vexing for the soul."

"Good," she said, pleased.

Sixteen
ALAYA GETS BACK TO PLANET EARTH

The village people came in droves to greet the cousin. The Western town was known for them. At the turn of the century one man had settled in that village and sent a letter back home, telling of his fortune. Others came to join him, and yet others, until fifty thousand of them arrived and stayed. They kept in close touch with one another and their country ways of back home never integrating, never melting in the huge pot of that new country of the many nationalities.

Cousin never divulged the reason for her sudden arrival to the land.

"See? I would have told everyone. I was not suited for the life down there," Alaya told her Sycamore.

"You need to learn that lying is only when one covers the truth that concerns people, help ease their ways. Anything else is not their business," Sycamore said.

"I will try very hard to remember," Alaya vowed.

Iris prepared a pot of coffee in a gurgling machine, as Jezebel arranged the Danish sweets on a silver tray in the kitchen.

They left cousin to deal with her many well wishers. She did a good job of things, as she understood how to speak to them. She told them of their relations, gave news of the village back home. The summary included people who died, and others who got married, political news of the front that fought with the archenemy. The fighting animated a screaming conversation where everyone spoke over everyone and not one person heard, truly heard what the other said.

"They like to hear their own voices," Sycamore noted.

"The very reason the dilemma in the region is unsolvable: all chiefs and no soldiers."

Morning coffee over, Iris and Jezebel went inside the kitchen to pick things up, load them inside another machine to get washed, and then prepare a spot of lunch. They took many slices of cold cuts and arranged them on a platter, another one held an assortment of relishes and pickles, and a third held sauces, of mustard, mayonnaise and ketchup. Soda drinks fizzed over their ice in crystal cups. The table was set prettily; decorated with white linen and place mats with embroidered edges.

The women sat down for a toasted sandwich.

"Their lives are so simple, so different. Lunch is a lengthy affair back home, which started at five in the morning and included healthy pulses cooked with garlic and onion, a roasted lamb, or veal, or pork, and salads, pilaf rice. It is a serious endeavour back home. Women started cooking right after their morning coffee through noon," Alaya commented.

"There is no time for elaborate cooking in this land. They are busy making money," Sycamore replied.

Jezebel ate the sandwich as though she had grown up eating nothing else. She looked towards Iris and followed her lead in constructing it. The mustard turned her stomach, and soon she turned yellow with the bile that churned inside her gut.

"Are you okay?" Iris inquired.

"I am fine, Auntie, thank you. Much of your food is new to my stomach."

"We will cook your foods tonight," sweet Iris promised.

"I will cook." Jezebel ran off with the opportunity.

"You know how to cook?" cousin interjected meanly.

"Of course," Jezebel answered. "Can't you?"

"Well, lucky cousin of mine," cousin noted sarcastically, "of course I can cook; they teach us very early how to cook in the villages."

"You are right," Iris, who understood the people, answered. "Your cousin is a very lucky man. This woman is the best that came from the old country. She is soft, well-mannered and a stunning beauty."

"Yes, a special issue." Cousin spat venom. "Why, what is wrong with my cousin? He could have married any woman he wished. She is the lucky one."

"I'll be..."Iris complained. "Surely we could be welcoming to this lady that has joined our family?"

"Yes Aunt Iris, you are right, of course. I did not say anything to the contrary. I am merely agreeing with you. She is so special." Cousin, new born in Christ, and self-appointed apostle, added sweetly.

Alaya sang to Sycamore:

I walk before my brother
He walks behind me
I walk behind some
They walk before me.
Teach me, Lord, teach me:
That the road is one;
The aim is to reach thee...

"This is lovely," Sycamore told her charge. "I did not know you could write poetry."

"Neither did I." Alaya giggled.

"How could you be lonely with a gift such as this?" Sycamore marvelled.

"I was never lonely. I was alone a great deal," she corrected.

The household slumbered in Michigan.

The cousin slept on the sofa with the television blaring. Uncle Howard settled on the easy chair beside her, snoring noisily.

"Jezebel is very ill," Alaya told her master.

"She will be fine," the old tree appeased her charge. "She is a brave girl."

They watched the bride get up to reach inside her bag for an ant acid pill.

"Is that okay?" Alaya asked.

Sycamore threw her head back and laughed, laughed the sweetness, and care of her charge.

"Stop worrying," she directed.

"I don't care to come into the world maimed by some pill," Alaya said.

"Ah, you are controlling," Sycamore announced.

"Not controlling, just hands on," Alaya laughed.

Once her stomach settled, her juices neutralized, Jezebel surrendered to a deep, drugged sleep.

Alaya flew back to the old country, where dawn broke to jerk tears from the harshest hearts. The return took a flash, a microsecond. She could return effortlessly to her sister if there were to be a need.

She hovered just over the horizon's line, above the bleached, sugar-white sand that got ready to receive the golden sun which had come each and every dawn to the mild Mediterranean tirelessly for millions of years; as though it anticipated the thrilling visit for the first time. That shore was a bride, a virgin, awaiting the receiving of her adored beloved. There, above the blue, and under the white, she soared in ecstasy, of love, of knowledge, of knowing that the world will one day see the love. So glorious was that dedication that God, Who made the sea, Had imagined the seagulls roaming over its foam, the sun that exploded the miracle of gold, whose rays bent down to kiss the tiniest of trees, brushed a hair from the eye of a bee, to fashion the diamonds that twinkled inside the waterfalls, and drop a tear of love on each and every flower in the fields. These scented blooms gave the fumes of their breath to invade the mountains, and cover the valleys. They suckled tiny lilies with elixir of joy. All that, so man, His beloved creation eats his food with joy and glee. He, the beloved, took unseeing and God the Father has not yet despaired. He repeats the miracles daily with the single hope that humans will see. All the work, for that one single glimpse from a single human is worth all the trouble. Such is the love of nature for this one creature that would one day see and behold the glories. The Creator is not whole until one human sees and beholds His awesome creativity. That was her beloved, the land of the middle earth – the heart of the globe. There, no extremes of any kind existed, neither black nor white.

The purity of soul, a splintering of the greatness of the Maker, grew eyes of the most scrutinizing where colours spoke symphonies of love to their Maker, and He heard, heard, and soared in ecstasy at the mysterious nature and its powerful gifts. Those abounded in man's very yard, as he rushed blindly through houses of worship to find, miss, come home to fight his fellow man over whose God was the greatest. The loss wrought a wave of sadness in Alaya, the depth of which rivalled that ecstasy which clutched it earlier, the poles, the poles of extremes, mirror of one another, mirror of the opposite, mirror of that duality of all creation.

Her parents' house slumbered in the darkness of the night. The dawn that broke, which Alaya witnessed, had gone missing by the dwellers of the bedrooms, shielded by curtains, and blinds. Father snored loudly, and her mother slept with one hand over her eyes, covering one ear, as if from years of blocking his nightly noises. He slept with an arm completely extended under her head, the other extended over the cover at a ninety-degree angle of one another. He smiled as he snored while she frowned as she blocked the obnoxious, intrusive noises.

The girls doubled up in other rooms. In the next room, where Alaya slept once with her second sister, there slumbered third sister in Alaya's space now. Fourth sister slept a mile away, due north of the house, over the village's only train tracks in her husband's home.

With the death of Dharma in childhood, Alaya's as a bride, Jezebel leaving the country with her groom, their once large family looked very small now.

Gone were the jubilant noises of the once busy house. There lurked vibes of sadness even when they slept; the different tragedies having imprinted the mortar and rocks with the sadness of those spirits that had lived inside the house.

Soon, Alaya knew from memory, mayhem would invariably break loose in the household with the first ray of the sun. Children will head towards the kitchen demanding sustenance, confusing parents with demands.

Alaya bent low to plant a tender kiss on her father's bald spot. He stirred and she stopped fearing his awakening. The man opened his eyes and looked up. If he were to have that other sight of prophets, the one Jesus spoke so often about, he would have looked straight into her being. A fly hovering on his bed post saved the day; he assumed it was its fluttering that caused the disturbance, extended his left hand, and brushed it away gruffly.

She lowered her form to snuggle inside her parent's bed sheets, just between the two.

"I miss the feeling of belonging to these two," Alaya thought.

Before Sycamore had time to object, Alaya regretted the attachment. She knew that the universe was part of all of its creation, that the whole was one, and the many, and that there should be no difference to a spirit between one set of parents, one family, and all the others populating the globe.

Seventeen
ALAYA VISITS THE IN-LAWS

Alaya flew south to the house atop the village. Furtive activity started before dawn as workers of the earth needed to beat the sun to do their toil. They picked the olives joyously grateful to the earth. They mounted the trunks of trees to shake them as others on the ground collected the shaken fruits, the shakers, and the gatherers, and those who sold water to the workers, and others still who loaded the sacks filled with the fruits onto trucks, and others who drove the bounty to the presses. Donkeys huffed during the crossing of the steep hill to different homes, heavy under their loads, so as to ensure the fruit got pressed and squeezed into oil and pickled by the owner's wives swiftly, lest it bruised during the wait which rendered the oil acidic. Work had to be done very fast before the bruised fruits turned acidic ruining the oil.

In the big house atop the hill that overlooked the village, which straddled the valley, its river and its cemetery, the women of the household cooked lunch.

It was to be a fried vegetable day, a meatless lentil dish and a salad. They packed the foods to send to the workers in the fields as the mother-in-law made a tomato sauce. She stirred a handful of crushed garlic over the thick olive oil, added the tomato wedges and stirred it. She covered to simmer before, Alaya knew, she would add the handful of dried mint they grew in the back garden.

The Egyptian servant laboured before the sink cleaning after both women resentfully.

Father-in-law fiddled over the roof with the last of the grapes he prepared for making raisins, and crossing to the far end of the roof turned the drying figs over to dry them for fig preserves. These were laid over a mess of bamboo sticks, and straw twigs so as to keep the air circulating under them lest they got mouldy from underneath from humidity.

"It is a regular food factory," Alaya thought. "These people live to prepare, hoard, store, cook, and eat food. There were never to be burdened by the Spirit."

"This is so unethical," Sycamore shrieked inside her charge's head. "We must never judge people. That is the duty of their God and Maker. When a human judges another, it is God Himself this human judges," she said angrily.

Down by the river of her death, Alaya happened up on a group of villagers carrying a coffin, heading towards the cemetery on foot. A woman in black cried and tore at her black hair.

Jezebel cried in a room. Sister sat alone on a dingy bed, in the corner of a small, airless room. Her crying wrenched Alaya swiftly back to Jezebel's side.

"They must have rented a flat," Alaya thought.

Alaya came close to her sister's hair, and fluttered lovingly, sending waves of love and compassion to her form.

"I miss you, Dad." Jezebel wailed loudly. "I want to go home. I hate this place, this dump especially," she cried.

"It is going to be fine," Alaya whispered tenderly to her spirit.

"No, it is not," Jezebel argued back. "I should not have married him. He is impossible."

"Oh, my Lord, are we spoiled." Alaya could see her own life in the body.

"You loved him," Alaya tried to remind her.

"I do love him. He is the kindest, most gentle soul, but shattered, splintered, confused, and oh, so controlling."

"You will teach him compassion. He has the soul of angels, and a good heart," Alaya told her sister.

"That is the reason I cry." Jezebel cried louder. "He is so gentle that his parents control him, and now me through him. I could never take this, regardless of how gentle he is."

"What happened?" Alaya asked Jezebel.

"He slapped her yesterday," Sycamore furnished the missing answer.

"Why?"

"He got a letter from his father informing him that her fourth sister's husband did not help with the expenditure of shipping her many clothes as they promised him. He had to pay three hundred dollars," Sycamore stated simply.

"That is a reason to slap her?" Alaya felt a rage that could have, if not checked, injured the man with its fury.

"Easy," Sycamore admonished. "You will pay badly for this. Besides, he is your future father."

Sycamore told Alaya that he had come home the night before after a long day's work, to a supper she had fixed. As they sat to eat, Jezebel realised that he sulked horribly and answered her words cryptically; when she asked him if anything was the matter, he threw the letter at her. She told him that it was not true. It was his father who had asked her brother-in-law if they could help with the luggage. Her brother had said that he would ask his friends at the airport. She had packed her stuff, leaving a great deal at his mother's home and gone to the airport. Nobody told her anything about the extra weight in her luggage.

"Where is the problem?" Alaya asked.

He got up from where he ate and slapped her.

"You are joking." The dead woman felt terrible.

She went back to the side of her sister, and patted her head, sprinkled her heart with joy. Her crying wrenched Alaya back to her side.

"Come. We need to go to the University, and register you for English courses."

"I will go to the University, learn, work, and leave him. I will never live with crazy people such as these. They are crazy. They killed my sister. I know this for a fact now. On some level, dear husband knows it also. For why else would he leave them so swiftly? Dad gave me to him as a punishment for her death. He took me as a remorseful gesture. I will not stay. Abuse is one thing I will not stand for."

Jezebel got up, washed her face, and went down to talk to Colleen, her new neighbour and the owner of the flat.

"Would you give me a ride to university?" Jezebel asked determined.

"Sure, honey. Give me five minutes to change. You could wait right here," the sweet woman with the southern drawl said.

Jezebel sat in the hallway. Colleen showed up soon after. She had a foot that was shorter than the other, but otherwise cut a beautifully handsome figure for a middle-aged woman. Hugh, her husband, she was telling Jezebel just then, handling the ancient vehicle like a stately Cadillac Salon, had two children, and she, his second wife, could not have any.

"You will be my child," she told her tenderly. "I will adopt you, and Hugh would love caring for you. He is a good man."

Jezebel's English, rudimentary at best, lacked much expression. She wished now that she had paid Mr. Joe, her teacher more attention; instead they had used his hour to play and laugh at the guttural sounds. Frustrated by her inability to communicate back, the young woman nodded her head repeatedly to show her approval, and gratitude.

"Thank you," she finally said, her words sounding alien to her own ears.

"It will be just fine," Colleen said, and patted her hand.

They arrived at the university twenty minutes later. Jezebel shook with nerves in the new environment. She feared being ridiculed for her accent. She grew anxious, riddled with nerves, and doubt.

"I do not know what to do," she told Colleen.

"I will stay with you. Do not worry." The woman appeased her.

They registered her for a French course, as the curriculum did not offer a course of English to foreigners. The registrar office suggested that she might learn from the teacher as she spoke fluent French.

"It is better than staying alone in the flat," Colleen suggested.

Jezebel agreed reluctantly; she feared imposing on her neighbour to bring her twice weekly to the university.

"I will study with you for the driver's test," Colleen promised.

"I cannot read or write English," Jezebel reminded her neighbour.

"I will help you translate it into French. It will do you good to learn it that way."

Jezebel returned filled with positive resolve. Something good had finally happened, and the world took on joyful hues.

"I will work and help my family. My father is preparing to retire and worries about the many children needing schooling," she said.

"What a wonderful idea, Jezebel. Yes, work towards that," kindly Colleen agreed.

And so it was that Jezebel took the first step towards a life that would prove frayed with many obstacles, but also brimmed with promises of hope and resolve.

She cleaned the flat until it shone, went to the kitchen and cooked an elaborate meal for their dinner.

As they ate the spiced fish, with the lemon, and olive oil salad, the girl felt the most awful pain in her head, and a violent nausea. She ran into the bathroom and felt very sick.

"What is the problem?" Husband shouted resentfully.

"I do not know," she said. "I have been feeling nauseated lately."

"We will go to the company's doctor tomorrow," he said.

"Thank you," she said gratefully.

The doctor said that she was with child. They looked stunned. He had just started his job, and had not gotten paid yet.

"What do you mean?" her husband proclaimed indignant.

"I mean you will have a child in seven months."

"How could you not know?" he asked his wife.

"I was too busy to count," she replied honestly.

"And your school, you paid tuition fees?" he shrieked, having forgotten the doctor.

"I will manage," she said, sounding hurt.

"She will be fine. Being so young, they never miss a beat." The doctor lent her a hand.

The ride home felt heavy and strange. Jezebel expected sympathy, a touch, a hug, something which would mark the auspicious occasion.

Nothing of the sort happened. As she stared towards his face childlike, insecure, fearful, he turned towards the window, brooding resentfully at the inconvenient timing.

"I am sorry," she finally said to appease him.

"It is not your fault. We should have been more careful," he answered.

Inside the woman, a well of fear swelled to drown her. University plans she had made, future work, a career, took a back step to this momentous event. She was scarcely ready to take on the responsibilities.

"I do not know how to have a baby," she said, pitifully frightened.

"We will figure it out," he said, still not looking her way.

"You hate it, don't you?" She needed to know how he felt.

"Not really. We could have waited a bit longer. Listen, about yesterday, I am sorry."

"I thought a real man never hit a woman," she said firmly.

He did not answer.

"My father always said that. He would not like it if he knew your father could rile you enough to strike me."

"I had told you specifically not to let my father pay anything. Is that better?"

"Even if you had told me, you should never hit people. That is so crass. I will not stand for it."

"It will never happen again, I promise. He took her hand in his tenderly."

They went home that night in silence. Husband felt very bad about himself; he fancied himself a pious Christian. The facet of his lack of emotional control he had just discovered confused him.

Jezebel vowed never to allow him to humiliate her again.

"Next time he touches me, I am leaving him," she vowed.

They ate dinner quietly, if disturbed, each roaming a private hell of confusion and mistrust.

"You made me do it," he finally said.

"Do not even try that one. Nobody makes anybody do anything. Obviously, you have seen this behaviour at your own home. Children learn things like that. Boys model their behaviour on that of their fathers, girls on their mothers'. I will not allow my child to see such barbaric behaviour."

Sycamore and Alaya cheered, hearing the grit of the young woman.

"She will be okay," they said in unison.

As the newlywed couple turned to their room to sleep, so did the spirits zip through the ether for a nightly flight back to the old country.

Eighteen
THE LAST FAREWELL

The pair sat suspended over the wings of the huge pine that sat for ages in the front garden of the village house, facing that balcony where everything happened. The mother and her daughter spoke of the day's events. The shrill ringing of the ancient machine inside the hallway briefly disrupted their discourse. The old man, his daughter, his wife, and the servant all ran from different sides of the house to answer it.

"Hello?" the old woman said in the mouthpiece.

"Who is it, America?" she screamed down the wires.

Both Sycamore and Alaya sat over the phone to hear the conversation.

"Who is it?" the old man asked resentfully.

"Wait," she shook him off distractedly. "I don't know yet. It is most likely your son."

"Yes, yes, how are you, my love?" she screamed louder still. "We are fine, all fine, how was your trip?"

"Good, good, have you seen your cousin?" she asked, eager for news, "and the mistress?"

"See how hatefully they speak of the in-laws?"Alaya pointed to Sycamore.

"She is fat?" she asked thrilled. "I told you she would get very fat."

"She looks wide in the hips?" the old woman repeated, "so fast?"

She exchanged an evil look of delight with her daughter standing beside her, while bored, both her husband and the servant went back to resume their disrupted tasks.

"She is eating like a pig, sure. Why else would they marry us two of their daughters if they could feed them? Keep watching them and let us know."

"He is what?" the lines ensured she missed some of the words spoken, "Besotted with her, I know, he is daft this way. Seeing how daft he acts around these women you would think the man was raised by nothing but males. Is that not unreal? See the suffering your poor aunt has to put up with? He is so stupid. They will ride his back like a camel. She looks pale, and withdrawn? She probably has some disease. Oh well, keep us posted, you hear? So good to hear from you, take care. Here is your cousin to say hello." She dropped the receiver in her daughter's hand.

The old lady went back to her kitchen duty shaking her head mournfully from side to side surrendering to the most shattering black mood.

"He found a job?" his sister told her cousin. "That is good. It did not take him long. He had such a good job that he lost to take time to marry Miss Jezebel, honest, you would think the world could not turn for my brother without a woman from this cursed family. She is what, a snob? Oh, how we know that. She is like her sister Alaya. These people think themselves the centre core of the earth. She sleeps until noon; what do you expect from princesses?"

"Poor Jezebel, what a mess I got her into," Alaya thought guiltily.

"Wait, wait, there is more," Sycamore nudged her charge.

"He caters to her every whim? Oh, my, God, this man never learns how to treat women."

"What did she mean by that last statement?" Alaya asked Sycamore.

"It is obvious, I should think. Do not worry about things like that," Sycamore suggested. "Keep detachment your focus. Keep the breath in the nose as you focus between the brows that would centre and remind you of whom you truly are. You need to practice this exercise until such a time that it becomes natural to you to breathe deeply from the nose and exhale deeply to the count of four."

"It is strange that she could still get to me in this way even in my current form," Alaya marvelled.

They returned to witness the sister giggle, giggle merrily; that mirth which carried all the woes of matters in the body and the ability to wrench Alaya from all things peaceful.

"Ooh, how I," Alaya started to say.

"Do not even think things like that," Sycamore stopped her charge.

Something had just occurred to the dead bride. These people, she remembered, hated one another to distraction. They had found a common enemy to unite them in the form of every new member that entered the family. The cousin spent her money to communicate with her aunt to irk her and rile her, not from any sense of justice or love, rather from a place of evil humiliation. She, her mother's sister, an able woman who had worked diligently at raising her children well, affording them the best education overseas, had suffered and sacrificed so as to make them something special. She was proud of her children; her daughter married to the richest man in the village had done well for herself, while her boys had accomplished much for their own future in wealth and material goods. Neither one of them were to marry a village girl. That irked the sisters that felt slighted.

"So, they are shooting their cousins down to hurt their aunt?" Sycamore said.

"Most definitely." Alaya felt sorry for her future grandmother.

"People of the body love nobody, not even themselves," Sycamore said.

They left the old village to return and find Jezebel lying down on the bed, yellow with sickness, reeling with dizziness. The pair understood that the newlywed couple had obviously driven to Michigan for a break with the village people and the family.

"What is wrong?" her husband asked her.

"I feel extremely ill," she told him.

"Get up, and help the women. We do not need them to speak about our lack of civility," he said.

"What are they doing?" she asked tired.

"They are cooking the noon meal," he replied.

The idea of food turned her stomach making her heave involuntarily.

"I can't think of food," she felt like crying.

"Do we need to see a doctor?" he asked her concerned.

"No, I will be fine." She tried to get up.

"Listen," he weighed his words carefully. "I just called my mother. She was very upset."

"Why?" Jezebel's mind whirled uncaring.

"She said that my cousin has just called them. It seemed she told them that you have gained a great deal of weight," he said, looking destroyed.

Uncaring to their opinion, Jezebel waited the end of his sentence. When he said no more, she felt confused as to the reason he shared such a silly piece of information.

"Do you understand what I am saying?" he asked anew.

"I can't say that I do," she replied, a bit more resentful.

"I mean, maybe, you should watch what you eat," he suggested.

"Excuse me?" She sat up just then. "You mean to say that your mother is dictating what I need to be eating from the old country, is this for real, are you serious?"

"Nobody is dictating anything to anyone. I am merely suggesting that you took care of yourself," he said.

"You are aware that I am expecting, right?" she asked as though to a toddler.

"Yes, of course I am aware." He felt slighted by her tone. "It is early stages yet, you must not pile on the weight."

When Jezebel weighed her answers finding no retorting, she stared dementedly at the floor, as though she weighed her options of what object

117

to break over his head, he saw the distress he'd caused her to awaken, frighten himself, and retreat.

"Listen, never mind, don't make a drama out of a simple remark. Do as you please," he said, leaving her.

She went outside to find his cousin coring squash for her aunt. Hate rose to blind her as raging hormones made her burn with nerves.

"Good morning Auntie." She kissed Iris' cheek.

"Are you not well, Jezebel? I worried about you," Iris announced sweetly.

"I am fine, fine. Listen, we are expecting a child. We went to check last week. I want you to be the first person to know that," Jezebel announced happily.

Her husband's cousin turned suddenly yellow with envy.

As Iris clamoured to kiss the young woman, the other woman left the kitchen to never return. That formed the nucleus of their relationship. She heard no more criticism from that side after that.

"Good riddance," Jezebel thought.

Nineteen
JEZEBEL SHINES AT UNIVERSITY

Jezebel finished her first semester of French at the end of that December. She was four and a half months pregnant. The professor, a young Mexican, was not aware that she knew any French. As she never spoke in class, he had no way of knowing. He spoke French with a horrendously incorrect accent, managing to mangle the grammar and the vocabulary badly. Still, Jezebel sat stony-faced as she took her notes of his English and listened intently to the translations.

One especially cold morning, she fidgeted uncomfortably on the hard seat with her growing tummy, the baby turning inside her abdomen. She was distracted by the somersaulting of the baby, which caused her to lose precious concentration.

When the professor made a mistake in conjugating a verb, she corrected loudly and without noticing what she did.

The pupils noticed nothing. He looked up, paled, stared at her long and hard, and resumed his teaching.

Jezebel sensed his discomfort and shook slightly from her error. If he were to ask her to leave, she would lose the four French credit hours she had accumulated.

She awaited his verdict with dread.

"You," he pointed an index towards her seat. "What is your name?"
She told him.

"Stay after class. I need a word with you," he commanded.

His English, being as terrible as hers, appeased her. She would not have to perform for him or think too hard.

"Sir?" she said after everyone had left.

"You are a French scholar?" he accused.

"Not a scholar, a native, sir. My native country is Francophone."

"Francophone?" he repeated.

"Yes. We were governed by the French mandate for years following World War I. Our former education is French."

"What did you study?"

"I studied thirteen years of formal schooling in French," she simply stated.

"What are you doing here?" he accused as though she spied on him.

Jezebel told him very briefly, and in faulty English the story of her needing to learn English for foreigners, and since the University offered no such course she took French instead.

The explanation pleased him, and he asked her gently to agree to his deal.

"You do understand that having you in my class unnerves me. I will find you distracting. That is not fair to the rest of my students," he said. "I will give you the four courses, but you go home. I will also give you A's for all of them."

"Okay," she agreed. Three months at the university, and already on her way with sixteen credit hours. Jezebel thought the deal advantageous.

"You come to register and pay for the courses, and I will mail your A."

"The major premise, sir, was for me to be with people my own age, and further hear your language as you explain the French to them."

"This is not happening," he insisted firmly.

"May I ask the reason for this? Is it against the law to take a course one is proficient in?"

"No. That however, makes the teacher nervous. Your mastery of the language far exceeds mine. That makes me nervous."

She went home relieved at not having to sit on the stiff chairs any longer, wondering what she would do with her days without the focus of the university.

"He kicked me out flat on my back with an A," she told her husband.

"That was harsh. What would you do now?"

"I will think of something to do. Maybe make some friends. A good-looking lady moved into the flat nearby, a Canadian. Colleen told me."

"She moved to which flat?" he asked, thrilled.

"She took the middle flat right across from our own. Colleen wants us to go visit her, and bake a coffee cake to carry over."

"Fine," he agreed.

She was a stunning woman, tall, red headed, lanky, and beautiful.

"I was a model," Andrea announced just as a fact.

"What are you doing here, all the way from Alberta?"

"I came with a job," she said. "Thirty-three is too old for modelling."

Jezebel, who had felt too short and dumpy, was delighted hearing that the stunning woman was over the hill, compared to her twenty years.

"What do you do for them?" Jezebel asked.

"Secretarial work," Andrea blushed perceptibly.

Something inside Jezebel stirred in knowing. Too lonely to make friends, she blocked the internal warning. She was way too green, and innocent then to know that secretarial work could shelter many shady women of ill repute under its banner.

"Something is wrong with this person," Jezebel noted consciously. "I am being warned to stay away."

Andrea could not have been a more charming, warm or more personable individual, however.

She prepared lunch.

"You must stay," she insisted warmly. "I need company lest I perish from hunger."

They reluctantly agreed to accept her warm hospitality. Seeing how gaunt she was, oestrogen surged through the mother to enlist sympathy and motherhood. Jezebel had to care for the pasty-coloured, poor, lonely model.

"I cannot stay," Jezebel, noting the time, said. "I need to prepare dinner for my own husband."

"Nonsense," Andrea dismissed the excuse. "He will come here and eat the rest of the chicken. Here, I will make two of them."

Jezebel admired the largesse of the woman envying the obvious flow of money. As they could not afford to make one chicken, never mind two of them, she felt awed by the tall, red headed Canadian.

"No thanks, he is not exactly the friendly, chummy type."

"I will invite him," she affirmed; as though he would listen to her and not his wife.

Jezebel resented the way the woman high-handedly moved on her husband, feeling a twinge of unease.

Another nudge came from Alaya's spirit, which she flatly ignored.

She cooked deftly and elegantly. Andrea raved about this recipe of chicken with pineapples, asking if they had had it. Both women shook their heads. Poulet a l'annas, she called it. Jezebel grew impressed by the elegant French accent.

She cleaned the chicken thoroughly, kept them whole, and proceeded to rub them with a generous amount of butter melted in the microwave, a contraption that impressed the poor woman whose country had just gotten television relay, poured dark brown sugar over them, salt and pepper, and stuck them dressed this way both in the oven on the highest possible temperature. The result was a golden blond chicken, crisply baked and succulent. Before serving it, however, Andrea added over the skin a mixture of the pineapple juice mixed with brown sugar. Minutes later she added rings of pineapple fruits, sending them back to the oven to get tortured for an added fifteen minutes into a deeper golden colour.

"Amazing," Jezebel exclaimed with the first taste. "I did not think sweet and sour could merge that well. In my culture, never do we use savoury with sweet."

"You are joking." Andrea proclaimed, "Owing your proximity to the Far East, one would think your diet was all a mixture of sweet and sour."

"No." Jezebel said. "It is not."

"Well, I have never had your food," Andrea finally announced.

"Now then, we will soon remedy this. How about you come next Saturday?"

"Great! Are you sure? Thanks."

"Dinner at six, shall we say?"

"Can I come a bit earlier, though?"

"Sure. Come any time you like. You do know, I am the cook, so I could not keep you company."

"I know that."

And on that lovely note, Colleen and Jezebel left their newfound friend. Jezebel beamed with positive vibes at the possible social life that loomed on her horizon. She delighted at the prospect of life, and the leaving behind the arid loneliness that had plagued her since leaving her large family back home.

"She is nice," Colleen said.

"Yes, she is."

Since Jezebel had made a friend, there was to be a conversation between her and husband after dinner.

"This is good," he exclaimed pleased with the chicken.

"The lady next door sent it."

"An entire chicken; how generous," he said.

She told him about Saturday's dinner invitation, their first ever, not knowing the way he would feel about the imposition on his free time, but he seemed very pleased.

"I will drop by the ethnic grocer in the city after work, and buy you some courgettes, yoghurt, and minced lamb," he offered. "You could make stuffed courgettes in a yoghurt sauce."

"Should we invite Colleen and her husband?" Jezebel grew excited wanting a party.

"No. Let's get to know her first." It was final.

The only fear that remained was the fact that she did not know how to core the courgettes and make the stew he asked for. She was planning on maybe a simpler meal, like koufta in a tray of potatoes and tomato wedges in the oven.

She vowed to wing it, lest he thought her an incompetent wife and homemaker.

She got up with renewed vigour and whim, attacked the house, cleaning it from ceiling to floor, shining everything. Nothing belonged to them, but she did her best to clean and dress things up for the new life of entertainment.

Saturday she awoke with severe back pains. She had entered her eighth month, with the baby growing more animated during the night, making her sleep-deprived. She dragged badly during the day. The woman wondered at the way she would finish the day without her precious afternoon nap.

Husband awoke sprightly and full of vigour, offering to go do the marketing. He believed in the division of labour: He worked at the office and she handled the household. This law, handed down on Tablets Divine, stood no chance of ever wavering, and allowed for no exceptions, lest the dire eventuality of death, her death, she understood, or a valued visitor.

It irked her deeply that he so looked forward to meeting the woman. A sense of doom hovered ominously over her chest that day.

She had twice seen Andrea since that first lunch. The woman had stuck to her unflinchingly. She would come from work and come by the flat, have coffee and leave.

"I saw a young child with you," Jezebel stated.

"It is not a child. He is ten years old. I babysat him over the week-end, the boss's son."

"Where is the mother?"

"They are divorced," Andrea said, closing the subject.

When a couple of days later, Jezebel saw a man leave Andrea's flat, she vowed to set up the borders. The woman acted like a swinger.

"Do you have a boyfriend?" she asked.

"No. I have just left a six-year relationship. Why?"

"It is odd." Innocent Jezebel marvelled, "I saw an older man leave your flat."

"Do you not sleep?" Andrea laughed good-naturedly.

"I wake up a great deal to use the restroom."

"Well, that was my boss."

"I thought you said he was in a relationship." Jezebel's heart beat fast.

"Ah, well! When did that make any difference to a man?" Andrea said.

"What do you mean?" Jezebel asked.

"Well dearest Jezebel, pure, innocent Jezebel. This is the new world. Things here stand confused; not clean white and black like you have in the old world. Men are men. They are swine. A man will get you pregnant, go to work and shack up his secretary."

"My husband is not like that. He is an angel of truth and ethics."

"They are all like that. Believe me, Jezebel, do not sanctify him, you will be more shattered this way. I can get, and have got any married man I wanted. Your husband is no different, believe me."

Jezebel felt deeply insulted by this obviously loose woman who insulted the high morals of her husband. She, now, deeply regretted having her in the flat, and the invitation issued on the weekend.

After Andrea had left that day, a new pathway of possibilities opened up to Jezebel's mind, filled with viabilities she had never before considered. Husband looked proper and acted with extreme decorum, but, she had never seen him with anyone but herself since their marriage a year before. What if he was to be acting proper for her benefit?

She made a solemn vow to find out.

"Andrea said that all men two-timed their wives," she told him that night.

"She did? She does not know your man."

"Would you, I mean, you know, with her?"

"Of course I would not. What a stupid person to put such ideas in your head. Do not worry about things like that." He sounded and looked angry.

The relief did not reach her heart. Something rankled deeply there.

"I do not even know her." What a response.

That was not an extremely good response.

She slept, angry with him, and admonished herself for inviting the woman over. Seeing, however, that she could no longer change events, she vowed resolutely to end the relationship right after that dinner. She could not wait for that Saturday to be over.

That Saturday, however, would never be over, not in this lifetime, not in numerous zillion others; as during this very Saturday, and he could deny through all ages, Jezebel's heart was to die, die to her, to love in all its forms. Jezebel's heart died to him, never to be resuscitated by any means or manner.

This would become the Black Saturday of their death, the death of her spirit, the death of dreams, and hopes; the death of life as she had known it, the death of their shared everything.

No other life she could possibly live could wipe away the scar the pair made inside her soul: Her friend and the man she put on a pedestal, acres over the best of men. She could never trust again. Her injured spirit, slashed beyond redemption to annihilate her, would never allow it.

For then, for that early morning however, hope reigned King. She cleaned the house as he went to buy her groceries. As she cut the parsley for their Tabouli a sharp pain in her carpal tunnel, a temporary side effect in some pregnancies made her hands spasm painfully, folding her thumb all the way inside her palm. She could not pry her thumbs away. Tears of pain ran over her cheeks as she waited for the spasm to subside and the searing pain to stop so she could resume her work.

As the attack abated, she minced the beans with the hand ricer, and cored the squash.

"Why did you buy so many?" she complained.

He did not deign answer her, but resumed the reading of his newspaper. The doorbell ringing luckily distracted them both from the suspended answer. Later, much later, she knew.

Twenty
A MOST HORRENDOUS REVELATION

A whiff of French perfume wafted through the kitchen to signal the arrival of their guest. It was only two o'clock in the afternoon. Jezebel remembered having said that she could come at anytime she chose. She came out wiping her hands on her apron, greeted Andrea kindly, only to feel a distinct energy, the likes of which she had never felt. It was like a current of filth coursing around her living room.

She sat with them on the couch, and they ignored her totally.

"Why do you not go finish your meal?" he ordered.

She got up and went willingly. The sauce was giving her a difficult time, as it wanted to curdle at all costs.

"Excuse me as I finish our meal," Jezebel said.

"Don't worry about me, Jezebel," Andrea responded. "I am in good company. Please ask if you need help."

"I bet," Jezebel thought, as she waddled ever so ungracefully towards the kitchen where they obviously felt she belonged.

Her energies diminished with something dire, Jezebel worked with no mind. As the yoghurt boiled, she unwittingly placed the stuffed squash inside the acidic sauce. She had always known that the vegetables would harden that way. The pair, beside her; distracted her.

"He never talks to me with this tone of voice." Jezebel felt shattered to discover he had a sexy tone of voice that he obviously used with other females.

"So, he knows how to coo to a woman, the son of a..." She stopped herself short.

"With me he orders like a master. He uses this gritty, cold, disdainful tone."

She brooded resentfully as she stirred and sweated. She rubbed her back, shifted her swollen feet on the ground, until, two hours later, he remembered her presence.

"What happened to that food?" he inquired.

"Well! I made a mistake, I am afraid," Jezebel answered gruffly, "maybe, darling dear, you could detach your bum from the sofa for a single moment, to come and tell me what to do next to remedy your meal?"

He ran to her aide. He informed her that she should have boiled the squash in salty water before dumping them inside the yoghurt, fished the yellow vegetables out, and proceeded to place them in hot water to remedy her mistake.

"When they are soft, place them back inside your sauce," he directed.

"Go back, go visit with our guest. I will talk to you later," she said.

To her utter disbelief, he ran out of the kitchen flushed with fear.

Jezebel served the meal on the round table as she shook from physical as well as emotional pains. She brooded as the pair cooed over her food, feeling generally as the guest and the pair the couple.

"That is an odd feeling," she thought. "I feel like her guest in my own home."

"She has an astute spirit," Sycamore told Alaya.

"That is a dimension my family possesses." Alaya looked livid with anger.

"Are you okay?" her husband asked.

"Fine, thank you, beloved," she lied.

Fine would have been the least appropriate adjective on earth to describe that feeling which raged within her. A raging torrent of unshed tears flooded her insides. She had removed her soul from her eyes, and to look forever inwards and upwards, never, ever to meet the eyes of another human, until maybe, years, twenty-five years later, upon meeting her soul mate, and real spirit friend, her pure sister for all lives, Lily of the Green Eyes. It was the second Jezebel stopped trusting humans. On the other hand, that signalled also the first time, Jezebel of the innocent spirit, realised her difference from other beings roaming the earth. She, obviously, had managed to remain innocent as the child that came from heaven, also, that other people lived differently; in utter disregard to morals, as well as others' feelings. Finally, women of ill repute did not necessarily reside in brothels, like in the films; they were good looking, tall women, with perfect speech patterns, that cooked and kept immaculate homes, went to offices to fish out rich, divorced males, ensnarled them, ensnarled their friend's husbands, ensnarled all ensnarlable males, so as to ensure for themselves rich lifestyles. These dangerous females easily hook suckers like her husband, who thought himself astute in the brain. Those in brothels, Jezebel had formerly disdained, became respectable ladies, going about fulfilling their needs, in an honest fashion, were much less dangerous than the sharks in decent neighbourhoods like hers, preying on husbands in their homes, making their pregnant wives cook for them.

Two and a half decades of arid desert living, Andrea the men Anemones, would give back as a gift of gratitude to the pure innocent, heavy-with-child woman, who slaved a week over her cursed meal.

Jezebel disdained the crass nature of the woman, but never blamed her, as she, the woman, owed her not a thing. Her mate, however, that was a totally different matter. Their pure love and commitment proved a fallacy to behold.

"How did you find her?" Jezebel asked.

"She is very nice. Keep her as a friend," he ordered.

"Sure," she thought cynically. "Listen, I do not know how to tell you this. I say this purely to save you from embarrassment." There, later, Jezebel would kick herself for having told him that. It was then that he got the idea, from her, to focus on the woman.

"What is wrong?" he asked.

"Andrea said that no man could resist her advances, not even you."

"She did? Do not worry about it," he smiled.

That was the extent of that conversation.

"Listen," Andrea offered days prior to Jezebel's birthing Arya. "As you are closing the flat to go overseas right after the birth, come and stay with me. Send your furnishings to storage and stay with me."

"Thank you," they both said.

"I mean it," she insisted.

Afterwards, Jezebel informed her husband that she did not want to stay next door.

"I arranged for a week off to see you through the birth. Three days afterwards I shall fly towards India. You will go home for a month then you will join me with the child in Madras."

"Fine, In the meantime, how do I spend six weeks with our child alone?"

"I arranged with a couple from church, you know them, John, and his wife Rachel. They will keep you with them."

"The couple with the adopted girl, what would they know about babies?" Jezebel asked.

"She is a nurse. She will help you deal with the baby."

Seeing how little choice they had in the matter, Jezebel agreed, and vowed to make a go of things.

"Don't worry, it will be fine." She hated it when he said that.

"Fine," Jezebel said.

He took her for a ride that day. June came to sear the earth in heat and humidity. Her husband ached to leave to his new job, so he pushed her to walk so as to ease her labour. They drove around the countryside. He stopped by the side of the road and bought tiny bags of cherries, apricots, and grapes. She gobbled the foods too fast then became nauseated beyond control. He stopped by the side of the parched park to allow her to vomit the acidic fruits.

"I want more," she asked parched.

"What is wrong with you, since when do you like fruits?" She did not.

Obviously nature ordered the meals that suited the woman's situation. She merely obeyed.

"You will vomit again?" Her behaviour confused him.

"I need more fruits." Jezebel felt a compulsion to eat the fruits.

He stopped again and bought more from a merchant off the road.

She kept the last batch of fruits down, feeling properly satiated. Pleased with her appeasement, he drove them back home, patiently, kindly, correctly; a man who saw it his duty, and kind Christian charity to care for the woman he had impregnated. His favourite word when she thanked him for something kind was his reply that it was his duty.

Funny, in light of the recent disaster, Jezebel would think that she should have but never had done something; take notice of this ugly word that she mistakenly took for love. That outing remained in her mind as the most blissful memory of a time filled with hope and the naivety of innocence, her innocence.

Three o'clock that early morning, she awoke with a sharp stab inside her abdomen that felt like no pain she ever experienced.

She sat straight up. His sleeping head resting on his pillow beside her, and under her tortured abdomen, looked like the most cherished sight she had beheld to date. Jezebel had fallen in love with her husband from the onset.

"I will not wake him up yet," she vowed, "let him rest. His night should be anxious and long."

The pain came every ten minutes pointing to the long hours ahead. As it was not especially sharp, she placed her hand on her stomach and talked to what she believed would be a daughter sweetly in her mind. Jezebel understood about this spiritual connection the two beings had established with one another, and knew beyond doubt, that Arya would understand and abide by her mother's wishes, to do her best to help ease that momentous adventure they were poised to undertake.

"Here, here, beloved spirit, you need to be strong for mom, help me birth you, work with mommy so we might come out safe and whole."

Safety was in the cards for them, but wholesomeness flew away as surely as a bird would take off from its cage, never, ever to be captured again. Doubt, the loss of all hope, would arrive with Arya.

When the pains came closer together, three minutes apart, Jezebel touched husband's head gently, fearing to unnecessarily startle him.

"What? What is wrong with you?"

She found his question odd, at four in the morning of that day of her due date, to ask her such a question.

"I think it is time," she said gently.

He jumped in one leap, and fell groggily over her.

"Would you please relax?" she asked giggling. "I need you to relax for me."

"Yes, yes, yes," he mumbled as he extended a leg inside a trouser and fell over the wardrobe.

"Come on, come one, come on," he chanted, a general with a mission.

She got out of bed, slowly, calmly and proceeded to calmly slip her comfortable navy blue dress over her head, slipping her feet into comfortable shoes.

"Could you please put my bag in the car?" she asked him.

"Yes." He went out and banged the door shut behind him.

She opened the main door noting his nervousness.

"We need to drive to the hospital. I need you to relax."

"Fine, hurry up." He was not getting it.

He ushered her out of the house and shut the door. He had forgotten his car and house keys inside their flat.

Jezebel sat on the top stair, held her stomach, and surrendered to the most pleasant fit of laughter. She laughed as she pointed to the opened window behind her over the bushes, and laughed harder when she saw him climb over the window, and fall inside to crash into the glass side table. She laughed hysterically by the time she noted he had returned having forgotten to wear his shoes.

"I am glad I amuse you," he smiled embarrassed.

"Maybe I should drive," she offered.

He sat in the seat and tore through the sleeping town, stopping at green lights, and proceeding on red ones, as Jezebel laughed all the more tears running down her face.

"You are getting us killed for sure," she said.

They did get to the hospital in minutes. He stood by her bedside through her entire labour.

"She hopes to become a nurse, and she will be a good one," he told her nurse.

"When did I mention nursing? I am a student of English, and hope to go into journalism," she corrected him to his displeasure.

"What are you doing?" she asked him when the nurse left after having adjusted her IV. "Are you keeping her company or supporting me?"

"Oh, you do not like to see anyone having fun, you selfish woman."

She simply could not believe her ears. She deferred the fight for after the birth, and concentrated on having this child, his child.

When next he picked up the conversation with the same nurse, Jezebel asked them to resume their animated talk outside. Having to feel jealous depleted energies sorely needed for tolerating the soaring pain she experienced.

She could not believe that he left with the nurse.

He came back to find his wife totally unresponsive to him.

"Listen," he awoke to say. "It is going to be fine."

"It will be fine for whom?" she asked. "You are obviously having fun."

"You are so jealous," he attacked her as a response.

He kissed her before they wheeled her away into the delivery room. At one thirty the next afternoon, Arya was born. Jezebel awoke having missed the entire birth; everything, for her doctor opted to use gas.

"Where am I?" she asked another nurse who fiddled with her IV.

"You are in your room. You had a beautiful baby girl," she said.

"Where is my husband?" Jezebel felt fearful.

"I did not see your husband. They wheeled you in about an hour ago. You were alone, no husband to be found. Do you not have any family, friends?"

That question remained for the longest time the most hurtful of that episode.

"My daughter, is she well?" Jezebel asked.

"They are keeping her at the nursery for special tests."

"Why? Is she not well?" Jezebel's anxiety threatened to kill her.

"She is fine, it's just routine. I will get her to you shortly."

Livid with anger, Jezebel called his office. They informed her that he had not showed up for two days.

"Where could he be?" she asked his sweet boss.

"He needed to close the house, and works with the storage people."

She called the house, but nobody answered.

She tried Andrea's house thinking it impossible that the vixen would be home, but she was.

"Is my husband there?" Jezebel asked.

"Yes, one moment." The world fell on its head.

"What are you doing there?" she asked.

"I am having lunch," he answered belligerently.

"Excuse me? You leave me here under anaesthesia, in a room by my self with not one person on earth who knows or cares for me, our daughter being tested, and you accept lunch from the woman I cautioned you about who said she wants to sleep with you to prove to me that I was stupid to trust you?"

"Well, I do need to eat," he replied cockily.

"Why is she not working?"

"She had a fight with her boss. She is leaving town."

"When did all that happen? Have you two been seeing one another? So, she is right, all men are donkeys. Do I need to find this out now, husband darling? Thank you."

"I will see you in half an hour." He closed the line.

Twenty-One
JEZEBEL MEETS ARYA, FORGETS THE WORLD

Men like these swarmed constantly vying for their own survival. Nothing touches Evil entities. God himself could manifest in all His greatness, still, this kind of man is incapable of beholding the glory; their sight turned outwardly, they see nothing but the pull towards flesh satisfaction. That, of course translated into the gathering of money, and the satiation of all the desires valued by the body. She, the woman that was raised with pure parents and purer ethics, understood a different law. To bind the spirit to another is God's blessing upon His creation. No lying is to be allowed inside this purity. Two bodies united become one. The Laws of the universe are all based on this law. Everything is paired in purity and form to its opposite to make that divine one. To violate the law creates disharmony that disturbs the whole. A family is the mirroring of that divine law; a man and a woman, a yin and yang, merged their energies to become Godlike. When one part of this equation is disturbed, the entire family is affected as a result. The family, being the prototype of all creation, affects the village, which in its turn disturbs the city that disturbs the nation, the region, and the world. That one family sets off a chain reaction, which disturbs all the energies to sadden God in the seventh realm. This is the pure law of two make one in marriage. Jesus Christ admonished against anyone disturbing the sanctity of holy matrimony because he understood this law.

Jezebel has always understood this simple law innately; her family having merged their beings completely to look and act as one had fashioned a living example. She lived totally in trust of her husband, and therefore, felt one with him. He, on the other hand, she had just realised, having lived with two people who hated one another, remained together for the sake of their children, was raised with the belief that keeping a low profile with his mate, to conduct a parallel life was allowed, even encouraged; for that way of life afforded the only possible method to uphold that major premise, which is to marry for the children but keep his parents' nucleus intact. These people lived according to that law of the body, and by the survival instincts; mainly, lies and deceit and contrary laws of the spirit, of God, evil.

What irked Jezebel most remained the fact that as unconscious as he was about her needs and those of her children, he saw himself as a good man, and even a piously religious one. That was hilarious to the pious woman. One person so divided that no two centres could ever meet. She noted the different people that manifested separate entities, amazingly different inside the one husband. That, being the state of the deceitful self, which could mimic God and all His virtues, His saints and the consortium of His angels, saddened the woman. There, he spoke of Sunday church, only to come back and shriek in anger and aggression at the slightest infraction. Now, Jezebel had to find the playboy who fancied himself a Valentino, and make sense of his multiplicity so as to survive.

"How do I grieve over having had my soul vomited upon by these two people as I offered my purest; this child, this angel, this difficult labour? That it is nothing to the swine maddens me. He shacks it with the whore." She felt like death.

That drove her mad. Piety hovered in their brains, as a concept of their own church-going routines, above and beyond evil thoughts, deeds, and ultimately hurtful actions.

She knew well about his spirit, but vied to hide it from her children, her parents, and the entire universe. The more evil his actions, the more protective of his reputation she became, yet the more he disrespected her, thinking her weak, concluding her fear for her children and her home as fear of his leaving her.

That was the furthest thing from the truth.

The better she treated him, the more tolerating, the more his weirdness grew. He grew abusive; for he thought her afraid. Jezebel knew no fear; she encompassed within her open womb all motherhood, their aches, grieving, and fears for their children. One idiot was not worth her shattering the heavenly angel she birthed into the world.

"I shall endeavour to be the best mother that ever lived," Jezebel vowed to herself.

For then, however, upon her birth, when life came in to show its ugly fangs to Jezebel, Arya pulled at her spirit.

"I need to see my daughter now," she shrieked demented with nerves.

"The doctor has left the hospital. We need to call him to get his permission," the nurse said.

Two hours had already passed since she had discovered her husband lunching with her best friend, teetering on the brink of a mad abyss, feeling in a limbo state of sheer solitude, Jezebel feared her own madness.

Jezebel dialled the number again.

"Do you mind if I spoke to my husband?" she hollered in Andrea's ear.

The latter dropped the phone, and ran to fetch him. Jezebel heard muffled voices, then the woman returned to inform her that he had already left and should be with her shortly.

Little demons dedicated tiny lives, and limbs to pull and tug at each and every one of her synapses. She shook with jangled nerves.

"I want something for my nerves," she rang a nurse to demand.

"We need to call the doctor." She left to call.

The nurse returned with a bassinette in tow and a minute cellophane cup brimming with pills. She placed them inside the palm of her hand, as she deftly managed to pour water in another cup.

Jezebel, the woman who was raised on herbs and spices downed the pills, washed them with water, hoping they would kill her pure unpolluted body, and jumped to catch the baby.

"What a beauty you are. Of all my stretches to imagine you, my fancy managed to reach nothing of this glorious perfection." She smiled, smiled, smiled the miracle of her real mate, and creative partner.

Arya smiled, smiled, and smiled during her reunion with her mother. The baby's eyes fixed steadfastly upon the innermost core of her mother's sight, delving through her inner core, the depth of her being, where light shone bright, and her true self resided at peace, separate from the body's filth and desires, its crude machinations, lies, deceit, and dirt.

Arya fixed onyx eyes onto her mother's spirit to fasten her sight, imparting wisdom, love and total security. Arya told Jezebel things, if repeated, the world would shackle the new mother and commit her to the nearest of asylum. Never had the new mother thought what occurred in her first meeting with the newborn possible in this realm of daft humans.

Arya told Jezebel that she knew her from before, and that she loved and appreciated her that she had picked her from among all other women to come to her as her child. She said that she would take care of her mother; that she would never, ever leave her.

There, Jezebel felt her being stir in response to the being of light, felt in clear awareness the changes that took place within her.

"How strange is that?" she thought. "The child speaks to my spirit. You know your mommy, Arya, don't you?" she asked the entity from heaven.

Not for a second did Arya's sight flinch or stray away from her mother's sight.

"I swear the doctors are wrong when they say newborns are unsighted at birth. I have never before this moment felt so seen. You are mine, mine, and mine, Arya. With you I feel complete, finally complete, creation and pure love all in one bundle, and here it is life. I have waited in desperate ache expecting this one moment."

She swore afterwards that the child winked and smiled broadly.

"She is a spirit I know well and love. That child of mine is as old as time, and oh, as perfect and knowing."

He came finding them thus, the mother with her face glowing, beholding a miracle of creation.

Jezebel stared at him flatly. Her soul was taken, and her spirit filled with an ecstasy the likes of which no stupidity of man could ever disturb.

He brought along a camera and preceded to take pictures, none, Jezebel thought, would come out well as he never got anything right, ever. Not one picture came out. She did not ask him where he got the camera from, she simply knew. They were playing the let's take naked pictures with the Polaroid game as she was in painful labour having his child, she thought.

He made a show of acting, acting, and acting, the dutiful father that he was, not daring to come close and kiss his wife's cheek.

"I hate you, and curse you, and your parents for growing such monsters through all eternity. I shall make my life as separate from you as possible, and you shall never find my spirit to break again, or my heart to shatter it. That would be my punishment on your cursed evil nature." She cursed, not knowing yet, that cursing is wrong, because it returned to the curser, multiplied.

"Where did you sleep?" she asked as a fact.

"On the couch in Andrea's living room," he said, sounding sheepish and cocky at once.

"Why did you not tell me about that plan?" she asked.

"I think I told you," he said lying.

"And I agreed?" she asked him sarcasm dripping venom.

"Yes," he repeated.

"Listen. I just had a baby not a lobotomy. Please, do not insult me any further. I have never felt less valued, more humiliated in my whole life."

"Listen," he went for the acting job.

"Shut up," she shrieked. "Just shut up."

"I am sleeping there tonight," he said.

"And you are not screwing the whore, right, just using her couch? You must not think too highly of me to try this lame excuse. Either that or else you are a bloody moron. I think, maybe both. How do you think you are going to resume your life with me after this event? You probably think that you will figure things out later, right? Well, good. We will see."

"I am actually not sleeping with her whether you believe it or not. The first night I spent there she paraded before me in skimpy, lace underwear, but when I did not react she said that you were right; that I was different than other males she had known. So, see, here you go."

"All that and you went back to stay, and back. Is that supposed to make me feel good? That I am left under anaesthesia while you play the underwear game with the whore friend?"

"You are such a drama queen," he said.

"He is trying to kill me." She felt her blood pressure skyrocketing.

"Do as you please. Whatever suits you is fine." She had never seen this aspect of him. "When do you leave?" she asked.

"The day after tomorrow," he replied.

"You plan to shack up with my whore friend until then?"

"Yes. I will take you tomorrow with the baby to the nurse where she has a room for you, I will sleep at Andrea's and she will take me the day after to the airport."

"How cosy." He is mad, she thought.

Jezebel concluded that she had married a demented man. Everything about his behaviour contradicted the laws of even adultery. The philanderer did not have the decency to hide his whoring, but then, it was in his blood.

"Do you have plans with Andrea then?"

"Of course I do not. Do not be ridiculous." He was asking her to allow him this fling.

"Demented Evil entity," she thought.

Dejection never felt more suicidal. If it were not for the slanted eyes of Arya, she would have easily killed herself, and finished with this world, and its evil inhabitants.

"I will see you tomorrow then." He had already had enough.

He left them alone. No mother, father, sister, friend, priest, nothing. She had just split her insides nearly in two, and all his energies brimmed in the vicinity of the camel with the red hair.

Hysterics and the sudden drop of hormones clashed at the door of her heart, as she laughed uncontrollably at the incongruous image of the shmuck fancying the taller, older, redheaded cow.

"You are crazy," he spat before he left.

"I must be because you are still breathing," she hissed.

"I am a snake. The asshole turned me into a bitter, poisonous snake. I shall poison myself and this infant."

She had studied somewhere, her psych classes somewhere, that repression poisoned the spirit. The woman could not remember through her jitters how they suggested the relieving of repression then, suddenly, she remembered, the need for expressing lest suppressing killed her, the expression, that was it. How? There was something about imagining the cause of one's agony in the face of the pillow, and beating it, beating it, beating that pillow and screaming inside it one's grievances.

"How to do this thing here?" she wondered.

"The bathroom." She had quickly found a solution.

There were not many options left to her; it was to be either suicide or revenge.

She dropped her feet off the bed, and a soaring pain sliced through her from head to toe, in a clean motion. She shrieked to get the nurse running.

"What is wrong, Are you in pain?"

"Yes." Jezebel tried to catch her breath.

"Strange! I have just given you a pain killer."

"Do you have anything for heart pain?" she thought, but instead she said, "It was probably my fault. I got up fast and furious."

"Let me help you," the woman said. "Why are you taking the pillow inside the bathroom?"

"I am dizzy, maybe you could support my head over the toilet bowl."

"Okay!"

"She thinks me dotty," Jezebel mused.

Alone, with the nurse's buzzer tucked firmly inside her hand, she waited for the door to close, then she started beating that white pillow, softly at first, then harder, harder, and harder still until the tears came, flowed, soaked her, soaked the tiles, ran into the corridor over the white floors that smelled of antiseptics and soap, through the elevator, flooding the stairs, the town, all the way to Lake Michigan, which ran down to the rivulets, met with the broad Mississippi, all the way to the graves of poor women like her who believed husbands' lies to shatter their bodies and rift their spirits and died having children of men like him who could not make believe that splicing her vagina in two halves to get him the angel he planted within her was worth his attention.

"You bastard son of a bitch, you stupid, stupid bastard," she chanted rhythmically with the slapping, "I hate you, will always hate you, until I die and then some."

Her blood ran like rivers to cleanse her internal organs of his filth. She cared not whether she lived or died, but relished the cleansing of that pure place she had given him in worship and devotion; her tabernacle of love, her offering of pure womanhood, the meeting place of their souls, her pure one, and the wicked entity that he presented her in deceitful manipulations as his covenant of eternal respect.

"It is not his fault," she beat the white pillow as she chanted, "not his fault, not his fault. I am stupid, stupid. That is it. Nobody is to ever come close enough to that pure fountain as to succeed in sullying it, ever again. I will close my spirit from here on to all humans."

There were definite flags, of all colours and shapes she chose not to see; from the second her sister met him, the flags flapped in the wind for all to see. For some odd reason, everyone opted to shield the viewing. Things were clear from the onset; the people of the dark had never attempted changing their realities, it was the innocent, naïve ones of her family, that chose to disbelieve that which they saw and skimmed over the filth.

"He cannot help what he is. It is up to me now to stay or leave." She could not see her way through this one as yet.

"I can't leave him, though, no matter what he does. My poor daughter needs to have a chance in this life. To leave him now would ruin that angel of light. I must buckle up and stay for her sake. My life would not amount to much anyway if it were to continually cause her misery. I am not that important." Having made the decision of love eased her heaving spirit.

"I will stay and shield my spirit from him. I will never be the same open field to him. He should sense my death, and shrink in horror at the monster he made of the lamb. That would be his punishment." She hit the pillows still.

Exhausted, and dried up, she stood off the toilet seat to reel from weakness and hit the floor. There, in a pool of blood, she remained as she awaited the world to cease its silliness and stop its reeling. As she waited, like an injured dog of no real consequence, an image of her once beloved crossed her mind, to bring about a renewed bout of hysteria. This time, however, she laughed, laughed, laughed hysterically at the idiocy of humans in their blindness of greed, and desire.

Suddenly, she felt fine. Calm reigned through the universe as the Lord God, the lamb of all sacrifices, rose on His cross before her sight, nailed and bleeding from His five wounds.

"Forgive them Father for they know not what they do."

He hugged her right there on the bathroom floor, as her life juices flowed from every orifice of the filthy, crude body. He kept her close to His chest, where her heartbeat finally stilled all her fury.

"What do I do now?" she asked.

"It is your destiny, Jezebel, your destiny. You must choose your path."

"Right," she said. "When were we allowed a path, my Lord? By the way, what have I done to incur such wrath, such an awful destiny with these entities?"

She heard him say as clearly as the day that shone bright, and the assurance that the stars of his night would soon follow on its tail, and the depth of night that would showcase them, that the man, as awful as his spirit may be, was blind, not bad, and that what was allowed to happen was a gift, a gift of growth and maturity.

"A gift?" she shrieked to bring back the nurse.

"Alright?" she asked.

Jezebel nodded sweetly to appease her, running right back to the gift idea.

"How could my total shattering possibly be a divine gift?" she asked, incredulous.

He was gone, but the idea with its strange possibilities appeased her. They would never leave her, she knew. She, a child of the higher realms, could not even understand the logic of the body. Her reality lay in the clutches of the wicked and lost but her spirit, she understood, belonged to the realm of heaven.

"They will help me. They are here with me. I need nobody else. My daughter the angel and the God on the cross dying to wash our sins away will see me through this hurdle. I could tolerate some of his vinegar. That is fine."

With that decision, Jezebel forgot everything, and knew beyond doubt that her life will encompass many more hardships, and that they would help her, and that the road to his divine abode was filled with such horrendous thorns, but that, the rose was worth reaching.

"The rose is beyond the thorns. The jewel is hidden behind bars. The rose is beyond the thorns, my beloved. Thank you for the opportunity of Love," she prayed.

When he came back to pick her up, he looked shattered by guilt, and remorse and fear of being attacked, instead he found her serene and calm, ready to go.

"I should always remember never to forget what an idiotic person this man is. He should have at least hidden his trail; that would have been merciful all around."

"I did not want to spend the money on a hotel," he said.

"So, you ruin our lives instead by staying with the whore?"

The heat of the earth felt like the hell of insecurities she had been thrown inside. A six-week jail sentence, solitary confinement with a new baby, she hardly knew how to handle, and a husband gallivanting the globe in search of fun, loomed beyond her horizon of fear.

"He has got it all worked out. He now had a wife and a child, security. Money overseas, and trips to the lap of mother, and sister dearest, who were pleased with the money he gave them, heavenly. That man will rot in hell for what he has done to me and my late sister," she thought as she smiled secretly.

He thought she had gone bunkers, lost it, but said nothing.

"I will take you there, and come back in the afternoon to say goodbye," he said.

She did not ask where he went, she knew, and did not care. Her covenant with the man of peace was done. She would leave his punishment and fate to her masters, the managers of the earth. He would definitely reap, and reap abundantly, she knew, as the law dictated that good deeds generated good rewards and bad deeds returned ten folds to their perpetuators. It would be fun to watch him squirm, she thought with relish.

Now as she extended her cheeks to her lover to kiss chastely, as his spirit ran to his whore leaving his child behind, she heard a chorus of angels sing.

> This load that breaks my back is heavier than I can bear.
> Yet, there is sure belief, beyond doubt, as I feel you there.
> As I ooze my life juice to birth this angel I hold tenderly,
> I feel your hand holds me as surely as I witness the rain.
> Do never let go, please beloved, my child needs your care.
> Hold fast, true, you would never give more than my due.
> Whatever you think I deserve, I accept in fierce humility.
> My brother, Father, your angels are now my sole family.
> Appease, fury overtakes my weak body so I might strive.
> Not for me, never, only my child, the pure tyke needs me.
> My life, enlist in your service with mirth and joyous glee.
> As my sight sets upon the intended destiny: Your peak.
> Take my life, take the hurt, do what pleases you with me.

Jezebel made her deal with the beyond as she sat, broken, badly injured, a dog whose accident had left him there, alone with no recourse left but that dejection and confused, fixed stare.

Violence and abuse were lost humans' legacy to the world. Some old Bedouin in her beloved plains back home had once said to her father, she remembered just then, that wisdom needs to be the prayer for all those one loved and cared for. When her father had asked, baffled by the old man's words for an explanation, the old man had explained: Wisdom, he said, is all that is needed to survive the stupidities of humans. Without it, injury to self and others is undoubtedly all there seems to be out there.

Her mate was consumed with his new beloved, she felt. He was in love. An energy that had taken him over ensured his loss. He could focus neither on their child, nor on that woman that had delivered her, for more than a few seconds. A flight instinct urged him to flee, to such a point, that madness roamed in his eyes. Jezebel settled her baby in the upstairs room of the strange house she had never seen before, to come down and speak to the stranger she had never known, to find her husband revving to leave at all cost.

"Okay, fine?" he said from the door.

"Stay and have lunch with us," the nurse asked him.

"No, I need to go."

"Why do you let him treat you like that?" furious, the nurse asked.

"Because my law knows nothing but love, that is why," she responded with assurance and calm.

"He leaves you to live with this woman? He is depraved, evil."

"Let the sinless one cast the first stone. That is what he wants to do, though I cannot shackle him to love me. He needs to want to love me, right, Rachel?"

But Rachel the Christian did not understand nor was she willing to understand such biblical drivel. Hers was the religion of control.

"The Bible said..."

"Spare me." She went up to her room for a rest.

Jezebel placed Arya in the crib, went to her bed nearby, and slept; each time the baby awoke, she fed, changed her, and went back to sleep as to feel energetic enough to care for her.

The next day, he arrived with Andrea at five o'clock in the afternoon. He had spent the entire day with the strange woman, as the nurse who attended Jezebel, nagged and cussed him.

"He brings her with him?" The woman felt deeply insulted.

"She wants to see the baby and wish you good luck," he said.

Jezebel said nothing to the woman, but sat across from her silently.

"I am leaving to go away to California," the woman said.

"Goodbye," Jezebel said.

"Listen," she hesitated. "He is such a good man. You are right where he is concerned."

Jezebel's fingers bunched up by their own volition to form a fist, as the body tensed to strike the woman who ruined their lives as she sang his graces.

"Oh, he is the best, the top absolute best," Jezebel said.

He kissed his wife, and rose to leave, to spend the last night with her friend.

"Why don't you sleep here?" the nurse asked him.

"The sofa there is more comfortable," he replied boldly.

Jezebel said nothing.

"I will see you in a couple of months," he said gruffly, hatefully.

"I would rather you died first," she said. "One fair day you will see me sleep with another man, one you have considered a friend. I would make sure you know how this feels, you stupid bastard."

"That would be a sin," the stupid bastard said.

"No, the sin is to sleep with a demon like you."

On the third day of Arya's life, the nurse told Jezebel that her family would go away for their summer vacation for a week.

"A week?" Jezebel knew nobody now, not a soul; that frightened her.

"Did he not tell you?"

"No. He told me nothing."

"We will leave a number in case of an emergency."

"Thank you." She went up to her room to take yet another nap.

On the fourth day of Arya's life, when hormone levels dropped, to bring down alongside them the ceiling of life, Jezebel awaited the onslaught of hysteria all morning, when nothing happened, she thought, "good, I must not be alone, after all." The angel in her ear had told her about the sacrifice and spilling of blood on the cross, and how this atoned for the sins of the world; she half-believed his words. Now, this morning, alone in the world; when usually all the family and friends rushed to gather around mother and baby, to celebrate life, and thrill at the joyous event, she was alone, and at peace.

"Your life is about you, you, not him, not anybody else," someone deeply intelligent, told her.

"Yes," she agreed, "It is my child, my life, my birth, my own."

Not even hysteria was permitted Jezebel as Arya needed her. She went up to Arya's room, where Arya lay, completely still and quiet. The miraculous child ate, slept, and stared at an angel overhead.

"Let us go shopping. We need some decent clothes to visit our grandparents."

Standing above the silent crib of her daughter, Jezebel made a vow to herself and a covenant with her child; to study and become independent of the man she married, even if only in an economic sense. So, in all practical considerations, whether he knew it or not, she had totally divorced him that instant.

The prospect of home, five weeks from then gave her the will to live.

Something else, an idea, whose dire need had just materialized; it was about offering all acute pain to the Lord in the heavens for the atonement of peoples' sins in purgatory.

"I offer the pains and suffering to your mercy for those who suffer different purgatories in different realms of planets; take them, receive them and forgive their sins my Lord."

That small prayer worked wonders. Suddenly, a sense of well-being suffused her body, and a sunny outlook overtook her being. Gone were the demons that pulled on her nerves and the black fog that invaded her chest cavity so as to choke the breath out of her.

"See?" she told Arya in her baby seat by her side. "Mommy will take you shopping. That will be your first shopping trip, ever. Is that not fun, going shopping with your mother?"

They went shopping each and every day of Arya's second week of life. Each day, the ritual was the same, she would dress up, then dress her daughter with the utmost care, then, carrying her in her chair, she would fasten her up in the front seat, and together navigate the roads to different malls and shopping sprees. They stopped for lunch, whereby Arya got her bottle first, then sitting happily in her chair, she would watch her mother eat, and try to hear the noise all about her. They closed the malls before they returned home with all the commuters who returned from different jobs to choke the highways, making driving impossible.

That stalling of traffic did not affect Jezebel; she relished it. They, the nervous commuters whose drivers tapped the steering wheels nervously, were all she had of a social life. She turned around to smile at those beside her, to get a weary smirk of annoyance in return. She needed them to see her; as she felt like fog disappearing with the first ray of the morning sun. They were, these harried commuters, all that she retained of contact with this world.

Twenty-Two
JEZEBEL AND ARYA TOGETHER

They went out again, and again, to return things, and buy others, and on the fifth day, Friday, she went to a supermarket to buy some meat to fix a meal for her host family's return. She would make them chicken with meat and pine nuts rice, and a fatoush salad.

Arriving back to the house, she was shocked to see their car in the drive.

"Where were you?" Her hostess looked genuinely frightened.

"I went to the Super."

"Women and babies never leave their homes for three weeks."

"We are not normal women and babies."

They chuckled and hugged, and Jezebel felt better at seeing them, and their little girl-child.

"What happened? You are early."

"There was a torrential storm in the park where we were. It grew miserable enough with mudslides."

"I see. Oh, well. I am going to cook dinner."

"That will be nice. We ate nothing but picnic foods."

She cooked dinner as the nurse tended to baby, and soon the days flew by, days during which time Jezebel never thought of him, his friend, or anyone.

Then, it was time to go back home. That would be the first journey back since her arrival to the New World.

Jezebel flew over the clouds right with the plane, soared higher than its tail, and the slow passage of time stopped its laziness and sped ahead to thrill her.

In Paris, they had three hours of waiting time. She got out with the baby held to her heart and the carriage at her elbow to walk down thirty concrete stair steps to visit a hairdresser and fix her hair.

"Can you do something pretty?" she asked the French hairdresser.

"You need a trim," the nice man suggested.

"Do what you like."

Arya sat by her side in her little carriage, as everyone in the shop marvelled at her sweetness. The baby did not cry, nag, fidget, move or whimper. She sat still and alert watching her mom intently.

"It is eerie the way she keeps your eye in hers," the hairdresser said.

"Well! She is very special."

"The way this child stares intently into you and the atmosphere," an older client offered. "She is reborn."

Jezebel had never heard the term before, nor did she know anything about the philosophy.

Arya chuckled, and was seized with a fit of hysterical laughter. The woman crossed herself quickly and left.

On some strange level, Jezebel, having seen so many children in her family born, sensed the different powers in her own child. Arya, she felt, emanated a form of communication that spoke to her mother, and further, understood Jezebel's thoughts and acted upon them. The child's nervous system received information like an antenna: When her father left, the child did not ask to eat all that night.

"Is this normal?" Jezebel had asked her nurse-hostess.

"No. It sure is not. I have never seen that before. Newborns eat on the hour sometimes, and usually every three hours. Arya has not eaten since her father left. That is odd."

On the plane, Jezebel noted with great surprise that Arya did her best to be accommodating. It grew so uncanny that passengers commented on her lack of conformity as a baby.

Once home, Arya grew animated; she still did not exhibit much fussiness, exert undue demands; the child showed alertness, as though she recognized the country, and smiled broadly.

The entire family stood at the airport to meet and greet them. Jezebel's dad wrenched the baby out of the bassinette and held her overhead like a trophy, a grand prize. He smiled broadly up to her, and pirouetted as the family, and other people stared.

"My grandchild," he repeated profoundly.

People cried, his wife, Arya's grandmother, turned beet red holding back her own sadness so as to not disturb the happiness of the occasion, even strangers cried witnessing the love of the giant man in motion. So unabashed, so lacking in self-consciousness he was. Jezebel's father revelled in being madly in love with his children. Showing emotions had never threatened his manhood. He had always been overtly loving; the very reason both his daughters suffered the emotional aridity, bleakness of their shared husband's desert.

When a person grows with emotional expression, he grows sweet and tender like a Lily by a riverbank. To shield this source of sustenance is to kill the being on the inside. Like the lily away from the source of sustenance, it shrivels and dies.

Jezebel also soon found herself thrown into the air. She landed in his arms. Like a child, her innocence exploded with the love, and all the rest, the preceding years; a hateful memory stuck inside a thick fog of the most violent hues imaginable, evaporated. There was the diamond white that shimmered eternity in the dew of his eyes. It ran down his cheeks, and stopped glistening by the corners of his mouth, and an anxiety which bespoke of his suffering her absence in the furrows of his forehead grown deeper in the last years. Those age lines seemed to plump up before her eyes.

"I missed you, Pappy." His gritty voice rasped its way through her heart. "How are you?" he asked.

"I am fine, just fine. I missed you too, Dad."

Mother swayed embracing her and Jezebel feared her collapse.

She looked up to gauge the state of her child, only to catch Arya laughing loudly; chuckling happily her own return inside the fold of love.

"She is absolutely beautiful," Mother said. "Just like you as a baby."

"She is much more precious than I could have ever been, Mother. This girl is strange."

"Did she have a mark?" Mother asked.

"What mark are you talking about?" Jezebel marvelled mother's timing, "What sort of a mark, mom?"

"Like anything different, like a veil, a white mandeel, lace covering, around her body when she was born?"

"What's a mandeel Mom?" Jezebel grew impatient with the conversation, needing to run and grab the child that was being passed like a sack of sugar overhead, from hand to hand.

"A mantilla lace covering that is born with the child," her mother said.

"What is it, a family tradition?"

"Your late sister Alaya was born like that. I was hoping. Never mind all that, welcome home. She is very special. She looks exactly like Alaya. Your father thinks the resemblance uncanny," the mother added.

"Arya would look like my sister Alaya because my sister and I resembled one another," Jezebel replied.

Jezebel, finally released, ran to reclaim her daughter.

The celebration heightened Arya's colour to make her eyes shine with joy.

"You liked that, you rascal, you did," Jezebel cooed her love to her daughter.

Arya threw her head back and sent forth the eeriest sound of mirth Jezebel had ever heard.

"She sounds like Father when she laughs," second sister commented joyfully.

"Yes, like a gritty record of these old phonographs our father used to play," Jezebel replied.

"She chuckles like a wino," Joe said proudly.

The children hugged and laughed at the second born in their family, the first grand daughter, and she was grand, as Father had commented, fourth sister having had two months prior a boy grandchild for them.

"Life is perfect," Father sighed in the car as the motorcade left the airport heading north towards the parents' house for a big luncheon in the new arrival's honour. "Children and grandchildren are the best things life offers; God would never give horrible, truly horrible people this gift," he said.

"They must be," Jezebel agreed, unsure that God punished his people that way.

"Is she good?" her father asked. "Do not worry. Your mother and I will care for her so you can rest during your stay."

"Thank you. I know, Father." Jezebel felt whole again.

"Did you hear what my mother-in-law said?" Jezebel asked.

"No. What did she say?" he asked. "Why are they not coming to lunch with you?"

"She picked the baby saying, 'oh, well, she is not much, but she will fatten up and be fine.'"

"Tact has never been your mother-in-law's forte. The woman is touched. She treated your sister like a slave. Alaya will soon haunt all of them from heaven." He chuckled with mirth. "There are definite recourse measures for people such as these. You would think that having had children of her own the woman would understand that one must never speak to a new mother in such a manner."

"It killed me. They always dismiss everything I do."

"Well! Do not let it bother you," he repeated, his colouring belying his cool.

"She is saying to me not to think much of myself just because I gave them this skinny runt," Jezebel added.

"Let it go, Jezebel. Do not analyse her every word. They will drive you mad. It is extremely damaging to create body pain by remembering hurtful words that evil people tell us. It creates psychological time which one could get stuck inside to create much misery and disease. One needs to understand the source of such words, place them in their proper perspective, chuckle over their stupidity, knowing that the entities; the sadists, that plan, hurt are very disturbed. Let it go," he said wisely.

"It is easier said than done, father," Jezebel replied.

"It is easily done. All you have to do, darling, is learn to live in the moment, that very now. Your now is this miracle of bliss. Look at her and know the glories of our beloved Creator. Look around you and see, see, not look, but see the gifts of the earth," he said as they crossed over the Mediterranean.

Looking up suddenly around her, Jezebel felt a jolt of reality. She suddenly saw the glory of the place, gifts of a deeply creative lover etched for her eyes only. She, lulling inside her miserable little head, had nearly missed the magic. The sun exploded overhead in rays of orange, burnished copper, and gold, dancing joyfully for her return. It ran to the navy blue sea to kiss the rocks, and lick the foam and bop and skip in ecstasy the happiness of the perfection. There, white frost detached itself, bubbled and jumped, over the rocks, over higher rocks, went back to the sea for momentum, and tried again, came closer, and closer, and a spray of the most delightful aroma kissed the tip of Jezebel's nose.

The air was a gift of the most divine. It smelled of all kinds of blossoms, orange blossom, lemon blossom, tangerine blossom, grapefruit blossom, and together they created a heady mixture, to madden, to gladden, to intoxicate her.

"That is the whiff of my home. I will never be able to leave again."

The earth gathered energies to offer its smells to her, and a tangy tartness prickled the inside of her nostrils.

Some people over by the side of the road that skirted the ancient seashore, fished, while others built a bonfire over whose flames they cooked the fish they had caught. Simple people having lived simple lives for centuries with the utmost of presence contrasted greatly with that plastic life she had just left.

"God has never left this land," she thought reverently. "Life is still pure here."

Finally home, Arya surrendered to a sound sleep. The uncanny creature just six weeks old, acted as though she revelled in the fact that they had arrived home.

Jezebel had worried about Arya's facial mannerisms when she slept; she frowned and smiled, sighed and made little crying noises of torture, as her little body spasmed, shook, and her mouth pouted. She, the mother, felt sorrowful for this child with her own memories of torture.

None of that happened once Arya settled at Jezebel's home.

Dinner, a feast of love prepared with Mother's heart, was planned to please Jezebel. It touched the woman deeply that they had prepared all her favourite foods. Father had sent his driver to buy the chicken she liked from a merchant a hundred miles away.

"Did Raymond open shop in this region?" she asked, as she admired the chicken simmering to perfection in a tray glistening with butter, and smothered with a bed of succulent garlic.

"No," he chuckled pleased. "We had him prepare it just for you."

Dumb with emotions, she wrapped her arms around her parents.

"I love you," Jezebel told them. "You must not spoil your children this much. How could they survive other people?"

They ordered the chicken from the Bekaa Valley, sent a driver to buy an entire barbecued smorgasbord from another region.

"That is too much. How much food do you think I can eat at one sitting?"

"It will be in the fridge for you. Not that you will have much," her mother said.

After dinner the girls congregated in Jezebel's room for a chat that extended through most of the night. They wanted to know about her life in the faraway land of mysteries and magic. She wracked her brain to remember points of interest in the huge place; its tall buildings, its many shops, and amusement centres.

The reality stood different to her mind. She found nothing in that huge land to blind her from their love, and could remotely compete with the intimacy of her nature at home.

"Are people nice?" her brother Joe, asked.

"They are nice, generally. They greet you in the stores, and smile. They are not deep enough to embrace you, though. Their friendliness feels like a moral duty," Jezebel answered.

Finally depleted, Jezebel fell into a deep sleep, only to hear Arya whimpering. Fighting the needed slumber, she managed to open her eyes, only to witness her father kidnapping Arya.

"Sleep," he said. "Mom and I will care of her."

"What time is it?" she asked disorientated.

"It is six o'clock in the afternoon," her mother said.

"Why did you not wake me up?" she said ashamed. "Did you get any sleep?"

"Yes. She sleeps fine. You needed your rest. What do you want to eat?"

"Some of my food," Jezebel giggled.

They warmed all the foods, sat around the table like old times and as if life had never changed.

"Why it is that home is always the best place to be?" she announced happily.

"Unconditional love," her father simply replied.

"I will be up all night through," Jezebel feared.

There was no need. As her body started recovering, it reclaimed all its lost sleep. The minute she placed her head on the pillow, she fell asleep. In her sleep, she again felt her father reclaiming the baby, and tending to her needs.

It took an entire week to make her feel somewhat human again. Jezebel could now resume her life.

"A visit to the in-laws is imperative," she told her mother.

"Yes. It is important that they see Arya."

The girl sent forth a mighty shriek.

"What is her problem?" They all jumped to her cot.

"Nothing, there is nothing wrong with her."

"The child has ancient eyes." Father announced solemnly.

"Yes. She is probably a prophet," Jezebel said for a laugh.

Twenty-Three
THE STAY THAT ADDS HORRIFIC DIMENSIONS

She worried about being with them for the first time on her own. She knew how difficult they both could be.

They ran down the lift to claim the child and her things, hurried with Arya up to their flat as though to claim their child.

"Wait," Jezebel demanded.

Nobody turned.

The house smelled of kibbe and fried aubergine, and her mother-in-law took her straight to her room.

"This is your home, princess," the old woman told Arya.

Jezebel's heart sustained a painful jolt whose source and meaning evaded her totally.

They made a fuss over the newborn, which she tolerated generally well, her head turning to clutch at her mother's eyes.

"She checks on you all the time," the grandfather observed.

"She fears we ate her mother," the grandmother joked.

Arya threw a fit just then.

Jezebel carried her child swiftly away claiming her need to be changed. She ran to her own room, and closed the door to breathe.

Arya, changed and fed, fell into a quick sleep. Jezebel put her head on the pillow to rest a bit before lunch. The door opened again without a knock.

"My madam wants you out now," a servant she did not know, said.

"Yes. Do you mind knocking next time before entering the room?"

"I feared waking the baby."

"Knock softly then. Thank you."

Jezebel, exiting soon afterwards, heard the maid telling the old lady that she was a stuck-up snob, to which the latter responded that the maid has not seen anything yet.

"Sure, the best is yet to come," Jezebel promised them.

They both jumped startled. The old woman, a hearty peasant with fierce attributes and few sensibilities, adjusted her attitude quickly so as not to appear caught. Jezebel knew that she was afraid for her hands shook badly.

"Your sister-in-law is sitting in the living room. She is dying to meet you, my dear. You will no doubt form a solidarity front and torture me, for you know; no daughter-in-law is ever to love her mother-in-law, ever. I don't care what anyone says."

"The woman has a stick wedged tightly up her bum, and shall never be able to chill," Jezebel thought.

"Give me a break, okay?" she said instead.

"I see a huge difference in you," the old woman admitted respectfully, "I thought you were a weak one like your sister Alaya. But, no it is good. Yes, sure I will give you a break lest you throw a fit and embarrass us before our neighbours and relations. But, once your husband is here, we shall see to your attitude."

Jezebel felt like hitting the nasty woman.

She left the kitchen instead, heading towards the living room.

The woman stood up to greet her. She was sweet and elegant. Husband's brother also stood up and planted a kiss on each of her cheeks.

"Welcome," he said shyly.

"Thank you."

"This is my wife."

The two women sized one another up, and kissed as a formality.

She had a foreign accent, and a high-pitched voice. They asked about her stay, and told her that they enjoyed her husband when he left her and the baby to spend three days with them.

"He wants me to take you to hospital for a check up. I have made the appointment for next Monday."

"I will take her," husband's father offered.

Jezebel resented being handled as if their property.

"I am sorry. I can't next Monday," she said softly.

"Why not?" new sister-in-law asked kindly.

"I promised my parents to attend a barbecue there next Saturday."

"No. You cannot go," her mother-in-law shrieked from the door.

"Excuse me?" Jezebel asked in sheer disbelief of the rudeness.

"You are excused. You are not going anywhere. This child is ours, ours, you hear, and you are our kin, and this house is where you stay."

Jezebel giggled softly, thinking the woman daft in the head if she thought she could still control her. Now that husband was technically in the doghouse, there was little influence of his mother's on her decisions. They carried no weight whatsoever, his sulking brother, or his sullen sister, nobody, none of them mattered any to her. She and her sister before her had sacrificed dearly to uphold the man's love, the blond man with the smile that could shame the silver sun. What he did to her as she gave birth to her daughter told volumes as to his character.

"It is true what they say about the apple never falling too far from the tree. It is crucial to be born to parents of character the lack of which could taint the best spirits before they are aware to drive the pollution away," she thought, as she smiled their way politely.

"Thank you, Auntie," she said, opting for a diplomatic route. "I appreciate it."

The response came with such soft sweetness that all of them were taken aback, prompting husband's brother to give an approving smirk with a raised eyebrow and puckered lips.

"We will see. It is early yet. You have just arrived." His mother turned to oversee their lunch.

Everyone knew she was defeated, even her, especially her.

"When would you like me to make the appointment, then?" New sister suppressed an obvious chuckle though her approval showed in her eyes.

"The Monday after, please."

"You intend to stay an entire week at your parents'?" Husband's father proclaimed.

"Yes," Jezebel stated simply. "It is very difficult to lug a baby and her needed things about."

They were called to lunch, which was followed by a nap, then by a stream of well-wishers, coffee, chocolates, and the incessant doorbell ringing, and nosy people needing to know her innermost thoughts, who thought they had a right to pick up the baby any time they chose without asking, and to plump her on breasts emanating cheap perfume and other smells.

"I would like to see the baby," an old, removed aunt announced heading straight to the room where the baby rested.

"Excuse me," Jezebel said, and took off after the bold woman. "She is sleeping."

"I will look at her in her cot, if you do not mind."

"But I do mind. I do not want her disturbed. She is an infant."

The woman never spoke to her again.

"You hurt her feelings," her husband's father said. "She is the wife of my second cousin."

"I am trying to protect my infant," Jezebel responded simply.

In all honesty, though, the visitors made the day pass. They offered a respite from the old woman's cutting tongue and erected a buffer zone.

Finally, this initial visit over, she packed her things, relieved to go back to her parents.

157

"Have lunch, at least," the old woman demanded.

"No, thank you. We have just had breakfast," she said sweetly. "May your home always remain prosperous."

"It is your home, and that of your brothers-in-law, my poor children. May the Lord give onto them for the generosity they show us."

"Sure," Jezebel said. "The Lord is good."

"He is good to those who treat their parents well," she plunged a barb into the young woman's side.

"Yes. Precisely, the very reason I am going to my own parents."

Having dug her own ditch, the shrew could do nothing but lie inside it. Jezebel pecked her cheek at the door, and left her thus with her mouth open, ready to reply, with nothing coming out.

Twenty-Four
JEZEBEL HIDES THE TRUTH FROM EVERYONE

The phone rang the second they arrived at her parents' home.

"It is your husband's father." A servant handed her a telephone.

"Yes?" she said.

He went into a liturgy of things then announced that her husband had just called from India.

"So?" she asked. "Is there anything he wanted from me?"

"No."

"Well, thank you," she said. "I appreciate it."

"Well, do you not want to know how he is doing?" he asked.

"I am sure he is doing fine, right?" she asked.

"Right," he sounded bemused.

"Then, thank you very much."

"How is the baby?" He did not want to leave her alone.

"She is fine, thank you. And you?"

He got the message.

"See you soon?"

"Yes, soon. Goodbye now."

She clicked the phone.

"Let us go to the big city of the north for some kenefe," she asked second sister, who was driving by then.

"Yes. Who is paying?"

"I am paying, of course."

"Can I bring my boyfriend along?"

"No," Jezebel said. "I want to be alone with you like old times."

"We'll watch the baby," their mother offered.

When the women returned from their brief outing, the parents informed them that Jezebel's husband had called from Madras.

"He sounded so sad not to have found you. It seems impossible to get a line from Madras. He had to wait hours around the flat before they connected him. I felt sorry for him. He sounds lonely. Let us call him back."

"No, Papa, there really is no immediate need. He works shifts. We will never find him. He will call back," Jezebel replied, refusing the offer.

She did not want to talk to him. Having to act for the sake of saving her family grief might give him the wrong idea. She was deeply hurt by him, and did not want to speak to him.

"He said he will call you next Monday at his parents'," her father said appeased.

"Sure, next Monday then," she repeated, trying to sound excited.

When next Monday came, she met sister-in-law in the lobby of the hospital, where the latter introduced her to her sister coming to visit from a sister state nearby, and the three of them huddled inside the elevator towards the doctor's office and her post-natal check up.

"You know, you are stupid," her sister-in-law blurted.

Jezebel looked behind her. She could not imagine that this woman, two decades her senior, could be so rude.

"Excuse me?" Jezebel inquired. "Are you addressing me?"

"Yes, yes, you," the woman repeated.

Jezebel noted the saucers her sister's eyes made.

"The woman is nuts," Jezebel thought.

"I am sure you have my IQ scores, right? Else, you cannot make a statement of this sort, especially as I just met you for a few minutes just a week ago. Care to tell me why I am stupid?"

"Yes. Your husband came here speaking behind your back. He told his mother that his brother sent you a hundred dollars last Christmas, which you sent to your sisters."

"So?" Jezebel scarcely saw the reason for the drama.

"So? What do you mean so? Does that not hurt you?"

"Of course it does. How could it make me stupid, however? That is my dilemma at this point. To my mind, that makes him stupid."

"Why did you tell him?"

"Because I am an honest woman who does not steal from her husband," Jezebel said.

"That serves you right, then." The verdict was final.

Jezebel wondered at the motives of the woman. As she felt her uterus tighten, the woman swallowed her injured pride.

"I would not interfere like that if I were you," she finally said.

"I want your good," the older woman defended her stand.

"You could be procuring my divorce with this piece of information. One must never gossip. It is a cardinal sin," she said with a gentle tone of wise finality.

"How is that considered gossip? I am merely looking after you. Should you not know what lover boy is doing behind your back?"

"Listen, it is gossip because I feel like cyanide poison has just been injected into my bloodstream, as my brain churns ways on how to kill the bastard I have married to offer my purest best and this child. See? Now, with your titbit of poison-covered care I feel a dementia taking me over as plans to ruin this new child's life whiz dementedly inside my thoughts. See? That is the reason gossip is sin. Not only is it deadly black magic that poisons lives, it is returned a thousand-folds-back to you as well. You, obviously, for some reason want to hurt us as a couple."

"Surely not; I had your best interest at heart. I merely wanted you to be cautious around him," she said looking grieved.

"Why would you care? I don't even know you. If you asked me, you care nothing for me; judging from the disdain you have shown me during our first, and this second meeting."

Awareness made the older woman shake upon hearing the explanations. Her eyes, saucers of fear and darkness, she looked confused as though she had never given credence to another human's explanation before.

"I care for you," she said lamely.

"You have a funny way of showing your care. Listen, please, this is your drama somehow, so as such fight it yourself. Only thing is I wish the world stopped dishing black magic about. I am so amazed that you consider yourself educated and work in the field of counselling young women out of their troubles."

"Do not insult me," she went for an offensive.

"Kindly, do not order me about. It is not about you. My concern is for all the impressionable young ladies you advise. Know the human being before you dish the information. Do you know my state of mind? I could be suicidal. Your juicy information could have made my child motherless. So, exercise a bit of caution when you speak." Jezebel thought the woman senile.

Both women looked at the floor, as they crossed the linoleum of the long corridor leading to the doctor.

"Thanks. I will take it from here," Jezebel said. "I appreciate your help."

"No problem. Don't you want me to stay with you?" she asked.

"No, thanks; I will walk back to the house. See you there soon?"

"Yes. Nice to see you again." She sounded confused.

"Yes. Goodbye, nice to have met you," Jezebel addressed the sister.

They were gone, and Jezebel closed the clinic's door on them.

"He has his nerve, the sonofa," she fumed.

Her check up went fine, and the doctor they picked for her was extremely pleasant and personable.

"You are young and very healthy. Say hello to your husband for me. I knew him as a freshman at this university." He showed her to the door.

"Thank you. I will remember you to him. Thanks." He bent down and kissed her face.

"I will see you with the boy next," he said, "very soon."

With a broken heart, heavy with hurt and dejection, she descended the stairs.

"I will not go to him," she vowed silently. "I shall find a job and raise my daughter on my own, somewhere, maybe run away to Brazil where nobody knows me. I will take the airplane and head in the opposite direction from Madras. They will think they are seeing us off to meet him, but no. Something is deeply wrong with the man if he could treat me the way he has done to travel the world and to gossip behind my back." She was stressed during the entire walk back to reclaim her daughter.

"Thank you for keeping her," she told his mother.

"No thanks over duty," the old woman replied, genuinely happy. "She is my baby, you know. My son's daughter is my daughter. This is the daughter of my beloved."

"Sure," Jezebel said. "Thank you then on your lover's behalf."

As the family slumbered the afternoons away, so did Jezebel for lack of activities. She awoke startled by an unknown fear.

"He is going to call." She felt it. "Not being able to show them dissent, I need to go out so he misses catching me."

She dressed Arya quickly, told the servant that she was going to visit her uncle on the other side of town, left a number where she could be reached, banged the door, took the elevator down, and hailed a cab from the entrance of the building.

"Where to, Madam?" the kindly man asked.

"Four El Choubak, please," she said.

In the back seat, Arya stirred uncomfortably in her baby chair. The child's face contorted in a series of gestures that broke her mother's heart.

"She dreams like an old, tortured man," Jezebel thought. "I wish I could help her."

No sooner did Jezebel finish formulating the thought than the infant sent forth a screech of the most heart-wrenching intensity. The driver stopped immediately.

"She is an old reincarnated soul," he said. "She is an old one, that one."

Arya stopped suddenly, and smiled broadly.

"She is smiling now," Jezebel assured their driver.

"She is reliving her death, and rebirth." His explanations unnerved Jezebel.

"We are Catholics, you know. We don't believe in rebirth. Ours is a heavenly religion."

"Yes, I know," he replied politely.

Something inside Jezebel recognized the truth of what the driver said, making her insides quake ominously.

"Do not be frightened, young lady. I meant no harm," he said softly, having noted her fear.

Jezebel appeased the man, seeking to allay any guilt on his part. She further informed him that they had no point of reference as to what he professed of other lives. He told her stories about his people inside the mountains who met and reconnected with their past lives' parents. He was a Druze, he said. Speech such as the one he blurted was commonplace for them. He told Jezebel that theirs was more a philosophy than a religion. As such, it did not clash with anyone's religion.

"If anything it is not about God but man knowing himself," he said gently. "Man does not know who he is."

"What an odd thing to say," she thought as she patted Arya frightfully.

"It is the oldest science on earth, dear madam. This is not some made-up superstition."

"Yes, I am sure," she answered politely.

"No, you are not sure." He challenged her to unnerve her.

"What do you mean?"

"If you believed me, you would have inquired," he stated angrily.

"I believed you." She felt defensive.

"Why do you not ask me what I meant then?" He was not about to let go.

"I was merely being polite," Jezebel told the man.

"When someone tells you a thing of the most crucial implication to your and your child's life, you need to ask questions so as to learn and help your baby."

"What are you talking about?" She replied angrily.

These were the most intelligent men on earth. Ten thousand years before the birth of the Man of Peace himself. Because your daughter is a rare specimen of those souls who suffered during their last deaths, obviously, to come back shaking, and shrieking the way she does, maybe, I thought, you need to look into it," he said. "Not that you could find any information as the science of the mysteries is a hidden one."

"What do you mean, hidden. How could a science that old be hidden?"

"It has always been hidden. It is not a science revealed to fools."

"But that is wrong. Be it science or religion it should not favour or divide people."

"It is far from being divisive, my dear lady. The science was hidden for the safety of the leaders: Through the ages, these people were killed for their knowledge, they hid in caves and mountains to survive what they had discovered."

"It is an elitist science, then," she said simply, if antagonistically.

"No; if anything, it is quite the opposite. It was the science of the fakir, the poor, not the rich."

"This is counter-prejudice," she announced, triumphant at having caught him out.

In reality, Jezebel felt stumped. It was as though the man had suddenly changed their native language, to confuse her. The words sounded identical to that common language the country spoke, but suddenly the meanings had been allocated different codes.

"I have no idea what you are speaking about. Could you possibly explain it simply, in a nut-shell-like?"

He threw his head back, and surrendered to a fit of laughter.

"In a nutshell, yes, that is good. Twelve thousand years of the most intelligent findings man ever made in a nutshell. It is impossible. Alajawid in our region study this science all their lives to die and come back again, to resume their studies and still miss it. In a nutshell, okay, let me see. It is like this. Some monks in Asia, Japan, I think, followed a man who spoke about the fact that man was, in essence, and by force of his soul, eternal."

Throwing a glance at his rear view mirror, he found the woman clutching the sleeping child, staring back at him dumbfounded.

"So? Jesus said just the same thing."

He wanted to explain to her that Jesus of the Nazarenes was an initiate of this science. He spoke in fables, and told of the need for secrecy, so people did not kill their brethren, those who spoke the mysteries, only to be caught by these killers and die a horrible death on the cross.

To tell this beautiful woman with the doe eyes of an injured deer caught in some headlight would not have been merciful, or compassionate. His aim was to help the woman with the burden in her lap, not confuse her.

"Yes, Jesus is a beloved man of these people," he affirmed simply.

His words relaxed her defences enough to inquire further.

"How could the Druze of this region be connected to the science of the Far East?" she wondered, giving him a new route through which to approach her.

"Yes. It is strange. Ten thousand years ago King Assoka sent his ships filled with monks and initiated sages towards the land of the kings of Egypt, the Pharaohs. There later arrived into Egypt sages from our region, Joseph, the vizier, and Moses, the esteemed prophet of the Jews. The Pharaohs shared the science with these Jewish people, taught them the Science of the kings. From there, it went forth into Palestine with the Jews who left with Moses. There, inside Palestine, these tribes, arrived to form the Kabala society, congregated and worshipped, taught it, and practiced it," the driver told Jezebel.

"All in secrecy," he added.

"How did the Druze of the mountains get the science?"

"We also came from that Egyptian branch. We have kept the texts hidden for thousands of years," he confided.

"Yes. I have heard that your religion was secret," she told him. "Also, that you have an affinity to the Jewish population on our borders. Now, I understand that the science binds you."

"It does. We initiate our people, the elite worthy of the sciences, in caves under the places of worship in the dark of night," he imparted to shock her.

"Are you initiated?" Jezebel wanted to know.

"No, Madam. I am not intelligent enough," he stated simply.

"This is a terrible religion which makes people feel more or less worthy," Jezebel told him.

"It is not about that," he clarified sweetly. "It is not about bias, but profound ability. It is a difficult science to grasp. Everyone, we are told, will sooner or later grasp its intricate details in some future life. Those who are ready in this life are assessed and initiated."

"What is it about, generally?"

"It is about the classes of man. See, man is not one man. Man belongs to several classes of creation: Man one, the one that cares for food and drink only and the pleasures of the body; this man is still primal in his outlook and abilities. There is man number two, who is a bit more evolved through several deaths, and rebirths; that one is more advanced mentally and has developed a critical mind. He is the educated person who has risen above the needs of body alone. Then, you have man number three. Well this man has started to feel the stirrings of conscience, of spirit divine within his being, and is trying to find out, much like you. You, Madam, are intelligent enough and need to study. Then, there is man number four.

This man is already a philosopher, poet, writer, an anthropologist a carer for society. His conscious has grown into consciousness: He feels all humanity's pains, and works selflessly at some way to alleviate miseries for all humans. Then, man number five: This man is focused on his spirit, and works diligently at nurturing it with deeds, prayers, dedications, meditation, and the like."

"Most people are what?" Jezebel wanted to know.

"Most people are probably within the first three ranks," he said. "I am probably man number two. My need to furnish food and drink to my family leaves me little time to cater to my soul, or that of others," he said, and sounded mournful.

"I see," she said, feeling his sorrow acutely. "The last two numbers then."

"Ah, man number six would be the monks, sages, the Pluto, Plutarch, and Einstein of this world, almost but not quite there," the driver told the woman.

"Would they ever reach there?" she asked unclear as to the destination.

"These humans are very close to reaching their intended destination. In their next two or three lives, depending on how hard they worked, they would attain," he explained. "Jesus," he added, "was man number seven. He was God in the body."

"What blasphemy. Jesus was God," she objected vehemently.

"I hate these Catholics," he said kindly. "Yes, Madam; that is the reason this science is a secret; no religion could accept its truth. Each religion wanted to make its prophet a God," he said finally.

"Excuse me?"

"You are excused." He exploded in laughter, which irked her.

She handed him the money, as they had arrived, and had been sitting in his car for a good fifteen minutes.

"Good luck," he bid her sweetly.

"Thank you. Is there a book I could possibly read?"

"Sure. There are several, but not in our country. In the East they speak of the science as though there is no other," he said, still chuckling.

"I am going to India." She had swiftly forgotten about going to Brazil.

"There, get yourself a yogi, and read the Baghavad Gita." He waved.

"Wait, what does yoga have to do with that higher science?" she asked him.

"Everything and nothing," he laughed as he drove away. "Ask your yogi."

"Do check it out," he almost begged. "One day you could help your child. She is going to need you."

Her heart ached a little upon seeing the stranger leave.

She picked up the heavy child's seat in her right hand, placed her purse on her left elbow, and carried the baby's diaper bag on her left shoulder. Ambling this way, she took the elevator to the sixth floor where her uncle lived with his new wife. There meeting her were her mother and sister.

Her uncle opened the door greeting them with a smile of delight, reached out to relieve her of the baby's belongings.

They sat in the huge living room with the many bay windows overlooking no bay but tightly closely–knitted high rises, on which balconies white wash hung swaying in the breeze of the dawning fall.

Her aunt ironed linens, as a cleaning lady attacked the white kitchen with some antiseptic solution, the fumes of which wafted throughout to elicit a coughing fit from the baby.

"The windows are all open. Place the baby near one," her mother said.

"It smells good in here," Jezebel said, suddenly ravenous.

"You probably have not had breakfast, right?" her sister asked.

"That's right. There is so much to do with a baby," Jezebel told everyone.

"Is everything okay?" her uncle asked concerned.

"Fine; I miss my husband," she lied to cover her shaky hands.

"Understandable, sure enough," he accepted the lie.

Lunch was a fabulous affair. They had outdone themselves to please and welcome her. As they sat, about to drink the coffee, the phone rang.

Jezebel knew instantly that it was her in-laws.

"How are you?" he always asked.

"Fine, thank you." She waited.

"Your husband just called here. He really needs to talk to you. We gave him the number where you are. I expect him to call you soon," he said.

"Fine, thank you."

"I need to leave." She gathered her baby's things as she spoke.

"You just got here," her uncle's wife said surprised, "Anything the matter?"

"My husband will call me at his parents' home within the hour," she told them.

"Fine, then. I will give you a ride," her sister offered.

They left.

No sooner had she arrived at his parents' than she received a phone call saying that her husband had called her uncle's house. He spoke to her mother.

"What bad luck, you two are having." Her mother sounded pained for them.

"Yes, is it not? Oh, well, I should be with him shortly." Jezebel appeased her mother.

"He misses you both terribly," her mother said, pleased. "He is such a model husband and father. How you have lucked out, my darling."

"Yes. I am so lucky to have had landed him, Mom, and my sister. It was a double whammy as our fate was concerned." Her mother missed the sarcasm.

"I would not call Alaya lucky, sweetheart, regardless." Grieved, her mother corrected her.

"But, she at least enjoyed the great man, Mom, even for a measly month." I am going crazy, she thought to herself. "I fear the man killing me too now."

"Yes. I guess." Her mother was not so sure.

Her postpartum syndrome, a gift of Arya's birth, raged within Jezebel. She felt like shrieking from nerves, and recent events. Her heart thumped nervously at the lack of pathways. Her energies spoilt for a flight, as life and her duty to Arya dictated wisdom. She asked his mother to watch the baby, and went to take a long bath.

Twenty-Five
JEZEBEL POSTPONES HER JOURNEY TO INDIA

Rage which stems from emotional abuse, the likes of which the pure Jezebel incurred, stood impossible to deal with. The body, wanting survival, did not stand much by the spirit in any dilemma, and far less when a rich man abused his mate while she had his first child.

Jezebel's body spoke to her during these decisive days of her turmoil to dictate wisdom.

"Wisdom, where would I find this divine trait?" the poor girl argued with the body's spokesman, the brain.

"You," she shrieked her silent impotence, "You have no morals, self-worth, self-esteem, nothing. Wisdom is the spirit. Wisdom is the state of the spirit under any circumstance," her angel said.

"The spirit is a dreamer. I know about survival. Yes, fine, sure, he screwed up badly, but what are the alternatives?" The stupid body advanced an airtight case against her. It had an astute lawyer that understood manipulation. "Where would you go, Brazil? Give me a break. You are not that independent. Tell your parents? That he killed their first-born and now tortured their youngest girl? Father would finally take a gun to the man and end up in jail for the rest of his natural life. Besides, you know how happy his mother and sister would be when they heard that your great love would not stay with you, but with a Canadian whore when you had his child and needed him desperately. Do it for the parents. Go there, and give him hell," that brain said. "To stay here and stew in rage is not so intelligent."

"I really have no choice," she thought sadly.

"None for now; in the future, if you played your cards right, you might have a chance."

"Fine, for now, however, for as long as it takes, I shall not speak to him," she vowed.

"Fine," the body's lawyer agreed. "Just go to him. You two could never fix things a continent apart."

"Right," Jezebel agreed. "I will go fight for the both of us. My sister died out of desperation over the stupidity of the man."

Her decision made, things felt uphill. Everyone breathed easier. Even his sister and mother acted courteous to Jezebel.

"This child of yours is an angel," his mother proclaimed in a rare generous mood.

She allowed him to contact and speak to her. His love could have melted icebergs. His wife thought him idiotic. As he gushed over missing her and their child, she replied coldly, if politely, in monosyllables. His voice turned her stomach, and his love made acid churn within dangerously.

"I will never trust him, regardless. Something is deeply wrong with this man. He is both angel and devil equally."

Jezebel acted normally, not to her own normal self, but theirs; as they never gushed over their mates, they found nothing wrong with her flat tone.

He explained in details about the manoeuvring he'd had to do to reach her, asked her about her health, that of the child's, generally speaking too fast and too much.

"When are you coming here?" he sounded breathless, enamoured.

"In another month," she said, having problems with the loving.

"No. I could never take another month. One week. That is it. I do not know if I could take that even."

Jezebel, having always thought the man honest, knew differently now.

"Next Friday, it would be three weeks," he added. "With the six weeks of your stay in America, that is what?"

"Nine weeks," she said, doing the math for him.

"My child is over two months," he exclaimed, hyperventilating his love.

"Yes," Jezebel replied, ice dripping venom.

"Are you okay?" the man asked, truly retarded.

"Fine, just fine, thank you. Could I be otherwise, with so many blessings?"

"I have been counting the hours to see the pair of you." He was seriously begging.

Noting the silence around, Jezebel realised that everyone was listening to her conversation. She opted quickly to change venue so as to irk them.

"You have been counting the hours?" she giggled sexily, "how sweet. You know I am counting the minutes, right?"

"Yes. I miss you so much." He sounded sincere.

"Oh, I miss you more," she proclaimed.

"You are so stupid," she groaned mentally.

Both women left the room as though on some cue she'd missed.

"How are your siblings, are they all well? What is new? Talk to me, I have been stuck in this place," he said.

"Oh, great, my family is great; especially with the fortune they had received at Christmas time. I heard so much about that. I need to thank you for being such a dedicated husband and mate. I am so lucky to have you. It is divine the way you support and protect me, and prepare your sweet mother before I arrived. She was so grateful and sweet when I arrived."

"Listen. Could we possibly discuss this when you come? I am truly sorry about that," he said.

"Sorry? Did you say that word? Wow. You must have awakened. Yes, we will discuss it. On that you can bet your life. For now, I need to tell you to please not call any more. You are controlling me even from the recesses of the East. I will see you Mid-October. One more month away, surely your love can withstand that. It will be good for you. Remember, you told me about suffering building character."

"I love you."

"Good-bye." She hung up quickly.

Upon hearing of husband's constant calling, at a time when phone calls from faraway lands were prohibitively costly, a luxury of the elite, her father, appreciating the dedication shown to honour his child, insisted she honoured her husband and fly to remain by his side.

Jezebel hated the mere idea of being with the man who had tortured, slighted and humiliated her during the birth of her Arya. She hated the way he dismissed her when she begged him to stay with them that last night before his sojourn, but hated most of all, the fashion with which he dismissed and discarded her at her lowest, most vulnerable weak point, to go with the whore she had cautioned him about; pointing to him that Andrea wanted nothing less than to destroy them as a couple so as to prove her point, validate her filthy lifestyle of whoring.

Jezebel was hurt over deep issues of morality, that age-old feud of the universe between forces of goodness versus those of evil. For her husband to consort against her with the entities of the dark pointed to her that he was an evil entity himself. She wanted to run away from him at all costs because she feared his proximity would sully the pure within her, eventually.

Looking for a way to escape the man without hurting her, already shattered, parents, she found none. To build her happiness over the rubbles of those she loved beyond dedication, and worship, was, to her mind, as evil as what her husband had done unto her.

She decided to save her parents, and further offer them solace in upholding their dream of having finally found that rare gem of a man they constantly bemoaned missing with the many marriages they had arranged for the many sisters.

"He is a gem, this man, a gem, I tell you. I told you that, Jezebel. Did I not tell you, Mother?" her father gloated to his wife and daughter.

"Yes, Father, you did," Jezebel agreed.

Mother, clueless as to the real world, smiled broadly at considering the luck of her daughter.

"You need to go to him immediately," the proud father urged.

"I shall, Father, I shall." Jezebel felt wedged between two walls.

Finally stuck, finding no viable options or valid reasons to convince her father as to her need to stay, she booked her flight to India.

The plane ride went well enough, except for the nauseating smells, which wafted from the cockpit to madden the young woman who had never smelled so many spices, and condiments before. When the food arrived, however, Jezebel spit out the first mouthful, knowing that hunger would be her second companion on the long journey, the first being dejection.

"I should have brought something to eat. The journey is so long."

She soon realized that everything the Indians made had to have a great deal of chillies, no doubt for their palates had grown deadened to subtler foods and the fine herbs of the Middle East, the cinnamon, and allspice.

Further, they believed not in any dairy products, such as cheeses, yoghurts, or soft butters. Even the bread grew alien in its preparation. She ate the apple, and decided to sleep.

Arya ate and slept in her cardboard bassinette, smiling angelically to her mother.

"You are no trouble, my darling, are you?" Jezebel appreciated her daughter's cooperation.

Arya threw her head back to give forth the most startling series of chuckles of merriment.

"This girl is not normal; she reacts like wise, old people," Jezebel thought.

Having read her mother's mind, Arya's laughter developed into a hysterical fit.

A kindly steward walking the aisle, having mistaken the laughter for a spasm of pain, came running.

"Is she in trouble, Madam? We have a doctor on board," the steward inquired.

That wrought additional peals of merriment from the two-month-old, who, looking around the plane seemed to laugh at everyone's stupidity.

The doctor ran towards the startled woman whose child looked as though on uppers, and inquired as to her diet.

"What did you feed her? She sounds high," he asked.

"Her formula, doctor, nothing else," Jezebel replied defensively.

"Well," he looked startled. "I have never."

Arya laughed still, squirming in her mother's arm, and starting to experience discomfort, as indicated by her heightened colouring; a deep red, that has started to take on hues of light blue.

"She needs to stop. She is having some fit," the doctor said worried.

That wrought more laughter from the baby.

"Do you think she is possessed?" Jezebel asked the doctor.

"I am not a shaman, dear woman, but a physician. Whatever you daughter is doing is not a medical problem, I assure you. Having said that, I have never seen a young baby act this way."

"Surely," Jezebel trembled, "someone must know."

"We, in India," he said haltingly, unsure of how the mother would take his words, "believe that some old souls come back from the dead with memories. I think that your daughter is a very old soul."

"That is?" Jezebel held her breath, not truly wanting to know, and yet...

"What religion do you subscribe to, my dear Madam?" he asked gently.

"The Catholic religion," she said, and sounded defiant.

"You will excuse me then if I withhold my diagnosis of your child's hysteria."

Arya had settled down by then. She played in the cardboard box animatedly. She turned her hands and followed their movements intently.

"Look at her," Jezebel said. "What could she have been dreaming of that might give her tears in her eyes, stomach spasms, and gestures of so much hurt and pain, to suddenly heal and play?"

"A previous life," he blurted.

"Jesus Christ was sent by God the Father to save humanity from sins," Jezebel said. "He promised heaven and hell. We don't believe in reincarnation."

"Do you truly believe that?" he said shocked.

"Of course I believe that." She pouted insulted.

"How did you investigate this story? I am not saying it is not real, I am merely asking for your own personal inquiry. Was there any?" the doctor inquired.

Suddenly her memory of the taxi driver, who had spoken about the Druze in the mountain hiding the secrets for two millennia, rose to freak her out. His words matched to the last letter those spoken by the Indian doctor. Could it be possible? Jezebel wondered, that a science of such importance is kept away from people? What could the reason be?

He spoke still, but she heard nothing of that which he said. Inside the woman a fear grew, and the inkling of excitement.

"I asked you, Madam, whether you have investigated that which you believed totally?" he repeated his former question.

"No," Jezebel replied. "How does one inquire?"

"One inquires in matters of crucial belief'- ones that matter greatly to one's life and death'- by reading other teachings, other beliefs, sciences, and philosophies," the doctor directed. "In your case, inquiry is crucial seeing the fashion your daughter belies that Catholic belief which states: Man dies, man remains dead."

"Religion is a matter of blind faith," Jezebel said. "It is sinful to double-check one's God."

"You give your most valuable asset, your life and that of your child, to someone who does not respect you enough to prove his story to you, my dear Madam?" he asked gently.

"Yes. That is our religion."

"Well! Mine is different. My religion is a philosophy that encourages its followers to investigate, check its viability, first- hand, urging the faithful to check for himself, and conduct his life, make his decisions accordingly. That is the difference."

"What is it about, though; how can one check the divine oneself?"

"The science is older than man and time. It started years before, many years before, but man can easily investigate it for himself."

"How could one check the divine?" she repeated, baffled.

"Man can find God when he stops the ticker tape of chattering thoughts inside his head, and there, all the mysteries," he said, "in a nutshell."

"Could you tell me more?"

"How much do you believe of what I have just already imparted?" He tested her.

"Everything," she assured him.

"Why is that? The reason you believe a stranger that rides in an airplane alongside you is simply due to your conditioning. You are trained to believe everything without self-inquiry," he finished confusing her.

"No," she thought carefully before choosing her wording, "because every word you said has found an echo deep inside me. I will investigate it," she promised him.

"Good," he also weighed his words. "If you wanted me to, I would tell you about your child. I tell you, mind you, because as a young woman you need help."

"Is she demonic, or something?" she stammered.

"No, it is nothing like that, poor madam. Your child is clearly an old soul."

"You keep saying this word. Kindly explain; I have no reference in my mind that understands the idea of old souls. In our circles, old souls are fallacies perpetuated by the Druze of the region. These simple Mountain people speak of old souls, we believe, from a vantage point of folk tales," she said.

"Old souls, born again, reincarnated, these are words that mean that a child is returned to resume a destiny that had been slashed, cut-off before its time. Or it can mean a soul that is returned to finish a life lesson. Everyone is born again, and again, Jezebel. This life is a big school. We come to this earth to learn lessons that we keep missing. The odd thing is, that lesson we keep missing is always the same one. In Arya's case, her being old is obvious. Your daughter has had a horrendous shock in her former life, one she remembers in this small body. Her jerks and spasms are not dreams, but the constant revisiting of that last death," he explained.

"Translation?" the woman giggled, feeling stupid.

"You could study the Buddhist religion, or the Hindu one, the Vedic Islamic, Sufis. Now that you are going to Madras, ask people, read their religious texts. Arya could grow either as your curse or else your blessing – that all depends on your readiness as a parent to understand her plight. As a mother, you could help your daughter come to terms with her past, by explaining to her the facts of her past or else she could become a nightmare of grief and confusion. That also is solely up to you as parents," the kindly doctor explained.

He stared towards the pretty woman, herself just a child. He noted the large, brown eyes, and the arched high brow that drooped with her fears. Hers was a sadness whose source he could not imagine, and it disturbed him deeply. She carried her pains like a cloak of misery whose black energies engulfed her body.

He, the doctor of kind Brahman discipline, knew no way of teaching this woman how to help herself and her child.

"I do not know where to start. You do understand, right?" he asked.

"Right." She waited hopefully.

"I was thinking that you explained to me your entire religion in one clear sentence. There is no feasible way to summarize mine in that way. Christians are lucky in this regard; their religion happens to them, like sheets of rain that assails them. Our belief system, on the other hand, dictates focused inquiry. As our religion is geared towards each human being learning on his own, it cannot blanket-teach. That is the reason,

Jezebel you need to go learn. Our premise of learning is the human himself. God happens when each human understands himself."

"It is that tough?" she asked.

"No. It is varied," he corrected, "and ever-so-fascinating."

"If it is not a religion, then what is it?"

"It is man studying man. It is the study by man of himself," the doctor explained.

"That is your religion? That is more like a waste of time. Each man and each woman understands himself. They, humans, are so different from one another, that you could not possibly lump them under one umbrella of study." Jezebel felt confused.

"Hey! That is good. We could start from there. You gave me a good idea," he said elated. "I know you uttered that by accident. But, what did you exactly mean by people being different?"

"You know, like we are five girls, and each one of us is completely different from the other," she said animated.

"Yes, the reason for that?"

"Genetics; each baby selects different attributes from the vast genetic pool. The combination could be endless," she stated. "My eldest sister was a scholar, my poor sister, while the rest of us hardly liked to attend school."

The baby awoke suddenly to send forth a mighty shriek. The wail, a siren of piercing tones, awoke the entire airplane. Passengers lifted their heads up to stare the poor mother down hatefully.

She picked Arya up quickly, placed her on her bosom and patted her back, rubbed her shoulders gently, if distractedly, wanting to resume the conversation with the stranger. Arya calmed down gradually, though she still gasped softly.

"Could you please help me?" Jezebel beseeched the man with her eyes.

"Tell me of your sister," he asked, lowering Arya into her crib.

"My eldest sister, Alaya, was a scholar and an astute reader. She died on her honeymoon; stung by a colony of bees. They are still investigating her death as a possible homicide," she stated the facts.

He jumped in one leap, uncovered the baby's body by pulling her long shirt up so as to bare her chest, then, he bent low to scrutinize the small abdomen.

"What is wrong?" Jezebel asked.

"These marks, has she always had them?" he asked the young woman.

"Yes," she affirmed. "Her doctor assured me that they were common birth rashes that should disappear as the child grew older."

"They are not birth rashes. They are faint bee sting marks," he corrected.

"She has never been stung by anything." Jezebel was baffled by the incongruity of the diagnosis.

"Yes, she has. She was stung in another life. Her hysterical dreams are the reliving by the super mind of that horrendous event."

"Hang on one second, please." Jezebel had had enough of his stupidity. "I am assuming that your science is right, even going as far as believing that Arya is truly the soul of my sister Alaya. How could this new body be that of my dead sister's? Arya got her body from me while my dead sister's was of that of my mother's body. That does not make sense."

"It has been known to happen. The mind does that. It transfers the marks of the last death to the new body. These stings are so imprinted on the mind, that it brings them along to the new body," he stated.

"That does not sound scientific to me. Science provides measurable results."

"There is an answer," the physician faltered. "It is rather complicated."

"Try me," Jezebel challenged.

"Well, what I am about to tell you is singly the most crucial aspect of that divine science. The ignorance of humans as to this aspect of their beings stands at the basis of all their bafflements and suffering. It is about intentions, humans' intentions. A person formulates a need for water, he gets up and fulfils it by reaching for a cup of water to drink it and feel satiated. The spirit mind is more powerful than the brain and the hands that fulfil its wishes. When the spirit wishes deeply, the mind, simply, moves to fulfil its wishes. The process is this simple. When humans understand the powers revving within their beings egging to do their bidding, they would use these powers to create a great deal of good."

"Indians understand this power of intentions?" she asked amused.

"Of course they do, Jezebel." He resented her smirk.

"Why do they not use it to get out of poverty?"

"Because they don't see their poverty as necessarily a bad thing," he said.

"What do they see as a bad thing?" she asked.

"Peace and happiness are the attributes coveted in the East."

"Say we agree that intentions on the part of the mind could transfer marks from the old body to a new one. What would be the advantage in this case?" she asked, needing to know.

"Nobody knows the reason," he told her. "Who knows?"

"Why did the baby stop when you spoke to her?" Jezebel needed to learn how to help her child.

"She understood that I knew her suffering, and stopped to listen to me, then believed me."

"Her mind is that advanced?"

"Obviously, all the memories she lived, the traumas, everything has been transferred to this body by the superior mind. The mind does not die with the body; only the material brain dies. Memory is also stored in the spirit Mind," he explained.

"Your science speaks of that?"

"It does," he affirmed.

"Does she know me as her sister?" Jezebel asked, and paled in fear.

"She picked you to come back to," he assured her.

"She also chose her own husband for a father?" she asked concerned.

"Of course; we are more comfortable with humans we know and love."

Jezebel picked Arya from her cot, and spoke to her.

"Hey, sister, darling, I will take good care of you," she cooed softly.

Arya opened her eyes, stared straight in those of her mother's, and smiled, smiled gently, and ever so tenderly.

"I think you are right," Jezebel told the doctor. "I will study all that science upon my arrival."

"It will do you a great deal of good, and furnish you with helpful understanding," he said.

He got up to leave her then, when she extended her right hand, and held his gently.

"I will always be grateful to the chance that brought us together," Jezebel said solemnly.

"There is no chance in life, Madam. I was made to help you on purpose. The universe that oversees humans arranges for helpers along the way. It is called synchronicity. As to whether she knows you as her sister, Jezebel, not on any conscious level. The soul mind knows, the body's brain is a clean slate on this level," he said. "Things will come up to confuse Arya. You need to understand and explain to her."

He left her baffled as she stared at his back, trying to decipher his new words.

Jezebel realised that for the duration of that hour, her own problems, ones that had governed her life since the birth of her daughter, were not present to tug at her body. Appeased with the respite, she found a measure of peace she vowed to maintain.

"I sent focus elsewhere and forgot my grief," she noted. "I will learn how to respect my body by listening to its pains, to block the past, so as not to accumulate further pains for the body by obsessing."

Arya slept soundly in her cot again, as Jezebel started feeling her hunger pains anew. She rang for the steward to ask for a sandwich.

"I am very hungry, would you possibly have a sandwich?" she asked.

"Indians do not know the sandwich, Madam," the man explained. "You could have the meal."

"Your food is very hot for me," she explained to him.

"I am sorry," he said embarrassed. "That is all we carry."

"I will try to eat the meal." She did not have a choice.

When he brought her the plate of hot, spiced rice, she tried but failed to eat the spicy food.

"We do have some samosas," he came back to inform her.

"What are they?" she inquired.

"They are spicy meat pies," he explained.

"I will try them." She thanked him gratefully.

She found them amazingly tasty, if also on the spicy side. She ate the meat wrapped in thin pastry gratefully, washing it down with water, and then she slept.

Twenty-Six
FAMILY UNITED IN MADRAS, INDIA

Although the nine-hour flight was scheduled to land in Madras, the flight attendant announced over the speaker that it would land in Bombay instead; owing to some mechanical problem. Exhausted, and hungry, Jezebel was unnerved; fearing to alight with Arya in Bombay. The doctor ran to assure her of his assistance. No sooner had the airplane landed, than a gust of hot air invaded the interior making everyone queasy and uncomfortable. On the tarmac the heat assailing them was accompanied by a strong fishy smell, as well as with another putrid one, to make her faint.

The drive inside the city loomed surreal; as the length of the shore was littered with shacks, tents, makeshift dwellings, where natives cooked on kerosene cookers.

"Welcome to Bombay," the bus driver announced over the loudspeaker.

Several Western passengers giggled. Jezebel covered Arya's nose threatening to smother her, such was the potency of the smells that assailed them.

"Do not close her nasal passages," the physician instructed the mother.

"I don't want her to smell this," Jezebel said.

"Smell what?" the doctor asked.

Everyone giggled anew.

"Honestly, Jezebel," he laughed. "Of course I smell it, I was joking with you. It is better for her to get some air, even tainted, than to choke to death, surely."

Jezebel removed the blanket from Arya's nose. The child slumbered, seemingly unconcerned with it all.

"Anyone that finds their life difficult needs to visit Bombay," she told the doctor.

"They are the happiest people on earth," he assured her.

"What is the reason for such happiness?" she needed to understand.

"Their sheer disdain propelled outwardly, they understand that they are not the body, but the spirit divine. That spirit, Jezebel, cares little for worldly possessions," he explained with pride.

Along the length of the sidewalks, an entire downtrodden country lived. They cooked on kerosene cookers, and raised their naked children on the pavements. Old people lounged on flat mattresses, just feet away from traffic. Women tended to domestic chores: Some cooked while others baked flat bread over skillets while others still, boiled their wash, as their mates and youths fished the sea beyond.

Men ran completely naked without a stitch of clothing, on by the sea, their bodies toned and perfect from the sun and exercise. Jezebel understood instantly that India was going to be different from anything she had known.

Anywhere one looked his vision was blocked by a sea of dark heads that stuck together like blades of grass which hugged the earth in her father's garden.

"It must be horrible being them," she thought. "Everything Western people valued was lacking in this place, security, shelter, money, comfort, gathering of things. They have nothing," she marvelled.

"Humans do not need much," her only friend told her. "Happiness is this. Things we accumulate, Jezebel, shackle us to them. We become enslaved by the things we gather. Very few humans understand the need to be free from possessions to be happy, truly happy. These people understand the need to die free."

At the hotel, Jezebel carried Arya to their assigned room, placed her on the bed, and went in for a bath, only to run out as quickly as she had entered, all the way to the entrance hall, naked, having slammed in her fear the door behind her leaving her daughter inside.

Alone and naked in the hallway of the strange hotel in this strange, foreign land, Jezebel felt like crying. Fearing someone seeing her, she knocked on the door of her neighbour, instead.

"Could you please hand me one of your towels?" Jezebel asked the Swiss lady that had travelled on the same airplane with them.

"What are you doing naked?" the woman asked laughing hysterically.

"I went for my bath when five huge cockroaches jumped at me inside the shower stall," she told her. "Could you please call management to get me a key?"

"Yes, immediately," the kindly woman said. "She is asleep, relax. We can hear her clearly from here."

"The cockroaches are in there with her," Jezebel exclaimed and shook fearfully.

"Did you not close the bathroom door?"

"I did," Jezebel said.

"She will be fine." The woman dialled the hotel desk.

"My bathroom is also filled with gargantuan insects. Is this your first trip here?" she asked.

"Yes," Jezebel answered, her skin crawling as though the giant insects crawled on her back.

"You will soon get used to the insects. We don't notice them any longer," she informed Jezebel as she smiled.

Jezebel could not imagine a day when she could ever get used to the giant roaches. She thanked the lady for helping her upon hearing her room door open. She ran out to cover her body with another towel before speaking to the two young men who came equipped with a rusty, ancient gadget to kill the bugs.

"What are you doing?" she asked.

"We kill the bugs, Madam." The man stopped spraying.

"What is inside? The chemical?" she asked.

"DTT, Madam, very good, kill good." He grinned, happy to please.

"Listen, stop, please. My baby is not to smell this, okay, thank you."

"No want to kill bugs?" He could not understand the woman.

"No," she said gently. "Go find me a clean room, please."

"So sorry," they sing sang in perfect synchronization.

They moved her to a room that was sprayed earlier. Arya slept soundly, still, unperturbed by all that took place about her.

She lay on the bed fearing to fall asleep and miss her flight. The long journey and hunger got the best of her, and she awoke to the ringing of the telephone and a voice, which summoned the passengers of her flight to resume their disrupted journey to Madras.

Twenty-Seven
RAGING SEA OF RESENTMENT IN MADRAS

They doubled right back to the airport. It had already become dusk. Things had changed within a span of three hours to entice and thrill. The change surprised Jezebel. Gone were the smells of people and fish alike. In their place, there rose the most enticing orange hue, which bathed everything in a warm, soothing aura.

The sea rolled in a bath of brilliant orange then, bathing, bathing the heads with shimmering gold. Bathed this way, the entire scene took on hues of majestic purity...children played on the sand of their sea, and adults strolled their toils away contentedly, smiling at the beauty, and grace, in perfect harmony.

The scene brought tears of joy to the young woman's eyes. Their happiness had somehow connected itself to her, and she finally found solace and grace.

"I shall forgive. First, I need to understand, then, I want to forgive. This episode shall mar and destroy all our lives."

Surely, Jezebel understood, these people had serious tragedies to tackle daily yet they forgave and smiled, and walked, and drank the dusk in deep gratitude for the majesty of that idyllic nature.

She quickly felt a wave of bitterness rise to choke her throat as she remembered that which she so longed to forget and forgive.

"They make the mistakes and we have to work on the bitterness they make us produce so our children survive in happiness."

Madras came into view. It looked majestic in the gathering night. Its streets were laid out in a grid and their gardens rose like crowned jewels above the rooftops.

"It is beautiful," she said aloud.

"It is the most beautiful of all our cities," a native answered her.

At the airport, which was more of a shack than a building, her husband stood beaming at his Harem, from ear to ear, surrounded by a band of men like the shah he was.

He ran and kissed his wife, handing the child to a man.

"Hey," Jezebel shouted, "excuse me. Don't give my child to anyone."

"Oh," he said, as he held her waist worshipfully. "Do not worry. That is our driver."

They walked out, leaving the luggage to be handled by the company's personnel, towards two archaic black vehicles.

He opened the door to settle her in, as a man took the child to another car before theirs.

"Where is he taking her?" She feared for Arya.

"Relax. He is taking her to her nanny."

"I do not want her to have a nanny."

Jezebel opened her side of the door to go claim her infant. "She will be with me. What if they are to have an accident?"

They assured her as to the safety of her child, further informing her that it would not be seemly for her to carry her child like a peasant in light of her husband's position in the country.

"Relax. She is fine." He wrapped a sweaty arm around her shoulders.

"How are you?" he asked, anxious with desire.

"Thank you. I am great. And you?"

He squirmed in his seat, and resumed the acting.

"I sure have missed you and my sweet baby."

"Are you acting in front of the driver?" she asked in their native tongue.

"No, why?" he asked.

"Because when you left me you scarcely remembered the fact that we were married. That is why," she told him.

"Let us not start with this," he said angrily.

"Oh, yes. Where do we start then, with what?" she asked. "Do you truly believe that you could shack up with my friend for three or four days, leave me like an injured dog by the side of the road to heal as I cared for an infant and forget that? Surely you are not that stupid! Unless, you think me stupid."

"No, of course not; what is done is done, however, and we need to turn over a new leaf."

"Sure enough, until such a time you befriend another good-looking girl and another leaf would need to be turned, and so on?"

"What do you want?"

"I need you to tell me what happened. I need us to understand the reasons it happened, and try to heal together. Do not underestimate what happened, or try to sweep it under a rug."

"Sure. We will do that." He wrapped his claws around her anew.

They rode close behind the car carrying their baby, as Jezebel felt her essence fly, fly, over the cows strolling between cars, over their dung, over the heads of shepherds, and sheep, over the dust rising at their backs, over the rickshaws, the bikes with bread and flies, over masses of humanity, over her own fear of the place, to the place where Arya huddled in the arms of her old nanny, Mary.

"We are at the fifth building from the left," her husband directed.

They carried everything to the flat. People, Western people, waved their hands to them in welcome. Others, dark skinned, and stunning, in their early twenties waved and welcomed Madam. She felt like a fake royal.

"He missed you so," two American ladies told Jezebel. "He could talk of nothing else."

She felt like striking him. He was obviously acting the good husband so as to catch some lonely woman.

"Can we see the baby?" neighbours asked on the stairs.

"Sure," Jezebel agreed and showed the beautiful Arya.

"She is beautiful," everyone said. "She is the youngest member of our compound."

Arya smiled and looked around, seeming to scrutinize each face as to commit it to memory, as her mother ducked her head in painful shyness.

"This place is a nightmare for me," she said.

"Why? They are looking forward to meeting you. Besides, there are some young brides like you, one from Burma, South America, married to an American Tony, and another, my boss's wife, and a third, Diana, the chief accountant's wife. They have an adopted son, Charlie, just a few months older than Arya. It should be fun for you. They play tennis, and have tea at the English club."

What he failed to tell her was the fact that he slept days, and worked the night shift, nights she would spend alone, in the forsaken place that does not sleep, but chants its nights awake with the first setting of the sun.

He kissed her goodbye, soon after, and promised to see her in the early hours of the morning.

"I will see you soon. We will have breakfast together."

He forgot, or had never noticed that she never ate breakfast.

She took the baby away with the nanny to cinemas, to parks, to the English club, so as to ensure him a quiet place to sleep away their days. The two youths that changed sheets came early, before dawn, to change and take away the linens, and towels, and Theresa, Mary's sister, who came early to clean house. Everyone left by eight in the morning to allow the master sleep.

And so it went, only the weekends were free from night shifts. The country was vast and densely populated, and Madras, the city offered little, but alien, and strange places of joy.

There was the posh and oh, so fancy, Queen's Hotel, furnished much in the style of Buckingham Palace where people wearing turbans on their heads served inferior foods on silver trays. The meat smelled foul, and its vapours nauseated Jezebel, who tried so hard to still her sensitive stomach so as not to look rude to others from the compound, who, lacking taste buds, looked as though they ate prime rib at Maxim's.

"Eat," her husband admonished.

"I can't. There is no way. What is this meat? It tastes gamy, sour; wild-like."

"It is not beef. It is buffalo." He grinned knowing her reaction.

There was no reaction simply because she had no idea what buffaloes were.

"What is a buffalo?" she asked him.

"These are the huge, shaggy creatures that sit in the swamps all around the city."

She got up, barely able to utter the words of apology and headed straight to the Ladies' room.

"Anything the matter, Madam?" the waiter asked noting that her sizzling plate sizzled untouched.

"Not a thing, thank you. Could you possibly remove this and get me a plate of vegetables, and fries, please?"

He did. The vegetables were sizzling hot with chillies, and the fries, they were just fine.

A rumour about her lack of eating circled around. She ate at the club, mostly, where bacon and tomato sandwiches tasted heavenly, missing the yellow dye, and the red spices, and throat stripping hot chillies everyone adored.

She befriended the young group and went playing tennis, hunting saris in the old market, and even went with cook through mudslides, and monsoons to the main bazaar to buy the vegetables and fruits for her household.

"You must eat, protein, Madam," cook often said.

"Yes, you are right. Could you possibly make me an egg sunny side up?"

He obliged, delirious with joy at her first request of him. She hung close by to watch him wash the outside of the egg, and watch the hot butter sizzle nicely in the tiny skillet, as he opened the egg; only to jump in consternation as there in the middle of a sickly pale yoke, sat a worm still alive and wiggling for survival.

That was it.

Jezebel was never ever to eat anything cook made at home again. She started cooking the meals herself, with the foodstuffs she herself gathered.

"You must try this one place in town," Liz, the boss's wife, suggested.

Jezebel's first reaction, of shirking, she quickly revised, and stilled; grateful for the invitation, she promised to do so and visit the place.

"I am not keen on the food, you know. My taste buds are still very mild oriented," she replied as gently as possible.

"Nonsense," said the friendly brunette. "We will change your opinion yet, next Tuesday, my treat, I pick everyone up."

Jezebel's day of reckoning dawned crisp and clear, affording no reason to decline; to insult the big boss's wife would surely cause brimstone to hail on husband's head for having picked the stupid wife with the boorish manners.

She vowed to do her best to eat. The group met at a street café. That was different, as it stood outdoors affording everyone a fresh breeze. It was brimming to capacity with Western youths, elements of some cult who believed in a different dress code, one famous in the West in the wild sixties.

"Is everyone on drugs?" she asked.

"Probably," Liz giggled, "on something, for sure."

"Are hair brushes out of style?" some old lady asked.

The group laughed, and Jezebel felt happy for having accepted their invitation.

"They make the best Masalladosa right here," Liz assured Jezebel.

"What are they?" She had made up her mind to eat anything so as not to offend her host.

"They are fried breads, pancake-like, but savoury, stuffed with an assortment of spicy, fried vegetables." That sounded divine to the seriously famished Jezebel.

"Try one. We could always order more."

"Fine, thank you. I will have one," she told the waiter.

Everyone had ordered the same Indian crepe suzette. The ladies started digging inside the yummy roll of delicious vegetables. Jezebel tasted hers and felt guilty at having so swiftly cancelled the entire cuisine after one meal at the Queens. As she rolled her eyes in genuine delight, Liz, their host, rolled her own in sheer fright.

"Do not, Jezebel, do not swallow," she ordered frantic with fear.

Jezebel froze thinking a fly had landed in her mouth, but instead, Liz extended her hand and to the sheer horror of everyone, pulled a thick thread yellowed by years of use, and as she pulled, a rusty needle came out straight from Jezebel's mouth.

"Okay," Jezebel announced shaken, "does anyone else have a needle and a thread in theirs?"

"No," they answered.

"I am sorry, darling," Liz said, blushing deeply. "We have been in this country for over eight years, and have eaten here regularly, as it is Bruce's' and the girls' favourite haunt, never, have we ever had an incident of this kind."

"I believe you." Jezebel patted her hand. "Do not worry."

Nobody asked whether she would have liked to reorder, and pick something else. In reality, this incident ruined the reputation of this place, as the compound housed fifty families.

"It is an omen," Jezebel announced. "For some odd reason, I am not supposed to eat out in this country. I have had so many incidents since I arrived that nobody else experienced. Things are manifesting to me to leave the cuisine alone."

"You are making it happen," A Fakir interjected from a nearby table.

"Excuse me?" the ladies answered in sheer rebellion.

"She is so finicky; her intentions to find dirty stuff are leading her to find them for sure."

"Shut-up," an older expatriate wife said. "The drivel these Indians get up to."

"You lady, have an extremely strong spirit. You are projecting the stuff," he said to Jezebel.

They all looked at one another and giggled thinking the man drunk, or else mad.

"Stupid Westerners," he spat disdainfully.

"What did you call us?" an old expatriate's wife, hollered.

"She is not like you. She is wise. Her intentions could make the world turn on its axis. Only problem, she is not aware of her powers. Go see a yogi. You are here for a reason."

She asked whether any of the ladies knew of a reputable yogi. One lady, who wore a sarong and looked like a weirdly demented blond-blue-eyed Indian woman, raised her hand from the far end of the large table.

"I know the best yogi in town. He is close by your compound," she said. "I will take you to him."

Twenty-Eight
INITIATION IN THE HIGHER SCIENCE

Pauline Simpson picked Jezebel first thing the next day and took her to the yogi. He was old, shrivelled, and kind. He welcomed the four ladies from the compound with soft courtesy, never speaking, and when spoken to he answered in protracted monosyllables.

"Yoga," his young spokesman said, "is the study of bodily control. When it is spoken of the spirit, however, yoga means to yoke the self with that of the divine entity."

The ancient straw mats hurt Jezebel's knees, but her soul got pulled by the ancient man who wanted no money from the people with the most money in India, and only accepted a fruit or two.

"You are different," he told Jezebel. "You have pink aura."

Jezebel, thinking everyone mad, smiled back, not understanding a word he uttered.

"Thank you," she said. "I shall bring you tangerines."

He loved the small, aromatic fruit.

"I thank you," he said, and placed his palms together and bent his back meekly forward.

That broke her heart. She learned to do the same meek gesture back to him.

He looked hilarious in his diaper thing and dark, wrinkled legs with nothing on his emaciated torso.

"Would you like me to give you some food?" She knew he was a vegetarian.

"No. No need. Man eats well, two fruits a day."

"Really," she marvelled at the vast and varied kitchens of the West and Middle East. "No deficiency in nutrients?"

"No, no," he giggled sweetly, "this invention of shopkeepers to sell more for money."

He rolled his eyes to the heavens and started laughing, laughing, laughing.

Jezebel thought the joke silly, but for some odd reason she could never fathom, he found it hilarious.

"Fine, then. If you were going to be insulting, only fruit."

"Thank you, yes. No need too much," he said again.

"But you help teach yoga." She could not understand the asceticism.

"That is humane duty," he stated vehemently.

And of course, she missed that last statement completely.

She, who had come from a long tradition that upheld merchandising as a holy trait, a culture seeped in work for excellent pay, and forefathers who became so obsessed by wealth that they cruised in their ships the four corners of the globe to exchange their natural resources for pay, could scarcely wrap her mind around the ascetic disdain of Indians such as this yogi.

It would practically be years, many years, decades, four of those to be exact, before she could want to remember the yogi teacher and India with an inkling of understanding of what his life represented, to benefit from his teaching. So engrained in money and the pride in making it she was, that she thought the man eccentric at best, idiotic, and went on compassionately to convince him take some of her money to put some fat on his loose skin.

When she did understand the value of such asceticism, Jezebel blushed at the realisation of her stupidity. It was, however, this experience that formed the nucleus of awareness of years of successful searching.

There, on the shores of the Ganges river, green with filth, and dirty bodies, there lived a human race so developed, so against everything she had known and upheld, so as to kill her with embarrassment; such was her disdain to them, and her stupidity – she was to discover later.

Still in Madras, the yogi stared her down in a strange way.

"You feel good?" he asked.

"Yes, great."

"You put weight," he pointed to his own waistline.

"Yes, a bit," she said surprised at his speaking at all.

"Something no right," he said simply.

"You mean I'm dying?" she joked pleasantly, never taking him seriously.

"No. Means you go get another baby," he said.

"How you know?" Jezebel amused herself with the strange man.

"Yogi read chakra. Yogi feels vibrations," he attempted to explain in his halting English. "Madam has new baby."

"Not possible yet to have another baby," she told him.

"No, baby can come," he said. "Baby boy come to you. Madam too much male inside her now," he said to confuse further her with his incoherent diction.

She was with child, the Indian doctor who tended Arya said that very afternoon when she went for a check-up.

"How far along am I?" she asked.

"Ninety days," he informed her.

"That's just perfect," her husband murmured.

"Shut up," Jezebel thought. "That is too late."

Jezebel left the doctor lamenting her life. They had told her at the hospital that conception was an impossible occurrence in her case.

Her husband grew agitated with the news; bemoaning their luck. Jezebel felt suddenly protective, and resigned, if a trifle bit disappointed at the closeness of her confinement. She had just recovered her waistline, hating to relinquish it to another baby so soon.

"We cannot have this child," her husband dictated.

"Do you care anything for my health, or is everything to you a matter of calculated convenience? What kind of a human are you? How could you be both angel and devil?"

"I did not allow for this in our plans," he answered flatly ignoring her allusion as to his duality.

"That is too bad, the universe has opposite plans for us, obviously," she told him.

"I will leave you," he threatened fiercely.

"Please," she motioned towards the cows outside the door.

"You have changed." He mourned the loss of the idiot.

"Yes, that is so very true. Incurring the shocks I have had, is it a great wonder I should change?"

"Please, honey, we can't care for two children." He changed his verbal course.

"Honey?" she noted. He must be truly frightened to cajole.

"No," she replied. "We should have been careful. I am not killing this child."

He nagged all night that Sunday, and all the week that followed, until, eight days later, having found some quack in the land of compassion to cows, and nature, he sent his driver to accompany her to the clinic.

"You want me to go have an abortion by myself? What if I were to die? What would you tell my parents?"

"It will just be a consultation," he promised. "I will be holding your hand through the actual procedure."

"I like the word procedure," she complained through the nasty receiver that buzzed and whistled asthmatically. "You make it sound like a life-saving medical need."

"Are we fighting over semantics, here, darling?"

The driver arrived soon after to escort her to the consultation. Leaving Arya with her sweet Mary and Theresa that moved the same five pieces of furnishings daily to clean under them, Jezebel felt deep guilt.

"I will see you soon," she gestured her goodbye to everyone at the door.

"Is madam okay?" Mary asked.

"Yes, fine. Just a check-up," Jezebel replied hating the lies.

The car drove through the compound, passed the residential areas where foreigners lived, through the main road, the main carriageway, left Madras heading due north, through lower Indian housing compounds, shantytowns, through a wreck of an area filled with drunkards, through shacks, and stopped.

"Here?" she exclaimed in sheer disbelief.

"Yes, Madam," he opened the door solemnly to her.

"What religion are you, Nadar?" she asked the driver.

"I am Buddhist, madam. Thank you."

That was the reason he looked terribly upset, Jezebel understood.

"Wait here." He settled her outside the shack. "I will call woman."

"She woman, no doctor?" Jezebel asked.

"Yes, madam, woman, no doctor, but very famous for procedure."

"Okay." The rattan couch buckled and disintegrated under her.

He rang the doorbell with a gong, and waited. Nothing happened. Jezebel noted the dryness of everything around. The scene felt appropriate; a woman that made her living from killing life would have gathered untold dark vibrations around her. Pure nature never strives in horribly tainted surroundings such as these. For years she would remember nothing but the arid dryness of all things around, and the ashen colour which surrounded the woman's life.

She came out, as Nadar's face had never left the door frame. It was as though the man hated looking at his Madam.

"She is a witch," Jezebel thought calmly upon setting eyes on her.

"Wait here," the old, wizened woman ordered.

She had claws; long, black nails that twisted and bent backwards. She had long fangs, on two sides of her mouth that went over her lower lip. Like her garden and her home, her colouring was ashen grey, even her skin.

"Unwarranted death had left its dark vibrations on her body," she thought.

"I will be back," she said before banging the door shut in Nadar's face.

She kept them locked out. Before she closed the door, however, Jezebel heard a tortured wail come from inside the shack.

"Let us leave, Nadar," she told the driver.

"Yes, madam, thank you, madam." He looked so relieved.

They doubled back the same way they came with not a word exchanged between them. Indians did not care for befriending their employers, especially foreign employers. They were not comfortable. Their situation forbade discourse altogether.

"You good being, my madam," he said.

She cried softly her fears and insecurities as he drove slowly, carefully managing the old, grey vehicle, through the storm of dust, generated by the sea of animals.

"We respect life, madam," he said for no specific reason.

She placed her dark shades over her red eyes, as to avoid having to explain the clandestine journey to any of the old cronies who, having no life, nosed their way into everyone else's.

"You did not?" husband asked upon her return.

"No," she replied.

They never mentioned it again. She soon started feeling ill.

"We need to tell the people."

She did not answer. This child she saved grew so dear and beloved by the woman who adored life like Buddhists, and respected Nadar, the driver, as being a higher form of entity than all the engineers, alongside whom her husband worked.

"Madam grow baby. Is okay continuing do yoga?" she asked yogi.

"Yes, yes, yes, very good, indeed, madam, good," he replied.

That constituted the only excitement over the baby.

"Madam also continue tennis; make baby strong," he volunteered.

Besides her long morning sleep-ins, nothing changed in Jezebel's life. She still went to the English club to play tennis with either Diana, or Irma, and had tea and English pound cake, as cook did not learn more recipes but the few ones that he got from some English cook, long ago, no doubt dead.

"The happiness here baffles me," Diane, the devout Christian droned her disbelief repeatedly.

"Their religion makes them happy," Irma marvelled. "It is all about dancing and playing with their many gods."

Jezebel was not so sure. Her ingrained Catholicism forbade mere imagining. She did envy their happiness, though; thinking them a daft, lazy population.

Life continued in this vein, Jezebel passing her days, waiting for husband to give her some time so they could have some understanding of one another.

The men planned a train journey into a famous temple, Mahabulapuram, husband informed her in one instance. It was to be an exception of sorts; as these executives never deigned to mingle with the wives. Far from being honoured, the woman relented begrudgingly.

"They want us to go along," he said, pleased.

"Sure," she said.

The three couples huddled in two cars, the harem in one, driven by Nadar, and the executive sheiks in another, driven by another driver the women did not know. Cook had prepared sandwiches and fruits, a thermos of tea and another of coffee. At five o'clock of a stunning Madras dawn, they started off towards the countryside, about an hour away. The group alighted before a monstrously old screeching train. The train, a plump, decrepit monster with no amenities whatsoever, creaked to a wizened, squealing, frightful stop before them. Jezebel noted how the group looked dubious as to its state to jump up the few stairs, yet, she did the same happily. It wound its way frightfully and asthmatically through a stunning countryside with villagers and peasants tending their dusty, dry lands. It then started huffing up a series of mountains to finally and blissfully manage to stop atop the last mountain.

They arrived at a rocky place, ancient and forgotten by time, but brimming still with activities only the sensitive should feel.

A chilling host received them; Mouhabulapurum Temple. The extensively carved monster jutting out of the red clay perched before them defiantly, uncaringly; having perched there for so long as to look surreally imposing. So uncaring to the world outside it sat so as to impose scrutiny; thrilling that spirit which humans shared, as to impose a form of silent analysis. It looked so sure of its placing, that it shunned its visitors; a king over the expanse of nothingness, brimming with everything, alone and complete in that unnerving aloneness the visitors feared continuously.

The survival of that temple, its silent abiding, the aura of contented peace, and wholeness it emanated, made it feel more alive than any temple of worship the group had ever attended. In its stark ascetic being raged a power few could ignore. If anything, and if Jezebel were to honestly trace back the instant of her flipping over to see her own backside, stare her falsity, one she nursed blindly over thousands of lives, that second of soulful inquiry would have been the moment to behold.

Not that beholding that temple were to stand as a blinding moment of self-discovery, it did not; if anything, at the second her spirit thrilled at the truth, her false personality, stood up frantically to discount and shoot holes of doubt as to the viability of that which the spirit whispered to the young woman of truth.

Jezebel, the youngest of six children, raised in a striving, noisy family that belonged and clutched at an extended tribe whose roots dug deep inside an ancient culture of forefathers that valued clutching for survival, could never see the beauty of that aloneness that this temple enjoyed.

It was more that its independence annoyed her for reasons that would not be clarified until years later. Suffering deep unease of insecurities upon leaving her family, whose strength featured solely in their clinging to one another in fear, the woman felt unnerved by the calm abiding in sheer disdain, of that temple.

When the different members of their group walked about the temple like tourists, taking pictures of gods and goddesses they neither understood nor cared to understand, acting as though these were oddities to snicker over their superiority of belonging to that one God in their Christian heaven of all beatitudes, Jezebel stood transfixed, immobilized by the truth that jumped inside her stomach that dictated a sudden need to inquire. And that seed of some other viability gaining strength, that need to question another truth out there was planted.

Westerners cancelled everyone else as they sat assured as to their superior placing in the world of ideas that are just so, with little regard to first-hand inquiry. Old cultures seeped in nothing but continual, lengthy survival, got ditched for the fact that they cared nothing for the money so valued, worshiped by the Christians. Yet, there in the East and the bowels of South America, the jungles of Africa, strived viable societies whose shamans snickered back at the short-sightedness of that younger society.

Had Jezebel been visiting that temple with Indians, it would have been doubtful that she learned anything. There, in the juxtaposition of West meet East, and the superiority of giggles and general snickering of the different members of the group, hid the woman's most precious of lessons, ones that would germinate in later years to a fruitful recognition, one she would enjoy and thrill, one that stood at the basis of her personal flowering.

There inside the temple were no ushers, monks, ticket booths, or anyone. The doors were flung open for all to take in the beauty and marvel at the mysteries.

Strangely alien to the devout Catholic that sheer disdain to proprieties loomed as to feel habitual suspicion rather than thrill at the largesse of the gesture. People, she thought, long institutionalized grew attached to the prison that usurped them, out of habit, hating to leave it. Further, long used to being told the way she should feel by noisy church elders, she again erred on the side of the habitual to resent being left to her own spirit to commune with that which screamed of loving care inside that temple.

Inside, an open span brimming with nooks and crannies, alcoves; where long ago initiates sat and learned from masters about their real beings of light, choosing to leave the world of the body and its desires behind to reach the beyond, now long gone, an energy remained to thrill. She wished there were some guide to explain the carvings that adorned the skeleton of the huge edifice. There were gods, both male and female, dancing erotically, some with many snakes jutting out of their hair, others sitting in the lotus position looking peaceful, and happy. Scores of worshipers brought baskets of fruits to sit inside the stone temples. They offered the foods to the gods to bless before they ate. They had placed red dots on their foreheads between both their eyes, to point to that mysterious place of their inner sight. They dabbed their different energy spots with oil prior to coming to ask for forgiveness of sins and blessings for their lives. The colours the Indians used were chosen for different reasons; the blues were intended for the healing from disease, the red for energy, white for purity, and yellow for spiritual seeking and attainment. The temple gods reflected the same array of colours. An explosion of blues, pinks, orange, and greens, looked as fresh as though painted the day before.

The entire scene looked mad, and the believers nuts.

Inside the temple huge gods towered high above the faithful, carved of the red earth that made the mountain that housed them. In the immense bowels of the tower-like edifice, nooks and crannies, candles and incense, people worshiped by sitting inside the carved shapes to stare.

Jezebel sat across from one temple of worship thinking how much like the sacristy of her Catholic church it looked. Lacking Christian adornments, icons, gold cups, and linen table cloth, this would have been the Maronite church at home, of her childhood. The differences were, she assimilated later, just on the surface and in the rituals.

"How old is this temple?" she asked Diane, who read a guide book.

"Six thousand years old," Diane replied.

"We, the Christians, have got hold of their science of the mysteries, and somehow managed to appropriate it, and refurbish it to look new," Jezebel thought and quickly grew guilty for having thought that.

"What a strange religion," Diane's husband commented nearby. "How many gods do they need?"

That question would cancel the entire philosophy right from the onset for her. Surely, there was to be but that one God. There, not following her scrutiny would manage to make her drop the sizzling energy her spirit felt. Later, she would understand, that although they were many gods featured on that temple, they were lesser gods, like the saints of her church, and one Godhead, that One and Only.

His mates giggled confused as to an answer, as not one western human having come to the land to work on its natural resources has ever given that religion enough credence so as to ever look into it, to soar the true riches, mine the real, eternal gold, more valuable than the gems they scurried to steal from underneath the poor natives, who saw and pitied, ignored and loved; for their state was beyond the earth, and their knowledge offered everlasting wealth.

"We think them quaint oddities, and dismiss them. I have a feeling they think us barbaric and ignorant," Irma, the beautiful Burmese friend, said.

"That is a culture," Diane said, "not a religion?"

Jezebel felt a definite stirring within as she sat staring across from the beautiful Krishna. Not that Jezebel revered the man giving him a second of viability, never; that never occurred to her at that age. It was more a soulful recognition of things true, if vastly misunderstood.

"These figures are mythical, like the Greek gods, right?" she asked her husband.

"I do not know. Surely, however, they could not be real. Since when do gods, if there were to be many, manifest themselves to mortals?"

"Jesus had," she reminded him.

"Ah, but," he stammered. "That was different."

Not knowing what to think, Jezebel got up and followed the group to the treacherous stairs, carved thousands of years before, from the side of the mountain which snaked their way around it, with a railing installed recently, to save the worshipers from a fall clear down the precipice clean to the steep valley below.

"Do not look down," her husband urged.

She did not.

The cars parked down in the valley looked like bugs. The drivers had driven the cars to bring the food and drinks. The sweltering heat made the food unpalatable. Yet, they ate the sandwiches cook had prepared and drank huge amounts of warm water so as to tolerate the oppressive heat, got in their cars to return to the compound, aching to join the century of their human family, so much ado about nothing; neither learning nor caring.

Twenty-Nine
A MOST FASCINATING SOLUTION

It felt strange returning to the world, the real world, not that even Madras felt like any contemporary world any of them had ever experienced. Still, and all, it was more normal than that faraway strange place of red rocks and colourful gods.

"Yogi Swaranami. You teach madam religion?"

"Madam, yogi no good English to teach. Buddhism no religion but science. Sure, our Lord Buddha wants to teach all human brothers their kingdom."

"He no say no to Christian?"

"No, madam. Before four thousand year he born, Buddha monks know the mysteries of God and powers of magic, but they hide it in mountains for only rich sects to learn and save. He comes four thousand years before now, and he say, no, I teach every poor and every person who like this science. It is all man right to know the kingdom of their Father. When the Buddha teaches, Jesus no come yet. He comes two thousand year after Buddha. How could Buddha not want Christian madam learn? He loves everyone. The Buddha, madam, he says, everyone is everyone. He no believes in division but thinks and teaches that in division all violence and war and abuse."

"Yogi, sir, please teach a little bit. Yogi English madam understands fine."

"I try. It is very difficult teach. Very long time science to understand. Yogi try because duty. If yogi no teaches now madam ask, it is no good, big sin for yogi," he said, and looked pained.

He suffered her request for he hated to speak.

"Try, please, Yogi," she begged.

"Long time before, Guatama prince was married to a good princess who give him little princess. His father was king of province. He, the king, he say to his kingdom nobody disturb my heir, and firstborn, nobody tell of death of body because my son very strong and proud of body. It goes that way, until one day, Prince Guatama go outside castle walls to stand and visit with friends. It happens on that day that one man gets dead and people take to the burning site for burial on pyre. He ask the prince what be wrong with the man on stretcher. They say simply dead. He says and what is dead? They say you know body stop. He no understanding idea

201

but feel very afraid. People no go live forever. Of course not, they answer, and they laugh at him. He goes to king, father, and asks the father why king hides this thing from his education, very important thing from him. Father answers for love for you. He says wrong to hide important things from children. When people love truly, they tell children truth. That, the truth make children strong, lies make children stupid, and give shock. I will go now and find out about this thing called dead. I need to know what happens after body stop. He leave his princess wife, and his princess, two-year-old daughter, and all his money, and take from father castle only one cup to beg food and leaves to the highlands. There, he finds many masters teach the mysteries of life and death. It takes him six years. He goes from one master that teaches one prayer to another, to another, to another. He prays well, he no thinks of desire, he stay up night doing the yoga and meditation, and praying, praying, praying, but nothing happen. One day, he sleep tired under the Bodi tree. When wake up next dawn, he look up to the last stars in the clear sky and his spirit goes to the stars. He joins God. He knows, Guatama, that after die we no die. This made prince happy, and he wanted people to know."

Jezebel sat mesmerized by the myth and the tale, thinking the story creative, and knowing that the yogi had never spoken that long, with that much passion.

"Why you tell madam this story? Very long story," she asked feeling a truth.

"Madam is good Buddha," he said.

"Excuse me? How many Buddhas are there? I thought Buddhas were only men."

He chuckled delightfully, no doubt enjoying some strange joke.

"No madam, more women Buddha then men Buddha."

"How is it so? Only males are prophets?"

He threw his head back and laughed with such mirth; chuckles rang like chimes his peals of delight, the expression of the pure spirit.

"Women are more Buddha natural. Women have baby, they go Buddha naturally. So natural for woman to love with abandon and give body and soul to everyone. Nobody thinks abnormal to call woman giving soul and body to creation Buddha. So rare for males, they go shouting on rooftops." This was followed by more chuckles and mirth.

"Can you please explain?" she asked intrigued by his male female speech.

"Madam, God is both woman and man. That is the reason he can make, creating the woman and the man because he has both inside him. The woman power is high in heaven, man on floor to do the land. So, woman is Buddha at her hut. Man goes to Tall Mountain to get to her level to pray. Many women are Buddhas in quiet of house, but when man sees light he shouts to everybody. That is the reason everybody who comes to the man knows about God." He laughed happily still.

Jezebel could not tell whether the story was fictional, or whether the man had made total fun of her.

"Jesus big Buddha," he said to shock her.

"What mean name Buddha?" she asked him.

"The Buddha means human pure light," he responded quickly.

"Jesus no man, he is God," she said.

"Yes, yes, all Buddha are God in body, madam, sure," he said to confuse her further.

"How can man be Buddha in body?" she asked him.

"He stop mind. Man Buddha stop mind," he said to baffle her. "Stop mind, very simple. Mind speak, speak when mind want lose human. Stop greed, mind stop."

"Nobody stop mind. No good stop mind. Man is stupid," Jezebel corrected him.

"No, use mind when need mind. All the time people use mind when no need for use. When no need, man must to be silent in mind. Make mind blank, no lie, no kill, no hurt, two years man be Buddha," he giggled.

"Are you Buddha?" she asked.

"No good say that, not humble," he smiled.

"I see. Be humble good?"

"More humble, more good," he replied.

"I say, so we sit in a silent place, and make our brains still, and meditate on humility, telling the truth, and we become enlightened." Jezebel summed things up.

"Correct, madam, very correct," he agreed and sounded elated for having made her understand.

"Thank you, dear yogi. I will stop coming because madam seven months with child now. Must go with family to homeland to have other baby," she informed him.

"God be with madam, and family," he said in parting.

She shrugged her shoulders, confused, thanked him, handed him the bag of fruits and left.

It would take Jezebel thirty more years to get both stories, and the temple thing in Mahabalapurum. When she did, she was already a mother and a grandmother. The yogi who told her the tale was right in all things. More women she knew were unsung Buddhas, and the few saintly men around did shout their normal loving to the rooftops for all creations to glorify them, such was their rarity.

For then, however, for that year winding sadly towards its end, she grew saddened by the acute love and depth of the people, natives, she had met, and they were numerous, not the least of whom was her beloved, selfless, emancipated teacher and yogi master.

They were also the flocks of black crows that flew so excitedly over the rooftop in the gathering dark, just before the world wore its orange cloak as the sea brooded over its beloved sun that tugged at her spirit. Yogi said that the sun was the heart of God. When she asked him which one, he had replied that it was the heart of the Godhead.

The young woman felt a deep reckoning upon setting eyes on the glories of that Madras of her earlier year. The land of the many gods produced the softest people, and the most pious. She tried hard to commit the cherished sights to memory for later recall.

There were the nights that gathered the earth around their bodies like a cloak of saffron, and the moon that flew silver overhead. Yogi had said that the moon was the shadow of the sun; as to replace the beloved love of the nurturing heart. For entire nights she, having cooked dinner for her family, sat watching the crows and orange sun flirt away in joyous fun. The crows came to eat crumbs right out of her lap. Arya shrieked excitedly as the black mates swooped low around her, she hated leaving the innocence of nature in Madras. They sat that way silently. Jezebel, whose sojourn neared its end, began to feel inklings of sadness, knowing that she would hate leaving the soft land with the scores of good people.

Although clueless still, Jezebel understood unequivocally on some primal level, that nowhere would her soul ever feel satiated within the confines of her body as during these peaceful periods over her roof in that setting sun of her beloved Madras.

The most poignant of all memories of that majestic country remained without rival the colour of the sun in India. It had a deeper colour, more translucent, deep orange the globe that went slowly beyond the horizon, as though reluctant to leave those who admired its beauty; those countless soft creatures in Madras. It played coquettishly for them, whispered words of promise, imparted secrets about other worlds, and the beyond, they understood and thrilled.

The energy Jezebel felt was novel, unlike anything she had ever experienced. When all her earlier joys were connected to homeland and parents, she, for the first time, grabbed a handful of bliss, separate of attachments, self-appropriation, communal living, bigotry, and belonging. Alone on that roof of the alien city, with not a human caring as to her whereabouts, with an infant by her side, and a flock of black birds all around them, Jezebel soared with the joys of being lost to the world of grasping and belonging, found a joy of just being with nature, a oneness she had never thought possible, to be forever hooked, a junky needing replenishing. That changed her forever, from ever needing, or depending on another for anything. That also offered her a gift beyond solace, a gift of herself, as a timeless entity with the universe as a parent, a tender, caring parent that expected nothing in return for the love it imparted. It loved all its children with the selfless gift for the sole pleasure of having been seen. That awareness of being one with her universe managed to change the woman from ever needing anyone's approval, to a deep, silent onlooker.

"I have never seen life before," Jezebel thought.

"Eleilyeih," Arya said her first word just then. She spoke her first Tamil word.

"Eleilyeih to you," Jezebel answered her child.

Jezebel picked the eight-month-old out of her chair and tossed her to the moon, to the stars, to the gods and goddesses of India, and the Sages of Madras, and the Buddha, and Krishna, Vivekananda and their dancing mates.

"You cannot wait to speak, can you?"

"No," Arya said.

She ran with the child down the two flights of stairs, called her father to his nightshift.

"She said hello in Tamil," Jezebel screamed down the line.

"No way," he marvelled. "Is she not too young for speech?"

"She is, but our child is miraculous." Jezebel brimmed with her love for the girl.

"That is nice." He sounded distracted with a clicking object.

"Goodbye," she said, and closed the line.

"What is wrong with you?" he called back to ask.

"Not a thing. Do not worry, honest. I will see you in the morning."

"Are you okay?" he asked.

"Yes, yes, fine, do not worry." She decided to sit by Arya's bed as she slept.

He sounded confused. She knew that he would never, ever get things.

Aware of the acute sharpness of her life, and the colours she saw all about her, it grieved her never to be able to share them with her mate. The fact stood clear to her mind that she needed to accept him for what he was, and that her life should be enough as a gift of clarity.

"I am a poet at heart," she thought. "He is an engineer. Somebody had to make the money around here."

When Arya fell asleep, Jezebel, with nothing to do, asked Mary to tend to her and decided to go back up to the roof.

She tried to practice silence of mind as her yogi master had instructed. It was not easy; the woman who had never noticed her mind chattering got confused with the faulty mechanism. Now, she was baffled by the fact that her mind spoke stealthily, silently, as though it did not want her to hear.

"Now, what is that?" Jezebel became upset at never having noticed the anomaly.

The physician of her journey into India came swiftly to mind to explain about man's needing to know himself as he did not.

She tried again to fix her eyes on the sun, now almost lapping the waters, to no avail. Her eyes bopped, jumped and watered. Tears streamed down her cheeks as she concentrated on fixing her eyes, making them like rocks inside their sockets. There, she got somewhere. Then, before she noted, she obsessed busily over the orange rays of the setting sun.

"That is a trick of my mind," Jezebel giggled, "she came in from the back door. What a wicked mechanism. How does that work?"

No answers occurred to her. The instance of inquiry got passed over, somehow, and she moved to other things over which to obsess went back down to her flat, to forget the experience for twenty years.

"Yogi," she interrupted a yoga class. "May I have a word?"

"Hold pause, and do other part of body same, and hold," he told his class softly.

"I can't keep my mind from speaking all the time," she told him.

"Your heart no ready. When heart ready, mind stop. One day, no worry, madam. Mind stops for you," he said. "When go?"

"One more week," she said.

He extended a warm, wrinkled hand towards her, and held it firmly.

"One day world know good heart of madam," he vowed solemnly.

"I say yogi master said madam be good then?"

"No matter," he said.

"What to do now?" she asked.

"Now, live a goodly life. Be good mother, patient like the earth, and giving like the fields, later, when they grow, your heart be big like a flame, and your spirit soft like flower." He left her hand, needing to disappear.

"Then what to do?" she asked, baffled by the way his words never made sense.

"Then madam, spirit brewing this Madras experience for long time, will teach madam what to do. Spirit awake, guide people, slowly, slowly, danger only when spirit sleep." Some directions, she thought, resentful.

Freedom was not a valued asset she could wrap her head about; the Catholic mind needed specific rites and rituals, incense and oil for atonement, hymns for every problem and occasion, rulers who taught what to eat what day for what purpose. That Indian freedom to seek by oneself stood frustratingly confusing. That freedom and soulful respect took years. She was used to quick fixes that worked, giving her authority to others, saints and heavenly bodies to run do her bidding; which really never happened, but, the possibility of its ever happening offered a panacea, a form of relief from pain for the right here and now.

Mary took baby to the Catholic church that last Sunday of their stay, as the couple dressed with undue care for a farewell party at the mansion of the president being given in their honour. Jezebel ached to collect two antique Krishna statues in bronze she had seen at the market earlier. She hated leaving without her statues, as her sweet husband fearing her attachment to the heathens as well as their gods, fearing the loss of his wife's faith that would affect their children's eventual growth, played at sabotaging the purchase.

"Could we please pick them on our way there?" she begged.

"We will see," he said.

Mary came back from church, brimming with uncharacteristic joy.

"Madam, mister, baby speak Indian," she beamed. "She sings hymns in Tamil."

"Yes, sure Mary," the parents answered dubiously.

"But she does," she heard the incongruity. "Please baby, sing ton can do la."

Baby started chanting, chanting, and chanting.

"Madam, she says right words; some bungled up, but others very good."

"Of course, Mary dear, it is precious," Jezebel answered.

"She is babbling baby talk," her husband muttered.

"No mister, please, baby says many word Tamil," the poor nanny insisted.

"Fine, good, teach her more. It would truly give her a leg up at UCLA."

"Who says she is going to UCLA?" Jezebel asked to divert the dilemma.

"Give me both a damn break." He ran into the room to finish dressing.

The couple left towards the boss's mansion, leaving Mary to sing with Arya, who kept her own end famously.

"Do you think?" Jezebel asked.

"No," he answered.

They passed the shops that started to close their doors. Jezebel's heart nearly broke upon seeing the old bazaar. She was embarrassed to insist. To leave Madras without a Krishna would be unthinkable. He did not ask the driver to stop.

However when he got to the mansion, feeling terrible about it, he asked her to instruct the driver about that Buddha shop.

"It is Krishna," she hissed.

"Buddha, Krishna, all the same to me," he replied.

She held out the card from the merchant. She took it out of her bag and handed it to the driver.

"Please hurry before they close," she urged him. "They are both reserved under my name."

He came soon after holding both trophies to her. Upon seeing them her husband went mad.

"They weigh a ton," he hissed, "How do you expect us to ship them?"

"I will carry them all the way home," she vowed solemnly.

They left towards Bombay, where they stayed for a night and a day to sightsee, and from there they travelled to the homeland.

"We probably need to stop in our homeland to have this baby. It should please my parents so to have it around for a little while," he cajoled.

"We need to go back to the US, collect our house furnishings, find a job, my university, our lives?" she grasped for an excuse.

"We made enough money to take a little break. It will be just a couple months, three at the very most," he said.

Thirty
HOME TO HAVE A BABY

A quick visit to the same doctor, at the very hospital of her last check-up, frightened Jezebel and doctor alike.

"You are orange. You probably contracted jaundice in India." He looked seriously concerned. "Let us test you immediately."

She knew it was not jaundice, but an overdose of carrots.

"Did you eat anything but carrots?" he asked when the nurse handed him her blood results.

"Yes, I ate some potatoes, and lentils."

"You are underweight," he said.

She felt very healthy and strong.

"I could not be suffering what with all the tennis, and energy. I feel fine. Stop worrying, really."

"You need to start eating proteins, and lots of them for the baby," he instructed.

"I already am eating like a cow. I am ravenously hungry."

Her husband, fearing the state of her depleted blood, came home with a rotisserie chicken that day, when his mother had cooked grape leaves. That provoked her wrath as she hailed insults over both their heads.

"This time you did it. Next time, do not interfere with the menus of this household. That is my job, you hear?" she instructed.

"She is severely anaemic. It is not good for the baby." He tried to elicit sympathy for the newborn.

"Nobody is starving around here," she issued the final verdict.

Listening to their discourse, Jezebel felt peaceful enough, if baffled. What was it that made her husband insist on torturing himself over and over again, subjecting his wife and child to unwarranted abuse? It rose from some deep need within him, a controlling need to impose his family on his parents; as though insisting on being loved and accepted. Try as she could, Jezebel failed to pinpoint the problem. For whatever reason, his sheer insistence on being loved by his parents placed the woman and her children in the line of fire. This maddened her, and him, but, he came back, and back for more; as though relishing the feud itself that had fuelled their lives, the feud having long replaced pure love.

Things continued in the same vein, where, having found a new part-time job to escape the den of abuse, he left his wife to deal with things, then he came back to take his mother out socializing.

"I am going to walk her over to her sister's; just for an hour or so," he told Jezebel.

"Why doesn't her husband take her?" She feared being alone in her condition.

"You hate me having fun," he would spit, and leave, anyway.

"Fun?" she would think. "You consider them fun, and me drudgery?"

They would leave her alone, taking sister along, waddling, waddling, along the streets as she watched sadly from the balcony.

"I had never noticed how he waddled from hip to hip," she'd think.

What irked Jezebel the most was the fact that they refused to let her go see her family.

"You are a wife of this family. This is your place. This is not a hotel for your convenience," his mother would reply to her requests.

He ducked his head down to madden her. She felt unprotected, and abused by all.

Seven weeks of this, Jezebel awoke with a start; a sharp pain piercing her body as with a hot spear.

"What is wrong?" her husband asked, sitting up in one leap.

"I don't know. I feel something sharp," she told him.

"Are you in pain?" he asked her again later.

"Yes. I think this is labour," she confirmed.

"Well, let us go to the hospital for a check-up," he suggested.

They left only to return an hour later. They were false labour pains, the doctor said, nature's dry run, a week before the birth.

"Listen, next time you awaken people in the middle of the night, have the decency to at least be having a baby," his mother said at the door upon their return.

"Let her sleep," he asked gently.

The house turned on its head just then. She took offence from things that would never offend anyone else.

She banged doors, screamed to the rooftops to hear, a litany of abuse about cuckolded husbands who tended nothing but their wives' demands and needs, and never remembered what their poor mothers did to raise them, what with the water hauling from wells, and carrying the heavy jugs over mountainsides, only to start their chores, the loads of wood to cut and carry on weary backs, and on and on.

Jezebel sat up thinking that theirs was a life she could not imagine. The girl thought the age of wood cutting for cooking was in their distant past, like the era of Jesus' time. Nobody she knew had ever used wood. Their region was so isolated that even kerosene did not reach it.

She truly felt compassion.

That was the first instance that Jezebel could identify with this woman's plight. Before, she thought her mother-in-law sadistic, jealous and hurtful. Now, she could see the pain that had created the resentments.

"What can I do to help, Auntie?" she asked, genuinely wanting to help.

"Do not ever, as long as you live, call me Auntie," she shrieked. "I am not your Auntie, and never want to be. Do you get that? Do not ever act like you like me. No daughter-in-law could ever love a mother-in-law."

"How would you like me to address you?" she asked her husband's mother.

"By my name," she said a bit softer. "I want you to get up and help me."

"I can't move, though. I birth this week, and it is so hot," Jezebel told her.

"You need to help with the chores." She walked away nervously.

"I could help with the food some, if you wanted me to."

"I would like you to clean this house, and come help me with the cooking. My niece and a group of her friends arrive from the west next Thursday. I have invited some fifty people to a formal luncheon and expect you to help."

"Thursday is my due date," Jezebel reminded her.

"So? We used to drop our children in the fields." She banged the main door behind her.

She came back with a boy in tow; he was laden with foodstuff.

"Do not, I repeat not, use a mop; get on your knees, and clean these floors," she addressed her as though she was her servant.

"I cannot bend down," Jezebel said.

"Try," she said as she handed the boy a few coins for a tip.

The delivery boy checked the pregnant woman sadly, sorrowfully, churning rage within her; she hated eliciting sympathy from strangers while her husband looked on unmoved.

"If you wish I could mop instead of her," he offered sweetly.

"Thank you," Jezebel said. "I am fine."

"Get out. Mopping is for women. Did your mother not teach you anything?" the old woman shrieked at the boy, who ran away swiftly.

Jezebel, having already mopped the entire flat with the mop, got down on her knees to redo it.

She moved furniture and plants, and cleaned the entire house, four balconies included, feeling proud of contributing in humility and acceptance to the general atmosphere of peace. Exhausted, but pleased, she ached for a rest.

"I finished the entire flat," she told her husband's mother.

"Come here and cut some onions," the domestic tyrant ordered.

Jezebel worked in the kitchen all day, until her husband returned. They served dinner at seven, and she collapsed into an undisturbed, deep sleep soon afterwards. They worked all that week unceasingly, until, the day of the party, that Thursday Jezebel awoke at six o'clock with another stab of pain. This one felt acute and more definite. It was followed by an unexpected piercing pain, and a gush of a thick liquid.

She, the mother, cooked eggs for breakfast.

"Come eat," she shrieked to awaken the region.

"I do not want to eat," Jezebel told her husband, who was shaving. "Maybe you should watch me bathe."

He locked the bathroom door, as he resumed his shaving while she showered.

Another shriek awoke Arya.

"Could you possibly tell her to stop screaming?" she asked him.

Husband placed his hand on the handle of the bathroom to leave and claim their shrieking child, when the entire door shook ominously off its hinges.

"Open this door right now," she ordered.

Neither one of the couple replied. They stared one another in surprise.

She resumed her banging on the door and cussing needing to know immediately the reason they were locked up inside a bathroom, and what possible lewd and disgusting things they were up to.

"She is in labour; I am helping her a bit." That was the worst thing he could have possibly said.

A barrage of insults battered the door to reach them about stupid men who knew not how to handle women. It was simply awful. They resumed her bath, and towelling, as she raved and ranted.

Finally finished, they exited to find the door blocked.

"Move," he said impatiently.

"No," she blocked the door with her body. "Could you tell me what is the reason for this stupid bath?"

"She needs help, mother, please move."

"Help with what?" She lost her mind with jealousy.

"Help shaving her legs, move," he said.

"You shaved her legs? Oh, my God, are you her slave? What man would do an unseemly thing like that? You are a strange one. She changed you, son. I have raised you as a man. What happened?"

He ignored her as he assisted Jezebel with the changing of Arya; all the while the barrage of insults continued pouring over their heads.

"Is there no way to stop her?" Jezebel giggled, disbelieving the incongruity of the event.

"It is surreal," he said.

Although he said little, he looked deeply hurt at being insulted before her, she knew, and at the little support being extended their way. Jezebel felt deeply sorrowful for him.

"You know we have to leave right after you deliver this baby, right?" he asked.

"Yes." She understood completely that their lives as a couple had become impossible among these people.

"They will divorce us for sure," he added.

She nodded her understanding, as she made the beds and prepared Arya for her breakfast.

"Could we trust her with Arya?"

He did not answer her fears. He was not sure, but they had little choice in the matter.

"Where are you going, mommy?" Arya asked from her cot nearby.

"I am going to bring your sister or brother." Jezebel gathered the child inside her arms.

"I do not want one," Arya said. "I want my mommy."

They shared a giggle together. Arya was almost a year old, and spoke fluently in two languages.

"I will be back soon," Jezebel promised her daughter. "Would you wait for me?"

"Tomorrow?" Arya asked, her only concept of time.

"Yes, tomorrow." She felt like crying for her child.

"Promise?"

"I do, I do." Jezebel crossed her heart.

"Good. I will call you," Arya promised.

"She is unreal," her husband exclaimed, in awe of his daughter.

"Yes," Jezebel agreed. "She is very special."

"Are you feeling well?" he asked Jezebel.

"I am fine. This is going to be an easy delivery, I feel," she said to appease his fears.

He came to encircle her shoulders when the door flew open.

"What a cosy scene of domestic bliss?" His mother spewed venom. "I could not believe I heard giggles coming from here. You must be happy that your mother is so deeply disturbed by your lewd behaviour, son, to encircle the great dame so tenderly. Yes, yes, spoil her a bit more, so next time she sits on our heads."

He removed his hand swiftly, and resumed dressing up, acting as though nobody spoke.

They never spoke, but left the house carrying the little bag, and thinking of their child ready to be born.

"I hope it is not one of your false alarms; anything to spoil my fun and my party." Then she screamed in their back her wishes of luck, and blessings of motherly tenderness.

His father hailed a taxi, happy for a change of pace, to find something which to occupy his hyper mind with, one that understood not the meaning of peace.

"The American hospital," he ordered the driver.

They arrived at eight-thirty to go straight to the labour room. It was to be an easy delivery. Three hours later, Edward, their son, was born weighing seven pounds, nine ounces, and looking as radiantly golden as the Madras sun that had conceived him.

"He is beautiful," the nurses announced.

Jezebel smiled contentedly. Her children were all that mattered in her life. They were love and creation. She felt the rightness of them, and knew that they would be the only thing that mattered, ever.

In her room, a garden grew. There were plants sent by her sisters and uncles. Mother and father were sitting on chairs across from her body when she awoke from an exhausted snooze.

"Hey, princess; he is beautiful," her father said.

"Who does he take after?" she asked them.

"He looks like a cherubic angel; all blond curls, and pink cheeks, and that smile," her mother explained.

That made Jezebel the happiest person on this earth.

Thirty-One
EDWARD, THE BOY WONDER, RULES

Humans live in drudgery and pain on earth, dreaming incessantly of a better future. The dream saves them from insanity. That constant thought projection into a happier future is their ultimate undoing, the thief that steals their present moments, the true enemy; an enemy hugged in sheer ignorance of its identity. We dream because we remember a better life. That, however, is not a blissful state possible for the body. The fact that humans know of a better state of being, points to their memory of that other place, a divine state, where bliss was possible and security was theirs without toil. That state of total bliss is, however, the state of humans in the spirit; a state of pure being where earthly clutches are deemed superfluous, even shunned.

That longing for that other state points to the divinity of man; a divinity man remembers to long for incessantly. That is man's spirit asserting itself on the greedy body.

The other state, the life humans experience inside the body, is one of sheer madness. Distraught at finding that blissful state of joyous being, humans work furtively, incessantly, feverishly at reaching the joyous state only to get lost in the maze of matter, driven further a field from their inherent bliss.

The more a human runs, the more mad his state of being. Like a person lost in the forest, he runs in circles returning angrier to his former spot, until, he sits down, relaxes and calmly attempts to figure out where he got lost.

Those among us who can sit and reflect have a greater chance at finding that which they looked for: Running in maddening circles is undoubtedly the ways of the body at shielding us from that divine truth we so earnestly seek.

The more a human sits, the more his stance resembles that of vegetables; a most shunned stance by those that uphold the body, the better his chances to stumble over his blissful divine.

Since time memorial, humans came to earth to get lost into the maze of the body; such is the focused and determined guile of that body to get us muddled so it survives unscathed, pampered.

Earth is the state of misery for all humans in the body; so to remedy the miserable state we either live in the future to drum up a blissful state or in the past to rehash some injustice hailed, most often by others, that they are never in the present where happiness is at the fingertips – all eternity simply is.

What helps perpetuate the fallacy of happiness is the fact that at some time in every human's miserable life, there occurs an event that makes him soar to heaven, touch the stars and kiss the firmament where angels play their harps, and the stars strike their cheerful tunes as the entire universe plays for them colours of the most startling shapes that match their soaring bliss.

Instead of getting the idea of living in the moment, humans self-appropriate the miracles in sheer stupid selfishness, thinking themselves glorious, never offering thanks, and never looking to the source of the miracle. They become absorbed, addicted to the desire of the symphony of life, to drop inside the abyss of sheer destruction at never finding it again.

That is precisely the state of humans who do not understand the idea of living in the present moment, of day-dreaming about it, either in joy, or else in misery. The state of the divine is ever-present, ever-accessible, if only one offers grateful thankfulness to the miracle, and keeps the self-absorbed ego in check.

As God is a jealous host; when he offers the party, he wants the human to thank him for the glorious event, not to think himself both the party and the host. He, God alone, is the Host of the entire universe, unequivocally.

And so, the snake of knowledge, the brain, the symbol of bodily intelligence, crude and slow, crass and ever-limited, fights the Lord, attempting to usurp that which He created with utmost love and wonder. The self is alive and, well stealing humans away from their own Garden of Eden. The Lord will never stand for that. Not that He holds a grudge, never; more that He had installed laws by which humans incur the same form of punishment they hail onto others while in their state of ungrateful selfishness. If they were to steal another's property, a divine energy manages to have the same and more stolen from them. A fair and simple law that affords no leeway has been in motion since time immemorial, Karma.

Those few that keep awake to the law of Karma are saved. By keeping the self ever-present, humans check that self, and further strengthen the light in their beings ensuring that self never goes haywire again, or rarely, and even then not completely. By so doing, man's duality, including his body and spirit, is brought closer towards a centre of goodness where extremes are not possible.

Even there, around the centre, one never gets a respite; for as others around one see the stability of being, and go after it in jealousy and greed wanting some for themselves, misery being their state, they assume erroneously, that they could steal or else destroy that human who smiles and gives thanks at all costs.

There being no saints born, and no evil entities created, the human himself goes towards one or the other by choice. It is all about that light born within each human. Either he strengthens that light with patience and good deeds to others to find peace in the body, and the realm of the earth plane, or else the body and its selfish resolve lead him onto the crooked path of desires and loss to suffer on the physical plane, and again in the beyond upon his death.

Having studied all that was written by humans in the form of their literary expression, Jezebel had learned that the only lesson needed by humans was the aforementioned. In one way or another, that is all that humans had ever attempted to resolve in all their writings. That simple truth imparted by the ascetic yogi in the dusty shack in Madras was all that was needed to learn. That she had learned. That lesson is what Jezebel managed to apply to save herself from sheer insanity with people in the midst of whom she managed to have landed to learn her most crucial of all lessons, humility and patience as she lived her present moment totally, painfully sometimes.

Edward's birth embodied all lessons in one sitting. It was an easy delivery during which Jezebel decided to remain focused on her pains so as not to miss that decisive life occurrence. She refused medication and sat about to calmly watch her weak body create a miracle of life, only possible, she knew with the divine intervention of that loving Creator of all things.

"I have given the family their coveted boy," she thought pleased.

He was beautiful her boy, blond, like the rays of a rising sun. Edward wrenched her heart from its cavity forever claiming it as his own. He had luminous skin, and large dark brown eyes with lashes that batted like angel wings and red pouty lips that never puckered to cry, but smiled incessantly.

"Thank you, my beloved God. Thank you for giving him to me. I am so weak, and could have never been able to do this thing. I offer his life to You to use and direct." She hugged the boy to her chest tenderly.

"Are you feeling well?" her husband asked.

"I am fine," Jezebel assured the man.

"I cannot go see you because I have come from work to care for Arya," he said.

"That is fine," she assured him. "How is Arya?"

"Arya loves the idea of having a brother. She, however, wants you to be here for her birthday."

She asked to speak to her daughter finding to her shock that the girl had developed yet more speech.

"How are you, mommy?" the beautiful child asked.

"I am fine, honey, you?" Jezebel inquired.

"I am fine, daddy is fine, grandma is fine, and everyone is fine. I want you to come home now," she broke down, to say.

Her plea broke Jezebel's heart. The child had never really had a present mother. Although Jezebel did her very best to be around her beloved daughter, circumstances in India dictated otherwise.

"I will be home for your birthday," she promised her.

"You won't." She sounded very negative.

"Of course I will, you'll see," Jezebel said.

"You won't, because you love the baby more."

That was terrible to hear. They spoke a while longer; all the while Jezebel assuring her daughter as to her unflinching love, and the latter insisting otherwise until convinced, Arya blew several kisses on the airwaves, kisses that landed inside her mother's heart.

"Edward has a fever," the nurse came to report.

"What is the problem?" Jezebel inquired.

"We do not really know, maybe a bug or something," she added.

"Is his doctor concerned?" she asked.

"Not in the slightest, we however cannot circumcise him in his condition. You have to stick around the hospital for another week," she informed the mother.

"I will leave the day after tomorrow to celebrate his sister's first birthday." Jezebel decided just that moment. "We'll pick him up three days later."

"I am sure that this will be fine. The doctor will speak to you," she said, and left.

"I am coming out the day after tomorrow," she informed her husband.

"That is a good plan," he said relieved, "I cannot care for Arya and do my work."

"Why are you doing that?" she asked.

"That is what my mother wants," he replied.

"I see, fine. Then I do have to go home," she said.

"I am afraid so, and listen, I will try to come see you today," he promised.

He had not been to the hospital for four days. He was with her through labour, and the delivery, arrived two days later to see the baby and sit for five minutes, and had gone home to care for their first child.

He came to the hospital on the day of her leaving. It was terrible for them both to leave the golden boy behind. Jezebel had called her mother to meet them at the house with a cake for Arya. She knew they would be there to celebrate her daughter's first birthday. Her father was not at the house when she arrived.

"You are here, you are here," Arya chanted. "Where is your big tummy, mommy?" the child asked.

"I left it at the hospital to come see you," her mother told her.

She kissed her cheeks, and her eyes and the empty tummy and her hair, jumping over the sofas, tripping the chairs, singing the Indian songs Mary had taught her and chirping her bliss.

"She has gone haywire," her father said.

"It is so sad," Jezebel told him. "I did not realize how she would miss me."

"You are all she knows, Jezebel, and trust," he assured her.

Arya enjoyed her birthday thoroughly; thanking everyone for the gifts of her dolls and toys, Teddy bears and colouring books. She sat on her mother's lap colouring on a notepad. The adults visited happily, as an unspoken sadness hovered over all their heads; the absence of Edward alone at the hospital with a raging fever. Jezebel read all their fears, but tried valiantly to still her own. Her son had travelled the universe to arrive to her safely. She had lifted him up to her Creator for care. To worry over his safety now would be akin to mistrusting His care. She kept her mind on her wondrous daughter in her happiness.

That night Arya slept in her mother's arms, stuck to her body as though fearing to lose her.

"When did her vocabulary grow to that extent?" Jezebel needed to know. "When we arrived three months earlier she spoke not a word of our language."

"I speak the words from before I was born," Arya told her mother.

The couple shared a rare laugh, one that somehow skipped the Gestapo's scrutiny, oddly, succeeding to steal a measure of intimacy the depth of which only his mother could fathom to torment herself. When he caught her eye, to go into her innermost recesses, places she herself ignored, he came out with a chunk of diamond to gladden and thrill them. That, to her mind, stood at the crux of all their shared joy as well as miseries. It is for these rare gems that Jezebel tolerated the intolerable in her life with him.

For that rare connection stood as her ultimate experience, one she scarcely could imagine forfeiting. That also, was what his family felt to hate her.

"I know the words from before I live here," Arya repeated.

"What is she babbling about?" Her father needed a respite.

"I have everything in my heart," Arya told her parents.

"Everything is in your heart?" her father, relieved, asked her.

"Yeah, everything, even the angels," she nodded.

They laughed hysterically at the imagination of their child, and generally felt blessed for both their children's health and wellbeing. They were allowed to feel like a family.

"You rest," he said. "I will go check on them."

"I see a woman and a man kill me," Arya came to divulge.

"Where did you see that?" Jezebel asked the child.

"In my dream," Arya said.

"Who were they?"

"I don't know. But they kill me with honey," she said.

Chills coursed through the poor mother's blood, and a doctor's voice boomed in her ear, telling her about her daughter's hysterical markings as being bee stings.

"You need never say a word of this to anyone." Jezebel's heart beat frightfully fast.

"But why?" the child asked, confused.

"Because I said so," the mother replied.

"What did I do wrong?" she asked, fearing to displease.

"You have done nothing wrong. We simply cannot speak of the honey killing us. That is all. I cannot explain things to you now. You have to promise mommy."

"I do promise," Arya said confused. "But the woman and her husband come back to kill me every time I sleep."

"Who are they?" Jezebel wanted to know.

"I don't know. They don't have faces."

Jezebel understood instantly that her daughter did not want to see the faces of her grandparents, and that, one day, she would destroy their family.

She hated teaching her daughter guile. There was no getting around that one.

Thirty-Two
ARYA REMEMBERS HER PREVIOUS LIFE

Jezebel ran from the room horrified, unable to tolerate the games they played; the minute a closeness grew between her and her mate, the old lady felt it and ran to plot her destruction, assisted wickedly by her daughter's counsel and her second son. Her old man sat and smiled; happy, no doubt, Jezebel thought, that their venom was directed away from him.

Now that they were appeased concerning the safety of their heir, they tightened the campaign against his mother. Thinking the dilemma through, Jezebel felt assured that they wanted her out as they wanted her husband and children in with them. It was an archaic set of rules adhered to in the land for millennia, she knew; the children of males were solely the property of their fathers and paternal grandparents. Owing these mothers towed the line of abuse or kindness imposed by their in-laws, these mothers stayed or left the fold singly on the strength of the matriarchal authority.

"Someone needs to inform these people of the century we're in," she thought.

She slapped cold water over her face and neck, trying to still her laboured breathing, and heaving chest.

"Are you okay?" Colette asked, having seen her run inside the bathroom.

"I am fine," Jezebel answered.

She would not tell anyone about Arya's being her late sister Alaya, killed by her own grandparents and come back with memories to atone for the sins others committed onto her. Chances were Arya would never divulge either; her daughter's subconscious mind would help block the truth.

What shattered the woman most was the fact that if her daughter were to remember more details, it would destroy their lives completely; her father would never stand for his daughter accusing his parents of a murder committed before she was born. He would invariably accuse her mother of having planted ideas in their daughter's head to undermine his family.

"It is disastrous," she went around the house muttering. "It is quite disastrous."

She also weighed the other eventuality; if Arya were to name and shame her grandparents, would that not vindicate her sister?

Finally, after a lengthy deliberation, she concluded that Arya's divulgence, if it were to occur to her later when she matured, Jezebel could divert matters before they developed into a disaster. She should tell the child that saving her father's feelings in the matter was more important than divulging the truth.

Unsure all around, even of the babbling one-year-old child, she decided to open her eyes, and say nothing.

"We go to church tomorrow?" she asked Arya as she tucked her in.

"We go get Edward tomorrow. Did you forget?" she replied.

"No. I thought dad could go get him, and the two of us girls could attend holy Mass, instead. I have not taken communion for a long time."

"Okay," she said.

They dressed prettily, in matching dresses made for them by an astute clothes maker in Madras. They even had hats to match, and decided to walk the few hundred meters to church.

"It is pretty." Arya enjoyed visiting the church.

"Yes, it is." Jezebel squeezed her hand. "Put this pound in the collection tray when the man comes by." She handed her daughter the pound note.

"Why?" the little girl asked.

"Because," Jezebel was not sure what to tell her, "the priest needs our money to help the poor," she said.

"Okay."

When the Mass was finished, they walked into the sunshine, and heat.

"We come back next Sunday?" Jezebel asked.

"Do you feel better?" Arya asked.

"Yes. Don't you?"

"I like Nana Mary's temple more," Arya stated simply.

Jezebel felt rage boil inside her, and guilt. Having assumed that Arya understood nothing of the rituals, she had allowed her inside Indian temples during feast time.

"That is blasphemous, darling. Please, please, do not say these things before the family," she begged.

"I promise, but mom, why?"

"Because Arya, the family would kill me if they knew I allowed you in a Buddhist temple," Jezebel said unthinking.

"See? Indians are better. They don't believe in killing. But also, Mary was Catholic not Buddhist, not like Shoshanna," Arya informed her mother. "Indians love everyone."

"Oh great, do not say that either." Jezebel took Arya's face in both her hands and kissed her. "I tell you what, don't say anything in front of them, nothing; keep silent to save mama."

"They are mean, I know," Arya blurted.

"No, they are not. We must never speak this way of our father's family. He would be so hurt."

"Fine," Arya agreed. "He knows that they are mean."

"How do you know that?"

"He knows. You don't know. He does not want you to know, but he knows," she chimed.

"How does he know?" Jezebel asked.

"He knows," she sang hideously.

"Arya, tell mommy," Jezebel insisted.

"She said bad things to my dad when you went to buy Edward from the hospital," she cried, hurt.

"What things did she say?" Jezebel resented the fact that they spoke before her child.

"She told him that she hated him," Arya shouted.

"What else?" she prodded her child.

"I can't remember." She wiped her eyes. "More bad things like that."

"Try, Arya," Jezebel encouraged, knowing her daughter hid things to shield her.

"She said that you are like a princess, like your sister. She did not let him go see you in hospital because she was not a maid. She said he needs to stay to take care of me." She sounded shattered.

"How awful," Jezebel said.

She picked the little girl up and placed her on her knee. The curls cascading over her back shone russet, wrenching her heart away.

"Don't worry about that," Jezebel appeased and assured her.

"Oh, I worry," she responded.

"You need to stop that. Mom and dad will take care of one another and of you and Edward," she promised, half believing herself.

"Why do they hate him, mommy?" she asked.

"I have no idea, honey," she told her truthfully. "He is such a good man."

"Lord Sri Krishna and his friend Arjuna will punish them by giving them bad karma," Arya said.

"No Arya, no darling. You must never speak of these people; they are heathens, you hear. Do not ever blaspheme against our religion, and God. It is very bad; you will get me in trouble. Do you want them to attack daddy for having raised you badly?"

"Who cares what they say? You should not care so much about that," Arya counselled her mother.

"Promise never to speak about any of that around them, okay?"

"I promise. But, I want you to know that their God is our God. Everyone's God is our God, mom. There is only one God," she concluded. "I will not tell them. I need to tell you."

"Thank you so much, Arya. However," Jezebel had no idea how to handle the dilemma, "Jesus Christ is the real God."

"Yes, of course," Arya shook her head affirmatively. "They have many Lords like that, also"

"Who told you these things?" she asked distraught.

"Soujaya and Shoshanna used to read the Bhagavad-Gita to me before I slept," Arya said. "I want you to buy it and read it to me."

"I don't even know what it is," Jezebel admitted.

"It is their science; the Vedic philosophy."

"Is that right?" Jezebel threw her head back and laughed.

"Yes, it is beautiful." Her eyes grew dreamy.

"Tell mommy what you remember from this Vedic philosophy," Jezebel cajoled her toddler, who could hardly form the words.

"It is very hard. Let me see. There was Lord Krishna, who was beautiful, he had a face like a lotus and a moon all shiny and pure, and he came down from heaven to teach people about the God so they could go to Him. He made friends with a man called Arjuna. He wanted to teach him about God. So, they talked a lot about that. He liked his friend a lot. Arjuna believed every word Lord Krishna had ever told him. He trusted him too. It is about stories of what they did. It is not scary, honest," she said.

"That is it?"

"No. He teaches him stuff to make him be a God like him. He listens to him and when he makes it, he gets a chariot of gold that five horses drove and took him to the sky for a ride in it. I saw the chariot, it is beautiful. Arjuna is no more like us after that; he is a God like Lord Krishna,"

"There is only one God, you said," Jezebel needed to point out the loopholes.

"Sure, I know. There are many Gods like Jesus, Mohammed, Lord Krishna, Arjuna, and the Buddha, but only there is the one Godhead, mom. He is the boss of them all," she said sweetly. "Everybody that gets the instructions of Lord Krishna, like his friend Arjuna, can go to the skies in a gold chariot with five white horses."

"That is terrible blasphemy," Jezebel started crying. "You are corrupted, polluted."

"Fine, sorry mommy; please do not be mad at me," Arya pleaded. "Don't cry, Jezebel."

"I am not angry." Jezebel found herself confused by her child. "I am afraid for you. Besides, stop calling me Jezebel. You should call me mommy."

"I would never let anyone hurt you, mommy." The way the child said it brought a chill to the woman's spine.

"You are going to protect me?" she asked laughing.

"Yes, I am." Arya sounded one hundred years old, and distant. "You never need worry about me. I will help you with my father, and Edward."

"How could you protect me, Arya? I am supposed to protect you."

"You cannot. You are soft and sweet. I have some strong from them. I know how to talk to them," she affirmed. "Could we buy the book?"

"What book?"

"The Bhagavad-Gita."

"Sure," Jezebel relented.

"Could we do it now?" Arya was nothing if not persistent.

"We need to run home," she said.

"The bookshop is right here," she begged.

They went in to buy the colourful book. Jezebel hid it inside a paper sack which she purchased.

Jezebel read about the chariot which represented the brain of Lumas. Although the two men sat inside it, controlled it, sometimes, the five white horses that pulled the brain along would pull both brain and rider astray if allowed to lead the rider.

Jezebel understood that the idea was to rein in the senses; horses in this case, lest they dragged the entity on a path of destruction and loss; the entity being in this case, the spirit within the carriage.

The woman found the idea ingenious. She decided to investigate; feeling within herself a stirring of knowing.

"See," Arya pointed to the colourful cover, "Arjuna sitting by Lord Krishna in the chariot. The five horses are the five senses, sight, smell, touch, taste," Alaya explained excited.

"You counted four senses," Jezebel corrected her toddler.

"Oh, yes, and the hearing," the child said.

"Who is the passenger?" Jezebel asked.

"That would be the master of everything, the spirit, the real me, the timeless," Arya said.

"You can't discuss this with anyone," Jezebel begged her.

"I promise," the little girl said. "You have to read it to me."

It was this book that started Jezebel on a long quest of discovery Like Arjuna, the young woman got instructed by Lord Krishna to the higher philosophy which thrilled and appeased her. Later, the book Arya insisted on reading proved to be the most prophetic of all the help the pair would need to survive the disasters assailing them so as to keep the family together despite all the adversities about them.

"That should not be our nightly reading," Jezebel admonished, "but our Holy Bible."

"They are one and the same," Arya said.

Jezebel decided to drop the subject for the time being, as they neared the house.

"You can't discuss this with anyone," Jezebel told her.

"I know, I know, stop being so afraid," Arya said.

Thirty-Three
DISTRAUGHT FAMILY DEALS WITH DILEMMA

The energy that governed her father's being defied description. It emanated soft power, palpable might; it hovered about his large frame with the chiselled features conjuring to those that saw it images of being in the presence of a king.

He came in to sit inside their living room dressed in a khaki safari suit whose simplicity evoked African warriors. That persona could not be more confusing as it got swiftly cancelled by the largesse of the man, his soft humour and palpable humility.

He embraced the husband tenderly, greeting the old parents gently and awaited his daughter's arrival with his precious grandchildren.

When Arya entered the living room at a run, her arms extended wide, her large eyes beaming her love towards him, he got up swiftly to pick her up and hold her in his arms.

She looked up to him adoringly, there having always been a worshipful connection of the most tender between them. He patted her curls as he visited with her father, who promised to go spend the next weekend with the family in the Bekaa Valley.

They left with Jezebel's husband waving tearfully his goodbye.

"The city is very stuffy," Jezebel said.

"It is already mid-July, honey, what do you expect?" her father said.

Arya spoke incessantly from behind them, periodically giving them news flashes as to her brother's state in the car seat.

"Mom, he is very red," she said.

"Leave him be," her grandfather replied.

"But grandpa, he looks unhappy," Arya objected.

"Yes, we will stop, Mr. Cronkite," he laughed in response.

"I love this child," he told Jezebel. "Does she remind you of Alaya?"

Jezebel's heart sustained a painful spasm; the events and machinations coming right after her delivery, and the fact that she hid them from her parents, had shattered her nerves. Now, she feared the mention of her late sister would get Arya babbling about the dreams and murders, the man with the long features.

"No," Jezebel replied cryptically, sounding short.

"She looks exactly like her. You would not know, you were not born," her father resumed his conversation innocently.

"I don't want her to hear about her aunt," Jezebel whispered.

"Why can't I hear about my aunt Alaya?" Arya asked her mother.

Jezebel turned around to stare her daughter down.

"What did I do?" Arya objected.

"How do you turn her off?" Her grandfather laughed amused by the child. "Alaya was just like that."

"Was she, dad? Sometimes I feel that she is not normal. Children do not have this extensive vocabulary at her age."

"It is the logic that is more baffling than the breadth of her vocabulary. It is not that she babbles stupidly, she makes much sense."

"Must not speak like that," Arya interjected.

"Why ever not?" her grandfather asked.

"It is vain. Vanity is the worst sin," she announced.

"Oh, she speaks divinity as well." He laughed harder. "What kind of a child is this?"

"How is vanity a sin?" Jezebel asked her, intrigued.

"It is the worst sin," Arya repeated, seriously mortified.

"Fine, you have already said that, Arya, could you tell mommy the reason it is so bad?"

"It is obvious; Jesus spoke about that a lot. He spoke about the snake of vanity. That is what got Eve in trouble, mom. It is the mother of all sins, the reason for much suffering and pain."

The grandfather pulled his car onto the shoulder by the side of the road. He turned around to the back seat so as to look at the child that so resembled his firstborn, suddenly shocked, intrigued by the resemblance.

"Turn around," he instructed Arya.

She turned around as asked. He pulled her trousers down to bare her bottom.

"What are you looking for?" Jezebel asked.

"Alaya had a huge mole on her right bottom cheek," he said.

"Arya would not have it," Jezebel said.

"You are so silly, granddad," Arya giggled, "How could I be a dead woman?"

"It is uncanny, the voice. She sounds exactly like your sister at her age."

"Genetics," Jezebel commented, but shook visibly.

He gave up just then, and Arya fell asleep with the rocking of the car that climbed higher and higher towards the peak of Dahr El Baidar, offering her mother a brief respite.

"Let us buy some watermelon," the giant man said.

Seen from that high mountain, the Bekaa Valley stretched below their vision like a Persian rug, painstakingly woven by the intricacy of the Godhead Himself, to take the breath away. A vast expanse of low hills dotted the vista, perching over the majestic colourful plains that hugged their skirts; children in constant adoration to their mothers. Grape vineyards languished about the breadth of one's vision to add the distinct colours of their fruits, hugged by fields of golden wheat, now bleached white by the sun, and orchards of all kinds of imaginable fruits finished the canvas with their constant worship and meek giving to entice and enthral.

They stopped before the Wadi in the big city of the Bekaa Valley, Zahle, built on several hills, bits of that extension of the mighty Sanine Mountain, to gather all their energies about the famed river which sheltered a cluster of restaurants famous for their delicacies to entice people visit from the world over.

Jezebel missed the scented, dry air, which cleared all ailments.

"Buy me ice cream from the Iraitim shop," Arya awoke to plead.

"There is no shop by that name, sweetheart," Jezebel said.

"Yes, there is," Arya insisted.

"Be quiet, you will awaken Eddy," her mother asked her.

"There is the best ice cream at Iraitim's," she insisted.

Her grandfather came back carrying a huge watermelon.

"It is bigger than you and Eddy combined," he said, happy to have the grandchildren.

She did not answer. Finding the matter odd, that his motor mouth would be quiet, he turned around to be faced by a terrible pout.

"Who made my little darling angry?" he asked concerned.

"Mommy," the child replied.

"You must never anger our motor mouth, Jezebel."

"What did she do?" he asked the child.

"She does not believe me." Arya cried louder.

"Oh stop it, Arya," Jezebel felt irritated.

"See?" Arya moaned, "See granddad?"

"I am going to get her in trouble for you, princess; I am her father, you know. I can do that."

"I know," she giggled sweetly.

"What is the matter with you two?" he asked his daughter.

"She has the most active imagination of any child you know. Sometimes she gets tiresome. She insists that she knows an ice cream parlour inside the Birdawni River called Iraitim." Jezebel sounded irritated.

"There was," her father said. "Iraitim was the most reputable ice cream parlour. His specialty was cream and toasted almond ice cream. How could she know that? That was Alaya's favourite flavour. Iraitim closed shop ten years ago. You were a little girl. You would not remember," he told his daughter.

"How do you know the shop, Arya?" Jezebel asked confused.

"I don't know," the little girl said. "I just know things."

They dropped the subject promptly; having both reached a dead-end of logical processes.

"Would a fruit ice cream stick do?" he asked the child.

"Don't worry about it. I don't want anything." She fell asleep.

Both children slumbered in the back seat allowing their mother a chance to take in the scenery. Memories came to flood her mind pleasantly. The very scent of the place brought joy to her spirit. As it was wheat harvest season, mounds of hay sat in squares in the middle of the shaven plain. The smell of wheat drying in the sun imparted that familiar scent which spelled summer. They passed the centre of their hometown as people waved and stared, passed the crossroad to go south, left the town, the stables, the river, all the churches, the small shops of Jezebel's childhood, then went deeper into the countryside that brimmed with nothing but stretches of grape vines, and brown earth.

People in Rayak, Hosh Hala, having lived so long with their French rulers had never dropped the habits adopted from their conquerors; these French army personnel, long gone now, had left their stamp on the town. Men pedalled their bicycles to and fro their fields, berets shielding their heads and britches wrapped around their legs fastened with pegs as to protect them from getting snarled by their bike chains. People sitting in outdoor cafes, sipping Arak as they munched on appetizers, looked surreally out of place; as though plucked from Valras or Toulouse and set there by a magician's slight of hand.

Horses crossed the town centre between motor cars and pedestrians strangely at ease as though it was the most natural thing, which affirmed the authenticity of the strange scene.

"This place never changes," Jezebel said. "I am so glad."

"I love this place," Arya squealed in delight.

"No, you do not," they responded as one.

"Oh yes I do," she twittered delighted.

"You think you do," her grandfather replied.

"I do. See, this is my grandmothers' parents' house."

While Jezebel ignored her daughter, the grandfather stopped swiftly just before the house that sat on the left side of the long road at the edge of the large town. He stopped before an intricately fashioned white, latticed, wooden gate, behind which a large house sat sadly empty.

"Which house is that?"

"This one," Arya pointed to the house.

"What do you know about that?" he asked, troubled.

"I know that we used to come here and ride in a buggy pulled by two mules. One time, my mommy got really angry because I messed up my Organza Easter dress. I was dirtied by horse dung from the back of the buggy. She changed me into my blue one to go visit the family."

"Ignore her," Jezebel said.

"What else?"

"They had many goats that lived in a shack behind the house."

"What else?"

"Some cousin lived there, just across the road."

"And?" he asked, leading her along.

"There was a shop by this house. The uncle had candies. The hairdresser nearby, who had cut my bangs which made you very mad."

The giant shook like a feather in a storm. Jezebel blocked them; thinking her child's babbling mere childish fantasy.

"Dad?" she asked. "Are you okay?"

"No Jezebel, I am not. This child knows things about us you do not even know."

"Is it true, then? Is this mom's people's house?"

"It sure is," he said. "Your mother and uncles were all born here."

"How would she know?"

"I have no idea."

The family awaited them on the terrace outside before the water fountain. Her mother watered the mint, as a young servant ran behind Dustin.

"Is Dustin speaking?" Jezebel asked her father.

"Some words, the usual papa, mama, bye-bye, good boy, you know, nothing like your Einstein there."

They kissed, sat around the fountain to sip the Arabic coffee. Her fourth sister introduced her newborn daughter, who looked just like their mother, the child's grandmother.

"She is a good baby," their mother said. "Lana never cries."

"Edward here is a regular prince," her father announced.

Drugged by the pure air, Eddy slumbered still. He had already missed a feeding, and was near missing the second one.

"Should we awaken him to feed him?" Jezebel asked her mother who looked baffled.

Their father said that one never awakened a child to feed him. Nature tells him what to do.

So, appeased by the love, Jezebel settled her children in the downstairs room to the left of the kitchen, while her sister took the room to the right, as the entire family moved to the upper floor as to afford the mothers optimum comfort and access to the kitchen. They took Arya to breakfast in the Wadi every day of that week. They rode horses, picked grapes, walked under the moon. It was splendid.

"We need to talk," he told his wife.

"Talk then," she smiled happily.

"I think Arya is our Alaya come back from the dead," he said.

"You are daft," his wife said. "How could you do this thing to a mere baby? Surely, it is blasphemy."

He told his wife that he once had a Druze friend from the Highlands who was sure beyond doubt that he had come back from the dead as his wife's brother.

"How horrible," disgusted, the woman said.

"Listen, who says that it is disgusting if it were the will of God?"

"I say it. It is disgusting. Do you realise the havoc such a system would wreak on the world? Do you imagine such a system?"

"Yes, I actually can," he admitted. "I sure can imagine it."

"Who would the system benefit?" she objected vehemently.

"Heaven could be the promise of release from the body. Hell could be life in the body."

"So, there is no actual heaven, and no actual hell?"

"It could be that way." He rubbed his temples savagely.

"I don't know," the soft mother said. "I don't know how to feel about that. Surely, that is not Alaya, no matter what. I would feel that I needed to reclaim her if she were to be Alaya."

"Yes. Jesus spoke about that also. When a disciple told him that his mother and siblings were outside, he told him something to the effect of who is my mother? Who are my siblings? All women are my mother, and all children are my siblings. That is the state of oneness Jesus needed us to achieve. That is the only way we could ever be happy. To appropriate our children, possessions, and things, creates a great deal of grief in light of this incarnation." He stared her way, knowing that she missed the crux of the matter.

"My children are my own. Do you expect me to feel about Arya the same way I felt about my first born, Alaya? I cannot. Alaya was mine and yours. Arya belongs to her mother and father."

"Yes, that is the body. Jesus did not speak of the body. He spoke of the spirit of all men. He constantly said that this spirit is one, referring repeatedly to the believers as his brothers, and of His Father as being all theirs. Alaya's spirit is nobody's but her own. Nobody belongs to anyone but themselves. If Arya were to be the spirit of Alaya, can't you see how she chose to come back to us? Obviously, in this science the child picks the parents, not the other way around."

"It is dizzying; it stands opposite to all things formerly believed," she marvelled, grieved.

"It takes a bit of adjusting and inquiry," he agreed. "I tell you, that Arya is more Alaya than you think."

He recounted Arya's recollections to her grandmother, who, upon hearing of the child's desires and tastes, broke down and cried.

"Does Jezebel know?"

"Jezebel knows more than she cares to share," he told his wife. "She fears telling us, lest we think her demented."

"What do we do?" she asked.

"We do nothing," he said. "We try to learn."

"What are you talking about?" His wife's mind obsessed over dinner.

"To my mind the One God that sent the many prophets could not impart violence to shatter His creation, now would he? It is obvious Arya has come to us to teach us acceptance and love."

"It is still an unfair law to my mind," the soft wife said.

"That sounds harsh, sure. However, because the aim of creation is to teach, how could a method be wrong? It is teaching by example."

"Why should Jezebel suffer so you, her father, might learn?"

Four weeks passed with Jezebel's husband promising to visit the family home in the plains, only to disappear from sight right on Friday, until he surfaced anew Monday evening. The family grew increasingly embarrassed around the people they had invited weekly to come meet the great man. It humiliated Jezebel's father, on levels her husband could not fathom. Her family, hailing from a tribal past, had always upheld specific ways and means of conduct, not prone to change. The set red lines when crossed spelled dire consequences, the law of in-laws forbade the slighting of one's father-in-law before his tribe. Jezebel understood about the troubles in whose path her husband had unknowingly placed her; to be forever targeted and shunned by her clan and the extended tribe that adored her father. The fact that he kept promising her to visit bode badly for him; had he openly explained his dilemma with his mother to her, Jezebel would have skirted the situation by asking to return to her husband claiming illness or such some excuse so as to save him face and her father embarrassment. Unable to hold his own end with his mother, and fearing to look unable to diffuse matters before his wife, he opted for guile and deceit. She knew that her father would never own the slighting hailed upon his person, but that he would soon act on the hurt.

"Call him. I need to know the reason he does that," the father ordered.

"Where were you?" Jezebel asked that Monday evening.

"Well, the Family goes up to the village every weekend," he answered.

"Why do you promise us though? That is so embarrassing for us."

"Well, every weekend I want and mean to go, but my mother wants me to go with her to the village instead," he stated dementedly.

"You have not seen your newborn son for the entire first month of his life," she accused. "Does your mother not care for your children? Do you have no backbone to stand up for us as a family? What is going on?"

"She believes your place is here with us not with your parents," he replied flatly.

"How about you, what do you believe?" she asked.

"Give me a bloody break, Jezebel."

She related the story to her parents. Neither one answered. They were people who deliberated matters. Later, she knew, much later, the verdict of their deliberations would reach her.

In reality the camps, on either side of her body, warred on lines of their rightful understanding of the world. To her in-laws' thinking and rules, Jezebel's needing to be with her family was a slighting to them; as the family that had claimed her as theirs. Further, carrying her children away from them, children they believe to be rightfully theirs by the laws that ruled their region, was a breech which they viewed as rebellious conduct.

While, to her tribe and family, people whose past dictated strict rules of conduct, their son-in-law's rejection indicated lack of respect to the father, the tribal chief of his clan and family. Verdicts as to his punishment would arrive shortly.

When Edward awoke the next day screaming for his first feeding, her father came to her room, wrenched the boy from her arms, handed him to his wife, and returned to speak to his youngest daughter.

"Your husband is a bad seed. You know I hate divorce, but he crossed the threshold of decent conduct. This is your home. You need to leave him. The man does not respect you if he could treat us this shabbily."

"Fine," she said. "I think he is incorrigible as well. It has been horrendous living with him. Not that he is bad. It is more that the man has long surrendered his powers to his parents. The games he plays, dad, are killing me."

"Fine, so stupid people do not belong in this family." His verdict was final.

"Do you agree?" he asked.

"Yes, I agree, dad. It has been very tough." Jezebel felt a deep calm.

"We go today, give him his children. We gather your belongings and return. I will start divorce proceedings immediately."

"Give these people my children?" she asked, confused.

"Yes. They are their children. Let them raise them. We care for our child as they care for theirs."

Her father had lost it. Jezebel understood instantly that some power had just closed the last exit door in her face, forever. Like a spy caught in enemy territory, the poor mother whose life was ruled by misery suffered an overdose of disaster that shattered her beyond redemption. Now, they had managed to lose her the only support system, her beloved parents.

"They did that on purpose." The revelation came instantly. "They knew my parents would feet slighted and ask for my divorce. They did not want me to lose my parents, but my husband. They figured things correctly; that my father would ask me to divorce their son, and that he would send my children back to them." Deliberation took only seconds.

"No, I want to raise my own children. To him, they are a night of love making. To me, they are life itself. Take me back to my husband's house. I will never have these ignorant people wreak havoc with my children's psyche, regardless. I will suffer, not them," she told her father.

"Fine," he said.

He took Jezebel back to her husband's parents where he asked the man the reason he could not visit his newborn son and his family for four weeks.

"Any reason, son?" the big man asked.

"Circumstances beyond one's control," the man replied embarrassed.

"There are no such things when one is in control of his own destiny," the man said. "I feel sorry for you. The mark of a man is in the way he can act fairly between his wife and children on one hand, his parents and siblings, on the other." With that he left, without greeting or turning.

"We need to talk," he told Jezebel. "We need to leave before they procure our divorce."

She heard the words, and knew that the man had long ago forfeited his powers to other people. He believed he had no right to conduct his life. She knew that running away would be the only recourse to saving their children from a broken home. She would have so liked to stay and give the children an identity, a country, a belief system, but that would never happen.

"Fine," Jezebel agreed.

"We leave Arya behind," he said. "We take Edward."

"No, I would die first. They will corrupt her."

"Two months at the very most. I don't have a job or a place to live. We cannot care for two babies."

She knew that he had made a deal with them. Her life would be a series of such compromises, and repugnant deals.

"I will stay behind with her; you go," she begged him.

"No, I will never leave you two together with them," he said.

"I can't let go of Arya, though. What kind of a heartless deal did you make?" she asked. "It is cruel to me and her. I don't trust them with her."

"She will be fine Jezebel. My patience is stretched beyond endurance. Give me a break, honey please?"

"Eight weeks, if by then she is not with us, I come back for her," she informed him.

"It is a deal." He sounded happy for having successfully negotiated the compromise.

It never occurred to the poor man to take a stand, a fair stand where everyone is properly treated. His life, one he believed beyond his control, wavered like a boat lost in a stormy sea.

Thirty-Four
JEZEBEL AND FAMILY BACK WEST

Jezebel looked forward to completing work towards her degree. The woman who understood the genius of her daughter, fearing that Arya would live misunderstood, vowed to educate herself to afford the child intelligent help. The young girl read books, watched documentaries on the tube and mothered her little brother like an adult. The mother vowed to continue her education so as to help raise her children in a progressive way. Husband went to work on the train, and came back in the evening, ate dinner with the family, watched the news and went to bed. It was not much of a life, but it had to do. The most rewarding aspect became the lack of fights.

"I will register at the university," she announced one night.

"Your English is not good enough," he replied dismissively.

"Well, I will learn, won't I?" she responded angrily.

"I took Psych. 101 three times, and ended up having to drop the course," he said.

"I want to try. I plan to take Child Psychology."

"What would we do with the children?"

"The university furnishes a nursery." She appeased him.

That was the end of this discussion. He accepted her proposal thinking that she would soon give up.

She registered for one English course and one General Psychology course. Her tests results shocked him. She earned two A's.

"I am surprised," he told her.

Life proved monotonously boring; the long winter months and constant snow adversely affecting all their moods.

"Do you want me to find a job back home?" he asked knowing her suffering.

"I don't know." She feared family troubles.

"Don't worry. I will protect us," he promised meaning it.

She knew better. They would never be allowed to be. Over there, their family was his family's property to do with as they wished. Jezebel feared her independence disappearing.

A week later, he announced that he had arranged for an interview back home.

"There is a hitch," he sounded fearful of her refusal.

"Which is?" Her heart thumped the constant pitfalls.

"It is over the Christmas holidays. You will spend them here alone."

"Why can't we go along?" she asked knowing his reply.

"It is the money," he answered mournfully.

"Fine," she relented.

So, he went back, found the job, and came back a month later with joyous pictures of his holidays with his own family.

"We will go back," he announced.

There, life turned on its head for the young wife; things happened with such speed to dizzy them all. Both children refused leaving their friends and schools, as Jezebel battled with her university and packing their belongings.

Jezebel had managed to complete an associate degree in psychology. As she turned, her children had grown so suddenly.

Packed, they proceeded towards their destination beyond the seas. They packed their few belongings, as they had little in the way of furnishings or earthly possessions.

Arya and Edward joined the American schools in the west side of Beirut, a walking distance from the flat their parents had bought overlooking the seashore.

Arya studied hard, and got good marks in all subjects: Only mathematics escaped the child. There existed a block she erected to baffle her professor.

She enjoyed geometry well enough. Arya's love was unequivocally the arts, music especially; there floating with the rhythm of the flute and drums, something within surfaced to soar with the eagles, the birds, over the tree tops, all the way into the skies. Music made Arya feel her being.

There above the blue waters the girl understood the chirping of crickets, harmonizing sounds of frogs, birds, even the smell of flowers, roses, and herbs in their garden.

As she flew, soon Arya found solace with the rocks of her garden, the leaves of the huge trees, scent of pine, and the music of God's running waters: There was to be no sweeter music for her than the rushing springs, and clashing, crashing sounds of waterfalls.

Attuned to nature and its mysteries, she thought that friends her age sounded bland, naive, boring. She simply avoided them, and sought nature and the outdoors, instead.

"You must have friends your own age," Jezebel voiced her concern.

"Yes," Arya said. "I feel ageless, though, old, as old as these mountains, and the rocks."

Never did Arya feel superior to anyone; on the contrary she envied her friends' normalcy. Her brooding nature grew as a burden, an isolating force of nature. It was never to be a contrived state, but her true reality. When she tolerated all things alike, she truly loved nature.

"We need to help her get along," her father told his wife. "She does not know how to play with children her own age."

"But she gets along famously with everyone. Although she looks aloof, detached, bored almost, she truly loves everyone well enough." Her mother defended her daughter.

"It is her maturity," he said. "I worry about her."

Their conversation made her feel odd somehow, abnormal even. She wondered whether she was strange. A little girl in her sixth form called her snob, a weird person. The insult cut deep inside her. It churned deep within her for days afterwards. Confirmed by her parents, the child's remark took on ominous dimensions.

"I wonder if I was weird," she thought.

She vowed to exert a greater effort to make friends of her own age.

"I will try harder to make a friend," she told Jezebel.

"Odille next door is very nice, I hear. Her mother had built her a huge entertainment centre in their basement for her doll collection. Why don't you go by there and visit her playroom. I am sure they would love it."

"I will," Arya said; feeling cornered.

All the girl's energies pulled inside, indoors, internally.

Seeing how she could not wriggle out of the dilemma without raising concern, she summoned enough courage to wander to the neighbours, next door. She crossed the road, and rang the doorbell of the neighbour's house.

Odille's mother opened the door smiling. She recognized her immediately.

"Come right in." She sounded prepared. "How are you Arya?"

"I am fine, thank you. Is Odille in?" she asked, faint with embarrassment.

"She is, come in." She closed the doors behind her.

Odille came out of the basement all freckles and red hair. Arya had met the girl once before.

"You want to play?" she asked, caring little about formalities.

"Sure," Arya said, feeling like an aunt to the tiny child.

They marched, Indian file-style, crossed the large living room, headed straight towards the stairs that went down to the lower floor, a basement. Odille flipped an electrical switch and pointed down to a narrow, carpeted stairway. The atmosphere felt gloomy, still and the air tainted, as though poorly ventilated. As Arya manoeuvred her way down, clutching at the wooden railing as not to find herself at the bottom and embarrass herself, they finally landed on the floor to look up and gasp.

It was amazing. The place looked like a page from a fairy tale, replete with all kinds of imaginable dolls, strollers, beds, closets, wardrobes, tables and chairs, china cabinets filled with mint-coloured china sets, with cups, saucers, animals in a make-believe garden. The garden featured grass, bushes, trees, a swing, a rose garden, a rocky herb garden, and an azalea garden. There was a kitchen, with its conservatory, a sun room, a gazebo. The kitchen had a fridge, a washer, dishwasher, and lighting. There, in the extreme northern corner, stood an almost life-size bedroom, where Odille busied herself seriously at making the beds and straightening the life size-dolls nicely. She gave one of them a bath, pleated another doll's hair, and like the regular housewife she was, noting her guest, she rushed to the living room so as to apologize profusely for her absence.

"Duties, the life of women," she said.

"It is fine." Arya nodded, extremely uncomfortable. "They think me strange?" she thought.

"Do you sleep here?" Arya asked.

"Sometime." She tugged at the bedspread.

"Why?" Arya needed to learn the way children's minds worked.

"Why?" Odille repeated confused. "Surely, you know; it is fun to pretend."

"Pretend what?" Arya knew just then that the girl was the normal one.

"That we are grown-ups." Odille rounded her eyes in amazement.

"I see." Arya never needed to pretend being grown up.

Arya did not see. In reality, she had not a clue what this other girl, a year her senior, spoke of. To pretend is to lie. Arya could not figure out the fascinating fun in that. Her entire life, from the first second of self-awareness in the body, encompassed nothing but clarity. So confounded by that seeking of self-deceit people her age needed, she vowed to find out about it. She felt a deep tension inside her stomach quickly followed by a strange nausea.

"If that is what normal looks like, I don't know whether I want to be like that. That is daft. Of all the things this little girl could be doing, from reading, to skipping rope, to even sitting outside on the porch to watch the sun set, to going to a movie, she instead burrows in this stuffy basement with stale air and the foul smells, to speak to a bunch of dolls. I am weird, indeed," she thought.

She suffered from the first second she spoke to the Odille girl, but decided to stick the visit out until a reasonable time to leave. Arya could not wait to flee this horrible place of plastic death acting at life.

"Is that not fun?" Odille handed her an empty cup of coffee.

The thimble-size green cup with its orange saucer, sat inside Arya's hand like a spit, as she looked inside, the emptiness drove her mad. Does this miniature woman expect her to act as though the cup had coffee inside it? She wondered, deeply disturbed at having to act the idiot, as though it were fun.

Odille lifted the tiny cup off its saucer with the thumb and index finger, lifting all other fingers strangely upwards. She then placed the cup to her mouth, bending her elbow in an elegant fashion, and she took a dainty sip. She shook her head in deep approval as to the excellence of the brew, lowered the cup back down to its saucer, and waited staring her guest fixedly.

"Are you not going to taste it, then?" she asked angrily. "It would be extremely rude to me, you know."

"Her mother must entertain this way, obviously. Where else would she have learned all these social mannerisms?" Arya thought.

"Sure," she said. "It is truly divine."

Odille beamed her pleasure through the blue opaque of her eyes. It made Arya feel less stupid to make this girl happy.

"Exquisite." She resumed the acting jaunt. "Where did you get it?"

Emboldened by Arya's approval, Odille proceeded to recite a long tirade of how her friend offered it, how she had sent her driver to go hunting the city for the rare Brazilian brew, and how when he came back with the brew, it had been the happiest day of her life.

"Amazing," Arya said, meaning exactly that.

"It takes so much more to make me happy," the little girl thought. "How am I to live my life with these people? Surely, though, somewhere out there someone is like me. Their teas, dolls and jewels mean nothing to me. They annoy me," she thought, as she smiled to the pretending girl who sipped still, coffee from the empty cup.

"Now we serve the cake." Odille jumped to the fridge nearby. "We are having a scrumptious chocolate mousse."

"Interesting," Arya felt a tightening of her chest upon seeing the plastic brown mound stuck to the orange tray.

"Is everything orange?" she asked, hysterical laughter bubbling painfully within her.

"No. Our motif is orange with red." Odille enjoyed discussing her decor.

"I hope your taste matures some in the future, it is ghastly," she responded in her head, as she hummed approval with her mouth.

"Okay, that was superb." Arya got up to leave. "That was truly an unforgettable experience."

"Do you mean that?" Odille marvelled at the pleasure of her visitor.

"Absolutely," Arya truthfully replied, "Unforgettable, honest."

"Swear you will never forget it."

"As long as I shall live so help me God." Arya swore solemnly never to forget this experience, and to run from people such as these like the plague, the cursed, bloody plague, in her future.

"But it is early." Odille enjoyed receiving guests.

"I have been here for forty-five minutes."

"Did you two enjoy yourselves?" her mother asked solicitously.

"Enormously, thank you, Auntie." Arya kissed the lady's cheeks.

"You are most welcome. Please come back any time you feel like it. Odille has so few friends."

"I understand. Thank you."

She never, ever saw them again.

The dream of death by bee stings stopped suddenly when she turned ten years old. For some reason she could not trace, it simply stopped. In its place, she started flying. She would start in bed, to awaken with her body paralyzed. Only her brain worked, and only marginally. That worked to the extent that she understood that she could not move. The amazing part about this happening became the fact that Arya felt great otherwise, better than she could imagine able to feel. Although her ears burned and buzzed; as though they had a mind of their own, her heart beat fast, nothing else happened. Only her nervous system overreacted to the paralysis in fear. Everything else felt ecstatic. That, she did not tell her parents about; she somehow understood to keep quiet; that it did not have a medical explanation. Although she felt happy, she could not remember what happened. Arya loved that these episodes happened.

Once, however, she saw herself suspended in mid-air. Her first awareness happened to surprise her.

"I am standing in the air," she looked at her feet suspended in the skies.

As the day had been an overcast one, and as it was early afternoon, the grey skies spanned the expanse of her vision; it was endless. It did not much matter to her; she was too enthralled by her body to care about the state of greyness. Looking down at her feet, she saw that they were white clouds. She was made of air, a white air-like material that felt like air, a bit denser than the clouds and lit.

As she mulled the mystery of her body, Arya soon realised that it was really hers; everything about her was there, her personality, emotions, even her mode of analysing things. As she looked into the vast greyness, she soon spotted a nun, about two hundred meters away, swinging; she was on a swing fashioned of thick, white rope. The nun sat on a white plank which constituted the seat. She wore a black habit, a black veil, with a white skullcap underneath it. A mess of tightly woven assortment of pastel roses, pink, white and yellow, twisted tightly around the four ropes which made her swing.

That entranced Arya. The girl's mind tried to find out what, in this thin atmosphere with no ceiling, were the white ropes fastened to. As she saw the young nun from her left profile, she had no idea who she looked at. As though feeling the other being a bit over to her left, the nun turned to elicit a gasp from the child. There was not a noise to be heard anywhere in this place; just a vast expanse of grey space. Even Arya's gasping was internal. As the nun turned sideways to look at the child, Arya went mad with joy. She recognized her; it was Saint Theresa of the child Jesus. Mulling the dilemma of the saint in her entity, Arya wondered if she were imagining the nun swing surrounded by roses in mid-air, the saint turned again and pointed with a move of her head to a spot just behind Arya. The girl knew that the nun wanted her to look behind her, but there was no need, as, and that blew her mind, she knew that her new friend from school, a sweet girl of the highest morals, stood behind her, a bit above her. The fact that she could see things all around her without turning thrilled her. Also that she recognized her friend, someone to share this experience with, had so thrilled her, to the point that something exploded within her empty cloud to thrill the world. So thrilled it grew, that thousands of angels started singing some devotional tune, and everything went mad. As one thousand sang one note, that note exploded in red inside a huge circle, with strictly confined border. She recognized that first scream as the note C, C in red. Then there was a chorus that blew another note that was yellow, and another one she did not recognize that was green. It seemed to her that the music they fashioned for her was the distinct echo of her own fireworks of joy inside her stomach.

"Oh, my God," she thought in delirium. "The angels sing my emotions of joy."

She turned towards her friend, having forgotten how to use her hollow body not to have to turn, to find her dozing, as though oblivious to the surroundings of mirth.

Just then, everything stopped, and she awoke in her bed. *Awoke* is not an apt description of what she had actually done. In truth, she was never clear as to this part of the episode, only that a partial awareness returned to her bed, where she found her ears buzzing to a burning, uncomfortable point, and paralysis. Her body roared like a chopper ready to take off into the skies. That sound confused her.

"Go, go, fly, fly away if you wish," she encouraged her spirit.

Nothing happened, but for the roaring sound and the burning inside her ears. She noted happily that her heart did not thump crazily any longer.

Having momentarily forgotten where she had been seconds earlier, she erroneously thought that her spirit ached for a flight, and encouraged.

Then, it felt as though some heavy object rammed the side of her back, the place across from where her liver was. As she slept on her stomach, the bumping made her back arch off the bed. Then, soon afterwards, a second or two, there came a softer bump with a lighter jolt, then, all animation returned. She opened her eyes slowly, trying to ease her body into functioning. She got up, drank some water, as her ears burned still, and called Janette, whom Arya knew beyond a doubt was also napping.

"Hey, were you taking a nap?"

"Yes, sure was. How did you know, though?"

"I saw you in the ether," Arya said.

"What are you talking about?" Jeanette sounded groggy, tired.

"How do you feel?" Arya asked.

"I feel as though a truck ran over my body, why?"

"You were very tired there also, anything the matter?"

"Actually, yes; I feel strange, like I went jogging instead of napping."

"Well, do you remember anything?"

"Like what?"

Arya tried to explain; only to find words impotent to relate that which is not relatable.

"I saw St. Theresa swinging on a rose swing," she told her.

"What a dream, how blessed you are, Arya. You do things nobody can do."

Jeanette adored the Saint and talked about nothing else. She had read her book in two languages and read excerpts from it to Arya.

"I think that seeing her in the ether startled me, I so wished you to see her that I had willed you to come. The flight must have exhausted you."

"What a brilliant dream," she repeated.

Seeing how there was no safe way to explain to her friend that she truly was there with her, Arya dropped it. Janette told everyone about the dream that Arya was pleased never to have explained what truly expired out there in the grey clouds.

The girl discussed these matters with nobody. Sharing, she understood, sealed her fate; her total ostracism by everyone. Studying for a diploma in Catechism, Arya listened intently to clues imbedded there, inside the many fables constantly stated by the Man of Peace, but missed them totally.

She wondered at the way the Lord of Christianity spoke in impossible fables, as though he shielded the knowledge instead of wanting to clarify its message. He called himself the Teacher. His role in this life, he told, was to guide his fellow man. Jesus referred to himself as the "Shepherd." Obviously, those students he taught were the sheep. Arya took offence to the branding of those he called his brothers, as sheep. If they were sheep, did that not make him a sheep, if he were their brother? What is the reason he uses animals?

Questions furnished no answers, at that time. One thing stood crisply clear to the little girl's mind, the fact that when Jesus spoke, he addressed an elite few of humanity. Those who had the mental capacity to grasp his words, the spiritual prowess to send these words to their hearts for translation, were the brothers He spoke about.

"Do not throw your jewels before swine, for they shall trample them," became his answer, to a disciple that had asked the reason for the use of codes, and fables.

"Swine, and shepherds, there were the lambs, the snake, locusts, a regular zoo," she thought.

Hidden messages escaped her altogether; asking the nuns muddled the matter worse; as these had been handed a master key of ready-made answers. Every time they got into trouble they pulled out the adage of blind faith.

"How can the shepherd leave ninety-nine sheep to follow that wayward one?" Arya had asked Sister Jean Marie Claude. "That does not sound wise. He could return to find the flock dispersed. He should have sent someone to follow the wayward sheep, as he escorted the entire flock home."

"I am sure, my child, that our beloved Lord and saviour knew better," she answered.

"How is that?" Arya needed logical explanations.

"We can't outguess the Lord's reasoning. He is our Master. We simply take the parable for what it says."

"Yes sister, true; blind faith is where things should be. However, if the Lord had worked so hard so as to come down and impart his wisdom, one that he wanted us to apply, fashion our lives by its example, there is a need to understand. What exactly is he telling us in this instance? To understand the surface of the words sounds unwise, there must be something deeper he is saying."

"We must never question our Lord, but need to believe in faith," the sister spewed the ready-made drivel, with the utmost of finality.

She studied the text as though it were literature, like all the others, to make a good overall mark.

She passed and felt like a total fraud. A knowing within her forbade guilt.

She followed the commandments to the letter, as they made terribly good sense to her, social as well as moral, and lived in the way her saviour and Christ did, as cleanly, honestly and charitably as her body could allow her.

There, stuck in a world that scarcely understood her, Arya opted to become a scholar of excellence. She studied hard, helped her parents raise her siblings, tended to the needs of all people around her, and prayed for answers.

"I need to know what is going on," she prayed. "Please God, show me your secrets."

Arya believing totally in her powers to ask and receive, receive answers to her prayers. Answers started pouring in to thrill her.

"There is something magical in the universe," she marvelled. "They are helping me from the skies for some odd reason."

All Arya needed to do was think of something for it to arrive and amaze her.

"It is magic," she thought. "There is magic in this world."

Stuck to a way of understanding the fables and symbols of her religion, Arya remembered her childhood's books from India. She decided to begin her search into the secrets in other books, other cultures.

"I need to buy the Bhagavad-Gita," she told the librarian.

"Could you write the name here?" She handed her a slip of paper.

Arya wrote the name of the ancient text, to look at the baffled woman who stared at her back, suspiciously.

"What is it?" The woman checked the child out suspiciously.

"It is an Indian story," she lied.

"I am so sorry, we don't have it."

"What do you have?"

"We have a collection of Tagor's poems." She smiled. "We still have two copies. I could sell you one."

"Okay, I will take one." Arya suspected that if he were to be banned, then he was good.

The woman handed her the heavy book which she had wrapped in a paper sack, charging the girl her entire monthly allowance.

Arya did not mind at all that she would not have a cent to spend on anything else. Only, when she got home to read the book, it was written in Pharisee. She laughed so hard that her father came running to her room.

"What is so funny?" he asked.

"I bought this book and spent all my allowance on it only to find it was written in Persian, papa."

She handed him the heavy, dusty copy.

"Lord, child that is a collectible book. It has been out of circulation for a half a century," he said. "Where did you get it?"

She told him. The money, turned out to be a mere pittance. Her father promised to find her a translated copy. They offered the book to a rich, American collector, who bought it for a fortune.

"Mother," Arya remembered the old book from India. "Where is the book Soujaya read to me in India? We bought it when I was a little girl?"

"What book, Arya?" her mother sounded surprised.

"You know, the fat book of the Hindu stories," she asked.

"Your father has been reading it. I last saw it in his night table's drawer," Jezebel answered.

Arya found the beloved book with crayon marks she had made a decade earlier, took it to her room to read, only to find that it was more veiled than their beloved Bible.

Arya read the Bhagavad-Gita intently.

There, reading the ancient Indian text, the young teen found all the deciphering keys to the fables her Lord, Jesus Christ hid inside his words.

"What could be the reason He veiled His words so jealously?" she wondered.

Then, a sudden revelation clarified to her mind. Arya remembered that Jesus Christ had explained his veiling of the mysteries; He spoke to the elite few who were able to comprehend His message of greatness. He said to His disciples, that, one must never explain the mysteries to swine; these people could easily trample over the mysterious solutions to the good life, and abuse the path by using for evil doing.

The path to the Lord's Father's dwelling is so powerful that it could easily, if abused by entities of the dark, work against goodness by abusing the good few entities of light.

That, Arya, summarised, conflicted in nothing with all the other messages from all the other prophets, the Bhagavad-Gita's included.

Thirty-Five
ARYA GETS TO KNOW HER GRANDMOTHER

Her darling grandmother knitted sweaters for her, and crocheted a bedspread in pink for her room. She professed to adore Jezebel's children, vowed to develop a sweet relationship with their mother. Their mother missed the west badly; she had taken a shine to that freedom it afforded people. Arya suspected that her mother liked being away from her grandparents' control over her husband and household. Father had found a job he liked well enough. His life spun inside the circle, much like the musical notes inside her circle of flight; things were confined strictly to his job, the house, but mostly his parents' home. Watching the man, one always got a feeling that he had never left that house, one he called, "our home", which maddened his wife.

The residents of their home spoke well of Jezebel in her presence, but out of earshot, things went into whispers, giggles and scheming. Arya had always understood the doubletalk; they were never too cautious around her, thinking her too young to grasp their scheme. As Arya spent a great deal of time at their house, she caught their plans easily.

"Hello to you," the old woman yodelled shrilly. "How are you, son?"

In the kitchen, Colette stopped the rushing of water so as to eavesdrop on the conversation.

"Now, she will ask him where he spoke from," Colette whispered in Arya's ear.

"Why?" Arya asked innocently.

"So she knows if she could speak freely. They never say a word around your mother."

"Where are you speaking from?" the old lady asked.

"Aha, see?" the servant exclaimed.

"He is at your home." Colette understood things clearly.

"Nothing new, Arya is fine," she said in her martyr fashion.

"No, thank you. Goodbye." The receiver exploded in its seat.

"They never talk when he is at home. She cuts the conversation short."

"Why?" Arya shook from their shared deceit.

"It is a mafia," Colette said. "Now, listen to them gossip."

Arya tiptoed towards the room where they sat. They started gossiping about her mother.

It was horribly offensive. Her father would have died hearing them deride his wife. Arya fought the impulse to tell both her parents of the way these people spoke of them.

"He was sweeping the kitchen floor," his mother spat disdainfully. "Her highness could not finish her work."

"See?" Colette whispered right in Arya's ear.

"How wicked," Arya mouthed. "I have seen my mother work like a mule. They are ruining the woman."

"Where is Arya?" Ever-vigilant sister asked suddenly noting the silence.

Both Colette and Arya ran inside the kitchen blasting the music to create a deafening sound.

"Hey," she complained. "What is it with the noise?"

Nobody answered, but allowed her to waddle in, stare them down, waddle out, and close the door behind her.

"There is more," Colette informed the girl.

"What?"

"She closed the door to ensure privacy."

"What has my mother done to her?" Arya asked naively.

"You are so naive. She controls them to separate them, so she could rule. You think she loves them? That is sad. People who love let the lover be."

"My parents will never have a chance," Arya stated simply.

"Not ever." Colette sounded so sure, depressingly so.

And so it was, that day hearing the schemes they concocted against her parents, Arya felt deep dejection, which quickly translated into sadness over the plight of her soft mother; enough to intervene in her way so as to protect her parents. Her sadness over the incident ran much deeper than the incident warranted however, as that night, during an especially deep praying episode, Arya felt a powerful energy inside her room. She slept in the guest room which overlooked the garbage dumps, and internal courtyard of several buildings. Before she opened her eyes, she knew he would be there. She had obsessed and fretted over all their plight not the least of which, her grandmother's, who clutched at her grown children in fear and stubborn resolve, fretting over her soul, and the state of hate she roamed, knowing that it was a huge sin.

"I pray to you, my brother, and Lord, to please, please help my family heal this wound of deep control and jealousy. My mother is a good woman who asks for nothing but her right to live a normal life with her husband

and children. Help us Lord of love, help us keep our unity in the face of hate."

"Open your eyes and look at me," someone spoke without words inside her head.

Arya knew that Jesus had materialized in her room. Further, that he stood in the north-eastern corner of that room; for a strong energy came from the direction of that corner.

"Please leave." She shielded her eyes, frantic with fear.

"You called for me. Here I am," he spoke inside her head.

"No, I did not," she spoke as silently as he spoke.

"Yes, you did." He insisted.

"Okay. I am sorry, please go."

"No. You called for me, speak to me." He so wanted to speak to her.

"I am so frightened to speak. Please go before I die of shock." She shook like a leaf in a tempest. "Don't you people have anything else to do but frighten me? I pray, and you come, the world prays, thinking you hear in your place in heaven, and grant wishes. Please leave, thank you so much for coming by, thanks, go now." They were both using her brain waves to communicate.

"Arya open your eyes to see me," he spoke gently, gently.

She did. In reality, Arya ached deeply to see him. He was all she ever thought about in one way or another. There was the light of a moon that spilled white on his face, faint, faint, the light, and brilliant the face of that Man of Peace. She opened her eyes for one second, to quickly close them tighter, so tight her eyeballs hurt.

"You are different. I have not imagined you like that." He was dark.

Remembering that he read her mind made Arya frantic with embarrassment. She hated it that she thought him simple, less ostentatious than any picture Roman artists had depicted him in. There were no bright blue eyes, no blond hair, and no lanky, long legs. He, on the other hand, looked perfect. His starkly dark looks matched the story of his life more than the blond-blue-eyed Caucasian dandy they had portrayed to entertain the West. There was no sarong anywhere in sight, and chances were, he never had seen one during his life. He wore aptly the Arab robe, or rather desert garb of his time, and he looked more amazing in it than any Roman could ever imagine.

"Please, go away." His power confused her energies.

"You called for me," he said softly. "What can I do for you?"

"Surely, you are joking. Do you think I remember now, under this horrendous pressure, what my name is? Please go away."

Her entire being quaked pitifully in the presence of the sheer power.

He left, and she knew, because the room stopped shaking.

When she uncovered her eyes, she knew the figure in the dark grey woollen camisole had left.

Later, that white night, as she sat on the balcony from where he came and left, over all the garbage, the cats that followed the scurrying rats to topple cans, and make hissing sounds, Arya sat under the blessed moon, her friend always, the witness of her miracles, and the only testifier as to her mysterious visitors, to rehash the events of that shocking occurrence.

"Why do these things happen to me?" she thought.

Her heart a flame of love, and her entire body feeling like a soft petal, Arya tried to still the body that shook, so as to remember what she saw. When one sees these entities, one is blessed, regardless, in greater ways than one could ever imagine. This strange episode affirmed this belief.

He, Jesus of the Nazarenes, was a Sufis. How she knew that? He told her inside her mind. Now, the most startling part to this became the fact that Arya had no idea what that word meant, not an inkling. So, with this reference word, she knew inquiry would invariably arrive.

He wore a woollen robe of the thick kind that shepherds wear. It was a coat, like an army coat, up and down, with sleeves, and no buttons. Underneath this, a dress-like, simple garb, of exactly the same colour, dirty black, dark grey. She felt like it would be itchy to wear. He had shoulder-length wavy hair, of the type prevalent to the Middle-Eastern person; very much like that of Arya, in colour and texture. It was dark, and wavy, a sea in calm weather. His eyes were the most startling of anything she had ever seen. These were widely set, large, long-lashed, and soft. They sat over, amazingly, a straight Roman nose, which in its turn towered over the softest, poutiest pair of lips ever made in the region. He had the olive-coloured skin of his people, and was not tall at all. Jesus looked barely two inches taller than Arya two months before her eleventh birthday.

"You are not tall at all," she had thought and felt horrible for it.

He had ignored her statement as though finding it stupid. He must have known it was the shallow body. He, however, looked extremely attractive. Medium in build and athletic for all the walking he did, Jesus emanated sheer strength and power.

There, in that corner, remained a powerful presence, an emanation, a scent of roses that never dissipated. Many years later, the room would become the sanctuary of her ailing grandmother. Miracles would take place in this room, empowered by the might of sheer energy left behind by the Man of Peace.

For then, however, loss of the spirit reigned and abounded all around. Fights and screaming matches over the reason her mother did not want to be part of their father's family maddened everyone alike. Edward, then nine years old, confided in Arya that he planned to run away to India.

"Why?" his sister asked him.

"I want to be a monk," he said. "I hate the way things happen in this family."

A dog Edward aptly named Bruno took to following him all the way from school, to sit at the door, until they trekked their way back the next day. Their father hated the mangy dog, as he called him, ordering him gone. Edward settled his Bruno under the balcony's columns in the shade of the huge willow tree ensuring him food and water. That made him escape all the fights; mainly their father's screaming, and their mother watching silently, if broodingly. For the time being, Edward forgot his plans of India, and stayed happily lost in caring for the dog that was in much worse shape than he was. He, at least, had parents.

After that night, Arya understood her total difference from those around. She neither felt special nor especially normal; if normal were to be that base where the majority roamed, she knew that she was different. Except for that other understanding she somehow got, that uncanny ability that she was afforded, to access the channels of other planes of existences, where spirits roamed, could be called and came to answer.

There, in this simple understanding, all her powers. There also, in the lack of this simple understanding, all loss of power.

That opened a new channel inside the girl, a channel of knowledge and other outwardly Mysteries.

And then, father got promoted to a very high post in the company.

He bought a car, a diamond set of jewels for Jezebel, whose support he appreciated deeply, and a bike for each of the children. Arya's was red, Edward's blue. They were so happy.

Thirty-Six
FAMILY FINDS SURVIVAL TOOLS

Then, true to her form, when things hummed at the house by the seashore, grandmother invariably threw a fit, to ruin everything for everybody.

She called to invite everyone to Sunday lunch. Jezebel begged off, informing her of former plans that they had already made.

"Who with?" she shrieked angrily.

"My parents," Jezebel answered calmly.

Arya watched the exchange shaking the belligerence of the old woman and marvelling at her mother's steely self-control.

"Aha, excuse me, ooookayy, we will see," the receiver slamming.

"She never says goodbye. This is so rude. It makes me feel terrible," Jezebel told her daughter.

"What did she say?" Arya needed to assess their situation.

"She will see," Jezebel giggled at the rudeness of the woman.

"That will ruin it for my father. The lunch is as good as ruined." Arya concluded.

"That is not true, surely. Your father is a big man," Jezebel of the dreams, said.

It was true, and Arya knew it, somehow. The child possessed uncanny insights into the dynamics that governed that family. She did not wear the rose-coloured glasses Jezebel chose to don.

"So true too," Arya persisted.

"Why do you do that? Do you enjoy sounding the doom alarm?" she raised her tone a notch.

"No. You need to see the true picture. If you did not, you shall put us all in the path of destruction, mom. The danger we see is less shocking than the one we choose to ignore."

"Fancy vocabulary for a little girl," Jezebel said, sounding hurt.

"I am on your side, honey, really. Wake up, please," the child appeased.

"Wake up to see how your father gets manipulated and suckered by these two women, Arya? I am much better asleep, thank you." She cried softly.

"Because you know the way they are, mother, act like you believe their love as you make your own plans concerning your family." The child taught her mother guile.

"How wicked is that? Arya, sometimes I feel you are as much a devil as they are," Jezebel said.

"Sure, yes. I am their child. That affords me a dimension they roam, while also, as your child, I roam that soft, other dimension. So, learn from what I have and remedy," she told her mother.

"Fine, so what do we do now, dimension genius?"

"Now, we are stuck," Arya announced to delight her mother.

They laughed hysterically at their situation until, spent, they sat down to fashion a counterattack before the man of the household returned.

"He will try to weasel out of my parents' invitation," Jezebel said.

"I know," Arya told her. "How can we offset his plans before he advances them?"

"So could you advance any new solution?" Jezebel did not want to lose to them every time.

"Tell my father, as soon as he comes home, that you should have lunch at your parents' and afternoon tea with his," Arya suggested.

So, as soon as her husband turned the key in their front door, she ran to give him a tender hug, to tell him the plan Arya suggested.

"That is an excellent idea," he beamed at the compromise.

They did. Everyone was appeased by the solution. She did it to give a respite to her husband, who looked about to crack under the pressure.

Jezebel understood that keeping the flow going was solely up to her. Things stood in cement, as far as his family was concerned. She started reading Arya's books, the poetry of the Sufis, and that Indian book her daughter kept by her bedside. At first, she did not understand the words. She spoke with Arya, who explained the little she understood. They had decided a year before that the science needed the assistance of a murshid, "a master." In a country where the science was banished to the Druze Mountains studied by those, who never cared to discuss it with anyone from fear of persecution, the doors to seekers stood tightly jammed.

"It is the best kept secret," Arya said. "I have no idea where to go for help. It just occurred to me that Jesus sounds and acts in the tradition of these Sufis; do you think he has learned the science?"

The Sufis were a Muslim group that sprouted in the gulf region, around Persia, Turkey and Saudi Arabia, at the dawn of the ministry of the Prophet Mohammed. Jesus, however, had arrived and left a century earlier. So, it stood as a baffling aspect to figure out how the Man of Peace, who lived in the Middle-East, could have encountered the science to learn and teach it.

"But the way the science worked, mom, from the Far East to Egypt, then with Moses and the Jews towards Palestine, it is very likely that Jesus was subjected to it. Not that he subscribed totally to its teachings, more that it is very likely that he was aware of it. Further, it is known that Nazareth, the village of his mother's birth, subscribed totally to the science. Nazar means, a man who has vowed; that, in the Druze's language means an initiate. Is that not enough proof?"

Jezebel had no way of knowing. They read the Bhagavad-Gita diligently, trying to decipher the symbols, sift the myth from the truth, to come up with some learning, to no avail. It was an impossibly difficult text to tackle for an uninitiated mind, made more horrendous by the intricacy of archaic language, and the impossibly confusing Indian names.

"That should offer you a space of peace and forgiveness," the young woman announced.

"Why should keeping peace be my burden?"

"Because you are seeking it; they are fine. It is up to you to forgive them."

Jezebel, frayed emotionally, doubted everyone. Even her beloved Arya, the soul of her soul had started sounding like a traitor to her.

"Listen," Jezebel said, feeling isolated in the world. "They are your father's people, fair enough. You definitely could not see them objectively."

"Oh no, I do mom, I really do."

"What then? What is the reason you defend them?" Jezebel started crying.

"It is for your own sake that things should become positive. The more you hate them, the more they enjoy poisoning you. Can't you see that?"

"As a remedy you ask me to forgive them?" Jezebel experienced definite problems with the solution advanced.

"Not only forgive them, but love them," Arya said, as she shielded her face instinctively.

Not aiming to disappoint, Jezebel raised her arm, and slapped her daughter. The smack resounded off the walls, came back to their hearing, like a bomb, to awaken the mother.

Arya neither flinched nor cried. The girl who understood she spoke the language of the Spirit, and her mother that of the body, could easily compute where the misunderstanding occurred.

"It is for my sake that you ask me to love them, Arya? Thank you very much. This is the reward I get for sleeping with the wolves; I birth a wolf of my own."

Now, that hurt Arya deeply.

She considered telling her sweet mother that she was not a wolf, and that she, in reality, was her own sister, that no human was better or worse than any other, except maybe for the amount of fear that ruled him.

"They are riddled with fear, mom. Can't you see that?"

"What are they fearful of?" Jezebel asked, as she got off the sofa, poised, muscles taut to finish off the battle.

"Wait!" Araya feared the furry. "Sit right back there. Otherwise, I will never talk to you again."

"Fine, You go right ahead and join their club, Arya, darling. There nobody speaks to me, anyway. The second I walk in the room they all turn into statues of silence."

"Fine listen, Listen, my father knows them. He humours their savageness so as to protect you and us. Believe this."

"You are so deluded, child. How could the wolf birth anything but wolf? He is them, exactly like them, cannot see anything wrong with them. When I say something wrong, he attacks me like a savage. Try to point one thing wrong with them, he denies and defends and fights you to the death," Jezebel explained.

"Yes. This is his loyalty to his clan. Behind your back, he also defends you."

"What is there to defend?" Jezebel sounded shrill even to her own ears. "What have I ever done to need defending?"

"Nothing of course, they simply find things. Like you cannot do the olive crops or wash by hand or even bake their bread. There is always something to say, mother, when one needs to argue. Surely, you know that."

"Fine, this is the end of this conversation. I am never talking to you either. Now that my father is dead and mother is too old to be burdened and all my siblings are too young to be shattered, I shall die close-mouthed. Surely, I thought you could have been less wishy-washy about them. That is fine, go. Please go. I need to be alone."

"No," Arya persisted, her heart shattered for her mother. "I will go after I make you understand what I mean. It is always better to love than to hate. That is all. If they could not love an angel such as you, that in itself, is their punishment. To hate is deadly. It poisons the spirit and kills the body, eventually. If they succeeded in making you that hateful, they would have succeeded largely in killing you. Is that not their aim?"

They sat still. Neither woman spoke. They looked like two statues with nothing to say, unable to move. There, for a long time they remained lost to the universe inside the hells of their private thoughts.

Finally, after what seemed a long, long while, Jezebel got up, took Arya in her arms and cried, still saying not a word.

The fashion with which the slight woman pressed her body to that of her daughter's made the latter comprehend deeply that peace and understanding of a finite, powerfully empowering concept had finally seeped through the body to reach the centre of the universe, where things are equal, pure and simple.

"Love, ha?" Jezebel finally said, giggling sweetly.

Arya nodded her head pleased. "Love," the girl said. "That is God."

"I will try," Jezebel promised.

"You need to do more than try, mom. You have to do it fast," Arya urged passionately. "The quicker you love, the faster you heal."

"It is impossible." Jezebel admitted. "The second his sister's name crosses my brain, it generates a quaking and shaking in my entire being."

"Is that not giving her too much power?" Arya asked. "Who owns you now? You are hers for the duration of hate."

"I guess. Never before did I ever give the power of hate credence or thought."

"Hate is a mighty emotion, mother; it runs five times faster before thought could ever catch it," the child said. "It creates psychological pain in the body."

Suddenly, Jezebel looked startled into wakefulness.

"How does a child know deep ideas such as these?" she asked baffled.

"Some people are born like that, mom. They have the gift of the Spirit. Hate is of the body. There are methods to help you change the dynamics."

"What kind of methods?" Jezebel was convinced to try the idea.

"You pray for them every day. You pray for your enemies first, before your beloved ones. In the early stages, the brain will freeze with shock of asking God to protect and free the people that tortured it. It is fine. As you keep up the prayers, there will come a time when the body gives up, and a new quality of grace happens; then, you know that you have made a divine leap. You are so powerful, invincible, beyond hurting. The power comes back to you. Now, you are in charge of your own emotions, not them. They could turn your whole body into a mass of quaking rubble, at their very whim, no more. Love that you have cultivated for those who, in the Man of Peace's very words, 'forgive them, Father, for they know not what they do,' she related peacefully, "will free you."

"You know," Jezebel reflected, "I thought this kind of unconditional love, the sole property of prophets. I have never taken the 'turn the other cheek' seriously. So, he meant it seriously?"

"Yes. Love changes the world; an old, tattered cliché having grown trite with overuse, does work. It so works, mommy. That idea is healing. Look around at God's creations. The flowers work all the time to impart their scent for free, to the criminal who has just butchered a little girl, as well as to the teacher, rabbi, and priest. There are no divisions in the eyes of the Lord, ever. His creation is one. The good, the bad, and the ugly are equally loved and nurtured by God."

"Okay miss, your mother is starting to get the picture of universal love," Jezebel told her child. "How is that fair, Arya? For God to love bad people as well as he loves good people seems unjust. What is the reason for being good then?" Jezebel battled with deep issues of morality.

"God, being nothing but love, seeing with the heart of love, could do nothing but love all His creation equally. As to hate, that could never be in the Heart of all that is Love. There is nothing else to be found in that big Goodness. There, no other options are available. Love is just that, love. In that place of total goodness, there is to be no judgment; that is of the body and selfish greed," Arya explained to baffle her mother with the simple impossibility of the explanation.

"That is so tough," the mother said.

Arya got up to leave assured of her mother's understanding.

"Where are you going?" Jezebel needed more.

"I am going to rest a bit in my room." Arya sounded removed.

"Why do you rest so much? Are you not feeling well?"

"I feel fine. I do not rest, mother. I meditate," she said, as she disappeared inside her room.

Jezebel watched the back of her little girl, not yet quite eleven years old and suddenly realized that there went a woman of the highest calibre among humans.

"She is right," Jezebel thought. "How could I have missed such a simple solution?"

Guilt at having slapped the girl tightened her heart, and pulled at the muscle of her chest painfully.

"I am sorry about the slap." She ran to hug Arya on her bed.

"It is fine, mother. It gave me the opportunity to show you how we grow when we turn the other cheek."

"How do we grow?" Jezebel asked.

"I mean were I to have fought you, we would have missed this lesson altogether. Because I did nothing, you got to thinking about slapping me, and come to make amends. That is good. Now, we are truly connecting the right way. Can't you see it?"

Jezebel saw it fine. Also, she saw that the child was not normal. No children she knew could logically explain a simple idea. To read the mysteries of the universe at this age, and teach it to one's parents stood frightening to the mother who knew not of the gifts of the soul.

When Jezebel asked about meditation, her daughter told her that to drop the senses, even for few seconds, turn the sight internally; there, all the knowledge was waiting, aching to manifest its powers.

And so, life's poignant lesson arrived to free the woman through the mouth of her daughter.

"I thought it was my place to teach you," the woman told her daughter.

"I am sure you will teach me many things. Make sure to read, though. That will make us friends, further cancelling any misunderstanding between us," Arya stated.

"I will. I promise you."

"I love you, mommy." Arya closed her eyes.

"I love you too, sweets." Jezebel left the room.

Before she could buy or read anything, Jezebel went inside her kitchen to prepare her noon meal, her heart filled with resentment: The prospect to pray for those who tortured her and killed her sister before her, confused her deeply.

There stood the knowledge as to the rightness of her newfound solution, advanced by the little girl, and yet, her body bucked, resisted. Jezebel's body schemed to undermine these people, shatter them kill them, even. Praying for their welfare stood against all these forces churning hate inside her.

"How does one pray for people like that?" she wondered.

She started praying for them, then she stopped. Hate, having grown like weeds inside her heart, startled her.

"Arya was right. I have become worse than they are." The thought frightened her.

Thirty -Seven
ARYA STUCK BETWEEN ENEMY CAMPS

While Arya got the wrath of the family, about one thing or another, Eddy smiled angelically, and got along with everyone.

"Why can't you be more like your brother?" father needed to know.

"Well, why can't you be more like Einstein? I simply am not, dad. You made me. Could you have not managed to clone us?"

He got up pointing to his belt then broke into the most delightful mirth.

"She is not real," he said to Jezebel.

"She is very real," she thought smiling sweetly to him. "You do not know what real is."

At sixteen, Arya felt oppressed at the house in the city. He, her father, never wavered, failed, or got bored. Every Sunday, practising a ritual, he got dressed, shaved, splashed after shave, and left to eat breakfast with his parents.

"Follow me later," he shouted.

"Fine," they answered in a chorus.

"No," Arya shouted back that day.

"Excuse me?" He poked his head inside her room.

"You are excused," she said seriously.

"Are you saying no to me?"

"Yes, father. I want to go out with my cousins, instead. It is so boring there. You sit around and stare either at the wall or the television screen. It is mad. I don't want to go."

"Fine," he said.

Jezebel grew angry by his quick giving up.

"I am not going either. I want to have lunch with my mother and sisters."

"No. You've got to go," he replied seriously.

"Why?" she rebelled.

"Because you are my wife," he stated.

He left.

That was the end of this argument.

Six years of studying the divine science had failed her still. At times such as these, when she felt like throwing an extremely heavy object over his sleepy head, Jezebel despaired at the futility of hours of meditations. Staring at the pure state of candle lights, numerous prayers beseeching saints and pure souls to lend their energies with the aid of which power to right her heart, wrench hatred, resentments, to believe herself healed, until an instance of his blind conditioning threw her back at square one to show her the futility of her focused endeavour.

"You look ready to murder someone." Arya giggled, seeing her father's back leave with a sharp bang to the door.

"Should not two play at this?"

"Impossible. One asleep, and one awake is the general rule," the teen snickered.

"What makes you so happy?"

"I don't give a hoot." Arya chuckled. "I have simply given up on people, mother. Tolerance is the key here."

They headed in two different directions, Jezebel towards her-in-laws', with Eddy, her daughter towards her own parents' house for a birthday party of one of her maternal cousins.

"Where is your pearl necklace?" the old lady asked.

"What pearl necklace?" Jezebel asked her mother-in-law.

"The pearl one he bought you for your last birthday, the one from Bahrain?" she stated slowly.

"Like it is any of your business," Jezebel muttered.

"Yes, where is that?" her husband asked remembering, to make her feel stupid.

She saw the sidelong glance of wicked mirth his sister threw. Jezebel wished he wised up to their machinations and stopped rising to their wickedness to embarrass her.

"At home, of course, where else would it be?" Jezebel smelled a plan.

"When you came back from your parents' home, I noticed the necklace missing," his sister seconded.

"What are you saying?" Jezebel squirmed, sensing a scheme.

"I thought maybe you gave it to one of your sisters," his mother elaborated.

That was it. Jezebel knew trouble had been started. The woman could not remember seeing the blasted string of pearls. She suspected the pair of having stolen it to plant suspicions inside her husband's mind. Whether it was given, or else stolen, things did not bode well for the woman who did not miss her husband's precious gifts.

At home she looked for it, to no avail. She could not offer a satisfactory reason for its disappearance.

"So where is it?" he asked threateningly.

"I really don't know. It has always been in my box."

He huffed leaving her looking baffled at his disapproving back.

"I will look for it."

"Do that," he commanded.

The necklace had disappeared. Jezebel searched the entire house, to find nothing.

Arya came back from her party to help search her mother's room.

"There is nothing, mom. It is strange. When did you last wear it?"

"Your grandmother was right. I wore it to my mother's last birthday, three months ago." Jezebel sounded depressed.

"You do not miss something valuable for that long?" Husband sounded displeased.

"Stop it, dad," Arya admonished fearing the escalation of a problem.

Everyone went silent.

"Guess who I saw?" Arya whispered to her mother.

"Who did you see?" Jezebel asked.

"I ran into my grandparents' servant; the one who lived with them when my aunt Alaya was killed. She is a beautiful woman."

"This woman has been missing for over two decades. The police are still on her trail," Jezebel told her daughter.

"She approached me at the entrance of the university. She works there still. She told me that she loved my aunt, and still believes that the family had killed her," she said.

"You are serious," the mother marvelled.

"She has never disappeared, mom. That is the thing. The entire village knows that she got a job in the city. Guess who arranged it?"

"Who arranged it?"

"My grandfather," Arya said.

"I do not believe it. He looked for the wench the hardest."

"He did not. You could talk to her."

"What does she think?" her mother needed to know.

"She thinks that my grandparents killed her."

"The reason they killed a young bride?" Jezebel needed to hear facts not allegations.

"They hated her because he was besotted by her."

"Good for her," Jezebel sounded very angry. "You want me to trust what this vile person says, Arya? She is an accessory to murder, honey. She ran away for money."

"No. She feared for her life. Besides, she was a child. She was fifteen, or sixteen years old."

"They will still kill her," Jezebel concluded. "Why speak now?"

"Statute of limitations as well as conscience pangs, I should think. She thinks that your life is in danger now."

"I have been with them for eighteen years, Arya. That is a bit too late." Jezebel defended them.

"You defend them?" Arya marvelled.

"Is that not what your science teaches?" Jezebel accused.

"No. My science teaches love, not stupidity," Arya retorted.

"I see. Okay, fine. I will see her."

"Thanks." Arya went to call a number from a card.

"She will come tomorrow."

"Now, my life is in jeopardy. If they find out, they will kill me to shut me up." Jezebel shook miserably.

"Yes, something else, she told me something else that might interest you; they stole all of your sister's jewellery and accused your parents of taking it." There came a most wicked twinkle in the child's eyes.

"Not true." Jezebel said, incredulous.

"So true, mom, from what that girl says. She asked me to go to my aunt's closet. All the broaches and wedding sets your father bought Alaya will be there. She saw my aunt wearing them. She would go to her closet, take the broaches off the lapels of her suits, and wear them. It was as wicked as that. Do you believe the gall of this woman?"

"Aha. You think?"

"Yes. I believe they are starting to undermine you also by making him think you are stealing from him to give your parents."

"That is ingenious evil," Jezebel marvelled, shocked.

"The crew is focused. Theirs is systematic planning of the highest kind. Things might not stop there. They might be plotting an accident for you as well."

"What do we do?" Jezebel grew fearful.

"We speak to the woman first then we formulate a strategy," Arya suggested.

"Great!" Jezebel groaned, "my daughter the detective."

The servant arrived the next day at eleven in the morning. Jezebel recognized her instantly from Alaya's wedding.

"I loved her dearly," she said, as she shook Jezebel's hand.

"Is that the reason you helped us find her killers?" Jezebel found herself resentful of the woman.

"Well, madam, I feared them."

"Why speak now?"

"I fear for you now," the woman replied. "If they were to kill you, I should never forgive myself. God knows I tortured myself over your sister's death long enough. She is gone. There was nothing left to do; speaking could no longer help her. May I ask you though, why give him another daughter?"

Jezebel took offence at the question. Although, as she thought of things, she realized that the girl raised an extremely important question.

"I don't know. Dad loved him," Jezebel said.

"You, do you also love him?" she asked.

"I was too young to know better," was all Jezebel could say.

"Something about your daughter reminds me so much of her. Bless her soul, she was beautiful." She wiped a genuine tear from her cheek.

"Thank you. Why did they hate her?"

"Oh, that. No. It was not about hating her, especially. It was more about him. They could not handle him loving anyone. He loved her beyond their tolerance. That was all," the woman clarified the dilemma.

"I have nothing to fear then. He has never loved me," Jezebel stated simply. "He never got over her."

"You are wrong, though, madam. You, somehow, have also become expandable. Arya said that they talked about your necklace. This is how they started with your sister. It is true. His sister wore her jewellery. I saw her. They used to giggle about your sister's stupidity," she explained. "The pair loved riling him against his wife. I heard them brag about causing them trouble," she said. "I never thought it could get to murder, though."

"Not that they respected their son more. His brother and father called him stupid all the time," Jezebel said. "He does not see it."

"He does. The man is intelligent," the woman assured them.

"Is there a tangible way to prove all this?" Jezebel was primed for a fight.

"No," the young guest said. "Not one person in the village would speak to the police or judge."

Jezebel thanked the woman for her time and efforts, promising never to speak to anyone of her source.

The woman ran down the long stairs fearing to take the lift lest someone saw her and connected her with the case.

"She makes sense," Jezebel told Arya.

"I will watch over you. You need to be extremely careful. How did they get to your jewellery box?" Arya asked.

"He gave them the key to our house," Jezebel informed her daughter.

"Why?" Arya screamed.

"This is how they are. They want to keep their clutches dug into every facet of our lives," Jezebel said.

"Have you missed anything else?" Arya asked.

"Sure. Gold coins, rubies, garnets, moonstones, diamonds, everything we have bought in India, thousands of dollars' worth. Your aunt wears them on rings. They had fashioned them for themselves, they smile, smile, taunting me to make problems. She offers me the coffee as she turns her ring finger up towards me." Jezebel trembled uncontrollably.

"Have you told him?"

"Yes."

"What did he do?"

"He attacked me. His parents were not thieves, he shrieked to awaken the dead. I dropped it."

"Fine, then. I will go to my aunt's house, and somehow look inside her home for your things."

"That is wrong." Jezebel said.

"That is called protecting one self, mom. It is different."

"How would you do it?" Jezebel did not have that dimension.

"With my intentions, that is how," Arya said determined.

"What are you talking about?"

"I will set the intention to find your things, and wait for the universe to offer a hand. In things fair, where right is on your side, the universe helps open doors," she explained.

The next morning, a Monday, Arya took off early from school. She called her mother with a proposal of drinking coffee at her aunt's house.

"No," Jezebel refused vehemently. "Keep me out of this plan, Arya."

"She will not be there. I promise. She roams the neighbourhood Monday mornings to buy her meat for the week. My cousin will be there on her own," the teen informed her mother. "That is a routine that never changes."

"How do you know that?" Jezebel marvelled at her daughter's awareness.

"I watch them closely, mom, something you need to do."

"Fine," Jezebel agreed reluctantly.

They took a cab which crossed the bustling city at a snail's pace, to reach the devastated building with the garbage strewn over the side curbs with the stench of sewers emanating from the air.

"You better not drink anything there," Arya alerted her mother.

The lift had not worked for years, so they took the filthy stairwell, instead.

On the fifth floor, the doorbell chime did not work. Jezebel shook from nerves and anger, as Arya looked relaxed and focused.

"No electricity either?" Arya asked surprised.

"They don't fix anything," Jezebel explained. "It costs money."

"That is the reason they wanted you killed. You are spending the money they could have," Arya told her mother. "Not even a blood relation, how dare you? Paris this and England that."

Arya used her fist to bang on the door. After a long while, her cousin Miriam opened it. She rubbed her eyes sleepily.

"Hello, Miriam." Arya bent down to give her cousin a kiss.

"Is your mother home?" Jezebel asked. "We thought we would have coffee."

She looked shocked; they had never dropped by before. Startled by sleep and surprise, the girl stood in her nightgown blocking the door.

"Why have you not called?" she asked politely, "I mean, sure, you are always welcome, but she is not here."

"Where is she?" Arya asked trying to move the child aside from blocking their entrance.

"At the butcher's," she said, and moved away allowing them to enter the flat. "I could go get her for you."

"Would you do that for me?" Arya cooed, as she kissed her cousin again.

She was a sweet child, and Arya loved her deeply. Her cousin was truly different, loving, tender and ever-so-sweet. She hated fooling her.

"I will go dress up; come in." She ushered them into the living room.

They sat on the only sofa in the entire place.

Miriam was gone in a flash.

"Hurry up," Arya said.

No sooner had the child cleared the landing than Arya was ruffling inside her aunt's drawers and cupboards.

Jezebel did not move from her spot. The woman feared being caught ruffling through the woman's room. That constituted sure death at the hand of her husband. She would be giving them a viable excuse to have her divorced.

"Come on," Arya pleaded, needing help.

"What if they came back?" Jezebel asked, hoarse with fear.

"It takes a long time to manage five flights of stairs. She did not take a key. Come on."

She dragged her mother inside the bedroom where she sat her on the bed. Arya opened the wardrobe and started shuffling the hangers about.

"And they profess cleanliness." Arya covered her nose.

"Make sure to return things exactly the way you find them," Jezebel instructed.

The woman's body jerked with each noise coming from the noisy streets below.

"Nothing in her box," she said, as she placed it right where it was.

"The left side of her closet," Jezebel pointed. "It is bolted."

"Can you see the key?" Arya asked.

Jezebel felt like a stunned stone. She heard the words, failing to wrap her mind around them.

"Let us leave now," Jezebel begged Arya.

Arya turned behind the huge wooden wardrobe, attempted to push it away from the wall, only to fail dismally.

"I cannot budge this thing. Give me a hand."

"No."

"Mom, please."

"What if they come back, Arya, what are we doing in her room with the closet pushed to the middle? How could we explain that one? You are all mad, mad. You are just like they are, wicked, Arya."

Giving up on any possible help, Arya pushed the closet with all her might, budging the monstrous wood enough to wedge her tiny body behind it, but only just. She proceeded to loosen the screws that secured a cardboard false cover to the back.

"Hand me her tweezers," she ordered gruffly, a thief on a mission.

Jezebel found the tweezers on the vanity table, and with a shaky hand she extended them towards her daughter's form.

"Get out," Arya fearing for her mother, said. "If they come back, talk to them, and tell them I am in the bathroom. That will keep you away from the scene. If I get caught, keep yourself away from it all. They never hurt family members. They would explain my presence away as childish curiosity."

Succeeding to remove the scanty back panel, she placed it aside, and entered the wardrobe from the back. Sitting inside the huge closet, she proceeded to find all of Alaya's things. She held the gold necklace in a shaky hand; that had nothing to do with the theft. She shook miserably as images of the day her parents, of that other life, her grandparents in this one, had proudly fastened it around her neck during her wedding ceremony, played to her mind. Each piece of jewels she held conjured up an image, a story, a tale that came replete with a visual as well as an audio. Arya shook her head aiming to stop the videos playing so as to resume her task and leave.

She managed to recognize her aunt's belongings to leave them in the pouch where they had sat; they were simply those that did not belong to her in that other life. Her mother's things, those she recognized, easily. Gathering their belongings in her skirt, she ran to the sofa where her mother sat, and showed her the bounty. She ran back into the room, fastened the board quickly, barely attaching it to the closet, pushed the wardrobe far into the wall, ran back into the living room, handed her find to her mother. Jezebel placed the jewellery inside a beach bag she had carried for that reason. Arya went back into the bathroom, where she washed her face, combed her hair. Inside her aunt's room, Arya straightened the bed where her mother had sat, double-checked the position of the wardrobe. Finding the tweezers on the floor, she quickly placed them on the vanity table.

Inside the wardrobe she ruffled through her aunt's clothes, to find some of Alaya's broaches pinned on different suits, others hidden inside makeshift handkerchiefs tied in knots so as to look like tennis balls, strewn in different old purses, bags, and boxes. Finally, she clutched her prize, her mother's necklace.

"Is that it?" she screamed.

"Yes. Leave it there," her mother ordered quickly, "and come out. Just bring Alaya's stuff."

"Why? I want your necklace, also," Arya said.

"Just do it fast, Arya."

Arya closed the doors locking them with their keys.

"They are all here," Arya announced, flushed with excitement and fear.

"How could that help us?" Jezebel voiced her concerns. "Now we are criminals."

"I will show them to my father. You cannot be a thief when the things you reclaim are your own, Jezebel."

"He will accuse you of having planted them, Arya. Your father does not want to face the facts of his family's wicked reality. He cannot, darling, as the knowledge would shatter him," her mother explained.

"We will have to stage an incident, then." Arya jumped from one scheme to the next deftly. "They are simply not getting away with murder and theft, to plan another murder, and another theft. It is not right."

"Let us leave." Jezebel wanted out of the place that so angered her.

They ran down the stuffy stairs, clutching at the heavy bag with the jewels they retrieved, to meet sweet Miriam coming up to see them.

"Where are you going? My mother is on her way back," she said suspiciously.

"Another time, darling, we need to prepare lunch for my father," Arya announced, breathless with anxiety.

"But I don't have a way into the house," Miriam fretted.

"Your mother is on her way," Arya told her cousin as she ran down the stairs so as to miss the woman.

No sooner had the pair reached their house, the aunt called asking the reason they had left so quickly. They gave her the same excuse, as Arya opted for the usual attacking mode subscribed to in the clan.

"So, where do you go for hours while people are visiting your place?"

The woman giggled happily, the love she shared with her niece, informing her that she had stopped at her parents' for a cup of coffee, but had doubled right back when Miriam told her they were visiting her.

"Oh well, another time. Just pencil it in your diary; do not say that we never go by your place," the teen humoured her aunt.

"You are wicked." Jezebel stated. "She obviously has not checked her closet, yet."

"Obviously not," the young woman replied.

"What now?" Jezebel asked.

"We plant them back on her," Arya suggested.

"You are worse than they are." Jezebel slapped her forehead in consternation.

"That is not a lie, mom. They did take them."

"If you were to plant them back on her, she would know and come after me." Jezebel fretted.

"Believe me, no. Once evil is caught, it shows respect. If you beat them, they will respect you."

"Is this seriously the way it goes?" Jezebel would have never known that.

"I promise you, mom. Watch and marvel," Arya said.

They planned to wait for an opportune time, plant all the jewels, some fake, others real, the string of pearls especially, inside her aunt's bag.

"How do we get to her bag?" Jezebel asked, clueless.

"I will feign an accident, hit the bag somehow, so it spills its contents before all their eyes," Arya announced. "Leave it to me."

"That was not the dilemma." Jezebel needed to ensure minute details got planned with precision so as not to create more havoc in her relationship with her husband.

"How difficult would that be, mom? They leave their purses around all the time. You simply stick the stuff inside her bag. I thought that this bit of the operation was obvious." She marvelled at her mother's simplicity.

The odd aspect of the operation conducted became the most telling: Nobody mentioned either the pair's botched visit, or the mess of jewellery lost.

"Do you not find this omission odd?" Jezebel asked Arya.

"That also is the state of deceit. You beat it, it does never dignify your success, but plans a countercheck to teach you a lesson; for having dared beat it at its game," Arya explained.

"How do you know these things? How come I don't know them?" Jezebel feared for Arya's soul. "You are not this dark human that roams the recesses of hell alongside them, please tell me."

"I am not. I am a good person like you, with a dimension that understands them. You are all goodness and light. While they can hurt you, they cannot hurt me because I know them; I am partly them," she explained.

It was six months later, and no more mention of the loss of pearls had been made. The women expected that the aunt had already found out about their stealing back their things from her home, had spoken to her mother and ally, and together had opted for silence on all fronts, fearing to lose the man.

"What do you think happened?" their silence unnerved Jezebel.

"Nothing happened. If they were to tell any of the men, they would blow their entire modus of operations out. They probably decided to get even in other ways." Arya tried to outguess them. "They have decided to let us have the spoils because we pulled an operation they could respect. They know that you are privy to their scheming ways, and that I am your ally."

"We have accomplished nothing," Jezebel concluded.

"You are wrong. They know we are onto them and fear our next move."

"We need to find a way to convince your father."

"Done," Arya promised.

And so it was that Jezebel, having so little faith in her child, as mother's do not, had forgotten about the episode quickly to resume her life of wife and mother.

Christmastime, father announced that they needed to have his family around for the noon meal.

"Yes. We need to." Arya jumped on the suggestion.

Jezebel gave the impetuous child a horrible stare of disapproval.

"It should be such fun, mom; the entire family will be eating here together. Is that not divine?" she rejoiced.

The girl and Edward, along with their father worked tirelessly preparing the house and the tree, while Jezebel prepared and stored foods.

It killed her that all her sisters planned to spend their Christmas at her mother's home while her husband and children never thought of her needs. She sulked as she prepared the foods and baked the deserts, and meditated over forgiveness and the sparing of hurt and pain to those she hated with the passion no meditation could possibly diminish.

They arrived around one in the afternoon, right after church. Jezebel served lunch, helped by the obliging children and her husband.

"Sit down," his mother directed. "Work is for women."

He ignored her remark as he continued to help.

Coffee followed lunch, then dessert in the living room, by the chimney.

As Arya gathered the small dessert plates to take inside the kitchen, she stumbled over the chair on whose arm her aunt's purse perched and an array of different jewels went flying for all to see.

"I am so sorry. I will pick them up," Arya straightened herself up to say.

Her Aunt turned yellow with fear as she watched the things strewn over the rug before the family's wide eyes.

"Is that not Jezebel's pearl necklace?" father asked confused. "What is it doing in your purse?"

Her mother looked sick with fear.

"Why is it in your purse?" she demanded.

"I have no idea," her daughter replied, her colouring washed out.

Everyone stared at the floor as Arya picked things off the rug. There were tiny rocks of different colours she gathered slowly.

"Bring them here to me," her father commanded.

The girl approached her father to place a handful of coins, and stones inside his extended palm.

"Are these not the stones Jezebel bought in India, mother?" he asked.

"Yes," his mother replied.

"What are they doing in your purse?" He stared both women down accusingly. "When we asked you about them, you said you had no idea what we spoke about."

It was a statement. He did not expect an answer.

The man got up, opened his sister's purse retrieving the remainder of his wife's possessions. He closed it, handed it back to his sister. He gathered the bounty together to hand to his wife, whose mouth failed to close throughout the revelation.

"Put these in your room," he ordered.

"Some of these things do not belong to me," she told her husband.

"They belonged to your late sister. Just put them in your room," he said gently.

Jezebel handed the bag filled with jewellery to Arya to deal with, her quivering legs having turned to jelly. Nobody spoke a word. His brother and father acted as though absent from the scene. Only the aunt looked bemused. Her eyes like two cracked saucers inside her pale face, she looked at the carpet, failing to process that which she had witnessed.

The episode changed things forever. All five women understood the lessons. There was no need to say any more.

Husband never pushed anyone to go visit his family again after that revealing incident. He became deeply sad; anger thus far absent in him, showed in the stiffness of his back.

"It is my duty to see them," he told Arya and Jezebel. "You are welcome to join any time you feel like it. I will never demand it."

"Thanks," they replied gratefully.

There lurked a stare of the most respectful in the eyes of the aunt and grandmother since the event.

"They thought you stupid," Arya said. "They have found out differently."

"I am stupid," Jezebel replied. "They were right."

"These people obey the law of the jungle. It is survival of the fittest."

"That is so crass," Jezebel replied. "The law is for animals, Arya. It pains me that you understand it. There is a higher law. Sure, they will beat me every time using that base, violent law of the lower grade human. An evolved person knows never to recede in growth so as to win for the body."

The teen that laughed seconds before the triumphant heist, puckered her lips, screwed her eyes, to suddenly surrender to a terrible fit of tears and wailing. Try as she could, her mother could neither put a stop to the tragic wailing, nor reach the child.

"What's wrong, Arya?" she asked.

"I can't tell you," she cried. "I would never tell you. It is horrible."

The mother jumped to gather her child in her arms tenderly. Obviously, her words about wickedness had somehow disturbed the child. Jezebel assured her daughter of her unflinching belief concerning her daughter's morality. Alaya wailed upon hearing her mother's words.

"That is something I can never tell you. I would like to see a psychiatrist. I think I am very ill."

"Ill?" Jezebel touched her daughter's forehead.

"Not that kind of ill, mentally ill," Arya snapped disdainfully.

"What is wrong with you? I have always thought you to be the most even-tempered, well-adjusted person I know."

"Ah well, obviously you did not know me well."

"Could you possibly explain what made you think such madness?" Jezebel asked. "Things could never be that bad."

"Worse," Arya cried uncontrollably.

"Talk to me," Jezebel urged, "Try me. We have always been closer than friends. We have pulled a jewel heist together; what are you talking about?" Jezebel pulled all the stops to gain her confidence.

"Fine, on my honeymoon, I slept with your husband, my father," she blurted out. "Is that not the most horrible thing you have ever heard? To make matters worse, I enjoyed it. Upon awakening, I felt horrible."

Jezebel blanched perceptibly. She attempted to swallow but failed, and her tongue felt like a piece of old wood.

"What do you mean you slept with my husband?" her mother asked.

"See? You could not handle it, either. What else could I have meant by it? Your husband was my husband. I was a virgin, and he deflowered me," she almost taunted her mother.

"Why are you being so hateful?" Jezebel asked, having forgotten that she had begged her daughter to tell her secret.

"Because I truly loved him as a man, mother. Is that sick enough for you?"

"Fine, you win. I will make an appointment with a prominent psychiatrist." Jezebel left the room to be sick in her bathroom.

Although she knew the hateful events had occurred in a dream, the fact that her daughter fantasized sexually about her father worried the mother greatly. For the first time in their lives together, Jezebel considered the possibility that Arya was truly, mentally challenged.

Thirty-Eight
ARYA SUFFERS FROM DELLUSIONS

The building stood longer than the city that housed it. So fragile that building seemed to stand against the blue skies that it looked as though it would fall and crumble at any moment.

They opted to use the stairs, as the lift with the many grills, looked dangerously ancient to brave.

The waiting room reeked of ancient inhabitants; mite, mould and mildew competed to choke the visitors that dared venture inside the place. A receptionist showed them inside an exquisitely decorated waiting room, replete with paintings, mostly oils, and antique furnishings. Arya's eyes stung and watered painfully as her mother coughed. The receptionist, they noted, looked at ease with the menagerie of doom.

"Why am I surprised? One does not expect such exquisite taste," Arya asked her mother.

"Things are not what they seem to be sometimes," Jezebel assured her.

He came to the door, a picture of elegance and beauty.

"Hello," he extended a manicured hand. "I am your doctor. Would you come this way with me?"

"Stay," Arya told her mother. "Next time you can come in."

"Fine," the mother agreed; happy to have found help.

The tall man with the amazingly compassionate eyes smiled gently at the mother.

"She will be fine. It will not take long," he said in a refined British English.

"Please," she said. "Don't worry about me." Jezebel's intonations rang simple in comparison.

"He wants me regressed," Arya came out to inform her mother.

"That is good," Jezebel answered. "It is, right?"

"I don't know. I want to do it, but I fear knowing."

"Can I be there with you?"

"Of course, I want you there," Arya told her.

They went out happily into the sunshine of the fresh spring into the world of streets and many pedestrians.

"Let us have a hamburger," Arya invited, "My treat."

They sat in a street café, where they could check and watch the season's latest fashions paraded before them, worn by the most beautiful women on earth, if Paulo Coelho were to be believed.

"We are a good-looking breed." Arya tossed her mane of deep russet.

"You are, my love. I, however, am getting old."

"You are still a beautiful woman, mother. Eddy thinks you the most beautiful woman that has ever lived," Arya told her mother.

"That is a son for you," she giggled embarrassed.

"Was Auntie Alaya pretty?" the subdued teen asked.

"Exceedingly beautiful she was. She did not look much different from you. She was a brunette, none of your red hair. Our family is an ancient one in this land. They come from a background of Christianity. They were allied to the foreign Crusaders and so escaped getting ravaged. Our women never got the legacy of blue eyes and blond hair. We managed, as a result, to keep our Canaanite looks intact. She was a typical Phoenician, olive-skinned, jet-black, wavy hair, brilliant black eyes, deep set and close together. Her best features were a pouting mouth, high cheekbones and a high forehead. She had a deep dimple inside her chin and mischief in her eyes." Jezebel tried to remember her elder sister.

"I am obsessed by her. It is like she has possessed me."

"I don't believe in that," Jezebel disagreed vehemently.

"How do you explain our connection?" Arya asked.

"We shall soon find out." Jezebel hated conjecture.

"I would like to see pictures of her." Arya grew excited about the idea.

"My mother had them banished to the attic. I shall try to find them for you," she promised. "It is so painful for the family, that time of our lives. Mother hates to remember it."

"Sure, I understand," Arya said, and felt a squeeze inside her heart. "How they must have suffered."

"It killed my father. We are all sure of this fact. Your aunt was the soul of his soul. He could not manage life without her."

"Is it not strange that whoever committed the crime got away with the perfect murder?" the young woman said.

"The entire village knows. They would never speak."

"How about the man who line fished in the river that day?" Arya asked her mother. "We could find him and bribe him to speak."

"What man?" Jezebel asked confused. "I am not aware of any eye witness."

"Oh, is that so? I thought there was a man fishing that day that saw my aunt," Arya related confused.

"Where did you hear that?" Jezebel grew animated.

"I don't know. Now, I am not so sure." Arya grew increasingly confused.

There was knowledge inside her. It sat like a slab of Swiss cheese, filled with holes. While the facts stood viable to use, they were weakened considerably by the holes.

The girl wondered if the fisherman were not one of these holes, or maybe facts. There was no way of checking.

They finished their lunch then walked up the road to the flat, only to find Edward sulking. He demanded to know where they were, and the reason there was no food at the place. They ordered a burger for him. He went to get it happily.

"I have the report, right here," Jezebel said as she reached inside a cabinet to pull up a stack of papers, yellowed by dust and age.

In one leap, Arya stood behind her mother's head as together they read the police report.

Edward returned with a carry-out box and stared at the women intently, baffled at the amount of bickering they had done lately.

"Stop it, you two. Keep the peace flowing in this house," he said.

"Shut up, Edward," Arya said.

"Mom!" he complained.

They decided to go back to the café so as to avoid disrupting the young man's life and peace.

Reaching the steel-on-steel decorated place, the women sat outdoors soaking up the sun and watching the pedestrians stroll before them.

"Where is that line fisherman?" Jezebel read the report. "Not one word mentions the presence of a witness. Where is that line fisherman? Who told you about the fisherman?" Jezebel asked.

"I am not sure, mom. Forget it. I probably dreamt it. You know me. What with the dreams of death and births, lives and other lives, this reality, I no longer know what is real and what is fantasy."

Jezebel felt a deep unease. Arya never made mistakes of this sort.

"You are not hiding evidence to save your people, are you?"

"Of course I am not. Do not be ridiculous," Arya said, blushing crimson at the implication.

"I don't understand you. I am trying my best to unravel this mystery that happened before my birth, yet, you attack and mistrust me. What ridiculous notions you get up to."

"If you were to defend them, it would be mighty nasty. To prefer saving them against my sister and the suffering my family incurred at their hands, would truly depress me."

"No mom, I am not defending or shielding them. Do you believe that if we were to find her killers we have legal recourse?"

"Of course," Jezebel said, relishing the prospect.

"We children, my father, your marriage; what would happen to our lives? Have you given these issues any thought?"

"None whatsoever," Jezebel shrieked. "You allow them to get away with murder, Arya?"

"What would that accomplish? They are very old now, mom. They are both in their nineties."

"And torturing us all the more? It will be just to see them in jail."

"Just for whom?" the child asked.

"For all of us," Jezebel's said, sounding demented.

"You mean, just for you."

"You were the one, Arya, who went after the servant."

"True," her daughter admitted. "I wanted to know for me, for us. As to doing anything legal about the knowledge, I am not sure. Some things are best left alone. This is, to my mind, one such instance. Let the universe deal with them."

"What do you mean?" Jezebel asked, failing to grasp the meaning of her daughter's words.

"I mean; if we were to trust the Maker and Manager of this world, we also need to understand the relationship of balance connecting destinies. It is as though humans are set up to function in a domino fashion. One action provokes a reaction; one that harmonizes with the whole, that ultimately serves the whole. If we were to outguess the forces in rearranging one domino, for instance, forcing the solving of this mysterious murder, we could be unwittingly creating a chain reaction of dire results to that whole," she explained.

"So we allow evil people to kill and ravage?" Jezebel asked, "So as not to upset the domino set?"

"We don't allow or disallow. Humans are to do nothing but follow their destinies in faith, and strict devotion of acceptance that their Father in the heavens understands the whole picture, and has their best interests at heart," Arya tried to explain.

"That stands as an impossible feat to accomplish," Jezebel proclaimed hotly. "We are to allow evil entities to think they got away with my sister's murder so as to grow emboldened by the victory, then to attempt and plan my death?"

"Something like that; not that you are to sit idle awaiting your death, more that in stilling, doing your best to show your love to them, the hope is that they awaken and get saved."

"So, the burden of murdering entities, sits on the victim's back as a responsibility. Do you ever hear yourself speak, Arya, my love?"

"Yes." Arya averted her eyes as she answered. "What is the worst that could happen?"

"I would be dead, as dead as my poor sister Alaya," Jezebel shrieked dementedly.

"So you will be dead. We know that only the body dies."

Jezebel pounced on her daughter faster than a cornered cheetah. In one leap she was tackling her to the ground. Over her child, a handful of curls in her hands, Jezebel awoke slightly to other people.

People stopped everything to look at the enraged woman killing the young person. Pedestrians stopped, a waiter dropped a tray of cold drinks and cups to awaken Jezebel further. She moved away from her daughter's chair, to look to her hand filled with red hair.

"See what I mean?" Arya laughed at the sleeping body when inside powerful emotions. "You could have killed me."

"Right," Jezebel, answered sheepishly, fearing that animal side she discovered lurking within.

"It is fine. Don't worry. See how we could all turn into murderers?"

"I am jealous because you love them so much," Jezebel answered truthfully.

"Why could you not see the reason they killed your sister?" Arya asked. "They were also jealous. They loathed the way he showered attention on her. He had no eyes for anyone else but his beautiful Alaya. That must not have been fun to watch for the two women," she said.

"How do you know that?" Jezebel marvelled at the breadth of her daughter's knowledge in the matter.

"I just do. I know exactly how he worshipped her. She once placed her hand on the back of his neck. He so felt her touch, that he rammed the car before them to total both cars." Arya got off the chair went in to pay for their tea.

Jezebel had never heard this story. When Alaya got married, Jezebel was a teen; she would have remembered such an accident, but did not. The woman made a mental note to call her mother and ask about the incident. If Arya were making stories up, that would prove detrimentally dangerous for her mental state.

"Let us go," she returned to say.

"Darling, could you remember who told you that story?" Jezebel asked, her earlier anger gone.

"Not really," Arya replied, "so many stories about."

"I had never heard that one," Jezebel said and ran to catch up with Arya.

"Let us not talk about it," she cried bitterly as she ran up the hill.

"Talk to me," she begged. "Whatever it is, we can handle it together."

"Listen as we have just seen, emotions, negative emotions are nothing short of that manifestation of what everybody calls evil. Except notice, nobody has evil within them, it is always in others. Every time you rile a person to a point where their sense of false self is threatened, presto, their evil entities manifest and jump to kill you. How is that different from a real murder? God has created both evil and good within our entities. The challenge is to increase one and decrease the other. That is the fate of all people."

"We are all evil?" Jezebel asked.

"Yes. Some are more so than others. One day, those who are evil could make a quick turnabout and become light. That is the only destiny possible for people in this realm called earth. That is all there is to life," Arya said.

At home, Arya went for her meditation. She placed the candle over the television set to get a better view of the flame. As she stared into the light without allowing thought to enter her brain, she pretty soon thrilled in seeing that tiny flame grow to gobble the entire room and throw long shafts towards the corners, the ceiling, even her own body.

Jezebel went to the kitchen telephone to call her mother. At first the woman could not remember an instance when Alaya and her husband had had a car accident.

"It rings a bell, though," she said. "Yes, wait Jezebel; they were not married but engaged. He had taken her to see my parents. He got home to call her. We both picked up the telephone receiver at once. Alaya did not know I heard them. 'Get back, Okay?' she asked, 'the roads are empty this time of night.' He told her that he nearly killed himself, destroying his car beyond repairing. 'I am fine. It could have been much worse. A car stopped before me on the red light. Dreaming of the way I felt when you placed your hand on the nape of my neck, I did not see the car stop, or the lights turn red. It was awful. I just rammed him as though nobody was there. I felt entranced. It was surreal.'"

"What did you tell her, mom?" Jezebel asked her aging mother.

"I told her that I had heard their conversation, also told her that the way he loved her was beyond comprehension. 'He is bewitched by you, Alaya.'"

"What did she say?"

"She said she knew that," her mother replied, crying openly by then.

"What was that, mom?" Jezebel needed to understand. "Ours is a calmer relationship. What did Alaya have that the rest of us children lack?"

"She had magic. Your sister could mesmerize anyone. That was a quality few people I know possessed."

Thirty-Nine
ARYA SUBMITS TO REGRESSION THERAPY

The woman wore white, all white. She walked down a steep hill, greeting nobody. Several people waved from both sides of the hill, from inside doorways. She could see no faces. Arya huffed painfully.

"Are you okay?" the doctor asked.

"Yes. It is so tiring on the calves, this hill."

"Where are you?"

"I am going down some hill."

"Why?"

"Just for a walk," she said.

The man came from nowhere to greet her. He looked frightening. Both his eyes bulged eerily, like frogs'. He was very sweet. He asked to walk her down. She nodded.

At the bottom of the hill, the man turned right inside a hut, where he kept chickens, and two pigs.

"Take it easy," the man said.

"You too," she said now.

"Take good care of yourself, pretty girl," he suddenly said, "how did your parents marry you to this cursed family?"

"What?" Arya exclaimed. "That is not nice. You are always at their house for visits and coffee. Why must you stab them in their backs like that?"

"Bless your soul, girl. You are so naïve," he said as he entered his hut.

The woman painted a frown of misery on her beautiful face, as she waved goodbye to the disappearing man.

"Where are you going?" the doctor asked.

"I am going down towards the river. Husband confuses me. He acts like he is ashamed to be with me before his village people, and his parents. I awoke to watch him dress up quietly. It is as though his nights are mine, to be spent secretly with me. His days belonged to his parents. His father follows him everywhere. The man acts like my jealous counterpart. That hurts me. I obsess over the fact that he makes me feel like a secret mistress that needs to be hidden, somehow. I can't understand how I will spend my life vying for his attention. And something else..." She knitted her brows.

"What else?"

"I don't know. Something strange...He hides and I cannot find in my background a clue to its unravelling. It is like they all hide something."

"Like what?" the doctor asked, intrigued by her depth.

"Being around them, one feels like a total stranger. There will never be a chance to blend in. They emanate vibes of aggressive oneness. I can't explain, really. It is more a quality of the air than anything else. It is like as a group, having seen dire tragedy in their past, they have made a solid pact, not to ever allow anyone else in. My husband, by loving me, had somehow broken that blood covenant."

"Strange. How did you feel that?"

"In everything they do. If one of them disagrees, they all join in to support him, unquestionably. They rally around one another unconditionally: That opens doors to much victimization. I think on these things now."

"What do you see?"

"I see vast blue skies, and white clouds that dot it sparingly. It is a crisp day, not cold. I feel a chill of fear course through my bones. I also feel a premonition of doom. I stop, look around to spot nobody. For a second, I want to go back. Seeing their hateful faces at the house above spurs my body forward, downward, to the river, the peace of the lulling trees and some rest."

"Are you afraid?"

"No. I feel shattered: Like the end of my life comes before living. I also feel sad and hurt at the way he never defends me. That cuts deeper than anything. I cannot find the reason for his lack of loyalty. The fact that he loves me is clear to all. Still, every time they attack me, he runs indoors."

"He is afraid to take sides, so they don't think he loves you and kill you."

"Yes. I think about that also. Men in our clan defend their wives to the death. They obviously do not subscribe to the honour code of man protects his woman."

"He could not protect you if he is afraid of them," the doctor attempted to help.

"Sure enough; what baffles me most, however, is the fact that he and his brothers support three gang leaders that torture them."

"Here you go," the doctor said.

"What?" She missed it.

"It is a strangely sick relationship. You called it a gang. The leaders in a gang control by intimidation and abuse. It is not a healthy relationship."

"What gives the gang members impetus to give their wills away? That was my preoccupation that day. And again I reasoned, if he were brainwashed to accept, I was fully awake, and as such he weakened my position. I hated that he looked drugged all the time while around them. The women use key words that trigger specific reactions. I grew to decode some of the words, and understood that his reaction to them would always be robotic, not prone to analysing."

"What do you mean by weaken your position?" He genuinely wanted to understand.

He found the woman brilliant. Her logic stood faultless and clear.

"I mean sleeping people do not make good leaders. As society appointed him through that marriage the head and decision-maker of our household, he placed me in dire danger by following their lead. We lost central control. He would tell me one thing to do as his mother would scream something else to do, as he stood watching her tear into me, baffled as to a way to act. They, mother, sister, and father, had a higher authority to veto any of his decisions. This is where the trouble happened. We have a huge breakdown in central authority. He, having willingly handed them his life, had never been trained to self-rule, had failed at ever knowing how to lead me. He expects me to follow his mother's lead, for she is the boss of my boss. That, I know, was not the proper way to handle a marriage." Arya cried softly.

"What were the key words?" he asked. "Give an example."

"There were many key words, a set for every occasion, so much so that they could speak for hours without a stranger understanding anything they said. The tradition is not new; so honed, so perfected that I suspect it of being handed down through generations, as a secretly coded language through whose use these people ensured their safety against foreign aggressors," she explained. "One such example is when they invariably asked: Where are you speaking from?"

"Meaning?" he asked.

"Meaning: We need to speak privately. Call from the office. We don't trust this channel," she translated.

"How did you learn to decipher this?"

"I felt threatened, and watched them closely. It was not easy. One had to use all sorts of intelligence so as to catch the least bit of conspiracy. The conspiracy is not straightforward, though. It gets more complicated, because the different protagonists double-crossed one another so as to skirt the central command chain."

"What do you mean by double-crossed one another?" The doctor grew increasingly more intrigued. "I have never heard anything like this."

"The spirit Mind, one that all humans possess, is never muddled. It is the brain that is conditioned. That other entity knows everything. Inside these people, the Mind understood the state of selfishness that made them robots. Invariably, when they fell in love, they vied to skirt around the scheme by play acting at being conditioned; they acted as if they did not love their mates, so as to survive the attacks, and protect their new families; as separating was not an allowed state. That created a duality of private actions, and public ones," she explained. "That was my first lead."

"Would you discuss it with him later?" He wanted to understand.

"Not really. What's to discuss? Things were plainly obvious. He thought himself free to act until they upstaged him. The power struggle happened among them. I was simply a chance bystander. I could have been any other woman on earth today. I was a variable. Besides, we were raised not to cause trouble, and the moral code; that creating a rift between a man and his parents, stood as the worst sin, a crime almost. I waited for him to see. I truly believed myself deluded, at first. It was much later that I realised that he acted to please them. His chief mistake was his failure to explain the reality of things at their home to me. Don't you see it? Had we both been acting together, then I would have made sure to help him succeed at deluding them that our marriage was a peasant-oriented one to deflect their wrath away from us as a couple. But, because his body was totally conditioned to put them first, he could not come clean to what he believed was an outsider. So, he towed both lines to lose both camps. He got both our wrath equally."

"No, I don't see it. What exactly should I see Arya?"

"The fact that he hid the horrible machinations from me, points directly to his awareness of its embarrassing nature," she clarified.

"Was he embarrassed?" the doctor asked amazed.

"Partly, as his embarrassment happened on the spirit level, and as his conditioning on that of the body, he was rifted, divided into two people, the saint and the devil," she explained.

"Did he ever get the whole picture?"

"He never did. Jumping from one extreme pole into the next, we all jumped with him. Sleeping people see only dreams. Reality needs wakefulness, or relative consciousness. That, I understood totally. This fact shattered my spirit. See, I was awake. I was born relatively more awake than even my own parents. My life stood like a fisherman's boat to be tossed by stormy winds. Emotions like control are erratic like the wind at high sea. They do not follow a logical course of action one could outguess and remedy. One is a victim at the whim of mighty forces. This state is horrendous to watch and live by."

"You felt like a victim?"

"Totally," she said. "They saw that I was awake, and felt all the more threatened by me."

"Did you tell your parents?"

"No. My father had a rule, once married you dealt with things on your own. To come back and rat on your new family constituted a dreadful lack of manners, and charity. I was stuck; I felt stuck."

"Where are you now?"

"I sit under a willow tree and think on these things."

"Is there anyone around?"

"Yes. There is a lone fisherman. He said hello, and nodded upon seeing me," she said.

"Do you see anyone else?"

She stopped.

The girl stared toward the horizon, in an upward motion to her neck, as if she strained to see somebody.

"What?" he asked.

"Somebody else is coming my way."

"Who is it?"

"It is our next-door neighbour. She is a good woman of virtue that likes me. She waves her shawl frantically."

"And, what happens, next?"

"She disappears inside the village. I don't see her any longer."

"What else do you see, hear and smell?"

"I see that the line fisherman moves a bit south. I can still see part of his back. He has just caught a huge fish. He turns back and smiles proudly. I return his smile. Birds of all kinds flutter in the tree, as crickets chirp happily in a nearby brush; also, a loud cacophony of frogs splits the sky. That makes me forget a little bit. Two old men pass me, and lower their heads in greeting. Their donkeys drag on the descent, heavy with their loads of vegetables."

Jezebel exchanged a distraught look with the doctor, who appeased her with a gentle motion of his hand, to assure her as to her daughter's safety.

"What is she doing?" Jezebel mouthed to the man in white.

He shrugs his shoulders to indicate his loss as to the reason Arya stares into the skies.

Just as the doctor opened his mouth to ask his patient a question, a blood-curdling shriek splices the air in the office to send Jezebel to her daughter's side in one leap, only to catch the doctor's arm which stopped her.

"Please," he asked, "go back to your seat."

"What is happening, Arya?" he asked, "Are you in trouble?"

"No, no, no, no, no, no, oh, my God," Arya shrieks.

The nurse rushed from her cubicle outside the office where the doctor had regressed the woman, to show her displeasure with a frown. Her furtive gestures indicated her distress at the sounds emanating from the place; ones that are swiftly emptying the clinic. The doctor motioned for her to close the door, shrugged his shoulders at the futility of his position.

"Why do you want to kill me? What have I ever done to you?" Her words came slowly, and demented with her fear.

"What? If he loves me, that should make you happy," Arya argued.

"You vowed to kill me because he did not listen to you? How could that be my fault?"

"Aha, I see. Go ahead then, and kill me," she said calmly.

She writhed and wiggled, sat on the floor, tossed and contorted her body in all directions.

"What are you doing?" the doctor asked her softly.

"I am trying to loosen these ties from my limbs," she answered him as she fought.

She jerked suddenly, stood up, and jerked her neck back.

"What is going on?" he asked again seconds later.

"My husband's father is tying me with my shirt," she complained like a child.

"Why did you jerk like that; did he slap you?"

"No," she said.

"What then?" he pushed.

"Wait," she gestured with a hand. "Let me hear what they are saying."

"Who is there?"

"There is poor Sycamore, my master, my husband's mother, and his father. They are arguing now about something. Okay, they have just made a deal. He is to get all her money if he were to help her kill me."

"How are they intending to do that?"

"I don't know," she said frightfully. "Maybe they want to leave me tied for the wolves."

"Leave me alone. Just go away. I am going to tell him what you are doing to me. He will know everything now," she screamed loudly enough to empty the remaining patients in the waiting room.

"Everyone has left," the nurse came back to whisper in his ear.

"That is fine. It cannot be helped." In reality he was enjoying this session.

The doctor had never subjected to regression anyone with such a unique experience. There existed no doubt as to the truth of this saga: Nobody could ever re-enact with such depth the horrendous emotions the woman facing him showed on her body.

The woman screeched like an animal now. A violent jerking of her torso, as she screwed her feet together clarified to him the mode of her torture. She was fastened somehow to some solid object, as she tried valiantly to loosen herself free. Only her torso jerked spastically, forcefully, this way, and that, to the left and to the right, until he feared she would sever her neck away from her head.

"What is happening?" He thought of calming her actions with the question.

She did not hear the question. Her internal turmoil and fears resounding inside her head, shielded her, cut her off, severed her from any world.

All her energies pivoted around wrenching herself free from her object of torture.

"What are you tied to?"

"This tree, this beautiful tree; the willow feels horrible," she answered distractedly.

"Where are your torturers?"

"They fled. They climbed up the cliff towards the houses above me. I can see their backs now."

And oh, what came next turned his stomach so bad, that a wave of nausea assailed him with a force he did not know possible.

The man had been seeing patients for three decades, thinking himself untouchable, but now, the reaction inside his body frightened him deeply.

The woman before him twisted herself free of her chair writhing like an injured animal on the floor of his office. Fearing for her head, he ran and proceeded to remove furniture pieces away from her body before she could split her head open. His nurse came in and together, they removed coffee table, side tables, vases, candelabras, and flower pots, running away with them into the waiting room. Her mother stood transfixed, watching the scene unfold, in sheer disbelief.

The fiasco of fear and demented, furtive movements stunned them all; as the girl shook and slapped, scratched, and contorted into the last spasm of what they knew was her death, stunned them into a shocking silence. It was so real, it felt as though they watched the murder happen making them feel guilty for not being able to help and save her.

Finally, she opened her mouth to the skies, eyes bulging; frozen, towards her Maker, she smiled, and stiffened into a board made of solid wood, a slab of marble.

"She looks dead," the secretary said.

"I hope that she is not." He touched the side of her neck.

Her pulse came faint, slow and irregular. She looked relieved, somehow.

"She is reliving her past death." He awaited her awakening.

"Let us not startle her," the nurse whispered.

"Yes. Get me some coffee," he asked shakily.

Jezebel ran out of the office all the way to the street below unable to stand watching any longer. There, she sat on the curb and cried.

"I will get you a cup of wine. You look like a ghost," the nurse said.

They sat there for five minutes with not a sound, a move from the woman who stretched corpse-like at the edge of the desk.

"What is she doing?" the nurse asked confused.

"I have no idea," he replied truthfully. "We will soon find out."

"Is she in any danger?"

"No." He prayed it be so.

He sipped his wine, as the nurse watched the woman on the floor.

"That could take forever." She lamented, wanting to go to lunch.

"No. I don't think so. Something is going on. I would like to find out."

"Like what could go on? Dead is dead. She could play this for as long as she wants."

She was wrong. The woman stretched her arms and shook her legs and feet as she smiled, smiled, unfocused.

"Where am I?" Arya finally asked, calm and rested.

"What?" she stood in one leap. "Dead, I am dead, but I don't feel dead?"

The nurse started to object when the doctor motioned her to be silent and go outside his office.

She stopped all movements, but remained. It was too enthralling to leave now.

"Who is she speaking to?" she wrote on a pad.

"No idea," he wrote back. "It's great, though."

"Ask her," she suggested.

"Life after death; she does not even know about her death. There must be a body, a form of a body, somehow, present with her. She has not as yet figured out the loss of her earthly form. That is strange. We never knew that. We thought..." he wrote furtively now, "that the spirit might survive. She is feeling her form."

"This could be a hallucination. We know that the body remains," she wrote.

292

They watched as the woman spoke to someone else, some entity she names Master.

"She is speaking to God." The nurse pointed to the skies.

He again shook his head negating her conclusions.

"Master, am I really dead?" she asked. "Why did I not feel my separation from the body? And what is it that flies through the ether?"

"My essence, what is that?"

"Okay." He wrote on the pad. "Eastern sciences speak of an ethereal form that covers the body. It must be that she feels."

The nurse could no more take in the intricate details.

"Let us awaken her. I feel shattered for her." She cried tears of sisterhood and compassion.

"No, a while longer," he said and wrote like mad.

"Oh, noo, my husband is crying." She cried for her lost love. "They have won, they have won. The evil ones have won."

The woman sat on the floor, cradled her head in her hands, and surrendered to a heart-wrenching bout of the most shattering wailing.

"I love you," she told him, "I love you. You should have defended me, protected me, and been aware of the danger. Now, what do we do now? It is too late for you to cry over my body, bring me roses I can no longer smell, as they smile, and whisper their glee behind you, keep up the pretence of loving you, as they vie for your money. Control, control is selfishness; where is selfishness from love? Selfishness is against love, the death of love, the death of lovers. Stop. Do not cry. Please, stop. I love you."

"Oh my, look," she spoke to someone to her right. "He can hear me. How does that work?"

"His spirit, his spirit can hear me? I shall help him heal then. I shall help him heal. I shall love him the way he loves, purely, innocently, spiritually, without greed, violence, selfishness, or want. I love you, love you, love you," she broke down anew.

Suddenly, she stopped.

Soon, a different quality of matter, solidness, heaviness, returned to animate the entity on the floor. Soon, the stillness grew to manifest itself into sudden self-consciousness. Quickly, she wrapped her skirts around her knees to cover the white legs. The woman looked about her in dazed timidity. At first, she looked confused as to her surroundings. She gazed about her immediate space, baffled as to her being on the floor to soon raise her eyes to focus on the desk, the doctor, the nurse, and then she spoke.

"What am I doing on this floor?"

"You have been telling us an interesting story," he said, feeling sorry for her.

Having had no time to control her coming out of her trance, the man could not imagine what she remembered.

"Do you remember anything that you saw?"

The woman looked towards her feet in concentration, which soon turned into a looked of utter consternation.

"I feel angry, mostly," she offered confused; "more like offended, sad, and abused. No wait, there is more. I feel as though I went somewhere else...Yes. I remember. I visited my death, right?"

"Yes."

"Is that not awful?"

"Yes. We have made a recording. Whenever you feel able, you could watch it. For now, however, a little while longer, I would not advise it. Whenever I deem you fit, I shall watch it with you," he promised her.

"It is so unfair to make me wait." She moaned, anxious to know.

"I know. It is solely for your good. It is shattering, I caution you."

"Obviously; death always is."

"No. Yours was most shattering," he informed her.

"How did I die?" she asked. "You could tell me the method."

"I don't know. You never said." The doctor told the truth.

"What do you mean? What did you not ask me?"

"Watching you suffer the actual episode shattered me into forgetfulness. I should have asked."

"What do you think?" she begged him to help her.

"Do you remember the faces of those who killed you?"

She stared into space attempting to reincarnate those faces that sat steadfastly behind all her nightmares, just behind her forehead, between her brows, there, yet gone.

"No. I really can't remember now. Did I say their names?"

"Yes." His heart ached from the imminent revelation.

"And who were they?"

They looked at each other in sheer consternation, the nurse and the kind doctor. How does one impart shocking information to this woman who suffered so much? The ethical dilemma shook the doctor to the very core: Is it more beneficial to uncover that which tortures this woman, or keep the lid on her murder so as to save her from sure annihilation?

"I have to think on this one," he finally told her.

"That is so unfair, though. It is most unfair. There must be some law against this. You uncover my subconscious mind, and hide it from me. Is this not theft of property? Surely, my mind's contents are my sole property."

"Sure." He giggled at the woman's keen intelligence. "Fair enough; your experiences are your property. I shall tell you. The people who killed you were your former father-in-law, and his wife, your mother-in-law."

"So, it is true. Yes. I have seen the contours of their faces in many a dream. My mother believes it was they who killed me. I never wanted to believe this fact, or face it. Here we are then. That is terrible."

"That is in your past where it should remain. Knowing will deter suppression and afford you a way to resume this life, instead of remaining stuck in a past life that is no more. Finish, put it behind you."

"Yes sure, I shall toss it right out." Her voice had a terrible, sarcastic quality to it.

"What do you mean?" he asked feeling horrible.

"They are my current life's grandparents. My last life's husband had married my last life's sister. They are my current parents. His parents are my grandparents."

"Your husband fathered you?" The nurse shrieked in disgust.

"Yes. I arranged it. I am sure, now. I must have picked them for parents."

"Why?" he asked disoriented in this uncharted terrain.

"Like a punishment," she said calmly.

"So, we seem to have compounded your problems." The man looked ill with the guilt for having told her.

"No. It is better. It is always better to know. That cancels confusion, diminishes virulent dreams and fosters consciousness. It is never good to live unconsciously to commit more mistakes. It is better. Thank you. I have survived death and two lives with these people; obviously, a lesson that is to be mine, was missed by me in both lives. That should become my focus."

"What are you saying?" The man had stopped understanding a while back.

"I mean, I need to find a way to survive them and find out the reason I came back to them," she announced.

"Let it go," he begged her.

"Why do you Western psychiatrists need to let go? That is wrong. You need to solve problems."

"Yours are not solvable." He resented her insults to his profession.

"No. Everything is solvable. Only, one needs to use the correct criteria, information, with which to solve it."

"Which is what?" He taunted her now.

"Finding the right keys that would unravel the riddle," Arya stated simply.

"Which are?"

"To believe in the facts of life; man is a product of his Maker. You want him to be studied on the force of your own sciences. A man abject of his spirit, disconnected to the other realms of the universe, sterile, and belonging to a body. This is where you fail. You are studying only a third of the human." She finished and stopped.

Having stated her opinion, she got up, straightened her skirt primly, reached down to pick her dainty purse from the floor, patted her long, silky hair around her ears as to regain some lost dignity, extending her hand towards his confused form, she smiled and shook his hand firmly.

"Thank you," she said. "You are a good man."

"Well, thank you. I will see you next week."

"Fine," she said.

With that, she closed the door behind her softly, and left like the soft breeze that tickles the trees in late summer.

"She is amazing," he said to no one in particular.

Shaken to the core, the nurse left without even a comment.

Arya met Jezebel, who sat still on the concrete of the sidewalk. They looked at one another in grief, but little else.

"Why did you leave me?" Arya asked her mother.

"I could not take it any longer," her mother replied.

"He said that we are making great strides; he wants to see me next week, same time," she said.

"How do you feel?" her mother wanted to know.

"I feel strange," Arya said.

"Did he tell you who killed you as Alaya?"

"Yes," Arya said. "It was them, as you had always suspected."

"Could it be that we spoke so much about the possibility to pollute your mind with suspicions about them?"

"Possible, but highly doubtful," Arya said.

Forty
ARYA SEES HERSELF AS HER AUNT ALAYA

The ancient city bustled with merchants peddling wares on carriages that looked as though sprouting from the concrete of the sidewalks. They had appropriated the exact, same spot for years, having inherited them from old parents. These claims were staked on the sheer force of having been used the longest. Housewives and servants heckled over the different goods with which to fix the noon meal. Women haggled over the prices of fruits and vegetables as a hobby; a cherished pastime for those who were afforded no fun in this life. The haggling had become expected, fun almost. Merchants playacted at anger to raise the prices, make a bit of extra money with these women as they checked them out; noting their shifts, the colour of their hair, commenting on their henna, and complimenting the scent they wore. Many alliances are made that way, many marriages concluded with the merchant handing the bag filled with cucumber; a familiar and expected form of social interaction. As they reached a point of compromise, a price in the middle, where everyone felt satisfied at having made the deal for the day, and nobody lost a prospective customer, jokes were cracked and alliances formed.

Nearby, next to the Valentino boutiques, Chanel, Ferragamo, Gucci, and other such foreign designer labels, there huddled young boys, delivery boys, drinking Turkish coffee out of cups that looked like tiny cymbals. They topped their drinks from a steamy thermos, as they awaited their employers to shout a need for a delivery. The contrast, while the most natural to those who lived there, looked incongruous to those who visited. Nowhere does the West meet the East in a more intimate fashion, more naturally, as in this Phoenician city, having done so for thousands of years.

Arya found the mishmash of cultures fascinating as she walked home that day. The doctor's office stood over the blue Mediterranean. She needed to walk southbound through the streets that bustled with the life of its inhabitants, where business mingled with culture, and banks rubbed shoulders with housewives who fed families that lived over huge institutions and the Souk.

"Hello, Arya," a woman greeted. "Are you well? How is your mother?"

Arya recognized the woman's face, failing to remember her name. She assured the kindly lady of her good health, and that of her mother's, and family.

"Give them my best," she said as she fondled a courgette.

"Thank you, I will," she replied never stopping.

With people knowing one another for ages, centuries untold, few secrets managed to escape scrutiny; the girl understood the fact; one that stood not a chance of changing.

"I wonder what they would say if they knew what I have known since my birth."

A caller for the noon prayer shouted his praises to Allah calling the faithful to noon prayers from a minaret behind her. Not to be outdone, the Catholic Church nearby, St. Nicholas, droned a bell signalling to the faithful a call for the noon Mass.

She laughed happily in approval of the many facets of her beloved city.

"They have all got it wrong, somehow," she thought. "Funny about the West; all its might and scientific prowess, getting as far as the moon itself, only to miss the crux of the mysteries and remain confused," Arya thought as she walked the streets. "Beirut, the city, knows how to hug all her children to her bosom, equally tenderly."

At home she found Jezebel cooking a roast. The servant girl chopped parsley for a tabouli salad, and fried vegetables to accompany the meal. That was structured. The entire country cooked one traditional meal at a certain date of the year's calendar. Roast day was invariably the meal for Sundays. Lentil stew was a Friday meal; only rich people added fried fish to the simple stew, and tomato and cucumber salad.

"How was it?" she asked without turning to look at her daughter.

"I don't want to talk now. I will tell you later. I need a nap before lunch."

"No. Come here and talk to me," Jezebel cajoled playfully.

"Later, I promise, mom." She left the kitchen. "Why are you making a roast on a Monday?"

"I have nothing else to make."

"Fine," Arya said but wanted to cry for some odd reason she hardly understood.

"Are you okay?" Jezebel inquired.

"Yes, fine. Do not worry. We will eat and talk."

A new quality of being entered her life just then, alien to anything she had ever known: It was as though she had suddenly become an alien in a place where nobody understood a word she uttered.

"What is the matter?" her father asked.

She shivered. In her sequence of death, inside her memory bank, some kind of memory she brought back from some death, that man had done things to her. Now, her love for him felt somehow strange; tainted.

"I am talking to you," he repeated insulted.

"Yes. I heard you," she replied testily.

"So?"

"I am fine. A little tired, that is all."

"Is she okay?" he asked Jezebel.

"She knows more than I do, dad, how I feel?" He was so controlling, the child thought.

"Fine, have things your way, Arya." He resumed his eating.

She ate little, and felt bored. There lurked within the girl a distinct feeling of caged imprisonment: She wanted to run away to the end of the earth, never to see him, his parents, or anyone she knew, ever again.

The realization that even at the end of earth, nobody would understand, would want to believe, or give the slightest credence to her experience, dawned on her and pained her deeply.

"There is nowhere to go," she thought shaking her head mournfully. "My death is the only solution."

"Do not even think this way," Sycamore shouted inside the girl's brain.

Arya's obsessive thought-pattern allowed no such soft communication to infiltrate the frantic channel of thoughts which frustrated her master who asked the child's angel to lend a hand in solving the problem so as to save the child. They decided to wait for a lull in her thinking to wedge their ideas inside her brain. They tried incessantly only to fail totally; the young woman's mind buzzed continuously with sorrow.

"Death could easily be the end of all my problems," Arya obsessed maddeningly.

"Stop it, Arya," both Sycamore and David screamed together on cue, "do not think about death."

"Stop what?" she finally heard.

"Talk of death is not allowed, darling. That is the test that needs surmounting," Sycamore reminded her charge. "Remember how we spoke about your tendency to give up?"

"What test?" Arya was familiar with the counsel of Sycamore.

"Wanting to die to interrupt the same destiny over and over again, Arya, that is the test we speak about. You do have to brave the lessons, learn them, live to the fullest and finish with all the drudgery the right way.

There is no escaping this life at whim. You have done so before in utter futility."

"Is there anything we could do to help?" her father asked, pained.

"No, father, you have done enough, thank you. Now, it is my problem to solve by myself."

"What does that mean?" He looked to his wife for clarification.

"Stop asking her. She has nothing to do with this problem." Arya felt hatefully resentful towards the man.

"What is your problem?" He banged his napkin on the table nervously.

"Ah, forget it. It is always about you!" Arya left the table.

"Where are you going, young lady? You come right back. I did not dismiss you yet."

"You know, father. Had you used this tone of voice with your parents and dear sister, we would not be in this mess," she spat venomously. "Why in the hell don't you use your prowess on them?"

"Are you using profanities in my presence?" He missed the crux of the matter.

"Oh, please, please, please," she shrieked, "leave me alone."

She banged the door behind her, and banged the huge oak entrance door before she left the house.

"She has left the house," he said in sheer disbelief.

"Let her cool off. She will soon return," Jezebel, perplexed by Arya's behaviour, told him.

"It is not like her," he exclaimed. "Anything happen today to upset her?"

"She would not talk to me either. Something is up with this child. God help us."

"What would people say?" he asked his wife.

"What people?" She hated the way he feared people instead of worrying about the welfare of the child.

"The neighbours, that's what people."

"Who cares?" Jezebel became highly agitated.

"I care, for one. Maybe you should care as well."

Jezebel resumed her work as if he did not speak.

"I am speaking to you, woman." His voice sounded threatening.

Having never heard him use this tone, Jezebel vowed not to let her heart skip a beat.

"Do not call her woman, dad," Eddy said softly from the door where he stood. "My mother is your wife, not some generic form of the female species. It is so rude."

"This is how he heard his father address his wife," she replied.

"What have I done, why do you all attack me today, care to share?" the poor man asked, shaking miserably.

He ducked his head to stare at the table shamed. That was not his wife who made the remark, but his son. That was different; men needed their sons to be proud of them. Eddy's remark carried weight behind it. His wife marvelled at the wrong options he picked from among the wide array of possibilities available to him.

"Mom is our mother. If you could not be nice to her, dad, you could spare her your generic form of address. By the way, father, we, neither my sister nor I, had ever heard you address our mother by her first name. May I know why?"

"That fosters intimacy, implies equality," she informed her son. "God forbid I should believe myself worthy of his friendship."

"No," her husband corrected. "I have never heard anyone address his wife by her first name."

"Not in your village where women are nothing but tools, yet surely, you must have learned a couple things in that West you so adored?" Eddy continued unrelentingly.

Jezebel resented the way her son spoke to his father. Upon watching, she discovered that her husband found it within the realm of the possible, even the very enjoyable that his son addressed him that way. Also, another thing came out of this discourse; he controlled his temper completely, showing no violence, but meek sweetness as he spoke to the blond, lanky teen as an equal.

While Jezebel hated watching her children attack their father, she hated it worse that her husband took it on the chin in sheer love and acceptance. When she made a remark, he pounced on her like a king rebuked his lowliest of servants.

"They are his children, his equals because they came from him, part of his lineage. There are to be other considerations attached to them. I am not as worthy." The woman marvelled.

They spoke with civility, as though her son had just paid his father the highest homage. Husband's tone grew conciliatory, as he explained matters of finance to his son while the moral discussion was promptly shelved. But she knew that he noted it, heard it.

"The bird you cage hates you," her father used to say. "The second you forget the cage door open, he escapes, never to come back. The bird you raise freely in your garden leaves to invariably return because he loves you. You have created a relationship of trust and respect which he never forgets."

The phone rang in the entrance hall to awaken her from her reverie.

"It is mister's sister," the servant giggled as she handed her the receiver.

"Yes?" Jezebel said into the mouthpiece.

"Is my brother there?"

"What is the matter?" her tone sounded crisp.

"It is my father. He says he can't breathe. Could you put my brother on the line, please?"

She handed him the receiver.

He spoke for a few seconds, got up, went inside the room to change his clothes, came back to inform them that he needed to meet the family at the hospital. He did not invite her to go along.

"I will call to inform you of the progress," he told them.

She did not answer. Instead, she and Eddy exchanged a knowing look of love.

Arya called to say that her aunt tracked her down on her private line, and that she was meeting her father at the hospital.

"Fine," Jezebel replied.

"Mom," Arya said.

"Yes, honey?"

"I love you."

"I love you, too, Arya. Call and tell us what is happening."

That day began two years of hospital visits. His heart drowned in water. They pumped his lungs out, gave him medication, and sent him home a week later.

For an entire week, Jezebel's husband came home only to sleep, get a change of clothes, shave and return. The odd part to all this became the fact that he looked as though he enjoyed the episode immensely.

"What is the reason he is so happy?" she asked Edward.

"They are making a party of it. They receive people from the village, and sit around drinking coffee, and then go out to lunch. It is odd, mom. It is as though they are on vacation. These people adore being with one another."

"Obvious for all to see," she spat venomously. "I cannot understand the reason they wanted to get married and leave one another in the first place."

"Well, they had to ensure their line of descendants." He giggled.

"Ah, yes. Excuse me. The royal family must do what it must do, obviously, noblesse oblige."

Forty-One
ARYA REMEMBERS, ASSIMILATES

Things changed after the hospital episode. Now, strange things started happening. The first, his father started giving orders. He called them at dawn every weekend to ask them over. The odd thing is that they loved being called to leave their lives, children and families to run and make believe that they were still babies at their parents' home. It was simply disgusting. To regress, they were to ditch their families. These felt properly ditched. It was maddeningly demeaning. Jezebel felt like a handful of sea salt sitting under the rain; her entity dwindled into oblivion.

"That was my father," husband said as they drank their morning coffee.

"At six o'clock?" Jezebel started losing it.

He giggled sheepishly.

"He wants to know if we wanted to go over there for lunch," he begged.

She felt like slapping him.

"Why, is he cooking? Your mother is bound to her bed after the fall from the tree."

"Well," he tightened his hand on the receiver, "the Egyptian woman cooks."

"No." Her chest tightened ominously. "I hate the woman's cooking. She puts tomato paste over everything."

"That is not the point." Husband sounded angrier by her refusal.

"What is the point?"

He opened his mouth to explain the point to her, when he remembered the old man on the other side of the receiver.

"Can I call you back, dad?" He sounded too solicitous for her taste.

"What do you mean you need to know now? It is only six o'clock, dad. I said give me five minutes."

"No, I do not need my wife's permission. We need to discuss this. I cannot drag her by the hair over there, so, discussion is needed. Besides, we had dinner with you last night."

"What do you mean, what do I expect you to do with yourself? Read a paper or something."

He hung up the phone roughly.

"What did he say?" She could tell he said something nasty.

"Nothing, do not worry about him. Let us go. He sounds so bored."

"No, we are not going there today. We have not been to my parents' house for weeks. Why is that? Do you never feel bad about me? Please, tell me only that."

"Of course I do, what do you think me blind, or stupid? The fact is, they are so old, and afraid."

"Being old is not an excuse to ruin your children's marriages, lives and jobs. Scores of other people are old. My mother is ailing. You don't see her issue orders about. This is selfish, not old. They want to rule everyone, and they are using their old age to achieve their end." She cried bitterly.

"So? What exactly do you expect me to do?" He sounded convinced that he had no options.

"I cannot hang about with our children for you to finish cajoling your parents through death. That is so stupid. It has been thirty years already. We have turned from teens to middle-aged people in constant bickering as we humour them because they are old. What if we were to die before they did? Do we then miss our lives so as they have everything, theirs as well as ours? That is daft." That was her longest speech to date.

"What should I tell them, go die, my wife is too busy thinking of her life?"

"Tell him no. We need to be around our home and family for a change. He is ninety-three years old, with children that care for him, a servant, a nurse, a dedicated daughter who has not lived so they do; what else does he want? Do living humans put their lives on hold so the old might be appeased? Who are you people? The faithful ones understand about death. They know that death is not the end. These understand that only that covering of clay is discarded for a new covering, as the eternal spirit migrates from one body through the next," she shouted demented with the usurping of her life.

The phone rang again just then to interrupt the litany. There were so many things she wanted to tell her husband; how she hated to have their every important moment stolen by them, how she hated waiting for their lives to start, how they had undermined their life to ensure they never had a harmonious moment, how she feared for her children learning these awful lessons of attachment and greed, valuing all things concrete and material.

"Yes?" He sounded mildly offended.

"It has been five minutes," the Egyptian servant informed him.

"What is the rush, Raghida? It is only six-thirty?" he said annoyed.

"Oh great, now he gets his servant on us," Jezebel ranted.

"No, listen. We will see you another time. We want to stick around home today." She hated the way he grovelled to her.

"Just say no. You do not need to explain," his wife directed dementedly.

"She wants to talk to you." He handed her the phone.

Jezebel took the receiver as she stared her husband down to make him flinch under the intensity.

"No, thanks, but no," she answered the woman gruffly.

"I am cooking your favourite food, madam. Besides, I miss the children," she tried to convince her.

"Not this time; my children miss my food, Raghida. We eat at the house all the time." Jezebel resented having to explain herself to the pushy woman.

"I have already rolled the cabbage leaves, please madam."

"How much did he pay you to get on our back today?" Jezebel giggled determinedly.

"In reality, ma'am, I am going mad here with these two, it would be good to see the four of you," she said to break Jezebel's heart.

"Fine, Eddy does not care for stuffed cabbage; could you please prepare pasta and a salad?"

"Anything you want," she said delighted.

"Did that hurt too much?" her husband asked. "Eat and leave."

"There is no other way, is there?"

"They are persistent." He giggled at her defeat.

Arya refused to eat. She ate crackers and cheese, and went to sit by her grandmother's bedside.

Jezebel had quizzed her on the doctor's visit only to get a promise of later. Now, she hated their relationship.

"Where are you going?" Jezebel pulled her daughter out of the sickroom, to ask.

"I need to talk to her." She pulled her elbow gruffly away from her mother's clutches. "Leave me alone."

"Arya, what is wrong with you? What is it with the violent outbursts of late?"

"Leave me, I said." Arya broke loose.

"She is unresponsive. Your grandmother does not communicate. We do not even know how much she understands. Let her be, Arya," Jezebel reasoned, to no avail.

"She is my grandmother, mom, don't worry. I won't throttle her, I promise you. Let me try to get to her before she dies," the young lady pleaded.

"What is so important about trying to reach the woman who has tortured my family and my children for years? Let her be, Arya. I am tired of making concessions to this woman, let her go, darling."

"No, it is crucial that I reach her, for all of us, me and you especially. I need to know what happened to Aunt Alaya. I need to understand how much evil lurks inside my being due to their tainted genetic material. I need to understand myself through this woman, please. It will be fine."

"I do not see the point," Jezebel told her, "I don't think so much importance should be placed on evil entities. If your grandmother had anything to do with that murder, she needs not be absolved, that is unjust. Do not intervene with God's wrath by offering her solace and forgiveness, Arya. That would truly kill me. What could this resolution tell the world? All they had to do is try to ask forgiveness as they died and that would wipe out all ills?"

"You wish upon them a dire end?" It was Arya's turn to marvel.

"I do not wish anything on anyone. Let the universe deal with her. Do not go changing my words," Jezebel hissed.

"They have changed you; no amount of meditation could save you," Arya said sounding hateful.

"What did you say?" Jezebel raised her voice to get her husband running.

"Are you two fighting by my mother's door?" he asked. "What is wrong with you?"

"Sorry," Jezebel told him to appease him. "God forbid we disturb her highness' coma."

"I need to know what you meant," she asked Arya, after her husband left.

"Meditation is a way for human beings to kill negative emotions," she reminded her mother. "How is it working in your case, mother, if you still harbour so much resentment?"

"She killed my sister, your maternal aunt, Arya. Do you not feel resentments?"

"She is dying, a slow, agonizing death; is that not punishment enough for you? Do you not feel the slightest inkling of compassion?" Arya turned the question around.

"Not in the least," Jezebel replied sounding consumed with hatred.

"Then kindly stop meditating; you are wasting your time. In your case, it is the false ego that is meditating to delude you into a false sense of goodness." She turned her back to her mother.

Jezebel ran and blocked her daughter's way. Placing a powerful palm on the girl's chest, she pushed her backwards.

"You are not going in; I will start screaming until you explain what you intend to do in there," she said, her eyes flashing anger.

"I intend to ask her the reason she killed me," Arya finally blurted.

"Killed you?" her mother repeated uncomprehending.

"Yes mother, killed me," Arya repeated sadly.

"Whatever do you mean?" Jezebel felt confused.

"You have always suspected that I am your sister Alaya, mom. Signs were all over the place to point to my having come back as her. Under hypnosis, I am her, Jezebel, having picked you to come back and finish this saga of confusion. If I do not speak to her, I will go mad with resentments and fury. I could not live, so please, move."

Jezebel moved away from the door promptly. From the door frame she saw Arya inspect the sick room about her. She then moved a chair from the desk and sat down by her grandmother's bed.

The old woman looked pitifully tiny inside the small bed. She slept on her back with her mouth gaping towards the ceiling. Her eyes, always half-closed, turned up towards heaven already; she looked as though she already roamed both realms simultaneously; too weak to live on the physical plane, and too evil to move to the higher one. She looked stuck in limbo.

"Grandma," Arya called to her.

"My soul," the old lady responded weakly.

"Do you love me?" the grandchild asked.

"More than my life," the old lady said and turned slowly towards the chair.

"Would you tell me something important?"

"I will tell you anything. What is it, Arya?" She sounded so weak.

"Why did you kill my aunt Alaya?" she asked. "I need to know."

The feeble woman, who had fallen months before, breaking not a bone, had sustained a shock which rendered her weak, and frail. The question startled the frail old woman, creating a storm of fear inside her so as to make her eyes spin pitifully inside the wrinkled orbit.

"What do you speak of, child? Who told you about that? Has your mother told you that?"

"No, Grandma. I know." Arya resented fearing for the evil wench's life. "Nobody knows, nobody will know. That is all." She patted the shaking ghost of the hand tenderly.

"Why? Why do you need to know now? I am dying. Could you not let it go?"

"No. I need to know. I am going mad. That is why. You are losing your speech. So please, grandma, tell me. It is not good for you either to keep it bottled up, as that should create untold misery. Dying spirits that leave this earth riddled with guilt go to miserable places of the darkest, possible environments to suffer their lack of meekness at not having repented and asked forgiveness," Arya explained, as she held the brittle woman's hand.

"What do you know about these things?" She refused to confess.

"I know, grandma, that you loosened the beehive. I also know that you rubbed her with the honey of the same hive so the bees attacked her. The boy who hanged himself had given her a pot of honey just seconds before. I also know what you told her. Why did you hate her so? She was a good girl who loved your son with purity. She was a very special girl. That is evil. I need to know the reason."

The old woman cried silent tears. Tears streamed over her face, got stuck inside the cracks of wrinkles on her cheeks.

"She was a witch. Your aunt Alaya mesmerized my son. I told him not to marry her. He, who never refused me, married her against all our wishes. We are peasants, my child. She was a city girl. All perfumed and pampered she was. Wearing these lace bras with matching knickers, a harlot, a harlot," she said hatefully, even near death she refused to release the jealous feelings of bitterness.

"He courted her for four years before she agreed to see him. He loved her beyond love. How could you assume such things? My aunt was a model human. You tortured and ridiculed her, called her names, chipped at her self-confidence, and because she neither hated nor abused you back, you resented her purity and killed her to shatter your son. For this you need to raise awareness, ask forgiveness, before you die," Arya told the failing lady.

"She was special, to be sure. What chance did his sister and I have with the likes of her around? We cooked; he bought her fancy foods from restaurants. We were simply not good enough for his princess."

"So, you killed her?"

"That was a murder that should not have happened. Later, of course, we knew."

"Who are we? Did your daughter know?"

"Of course she knew. She was the mastermind of the whole thing. The time, and mode, was impromptu, but we had discussed ways and means to shoo her away. We stole her jewellery, clothes, pieces of her trousseau, everything. He did not care, but defended her and her family totally. We killed her, we had to kill her," she rambled feverishly.

"I see," Arya said. "Evil spirits cannot abide the light. That explains so much confusion for me, thank you."

"How did you know all these details? Did my daughter tell you?" The old woman grew muddled.

"No, my aunt does not speak. She knows the darkness that lives inside her, and she fears speaking lest it seep through to drown the world."

"May God forgive us; now that we are going to see Him I am very afraid. In the heat of emotions, we had been rendered mad. Madness is where the conscience stops."

"You do not need to be fearful. God has forgiven you already." Arya assured the dying woman.

She looked at the pitiful, little form that lay like a lump of feverish coal in the bed. Wizened and shrunken, her eyes sunken inside the bony crevasses of their sockets, the leathery skin, too loose from lack of water absorption, the mouth, a mask of torture and fear, Arya marvelled at the way the body failed the people that had worshipped it all their lives, so as to believe in the sanctity of its eternal viability.

The woman of her regression who thundered with power; that sheer might that only the most fit in the body possess, disintegrated like parchment paper inside her covering of clay. She looked lost as to any direction.

Her grandmother slept pitifully, mouth gaping still, trying to save what little breath she had left to extend her temporary stay on earth.

"I want to go," she finally said, "I fear leaving, and feel stuck inside this body. Is that not a quite the predicament, my love?" she awoke to ask Arya.

"That is a definite by product of a life spent in the desert of the body."

It shocked Arya that her grandmother, never a listener in her life, listened intently to every word her grandchild now uttered. In this intent listening, there was the most startling power. Her body sat like a log of meekness, as her spirit rose, rose to meet the words in vibrant attention, the now, and its magical power.

"I worked so very hard all my life," she gasped as she spoke, "to leave it all out there." She motioned with a weak hand that shook towards her house. "The houses, furnishings, money, silver, gold jewellery, are all out there for the people who are alive."

"Do you care now what happens to them?" Arya asked.

"I want you to have all my jewellery," she said weaker still.

"Grandmother, I don't like things, see?" Arya showed her that she wore none of it.

She shook her head disgusted by her stupidity, trembling from the anxieties of that unknown beyond.

"Where do we go, Arya?" she asked. "Is it painful?"

"No grandma, it is not painful. When it comes, death is blissfully peaceful, and almost pain free."

"Why do Muslims call death the throes of being stuck, then?"

"There are those who speak of moments of intense pain as the spirit travels the light tunnel. I know nothing about that." Arya informed her truthfully.

"I wish I could undo things. God is merciful beyond our imaginings." She sounded so pure.

"Pray, grandma. You need to pray for forgiveness. Alaya has forgiven you both a long time ago. Believe me," Arya told her grandmother.

"I learned to read the Bible. I taught myself," she smiled like an angel as she told Arya.

"I know. You are a brilliant woman." Alaya loved you very much.

"She did, I know. I loved her very much. It was easy to love your aunt, child. She was an amazing woman, that is the reason my daughter hated her. She could outdo anyone in anything. That was the reason we knew that we were doomed as far as trying to please, or impress him," she said. "Fear is a mighty powerful emotion."

"Fear is at the core of all evil," Arya agreed.

"God curses me for my wickedness." She twisted her mouth in remorse.

"Ask for forgiveness. Do not curse." Arya admonished gently.

"She was such a young woman though, grandma. She should have had a chance at happiness. He loved her very much. Did you not fear your son's misery?"

"We don't believe in love," she said.

"Love is God," Arya told her.

"We are not about God," the old lady said. "We are about survival."

"You still feel the same way?" Arya asked sadly.

"No, obviously; now that the body is useless, we understand that the spirit is what should matter." She actually giggled. "Tell it to a raging, youthful body, though."

"Did you plan her death?" she asked.

"No," she cried softly. "We wished it deeply."

"Wishing anything deeply makes it happen," Arya whispered. "We make our lives strictly with our intentions."

"I am losing the little energy I have to tell you these things, but it does not matter any longer. I have very little time left."

"How do you know that?" her grandchild asked.

"You do, you feel the energy dwindle and ebb away," she stated calmly.

"Are you afraid?"

"No, more tired than fearful. I feel like a prisoner inside this useless body." She fixed the ceiling for a long while.

"How did you know about your aunt?" she asked intensely. "You could tell me, Arya."

"I will not tell you now, grandma, but soon you will know." She got up to leave.

"There will not be soon for us to speak, my child, tell me now," she begged.

"No, there will be another time for us; I know these things," Arya promised. "You have more time left. Use the time to pray and repent, lest you land in a dark place of misery."

"God is merciful," she wished aloud.

"God has nothing to do with your actions, you do. You did the bad deeds; only you can change their outcome," the young woman imparted.

"How can I do that?" She genuinely wanted to find a way to remedy her sinful condition.

"Revisit your past, ask forgiveness for each deed you have committed, imagine that you have been forgiven, pray for compassion, offer your current pains to the skies so as to alleviate the suffering of others. Pray for all those that are suffering today, start from the people you hated in your life, pray for them. Go around the world, pray for all humans. Enlist angels and saints alike to help you atone for your sins, remain inside the suffering body for as long as you can so as to pay for some of the sins you have committed. Pray God to allow you to reach a soft realm of relative peace when your spirit leaves your body. And grandma," Arya said then stopped, thinking the woman dead.

"Yes Arya," she answered softly.

"Imagine a soft place of beautiful colours and sounds. Do not imagine a bad place; the spirit will reach it. The beyond is strictly our making. Evil entities imagine a hell they reach, and pure spirits a heaven they find. The afterlife is what we make it to be with our wishes and intentions. Go on imagining all that you wish to find," she directed.

"Thank you, Arya, come back again."

"We will speak again soon," she promised. "Sleep now, grandma. Do not forget to say your prayers."

The old woman looked comatose in sleep. Her features contorted to give her an appearance of tortured spirits, a terrible mask.

"She is asleep again." Arya returned to the living room to announce.

Jezebel gave her a cross look. Arya made as though she did not see it.

As soon as the old man started dozing off on the chair, opening his eyes with each movement, lest he missed anything, Jezebel gestured goodbye to her husband.

She walked home with the children, as he went inside to sleep in his mother's room.

Forty-Two
THE LAST HOURS OF LIFE

There hovered an ominous cloud over the many children whose parents held their extended family under siege in a suspended bubble so as to appease their own fears. Although they came to visit the home, as they labelled their parents' abode, to sit and ask the same repetitive questions as to medicine taken, and food ingested, with utmost care, things sizzled beneath the amenities with unspoken violence. Nerves rattled their obvious fraying; sustained anxieties over years, erupted in shouting matches, triggered by the silliest infractions. Although the fights started over simple events, these were but a trigger for frayed nerves long over stretched by too much control. While the wives opted to stay away as much as possible; without causing trouble, the different members of the household stuck tighter together as a reaction to their respective families' objections to bow to the traditions their parents imposed.

"Your grandmother is doing very poorly. She has stopped eating altogether," Jezebel announced. "Your father is very disturbed."

"Let us go see them today," Arya suggested. "We will order some food to take over."

The old lady had developed a fancy for store-bought pizza in the last year. They ordered three large pizzas and headed towards the house, finding it dark, and gloomy. Arya went to see her old grandmother. Her father and uncle were at Church assisting holy Mass, as the aunt cooked for her children, and the servant fiddled in the kitchen.

Around everyone else, the old woman acted resentful, as though she were on strike, refusing their presence around her, or whatever they thought they did to appease her loneliness and pain.

"How is it going?" Arya asked.

"Great, Arya, just great," she snapped her answers, sarcastically.

"Are you in pain?"

"Not really."

"Why do you sulk so?" Arya needed to understand.

"I want God to take me already," the old lady ordered.

"He will when He is ready," Arya said and laughed. "Even God has to do your bidding?"

"There is no reason for me to stay. That is all."

"He takes His angels early." Arya did not mean any offence.

"And I am a bad woman." The old woman stated a fact.

"No, that is not what I meant. It is more that you do not really want to go while they can't wait to see Him."

"What?" She sounded a bit angry. "Of course I want to go. I have had enough of this." She gestured towards the bed and her own body as one.

"The oil is not finished." Arya giggled.

"So much oil for nothing, I feel dead already. How does it happen?"

"How does what happen?" Arya did not understand the question.

"The process, you know, Arya. Does it hurt?"

Although having forgiven, the process of her own past death rose before her to anger the girl, refresh hatred, and quake her body.

"There is a story I read. A devout Muslim was asked about this process, said that..." The girl paused. "Do you really want to know?"

"Of course, do tell me, Arya. It would help."

"Well, the sheikh said: God finds a man needing to die, and He sends His angel of death, the most beautiful of all His angels, to bring home the faithful. The angel goes down to the man's room, stands in a corner and asks if the man was ready to go along with him to the Father. The ailing man saw as only the good ones could see, and said, no. He asked him to allow some time to put his earthly affairs in order. The angel went back and informed his boss of the facts. They gave him three months. As God saw the faithful suffer, He again asked His angel to go down and bring home His beloved faithful. God instructed the angel to carry down a handful of heavenly herbs and perfumes. The angel again stood in the corner of the suffering man's room. The ailing man smelled the smell of his heavenly home, and felt a nostalgic feeling of sadness. He opened his eyes promptly to ask the angel to take him along."

The old woman closed her eyes in the middle of the story. Arya resumed the story, unsure of whether her grandmother slept or heard.

"And so?" she asked then.

"So?" Arya said.

"No angel in my room and only food smells in this house."

"Well. That is what they say happens. The faithful are never allowed to suffer," Arya said.

"The wicked ones, what happens to them?" the old woman asked.

"The wicked have to pray for forgiveness of sins. They have to pray fervently, and mean it."

"I do. Nothing happens." She pleaded; her eyes pools of black tears.

"Then, you need to drop all your earthly attachments," Arya instructed. "These weigh the body down, making the spirit dull and heavy, blocking the seeing of the angel and the hearing of God's summoning."

"What earthly attachments? My children resume their lives joyfully, interested in their respective spouses, and my husband, you know the story. He resents my dying for that usurps him of his slave. He is mad, this one."

"These are attachments. Forgive him his weaknesses and bless your children and their spouses. Let them go, grandma. These desires, resentments, will never allow you to fly away. They are your punishments made by you to remain inside the cage of the body," Arya explained.

She, the old woman, nodded her head several times bitterly, missing the subtlety of the younger woman's explanations. Her self-pity had created horrendous psychological time; the ephemeral time the selfish body creates to appease itself with, enlist sympathy, shielding the truth; that crisp, ultimate spiritual truth. Knowing this fact, the grandchild attempted to furtively explain; as clock time forbade long-winded explanations. There was an immediate need for swift explaining, so as to extend a hand of real solutions; lest the old woman fail to fly into the ether due to self-delusion and hate.

Arya sat holding her wrinkled hand sensing the battle raging within her grandmother's body that ebbed to lose precious breath fast. She mulled over the fact that most abusers foresaw themselves as victims.

"Go. I want to sleep," she waved her hand, dismissively.

"Should I call my father and uncles to come see you?" the child suggested.

"No, let them live." She turned her face to the wall.

"You feel the ebb of energy?" the child asked.

"I already feel as though part of a different reality, not all here," she looked confused, spaced.

"Sleep, now," Arya suggested as she got up to leave the sick room. "I will check on you later."

"No, no, no," she motioned with a hand that shook. "Stay, help my body fight. Sing me into this battle. Sing me into the skies."

"I thought you wanted to sleep," Arya said, confused.

"This tiredness is not about sleep, death, death is here. No more time to sleep."

The child suddenly understood that her grandmother wanted her by her side to see her off through the heavens; her body was fighting a losing battle for staying. Panicked and confused, she furtively fumbled inside her mind for a tune that might ease the woman's fears, and help release her spirit.

"Jesus loves me, yes I know, for the Bible tells me so, oh, yes, Jesus loves me, this I know, for the Bible tells me so," she sang as tears streamed down her cheeks.

"I will call your children," she said, running to the dinning room where they ate and visited.

The old lady caught her hand, and shook her head.

"You do not want them?"

"Don't leave me, too late, sing, sing me into heaven," she said haltingly, breathlessly.

"What should I sing?"

"Sing, God let Rima sleep," she asked.

It was an old song that the old woman sang to the child before her sleep. She remembered bits and pieces of the melody, and sang them, for the rest of the melody she made up words.

"Let my grandma sleep, let her surrender to slumber. Let this woman sleep, let sleep take her to realms so sweet, where pain is not, and disease is absent. Go, sweet spirit, run and escape the jailing body, run into the heavens. Soar, and go you powerful one. Let her have mercy in Your arms, oh, Lord and Father, let Your beloved Mother receive her inside the folds of her robes, and appease her fears, those of the body, for she is a pure soul, the spirit of your Father, our beloved God," she sang with all her heart.

"Arya, it will be soon, thank you," she told her.

The old woman rolled her eyes around egging to communicate, hating to leave this earthly realm of habitual suffering, then, she asked for water.

Arya felt a sudden panic. She ran to the kitchen to fetch a cup of cool water, returned to place a few drops on her parched tongue. There lurked a different, foreign energy inside the sick room. Her grandmother saw it, a bit over Arya's head, for she gave it a sweet smile of welcome.

The old woman looked dead already. Arya, fearing her motionless body, approached her gently to stare at her still form.

"Is that you, child?" she muttered.

"Grandma," Arya answered, startled.

"Where is everyone?"

"Should I call them, grandma?"

"No need," she said. "Some privacy for this undignified release is good, good. Hold my hand, and say nothing to anyone."

Arya held the hand tenderly, feeling unusually peaceful.

"Go. Go with God, my dear grandmother. Escape the pains of this body, and rejoice in the strength of the spirit form in which you fly. I know you are here watching me. I feel you here. Just go, you know to come back whenever you like." She bent down to kiss the sweet, sunken, hollow cheek.

The old woman turned her head slightly to look at the grandchild she loved, a look of sadness filled her eyes; she tried to speak but failed, expelled a breath, her last, and stiffened into a death mask of shocked resentment.

Having never been with a dead person before, Arya marvelled at the lack of fear present inside her. She, realizing the need to inform the woman's family of their mother's passing, left the sick room in the direction of the family.

"My grandmother has just died." Arya whispered in her mother's ear.

"Oh, dear God, help us." Her mother shook visibly.

"Uncle," Arya called out to her eldest uncle.

"Yes sweetheart," he said and ran from the living room.

"It is grandmother, uncle. She has just passed away."

He ran towards the room to look to the bed. There was no great change in there; his mother had died slowly over the past months. The eldest of the woman's children bent his form solemnly over the figure that looked peaceful in death, placed his finger on her still neck, checked for the pulse that had stopped beating.

The man closed his mother's eyes, keeping his finger firmly planted on the lids until they were sealed shut, forever.

"That has always been her wish," he said sadly. "I thank God for having fulfilled that wish for her, and me."

Although no sound was made, the other three children, Arya's father included, ran towards their mother's room, to find the girl, and her uncle standing solemnly over their mother's still form.

"What?" Arya's father asked.

Her eyes told him volumes. He ran and hugged the still, warm form of his mother on the bed. His sister came to wrench her brother away, only to do the same thing. Her middle uncle cried from the balcony outside. The sounds that he made would haunt his niece, and others who heard them, for as long as they lived. His were the cries of a child, abandoned, and desperately lost.

Arya informed Edward, who sat speaking joyfully to the Egyptian lady, who packed the remainder of their discarded meal.

"You better go speak to our father," she said. "He is all cut up about this."

"What happened?" the dead woman's husband asked.

"Have you not told her husband?" Jezebel asked her children.

"I don't think anyone has yet," Arya said.

"Grandpa, grandma has just passed away softly and quietly," she said.

He looked stunned, as though the words did not add up to anything he could relate to.

"What do you mean passed away, Arya?" he asked confused.

"Everyone is inside," she said, pointing to the room.

To her great discomfort, he opened the front door and ran out.

"Where do you think you are going? Come right back here," she ordered him back. "Go in and bid your wife goodbye."

"I will be right back," he said as he pushed the button of the lift to escape.

"Grandpa," Arya said pulling at his sleeve. "Get in here, right now. Go in and say goodbye to your mate. You lived with this woman over what, seventy years?"

He ran up the stairs instead. She let him go, leaving the front door open.

"Where is my father?" his son asked her.

"He ran outside. He will return," she informed her uncle.

That was the way she left, helped by the beloved granddaughter she adored, the woman she herself killed for having married her son in that other life.

Forty-Three
THE MOTHER GETS BURIED

Upstairs in the hospital's chapel where the mother lay, yellow with pain and cold with death, things looked and felt surreal. She, the dead woman, looked the surer of things. Her daughter cradled a cheek confused, startled by death of a mother who lived her last breath, fully. The three men looked small, like boys, confused, awaiting a foothold, a place, a dock, to place their lives upon to sail the remainder of their journeys.

Oddly, her old husband shook the worst of them all; fearing his own mortality, as though death angels spoke inside his head taunting him, come, come, come, dare and come over with her. He stared toward the cold box, sitting strangely on the brown wooden table, only to get lost immediately in his own head of fear, and memories.

He shed not a tear. Stone cold he stared, and crestfallen he sat; only the pale yellow of his skin showed his state of shock.

His daughter got up from her chair by her second brother, went over to throw a look to the form of her mother dispassionately.

"She is tough, this woman," Eddy told his sister.

"It is her faith. She is extremely pious," Arya's father proclaimed reverently.

"What faith? Is your father getting dotty in the head?" Jezebel asked Arya, who sat calmly watching the scene as though from Dante's Inferno.

"We must not say things like that, mother. We are getting worse than she is," Arya hushed her mother.

"God forbid someone says the truth in this family," Jezebel exclaimed.

"That is not our problem, though." Arya insisted on not gossiping.

Her father gave her a stern stare which bespoke of deep aversion to the disrespect they showed the body of his mother.

"We come before you, Lord, to ask forgiveness of sins, and the committing of this woman's spirit back into Your keeping. We ask You to keep her safe in Your blessed abode, as we are assured of Your everlasting love to all those who believe in You. She has been a dutiful mother and wife, daughter and grandmother. Our dear departed was a precious person who has jealously kept Your covenant, acquiring a multitude of Your blessings, receiving many graces. In Your keep we are confident she shall find a blessed and peaceful rest," the minister prayed over the casket.

319

Her children wiped tears that rolled of their own volition. The service over, they went to where she lay, to say private words of the most touching. Arya's father bent low to plant the last kiss on his mother's cheek, kissed her hand, straightened up, and left her.

He ran towards Jezebel, who held him tightly.

"Here, here honey, she is fine with God now. He has taken her pains away," she said, her heart broken for him.

Outside, in their different black cars, they were driven back to the empty house that would never brim with life again.

They ate quietly, if sadly, and wiped wayward droplets of tears away from eyes that forgot to remember the shame taught about the showing of emotions.

People started dropping in soon after, as village compatriots read the papers that announced her death.

These showed an insatiable appetite for details concerning her last words, days, weeks, and circumstances surrounding her death.

"Dad sure needs to talk. I have never heard him speak so much," Arya told her mother.

"It is nerves," Jezebel said. "It helps to speak of the beloved dead."

Coffee, black to share the bitterness of death with the family, was served non stop, and the cups collected, only to offer more. Droves of people came, sat, shared, and left when others arrived so as to make way. Such were the laws of the land concerning death.

"May you take the remainder of her days," they said before they left.

"What remainder?" Jezebel asked silently. "She left nothing to anyone."

Arya gave her mother a painful nudge in the ribs to make her squeal in pain. She feared the family hearing such remarks and creating a scene.

"Stop talking," she smiled. "Your joy is ever so apparent. Do not confirm their suspicions."

"Nothing to either confirm or deny; this is life," Jezebel said. "When one dies at ninety-five, it is expected. That is the entirety of man's lifespan."

"Fine, thank you. Now, go help with coffee, and speak to nobody unless I am around." Arya pushed her mother towards the kitchen.

They worked silently in the kitchen. Womenfolk from the village had brought down fresh vegetables, green olives, and cheeses for the family. All this they put away for the coming week. Some of the neighbours in the city had made foods for the family's immediate needs.

"It is exciting," Eddy said, as he checked the food.

"Hush, and go away. Stop munching as though it is a cocktail party." Jezebel shooed her son away.

"Sure, mother. I am hungry, though."

"Go." She handed him a piece of cake and pushed him out.

"What are you going to wear?" second brother's wife asked Jezebel.

"A black suit, of course," Jezebel replied, finding the question strange.

"Are the children going to attend the service?" she asked Jezebel.

"Of course," Arya replied for her mother.

"I am sleeping here," her husband informed his family.

"Sure. We will see you tomorrow, then," Jezebel replied.

She knew he would sleep in her bed. That was his way of bidding his long childhood farewell.

She kissed him at the door, and promised to see him first thing in the morning.

"I will bring everyone breakfast," she promised.

"Thank you so much, we appreciate that," he said, distant.

At her home, Jezebel wished her children would turn in so they could face the difficult week ahead. However, they were too excited for sleep. Trying but failing to sleep, she tossed in her bed until, desperate with nerves, she got up and made herself a pot of coffee.

Jezebel went back to her room to get ready for the day. Clutching her church clothes inside an overnight bag, she proceeded to leave the house for the baker to buy the family's breakfast.

They had been awake for a long while, she could see. She made mint tea and settled everyone for a breakfast of spiced pies, and cheese torts. They looked stunned to her, lost still; the night having added burdens to their hearts rather than alleviating grief.

"How is everyone?" she asked.

"Fine, fine, Jezebel," they answered in unison.

They ate fast and got up quickly. Their mother awaited them at the hospital, from where they would escort her to her final abode, final rest. The urgency of their task made them edgy.

"Let everyone go in his assigned vehicle," the middle brother issued the order.

He had somehow appropriated the seat of power, wrenched away in sheer violence.

"Keep to your respective cars after the service. We do not want to lose anyone. Do you hear, Eddy?" second uncle shrieked.

"Yes, uncle," Edward sounded slighted by the order, "I am hardly going to get lost."

"It will not look good." The father seconded his brother's ideas so as to ease matters.

"Let us go, then." Their sister had to place a word in.

They cried unabashedly at the hospital as they wheeled their mother's body out. Their sobbing shattered the hearts of technicians and patients alike. The controlled brood of industrialists who had so long sat on their emotions allowed the eruptions then. Tears long suppressed exploded with power. Old men, in their seventies carried on so over the death of their mother, enough to break the heart of those strangers that watched them.

They escorted her through the hospital, through the lifts, down to the basement of the church, into the car decorated with the wreaths of white blooms they had ordered lovingly. Once settled, they went back to their own vehicles to cry some more. They marched in a motorcade. The cousins followed in their private vehicles, all the way to church that sat smack in the middle of the city.

"That is your last ride, ever," Jezebel's husband bemoaned.

"She hated riding in cars, dad. That she will not miss," Edward told his father.

Getting kicked in the side by his sister's bony elbow brought forth a squeal of pain from the young man, whose thoughtless remarks bespoke of a mind that was not conditioned. Jezebel felt a giggle rise inside her chest for some odd reason, one she tried hard to swallow, to barely succeed.

"I am getting the giggles," Arya whispered.

"Do not look my way, then," her mother suggested.

People sat in pews leaving the three first rows for the family and cousins. Everyone wore black. They sat each next to his wife and children, awaiting the tragic ending of the century-long life.

A woman struck the organ to startle them into a sudden bout of fear. Music thundered through the ancient church churning their stomachs, and their hearts into pain.

A choir dressed in white appeared from the back walls of the sacristy shrieking violently in threatening tones how God was their shepherd, and how they shall never want.

Arya placed her hand on her father's shoulder and pressed her love hard into his skin.

He turned towards her pleadingly and cried openly, uncaring as to being seen and judged.

That was a first, Arya thought, and how very liberating it should prove.

"She is gone," he muttered in disbelief.

"Yes, father. She is gone."

"What a shame. I never thought she would ever leave us," he said.

"I know, father. None of us ever did either. She looked invincible," she replied.

"She worked so hard," he groaned, "so very hard."

"Life, father, is about dying," Arya spoke tenderly. "To be shocked by death is madness."

"If only I knew where she is now. You look at her, and she is like a wax dummy. Where do we go after we die, child? Are we just gone, or is there another place?" It was odd to hear him even venture into such deep topics.

Arya grew sullen with nerves. She had attempted numerous times to explain, read, and speak of spirits to him, to no avail. Father had refused to enter into discussions concerning the spirit.

"Oh, well. Obviously," the girl groaned, "as spirits are energy, they go back into the universe, where all is energy. Where else would energy go, dad?"

She understood that he dreaded his own mortality, and that her answer lacked tangibility: He obviously needed a more concrete answer, a place, a space, a heaven replete with angels, a huge entity called God, and harps.

His high colouring pained her. How she wished she could say something that made sense to him. To her great sadness, she could not. The answer to life was in death, and the answer of death was in life itself. Whatever is born shall eventually die. That stood as the most basic of all deductions. Yet, humans lived, and hoped for eternal living.

"Death should be a cursory course taught in primary schools. They teach children about everything except the most crucial lesson; the way to die in dignity and lack of fear," Arya thought.

Forty-Four
THE OLD MAN DIES SIMPLY, QUIETLY

Her grandfather had stopped speaking. From the moment his wife died he spoke not a word. He sat stooped with fear and anger, and stared at his shoes. He never once addressed his children, or the many people who came to console him. The old man nodded absently, and his gaze remained fixed on the ground.

"Father is in shock," Arya's father proclaimed.

"It must not be easy losing a lifetime mate," Arya said.

Like a toddler lost in a marketplace, the man wondered, wondered, wondered confused. He rejected flatly all efforts to comfort and appease his fears.

On Wednesday of the fourth week, his wife dead for a mere three weeks, and two days, he awoke in a state of frantic fear.

"Call my daughter," he asked his servant. "Tell her to bring a doctor. I feel very sick."

They rushed with the doctor to the house by the huge tree, to find him shaking like a leaf in the fall and just as yellow.

A preliminary test showed that his blood sugar level was very low. They mixed sugar with water and fed it to him. A second test showed that his sugar level had risen to a normal reading. The doctor checked his blood pressure announcing that it was perfect.

"He is fine now. He should be fine," the doctor assured the daughter.

"You are fine now," his daughter said. "Get up and watch some television."

"Leave me be," he said weakly. "I feel tired. I shall rest a bit on my bed."

"Thank you so much. We are sorry to have bothered you so early in the morning," she told the doctor at the door of the sick room.

"It is fine. He will be fine now." He shook the woman's hand.

Suddenly, a loud snorting sound made the pair at the door turn around to check the occupant of the bed. The man opened his mouth, snored once more, and stiffened into a mask of yellow death.

Both doctor and daughter ran to the old man's side.

"He is dead," the doctor announced, deeply embarrassed.

"What do you mean?" the daughter shrieked in shock. "You have just said he was fine. How could you get things that wrong?"

"Listen," the doctor answered sheepishly, "when God wants a soul, he just takes it. He does not ask our permission. His time had just run out."

He left quickly without saying another word. He neither asked for his consultation fee, nor did they offer it; such was his state of embarrassment.

She called her middle brother.

"You are not going to believe this," his sister said into the receiver.

"What?" The man asked, already stretched beyond human endurance.

"He is dead," she said shocked still. "Our father is dead."

"No," he answered groggily, "just like that?"

"I am telling you. One minute he was speaking to me, the second minute he was dead," she repeated, sounding hysterically calm.

The phone rang loudly, shrilly at Jezebel's house. The family, exhausted by the recent events, had overslept. Arya ran to answer it. She heard a wail from her aunt.

"Your grandfather has just passed away. Awaken your father."

Arya stood transfixed, unable to move.

"What is going on?" her father asked from the hallway.

Arya stared his way fearing for his heart.

"What is it, Arya?" he asked, sounding fearful.

"It is granddad," the child simply said.

"At the hospital again?" her father asked.

"I am afraid so, dad. You must really take it easy. It is very frightening what is going on."

"Well, we have all anticipated this." He turned to change his clothes.

"What happened?" Jezebel inquired, already shattered.

"He is dead, mom. I did not tell him." Arya could not cry any longer.

"Well done. Now, he will be prepared a bit."

"What did your aunt say?" He struggled with his socks.

"She said an ambulance came to take him to the hospital. My uncle is on his way to the house. They want you at the house."

"Why at the house?"

"That is what she said." Araya could not look her father's way.

Her father, having noted the shifting of his daughter's stare, suddenly stopped getting dressed. The man sat heavily on the edge of the couch, back bent, as though he had heard another message.

"He is dead, right, Arya?" the poor man asked not wanting to hear the answer.

"Yes father, he is dead." She still did not look into his eyes.

When she did steal a glimpse his way, however, his eyes had changed instantly; fear made them seem rounded, haunted.

Jezebel froze in place. Nobody moved towards the couch where the son who had lost both his parents within the span of a month, slumped pitifully.

"So, I am an orphan now," he announced.

A smile of the most untimely appeared on all their faces.

"What is so funny?" their father wanted to know.

"It is not about you, father. Can't you honour the dead man for one second?" the boy asked.

"You were saying, Arya?" He needed to speak.

"Father, an orphan is a young child. A child of three or four years of age is an orphan, dad, not men in their sixties and seventies. It is ridiculous, dad. You must see things as they really stand."

"No, any person that loses both his parents is an orphan." He tied his shoe laces meticulously as he argued.

"They are infants," Arya thought.

"They had never been allowed to grow up, or separate. Technically, that makes them infants, and as technically, they are, and would feel like orphans," Jezebel thought, saddened.

"Go get dressed." His tone sounded harsh.

"Yes." Jezebel disappeared inside their room.

"I don't know what to say to comfort you," Arya said and hugged her father's neck tenderly.

"I know, I know. They were very old, but they were still my parents, and you know, the longer they lived, the more I relied on their presence, believing in their immortality." A newfound lucidity walked in right then.

They left. He kissed his children tenderly. They looked startled by the change. Usually a goodbye kiss would be like jumping to the stars. It was simply not allowed in the stoic family.

"He looks fearful," Eddy whispered to his sister.

"Of course he is afraid. His entire support system has just crumbled. He still has his brothers and sister, though."

"Do not bet on it," Eddy sounded spiteful. "They, too, shall crumble. A crumbled mass cannot support itself, let alone other masses."

"What are you talking about, Eddy?" Arya grew impatient with her brother's rambling.

"I am saying that control could never lead to harmony. That is what I am saying, Arya."

Now that the family knew the drill of burial, they contacted the same funeral home, told the overseer to arrange for precisely the same arrangements as they had for their mother earlier in the month.

"You have lost your father as well?" The manager could not believe his luck.

The same minister, choir, friends and relatives conducted the same ritual for the husband of the woman who had just died earlier in the month.

The old man's funeral proved to be shattering. An inexpressible sense of acute grief hovered over all their heads, the sad state over the father's death; he had so hated dying that the fear managed to manifest so as to fulfil his wishes.

"Should we go home?" Arya's father asked his wife. "I am exhausted."

At their house, he asked her if she could cook something substantial for them.

"I am hungry," he admitted apologetically, "if you could cook something substantial, otherwise we order."

They had eaten nothing but fast food for the last six weeks.

"What are you hungry for?" she asked him tenderly.

"Some of your amazing grape leaves," he said.

"Yes mom, and yogurt salad," the children seconded excited.

Jezebel called the butcher asking him to send the meat over, as she started coring the squash that would accompany the steaks and stuffed grape leaves in the pot.

"Go take a shower, and a rest," she told him.

"I am way too tired for a bath. I will sleep some," he said and wobbled through their room.

No sooner had his back turned to her than he returned to give her a warm, long hug. It was odd, as her husband had not demonstrated his love this openly, ever.

"Are you okay?" she asked him fearfully.

"I am fine, don't worry," he said, as he walked back to their room for his nap.

"Thank you for everything, my love," he muttered tenderly enough to break her heart.

Forty-Five
AN ANGEL IS FOUND

It was when she stuck the corer inside that first yellow vegetable, while all the others stared softly towards her form, that the woman felt a surge of energy rise within her, to blind her with its power. So powerful, so pure, that pure light, that it came to blind her eyes with its softness.

It was then that she fell utterly and madly in love with him. Not that she had not loved him before, she had; what she felt at that moment, however, was the pure kind of love that comes with seeing another, truly seeing that other person as though for the first time, with the eyes of the spirit. Knowledge arrived clear, crisp and unpolluted by the body's jealousy, its control.

The events of their lives assumed different decoders to her mind at the moment that revealed the utter brilliance of her husband's depth. He had obviously understood what lacked within their marriage, had attempted to please his wife and children minus the expression, understanding that his mother could never tolerate it.

Worse still, it became obvious to Jezebel that her husband had suffered the most due to his parents' lack of expressing love and did the same to his wife and children, having learned the isolating behaviour.

Suddenly the couple ceased to be two bodies but one. There, no division, no greed, nothing could happen but compassion. His parents stopped being his alone, but theirs, and in that state of shared oneness, Jezebel understood how perfect they were, how fearful, and correct.

It was the wife's spirit that saw the man, alongside whom she had spent all her youth, as though for the first time. His deceit gone, he shone with an orange and saffron light. So ecstatic her soul grew that fireworks exploded within the woman's abdomen to delight and thrill her. It was too intense a feeling, however, which got translated by her nervous system into edginess; as though it would soon short-circuit to incinerate her into oblivion.

"What was that?" she asked herself, wanting to trace the moment of discovery.

The feeling of joy had come from her spirit recognizing the pure man, not through one instance, but suddenly; the accumulation of many such events had arrived to show the greatness of the man's being.

"He is a being of light," she thought.

"Why have I not seen it before?" she asked abashedly ashamed.

"He did not want you to see it. No matter what the state of his parents, he wanted them accepted and protected at all cost," some spirit said inside her mind.

"From me?" she asked, already knowing the answer.

As surely as the recognition happened, so did the stupidities of Jezebel's past blindness. Seeing partially that he covered for all the sins his family committed, the woman had got stuck inside her own mind so as to cancel the possibility of his greatness. Now, however, as she saw him naked, without the walls that vied to shield him away from her sight, she not only saw how strong he was but also, how saintly, and wise.

"He knew them all along." She felt a deep sense of shame at having so harassed him.

No sooner had this block been removed, that another facet to his character clarified to her sight so as to annihilate her with her own shortcomings in sheer embarrassment.

"He was caught in the middle between me and his parents to suffer both our wrath equally, never complaining, never caring as to his own safety. He so loved us both, equally, and fairly. He probably defended me with them as he defended them with me."

"Would the heavens send the marked, a lesser man than an angel?" Sycamore said.

"Who is that?" she asked.

"I am your daughter's guide," Sycamore said. "See, what an angel the heavens sent the both of you?" she asked proudly.

Jezebel cried hot tears of shame upon remembering her father. She and Alaya had so blamed him for the union he stuck them into, fearing his senility at that time.

"You should see where your father decided to land me," Alaya had told all her sisters, "at the house next door to hell's own door."

"What with the parents and siblings, though? What was that all about?" she asked the tree.

"That is the bridge of great inequities. It is not easy to cross from this earth to the higher planes of great beatitudes. That step takes courage and unflinching faith. The bridge is to love those that hurt you. He did knowingly. Do not underestimate the spirit of the man." That knowing shocked Jezebel.

"I feel horrible, just horrible. Years of studying to realise this fact; my sister and I were deluded in our knowledge?"

"That is the wrong conclusion to draw," Sycamore said. "Years of searching had gotten you here, to see him, see your failings, and remedy. That was your reward, not your punishment."

"That is not right," Jezebel objected. "Surely, the burden of righting their control, and abuse should not fall upon my sister's shoulders and mine as they jumped into death, and the beyond Scot free."

"They are not jumping into any sky to run freely," Sycamore corrected, "the universe has a reckoning with the pair of them that has nothing to do with you. They will have their own karma to pay. That is not your problem any longer. Your duty is to see that these two people were placed in your path to teach you a difficult lesson in obeying the will of the universe, shed a light onto your false personality so as to see it, fix, and get saved. As such, you need to be grateful for their lives, the teachings they imparted; for they will pay for their faults regarding your suffering." Sycamore taught.

That was the narrowest part of that bridge, Jezebel understood. From then on she needed to hold Arya's hand and brave the ascent over the gulf of hate, and greed, walk bravely with their sight focused on the divine so as to arrive in forgiving grace.

She attacked the cooking with a sense of depth, she had never felt before. It felt as if her cooking for her husband had suddenly turned into an act of worship, her kitchen suddenly turned into a temple of devotion.

"He worked for us with this kind of devotion," she thought. "I have even begrudged him his toil thinking it a way of escaping from being at home with us."

She left her kitchen to find Arya sleeping on her back writing in her journal.

"What are you doing?" she asked, somewhat dazed.

"What do you want?" the teen asked.

"I need you to come by sit with me," Jezebel asked her.

"I am not rolling grape leaves, mom. That is too masochistic for me," Arya proclaimed laughing.

"Listen, listen, in the kitchen. You do not have to help, but you do have to speak to me. I am freaking out."

Feeling her mother's urgency, the young woman ran to sit in the kitchen. She watched her mother attacking the insides of a poor vegetable as though hate were her sole aim; she wanted the vegetable released of its insides like a butcher wrenching the entrails of a animal that had bit it.

"Your precious Sycamore had just imparted the most shocking of truths," Jezebel told her daughter.

Arya listened intently if disbelievingly. It was like Sycamore to impart knowledge if she were to consider her charge blocking her voice.

"What did she say?" Arya asked.

"She said that your father had been sent to us, you and me, because he was the angel that would make us arrive," she said.

"I have known that," Arya said showing relief.

"Also," Jezebel resumed, "his parents were to have been the bridge of inequity."

"How do you mean?" Arya asked confused.

"Meaning, Arya, we need to stop hiding things from one another," her mother said. "As allies, and fellow travellers on that bridge, you and I need to start speaking truthfully to survive that ascent, and avoid falling inside the crevasses of the valley."

"I thought we have always done that," her daughter told her.

"I need to know all that the therapist unearthed of your past with the angel man. There could be clues there that could help us."

"Fine," Arya agreed, somewhat relieved. "Do we tell him also?"

"I need to hear the tapes he made first. We will decide later what to do about your father," Jezebel explained.

"Fine," she said. "I have the tapes in my room. You are welcome to hear them. I caution you, though. They could be disturbing for you."

"Disturbing, in what way?" Jezebel asked fearing to hear the answer.

"I was madly in love with him, it seems," Arya said blushing. "Don't you remember that?"

"No, mom, I have no detailed recall of anything." She turned to leave.

"Do you still love him this way?" Jezebel froze in anticipation of the answer.

"Yuck no, he is my father. That last life is not real to me. Hearing the tapes felt like listening to someone else's story."

"Where is the danger then?" the mother needed to understand.

"No danger," she said, "unless you wanted to hold my last life against me."

Jezebel stated, "I hope that I am more intelligent than that."

"You are," Arya said. "Your wisdom baffles me."

She came and held her mother, who quickly dropped the poor squash under siege, to encircle her daughter's waist in her arms tenderly.

"Whenever you are ready," Arya informed her. "I will be in my room."

She finished an hour later, placed the pot on the stove, washed her hands and ran to check on her husband. He slept on his back, as if on the cross. His arms were extended away from his body, and his mouth twisted like the Roman soldier had just removed the spear from his side.

Inside her room, Jezebel found her daughter still writing furiously in her diary.

"What do you write?"

332

"I am writing a novel, mom,"

"Is it your autobiography?"

"No, it will be a work of fiction. It might as well have been a fictional life."

"I bet it will be a good book," Jezebel said, thrilled at the prospect.

The mother had always felt that her children lacked direction. She had attributed the fact to their having been pushed to achieve by the family, and the many pressures of being compared to other children in the village who had achieved so much career successes.

"You have always been good at writing," she told her.

"Thank you, sweet Jezebel," Arya smiled. "It means so much to hear you say that."

"Why do you insist on calling me be my Christian name?" she asked.

"Your being my youngest sister has always been one of my real memories of that other, past life," Arya admitted for the first time.

"Is your book about that last life?" her mother asked.

"My book is about many other things besides that," she imparted sweetly.

"Why, why do you need to write?"

"Because it is my destiny," Arya informed her mother. "In my past life as your sister Alaya, as I walked the beach, I had distinctly heard my destiny described to me. 'You are going to be a great universal writer,' the voice had said.'"

"How old were you when you heard that voice?" Jezebel asked.

"I was four years old," Arya told her mother.

"How do you know that?"

"I know because I had answered that voice by saying that I was four-years of age and asked: What do I know of the universe to write for it?" she giggled softly.

"Speak of a loud destiny." Jezebel marvelled amazed.

"So, having cut my last life short by not minding my destiny, it has returned to claim its stake now," Arya said.

"Could we listen to the tape now?" Jezebel could not wait any longer.

"Sure," Arya replied and got off the bed to play the tape recorder, "if my father were to awaken, what then?"

"Do not worry, it will be up to me to deal with things," Jezebel assured her.

They heard an hour's worth of taping. It was a horrendous ordeal to share with the young daughter who suffered from that past life reliving.

"That is horrendous," Jezebel wiped her tears, "I had no idea."

"It is okay, I don't remember it, you know. It has relieved me, somehow. I feel lighter, more positive, because of it."

"How you loved him," her mother concluded.

"I still do," Arya explained.

"We are so lucky to have him in our lives," Jezebel said hugging her daughter.

"We sure are," Arya affirmed.

He awoke demanding food. The smells that wafted through the place had tweaked his appetite. They went into the kitchen and attacked the pot.

"My mother is the best cook, ever," Eddy proclaimed solemnly.

"All sons think that of their mothers," Jezebel deflected the praise.

"You are not my mother, and I think that," her husband announced.

"You are just sweet." She kissed his forehead.

"I love you, Jezebel," he said.

"Oh, yuck," both children said, running away, leaving the parents to tackle the cleaning up.

The next day was the open house at the church hall for all the people that did not make their father's funeral to come and offer their condolences. A catering company hired to prepare and serve coffee, and cold drinks was to take the load off the women. It was the matter of sitting for hours on end on the hard wooden chairs that concerned Jezebel. The first instance had taxed their backs, and knees.

"You do not have to be there all day," he said worried for her. "Come for the afternoon session."

"No, it is fine." She refused his kind offer. "Listen, what now? What would they do with the house and furnishings?" she asked.

"I have no idea, and I don't care. Nobody has said anything to me," he said nervously. "Why do you ask?"

"No reason, just curiosity," she told him truthfully.

"We have not had a vacation in years." Eddy returned to complain.

"We will go anywhere you want, soon," he promised. "Let us finish first with all that needs doing."

Forty-Six
JEZEBEL AND FAMILY IN PORTUGAL

Truth be told, Portugal would have been the last country on the globe Jezebel wished to visit. Of all her dreams and aspirations, Japan, China, Brazil, among other countries, Portugal was never on her wish list of countries to visit. Seeing, however, how her children insisted on Club Med, and how everything else was taken, Portugal became the destination of necessity.

They landed at Faro Airport just before noon on the 25th of August, Jezebel's birthday. She only noticed the fact when she saw the date over the luggage collection belt.

"It is my birthday today," she told her husband.

"And so it is," he agreed, "happy birthday."

"Have you planned it this way?" she asked.

"Of course, when did I ever forget your birthday?" he asked, pulling a suitcase off the luggage belt.

She lowered her gaze sadly thinking it unseemly to burden the man with trite matters when he was distraught with his grief.

"Let's go," he commanded.

They marched towards the doors behind him when suddenly Jezebel realised that she had no idea where she was or where she was going.

"I should learn to ask more questions," she thought.

"Where are we going?" she asked him.

"Club Med is an hour's drive due north. That is all I know."

He hailed a cab, handed the driver a slip of paper with the address; the man nodded and drove. The place looked very much like their country, with a different style of building. Theirs were more white, somehow, less serious. The landscape was reminiscent of all Mediterranean countries; that made her feel less alienated, less fearful, more prone to relaxing.

As their cab approached the site, the sea peeked out its beloved head from behind the land to welcome them.

"Ah, look, what a marvellous colour the sea has; it is green, aquamarine green," Arya shouted excited. "I like it here."

She had always enjoyed a deep connection with the sea, they all knew, the very reason her father opted to pick a seaside location for their annual week together. Ever since her childhood, Arya had begged her parents to go to the sea.

335

The site of their camp was picked for its sheer beauty as always. Tucked away from the village, the hotel perched over a rocky elevation, behind which the sea stretched into infinity. All around the place, manicured lawns of the greenest turf, golf grounds, tennis courts, back riding grounds, walking paths, surrounded the hotel. They walked into the clean, aired-out place to be welcomed by a staff that showed them to their rooms. These were bungalows on the main first floor, each with a private terrace, to its back.

"Lunch is served until two-thirty in the main dining room, and the terrace," the sweet young woman said as she handed them a map of the premises.

"How do we get there?" the husband asked.

"Go down to the basement, sir, and come up from the gym area onto the other side. If you were to ask, they will direct you right to the restaurants," she said.

"Let us go eat," Eddy suggested.

"Let us go," everyone cheered at the prospect of hot food.

Once in the main internal courtyard, a most baffling sight opened to their vision to enthral. The restaurants sat over the sea, inside different gardens that opened one onto the other magically. People milled about on different terraces which umbrellas flapped in the sea breeze, in terraced rows went all the way to the swimming pool. Blooming acacia, almond, and pecan trees sheltering some of the guests, while others sat among the blooming bushes, and raised gardens. The overall effect was dazzling in its beauty.

They went up two flights of stairs, crossed the terrace where people looked up to check them as newcomers, and entered the vast dining room in the middle of which tables covered the majority of the space. There were fish counters with an incredible assortment of seafood. Cooks stood behind their stalls, waiting and eager to dish out their concoctions with a smile of pride. There were pasta bars, salad ones, bread and antipasto bars, the fruit bars, and finally, soup and cake bars.

They selected the foods of their choice and went out onto the terraces to find a vacant table to occupy. The man had picked relishes and braised vegetables for starters, while the women picked cooked salads and legumes for theirs.

"It is funny," Edward told his father, "even foods are gender-oriented."

When the men went back inside for their main course, Arya kicked her mother from under the table.

"What?" Jezebel asked.

"Don't look back," she admonished, "the man behind you is checking me out."

"Since when does that faze you?" Jezebel was surprised at the remark.

"If you were to look behind you, you would understand that since this moment my life is doomed," Arya said, flushed beet red.

Completely amazed by the newfound boldness concerning the daughter that never cared to be a young woman, Jezebel tried to turn to check the phenomenal manifestation, Arya forbade her with a frown and a hand.

"Please, do not turn, mom. This man has gone into my soul," she said. "For him to notice that I told you would mortify us both."

"What is going on, Arya, how could this happen?" Jezebel asked.

"He is gorgeous, mom. He has the most startling green eyes, dark long lashes, and a pleasant smile that wrenched my heart away."

"Do not have, I beg you, a vacation tryst. These are shattering."

"Do I look like a tryst's type, Jezebel, shame on you; how little do we know one another." Arya paled perceptibly.

"I know, you are not, honey. A mother cannot help but fear for her children. I am confident that you would never submit to stupid activities."

"I would not, so relax," Arya said.

"Let us go get our food," Jezebel got up slowly.

Arya followed her inside the restaurant, and, when they came back, the man had already left.

"That is a strange spot to visit alone; these places are mostly for families," Jezebel remarked.

"Did you see him?" Arya wanted to share.

"I did. He is a good-looking man," her mother approved. "Surely, he has a wife tucked in one of the bungalows behind us, though."

"Thank you for making me miserable," Arya responded heavily.

They went back to their rooms for a rest. Their journey having been long and tiring had managed to shatter. The children shared the bungalow beside their own.

"What are your plans for tonight?" their father asked.

"Dinner with you two, then we hit the town," Edward answered.

"Good, stay together, and call us if you need help; call us anyway," he added.

Dinner was a startling affair as well. They offered a cocktail hour with entertainment, after which people walked on the beach under the moon.

They kissed the children goodbye, held hands and walked by the swimming pool towards the long stairs that wound their way up, sheltering under much vegetation, towards a strange summit which hid the sea behind it. They scaled the height, braving ancients stairs made from that rocky elevation so as to land on the reverse side all the way on the seashore. Once in a clearing, with the sea vista opened to their sight, they both stood in reverence.

The setting sun dipped inside the horizon bathing everything in the most mesmerizing gold. Rocky Mountains and hills which feet dug inside the sand of that shore firmly, imparting such intimacy; confident of their ownership, willing to share but not impart to the visitors. The intimacy of that union screamed the oneness few people managed. These rocks had changed from red right before their very eyes, to deep magenta, yellow, then orange.

"Is that amazing?" he asked.

"That is," Jezebel responded, breathless with the beauty.

People walked in pairs, glowing with the golden sand, the golden rocks, and golden sun. They walked barefoot on the edge of the shore. Tiny shelled creatures came up with the tide towards the sand to be entangled with their feet. Miles upon miles that shore extended all around the people so as to seem endless, boundless. Cafés served coffee and fruits, figs and grapes, the produce of the villages nearby. The pair entered a shed-like formation that straddled the shore, and sat down. He ordered a beer and shared it with his wife.

"Coffee?" he asked.

"No, I am fine, maybe a bottle of chilled water," she asked calmly.

She stared into the vast blue to feel a shift of consciousness, and remain with it. Her eyes half-closed, she stared and kept her thoughts at bay. There was to be no struggle, not a wave, not a ripple to disturb the magic. There, the entire universe rushed to heal her. The sadness and fears of the past months evaporated in that single moment of joyous presence. There, before the red rocks, and behind the sea, in the midst of a bustling café of no real worth to anyone, sitting across the man she had married for no specific reason, had resented for specific numerous ones, the world was healed finally for her.

"That is my graduation." The thought crossed her clear sky.

He knew when she shifted and stayed away. That was one of his powers, she noted. He also turned as to see what dazzled her. She did not know if he could see the luminous quality of the reds, bricks, and gold. She suspected that he did not as yet scc. His eyes were not clear yet, but also knew, that they will soon be.

A flock of seagulls shrieked and crossed her field of vision, making her smile. She followed their course with her sight until they started jumping over the waves for dinner.

The skies started changing with the sun, the more that dipped, the more its rays beaming around the people deepened, making the sky look violet, then blue, then dark grey. It was then that tiny dots of light clarified inside the translucent crystal firmament.

"I have lived inside my head for the last year," Jezebel thought.

When the black deepened and constellations appeared to dance for their Maker, a moon came up from behind the rocks to check the scene. It sat over their heads threatening to crush them.

"Did you see the moon?" the man asked.

"I saw the moon," she confirmed.

He got up to pay their tab. They walked silent side by side, their feet shuffling the sand that made a sound with each step they took. He never touched her. She felt that he had entered her spirit, and thrilled the miracle. He neither spoke about the house he would buy her so as to apologize for past mistakes, nor did she feel the need to ask him how things worked, or whether he thought the universe a fair place. They simply walked inside that silence that spoke volumes of the journey they shared, the trials they braved, the joys they spun, and the woes they together shunned. There inside that one silence, one person remained, not two. That one person strolled all their decades, which faded into a blur of fortitude and steadfast resolve to remain one with the other. They remained despite the turmoil and machinations that could and should have broken mightier humans. That endurance created a base, a foundation, a history which stilled fears and forbade nonsense.

"If you were to remain with a problem," he now said, "it too would dissipate."

"How could it dissipate just because we remained?"

"It does evaporate," he said. "Either that, or you dissipate; either way the problem is solved. That had always been my way to look at glitches."

She knew that he was explaining the strife they received as a couple on the hands of his family. A wave of pain rose to shoo the soft stillness away out of habit, and accumulated grief.

"It should not be that way," she said, instead.

"Of course it should not be that way," he agreed.

"Why was it, then?" she asked.

"Who knows?" he mused.

"Could you not have deflected the situation?"

"No," he said. "I tried."

"So, we get old and wither instead?"

"Who knows? To outguess God is a sin. The question is: did we learn, grow, from all the grief? That was the design, the scheme that we should come and learn."

"We have," Jezebel admitted. "Was the lesson worth all the grief?"

"That is for you to figure out. Today, I know that I am that much richer for it. I feel that I made a leap of faith that got me out of a hole, I suspect, that tortured me many lives. How about you, what did you gain?"

"I feel that I paid exorbitant dues to give my sister's life, my own, my daughter's suffering for this one lesson. It better be good."

"What does your daughter have to do with this?"

"Did I say my daughter?" she asked.

"You did," he said.

As they had arrived at a flat rock, his wife sat down. He could not see the yellow that rose to invade her earlier pink.

"What do you mean?" he asked firmly.

"I don't remember having said my daughter," she said opting for an escape.

"You did, though. What are you hiding?" he demanded to know.

"It is not the time," she felt like crying for having made the mistake.

"It is always time for the truth. I have lived with you long enough to understand your moods. I know you and Arya hid something from me. That would ruin our relationship."

"To tell you is to ruin you completely. Nobody could have a relationship with you afterwards, least of all yourself," she said.

"Do not protect me, Jezebel. Trust that I can handle things at least as well as you could," he said.

She told him about having heard the tapes that their daughter spoke of having been her sister Alaya, his wife, in that other life.

"Oh, that," he laughed, "I have always known."

"You have?" she sounded angry, "why have you not told me?"

"I did not want to hurt your feelings," he admitted. "She has always had the memories of her aunt Alaya. Don't you think I would recognize my wife?"

"Such a distinct personality as my sister was, you would, yes."

"Anything else I need to know?"

"No," she lied.

"What else?" he asked.

"Your parents killed her," Jezebel blurted.

"She remembers that?" His concern was for his daughter.

"Yes, she did under regression. She is fine with things, though. She blames herself for a great deal of what happened."

"How could she blame herself?"

"She thinks that her snobbism spurred them along to attack her."

"She could not help what she was and how they were," he said. "They are both dead now. Let the Lord deal with their souls. I am ever so sorry. I wish you could forgive them."

"She told your mother and they made peace," she said.

"How about you, Jezebel, what is your take on this?" he asked her.

"My take is one of glory to God. What else could my take be, dearest?" she said softly.

"What do you mean?"

She told him of the truth she heard in the tapes made with her daughter's voice. How she learned about soul groups in the other realm who told that spirits are pure and innocent, how in that state of purity, spirits judged their own faults in the scheme of things, and how in that realm things stood opposite to the way they did on earth. There, Alaya had said, selfishness was not; that only a universal love was. That dictated that all spirits made of the same energy understood the need to learn lessons so as to move the whole towards purity, and that a faltering meant the ultimate destruction of that whole. As such, Jezebel explained, her daughter understood that her ultimate test to have been furnished by his parents should have been handled in meekness. How she accepted to come back as his child while she truly loved him as a wife. Alaya was a pampered little girl come back more advanced in the spirit of humility and meekness.

"She has none of my late sister's attachments either to the things of the mind, or the material world. Part of your tradition is about hard work, and strong work ethics. That added a dimension to our child my sister had never had. That was good. So, if the universe were to have been made like this, exactly by a great Creator that sees all things, and wants the best for His creation. How could any of what happened be less than perfect? Does our Lord make mistakes, and who am I to judge His ways and means, His designs for His people?"

"You need to see their behaviour in the light of their fears," he said.

"That is the reason I could take it all fine; because love is all that I am now. He, the Manager of this great universe has prepared me to be as humbly accepting as my daughter had been so as to still and abide when she became ready to brave her endurance test. It worked fine, just fine. Through my initiation by my yogi, and the help of scores of good teachers on the path, I was prepared to accept in meekness and steadfast trust all that came my way. Seeing how your mother had gradually changed, softened, and grown, was all worth my while. We were all walking on that path of growth together although our bodies felt apart. So, that was good, very good. Look where we are today. Our family is in a good place. Love is possible now between us because we have learned that our differences are only skin deep. Love is what matters."

"They were very loving in their own ways," he rose to defend them.

"There is only one way to love: The Way," she said calmly.

"She was not an easy woman, my mother," he relented in light of her truth to honour her.

"No, she was not," Jezebel agreed.

"I don't want Arya to know that you told me," he asked.

"May I ask the reason?" she asked, hoping.

"Because, I love you," he said, "beyond love."

She bent her head to kiss the sweet bald spot a little below her. He turned around to take her hand in his to kiss and keep close to his chest.

"I have never loved a human the way I loved you, doe-eyed-Arabian angel of mine," he announced.

There, she looked up to witness a star streak a line into that dark surface of the sky above them to suddenly feel, that God, the all-knowing, had made the show just for her for this very moment of her joy. Knowing that she would see it thrilled Him. The sea beside them ruminated and hissed in the most thrilling sounds; its whoosh whooshing secrets of delirious lovers all around the globe reached both their ears to get translated by the spirit that understood sounds, and murmurs.

That took her breath away. She did not need the touch of his lips or that of his body, but his words to fill her to brimming. They, perfect in every way, had changed all realities between them from that sheer hell of insecurity to that calm trusting of being in another's full care and honesty.

"That is the gift of your parents, and my endurance," she said. "I thank them for this moment."

"What was?" he asked, pleased.

"You had asked me whether the lessons we learned were worth it," she reminded him. "Yes, they were worth each tear and each torment we lived through."

She knew that his parents listened and cheered their growth along from that sky.

"Nothing is worth that much suffering," he said, sounding sad.

"Yes, this single moment of perfect union is," she said firmly. "Lives upon lives that poor spirit sits buried inside the body for one single moment of reality such as this one. The body is like the candle that burns its flesh to light the way for others. It is the light that matters not the wax."

"Are my parents in a good place?" he asked her to startle her.

"I don't know what happens to people like that," she said truthfully.

"You need to pray for them," he asked.

"I could not. I tried. I am not that good," she told him truthfully.

"That means you are still angry with them," he stated.

"I probably am," Jezebel admitted. "Our daughter is the saint here. I still feel a chill course my blood when I see how so totally pure and loving to your family she had remained. One day, that will be my last challenge; I will achieve this pure state of love in the body."

"It will take some time," he said.

"It will," she agreed. "They test me still from beyond their graves. I have achieved the stilling of mind that wants to curse them. Eventually, I know, I will be able to pray for their souls."

"You need to teach me," he asked humbly. "I need to know now."

"I will give you some of my books," she promised. "You need to learn fast for otherwise the science will break us up. We will separate naturally otherwise."

"Do we need to be of the same religion to be married?" he asked angrily.

"No, we do not. First of all, this is not a religion; it is all religions and not one of them. The biggest fallacy concocted by man to abuse his fellow man is religion. When the Buddha was asked by his students how they could meditate, he told them to close their eyes and make the thoughts disappear. Also, he told them, 'If when you are meditating I happen to come along into your thoughts, shoo me away, away. It has nothing to do with me, and everything to do with you.' That is the purity of the man."

"What is that, we are Christians?" her pure husband said.

"I am nothing, not one thing," she said. "I have never had the need to be like you. Labels are not important to me, in fact, they shackle me like a slave. I am nothing, and everything, as such I have no need for an institution to label and file me. If you did, then, the science is not for you. The science is for the strong and wild like me."

"There is nothing wild about you. I am the tough one," he said surprised.

"I am wild in the spirit, and adventurous, you are wild in the body," she corrected. "The toughest bit about learning this science is to learn to distinguish between the two facets of your self, and learn to distinguish between their different manifestations."

"Why is that?"

"Because the body is very crafty; it knows how to mimic the spirit to neutralize it," she said.

"How could it, though? The spirit is much faster, stronger and more powerful."

"True, but the body is more focused, crude, conniving, and threatened. It has learned through many lives to watch and imitate the soft spirit's manifestations. The dim-witted would easily believe it and get lost," she said. "I have seen it happen numerous times among my friends."

"In me as well?" he asked.

"Yes, you are a master at hiding, and self delusion. You think that you are the body. We need to know who we are in reality."

"Who are we, really?"

"We are that timeless spirit we carry within to forget and get lost. The body is not our friend. The body cares nothing for us; it lies to us to survive. That is its state of badness."

They got up to go to their room. Walking slowly side by side towards their room, they heard the sound of loud music.

"There is a band playing," he said.

"A live band?" she asked.

"Yes, come, come," he pulled her inside the dark room.

People of all ages danced to the tune of Frank Sinatra's crooning, "I did it my way."

"That is my song, you know." He pulled her up, "dance with me."

She felt self-consciously old to be acting like a teen in love when he had forbidden her any fun or frolicking when she was young.

"It is okay," she said. "Let the young people dance, sit down, come."

"No," he pulled harder. "You get right up, right now before I scream above the music."

She got up to dance with him, finding a place at the very edge of the group, right by the door so as to escape notice, when to her utter mortification, the lights shone bright and the music stopped.

Everyone had magically disappeared from the dance floor. Couples, who seconds before had surrounded Jezebel, had vanished into their seats behind her, leaving the band to stare at her. It was surreal, her worst nightmare materializing to mortify her.

"What happened?" she asked as she hid inside his lapel.

The music started playing the most heart-wrenching tune just then. She tried but failed to place the beloved melody. They had played it for her graduation party, years before. When Frank Sinatra's stand-in started belting the words, she knew, it was the "Wind beneath my wings" of her beloved Bette Midler.

"That is my song," she said. "You remembered."

He spun her on the dance floor, all the while her legs felt like buckling with the knowledge that the people watched them.

"Happy birthday, beautiful Jezebel," he announced.

The band exploded with the tune of her birth, as people came from nowhere to cheer and congratulate her. Five young ladies and five young men dressed in a black and white uniform came running from the direction of the kitchen singing some cheerful tune she could not catch, then her children came in sight wheeling a huge cake with "Happy Birthday Jezebel" written all over it.

"What a sneak you are." She nudged him. "You could have tipped me for the pictures at least. I look a mess." She attempted to fix her hair.

She tried to straighten her hair with her fingers as flashes exploded in her face and people cheered joyously.

"What would they want with my pictures?" she asked.

"They are taking pictures of the cake," he corrected to relax her.

Everyone ate cake, as Eddy popped the champagne which the staff handed about in tiny plastic cups. Strangers came to offer their best wishes; some even planted kisses on her cheeks as they congratulated her over her husband and children.

"This is great," she said, finally needing to disappear.

"Good," he laughed, "we knew you would hate it. I had suggested a calm dinner in the village. Your children wanted to surprise you half to death."

"It was fine, surely surprising," she smiled.

They waved and ran outside the stuffy room.

"This is for you," he said handing her a small box.

"That is not necessary. You should not have. We are in mourning." She felt bad.

"Happy birthday," he said and kissed her.

He had finally managed to buy the watch she had been wanting for years.

"That is so beautiful, thank you."

"Should we go to sleep, you think?" he asked her.

"Yes, I think we should. It has been a most thrilling day."

Forty-Seven
ARYA FINDS HER SOUL MATE IN FARO

The aroma of coffee wafting through the room made her heart beat in sheer anticipation. She opened her eyes to find him standing over her bed with a tray filled with stainless steel pots. Some had sugar, others cream, a plate filled with sweet pastries, Danishes, rolls, tiny jars of locally made jams, sausages, breads, and croissants.

"You sure are hungry." Jezebel proclaimed groggily.

He poured her a steaming cup of coffee and placed it in her hand. She wondered at the fact that neither one of them had checked or asked about their children, ones they followed like hawks at home.

"Are the children awake?" she asked.

"Very doubtful," he said.

"Meaning?" she frowned

"They were probably awake for most of the night," he assured her.

"That is good to know." She sipped at her coffee.

They tried to watch the morning news on TV5, the only available channel that did not broadcast in Portuguese, to realise that they understood nothing as it was local, French events these covered.

"That is the only drawback of a vacation," he said, pained.

"It is intended to change the monotony of our lives," she replied.

"The world could be crumbling as we sit munching on croissants," he said.

"What could we possibly do to help a crumbling world, anyway?" she asked.

"You are right, of course." He sipped his coffee as he snickered. "We get so used to doing the same things over and over."

"Yes, we do," she agreed.

Portugal offered a welcome, if strangely alien, respite from the assaulting emotions of late; as they knew not a soul in the country over whom to fret about the reputation of their children and their conduct.

Edward and his father played a great deal of tennis while the ladies indulged in hours of massaging, swimming and yoga classes.

The different members of her family dispersed to different destination of interest to meet only over meals. Having missed the dinner the night before, Jezebel had seen them over lunch last. As the men ran towards the bar, Arya and her mother had remained on the terrace overlooking the ocean.

"Who is the young man you spoke to just now?" Jezebel asked.

"He is a doctor on vacation from Dallas, Texas." Arya blushed to worry Jezebel.

"An American?" her mother asked fearing other nationalities. "Is that the young man you admired upon our arrival?"

"Yes," her daughter replied simply.

"You seem close. When did you have time to get close to anyone? It is not like you."

"I like him. Steve is sweet, compassionate and deeply caring."

"Where did you see him?"

"At the night clubs, the pool, everywhere," Arya smiled enticingly.

"I see. There will be no telling how your father should take this new development in his life."

"Try to soften him up, won't you?"

"I will," Jezebel promised, unsure.

That night Steve ate dinner at their family's table. They went to their rooms knowing that Arya and Steve were deeply in love. Such were the vibes emanating from their persons.

"I like him." Father beamed for his daughter.

"I do, too. He is so sweet. They will make a great couple," Jezebel agreed.

Two days before the family was due to return home, Steve came to the swimming pool where they shared a morning cup of coffee, to ask if they would consider delaying their trip back as to give him and Arya additional time to get to know one another. They agreed to look into it. They went down to administration and succeeded in stretching their stay for an additional week.

"I called the hospital to ask for an extension. They were not too happy, but they approved it," he returned to inform them.

Now that the week stretched before them, everyone seemed to relax, opting for delaying the fretting over the unknown they all sensed looming ahead.

Jezebel went for a facial and a massage alone, as the three men joined the early morning gym class. Nobody knew where Arya was.

Feelings of the most confused assailed the parents; the prospect of marriage looming over their horizon. The man their daughter loved was every bit the gentleman they had hoped her to meet. There hovered over them the nagging feeling that she was to marry a foreigner. Jezebel understood how this fact could depress her husband.

He was a tall man, with a superb physique. His Celtic background accounted for the deep blue eyes, and sandy blond hair. Above all else, Steven was a decent, if boring, human being.

"Decent males are never enticingly spellbinding," her husband explained. "If they were to be riveting characters, females would not allow them to remain decent."

"I don't know about that," she mused. "My father was both, spellbinding and decent. That is not an outwardly bound trait, but ingrained and rooted in the being."

"Yes, sure, you are right of course, still on the whole it is easier to remain grounded when a man is less riveting," he insisted.

Riveting or not, Steven possessed a togetherness about him that bespoke of deep breeding on lines of decency, she thought. He would make some woman a fine, decent husband. One never needed worry about his whereabouts, or fear some strange woman wooing him away so as to make a point of her own. Steven exuded self-control as well as calm confidence.

Over that lunch they shared, he spoke about his family. They were of European roots, he said, on the paternal side, of Eastern, Russian ones from his maternal side, come to the country some hundred years before. They had kept the cooking intact, handing it down through the generations.

"My mother had converted my father into the Greek Orthodox faith as a condition for their marriage," he said, laughing.

"It is the opposite with my parents," Arya's father confided, "my father converted my mother from Greek Orthodox to Protestant so as to marry her."

"That is the East for you," Jezebel commented, "the rule by males."

"Not in the US," Steven commented. "There, women rule."

"Good for them, then," Jezebel thought, pleased for her Arya.

"Not so good, either camp loses by generating resentments," Steven added. "There should be a fluidity of oneness."

They stared each other in shocked respect; the man Arya loved was a being of secure fairness, one he wanted to extend to women as to share in love, not authority.

"So, Lebanon is beautiful," Steve stated. "Has it survived that last civil war intact?"

"It is on its way back in a slow, if sure, recovery," the father assured him.

"Is it safe for Americans to visit?"

"There lives a huge American community there still from before the war," Jezebel assured him. "More are arriving daily, I am sure."

"Good to know. It is a shame what happened there," he said.

Soon they dispersed to different bungalows for a brief rest before the cocktail hour. Jezebel and her husband left them sitting at the table still.

"We will see you later," the parents chimed.

"Later, mom, dad," Edward responded, "coffee by the pool, later?"

"Yes," they said.

"Steven and I have signed up for a Swim-Gym," their son informed them.

"See you there then," his father said.

They left them exalted over their vacation extension, the girl especially, making plans to hire a rental car to tour the country.

"I will be their chaperone." Edward swore solemnly.

The week flew by with the parents seeing very little of the young people; who booked early-morning tours, and flew by the land as to enjoy the sights and one another.

What with the free time, Jezebel and her husband spoke a great deal; a curious habit never afforded them in the past, what with his incessant work travels, and his parent's demands. She felt like a stranger speaking to him, also found that she kept a great deal tucked away nicely from him without noticing it. He had grown mistrusted over the years. He, she found, spoke freely, scarcely noticing the lapses in time that had separated them; as though he expected nothing from her, had never done, harboured no resentments, hid nothing. It was odd to see the man just be, without a past.

His was purity in motion, needing no analysis, wanting none. That facet of him startled her. When once she thought him wickedly scheming, she discovered that what she thought he hid were things he did not deem worthy of raising a stink over, so he dropped them.

"What makes you angry?" she asked him that day.

"Someone disrupting my peace," he answered quickly.

"You?" he turned the question on her.

"Someone insulting my intelligence," she said.

"You people are hugely egoistical," he alleged.

"I guess we people are," she answered, and laughed.

She remembered having asked him that first week of their honeymoon not refer to them as you people, to no avail, four decades later, he still did that.

"What is so funny?" he asked her.

"Nothing is, honest," she'd replied.

"You make fun of me, I know," he presumed.

"Honestly, no, it is just a passing thought," she skirted the subject.

"Do tell, Jezebel," he encouraged.

"It is okay. It no longer matters."

A week later, Steve asked to meet Arya's parents again. He had sent Edward to find them. He came over to the coffee shop, hut, by the seashore, to find them sharing a stack of French fries. He said that he had been looking for hours.

"Why do you two hide?" he admonished.

"We are free agents, Edward, with nothing to do but hide," his father said.

"Steven wants to speak to you," their son said.

They went up the long winding stairs, to halt, and resume their climb, all the way down the other side, the poolside, where Steven sat under an umbrella awaiting them.

"I would like to ask for Arya's hand in marriage," he said softly. "I have never met a more amazing woman than your daughter."

"Thank you," the father replied nervously, "it is a bit sudden. Don't you think?"

"It is soon, however, we are both very sure. I never get a chance to take a two-week vacation, so it is now or in two years." Steve sounded reasonably logical, if nervously breathless.

"Can we discuss this and get back to you on it?" the father asked.

"Sure," Steve said, and jumped in the pool.

Jezebel smiled at the prospect of her daughter's happiness, though fearing the distances that would separate them.

"I have no objection. Arya is a wise young lady," she told her husband.

"Oh, I don't know," he vented his worries. "It is too sudden for my taste. We don't know this man, the family he comes from. To send our only daughter to the end of the world disturbs me on more level than one."

"We will meet his parents before the wedding, surely. As to the end of the world, Arya is the only naturally-born American member of the family. The child relates to her birthplace. While it stands alien to you, the US is home for her. To her mind, our daughter is marrying a compatriot, not a foreigner."

"True, and all, but there is still the matter of his background. In our country, we know people, their backgrounds, genetic strength and weaknesses. We are flying blind here. That is dangerous."

"That is the global village. Young people cannot see that division. Steve looks like a good sort."

"I still believe it is a rash decision to make. We need time to investigate this man. When once a man came to ask for a woman's hand from her parents, her entire clan met to investigate the matter seriously. They sent people to ask of the family inside his village. There were specific topics needing tackling: His bloodline, diseases, temperaments, characters. Mostly, however, they asked about usage of alcohol, gambling and womanizing."

"Surely that is unnecessary." Jezebel giggled. "If you so cared about these archaic concerns, why then did you raise these children in the West?"

"I raised them there to offer them opportunities of education, of travel, hoping to bring them back to our country and settle them down."

"They have nothing in common with the young people of our country, though, would never marry inside our culture. I cannot imagine progressive Arya settling down with some bigot who expects her to obey, serve him and raise his brood."

"You are right, of course. But, Jezebel, to plant Arya and Edward in the West means that we would need to move back there ourselves. The West is very hard on old people. I have hankered growing old in our country with friends and family." The dilemma at hand distressed him.

"Let us bless their union while we check on his background," she suggested, advancing a temporary solution.

Jezebel had always projected her family in just such dilemma. It pained her to see him thus shattered, as she bemoaned his lack of projection. Their children belonged to an international community; having roamed the world of their brethren in sheer boldness. They had left the US to live in India, Lebanon, back to the US, back to Greece, back to the US, back to Lebanon. Among other places of residence, they had visited for their vacations the four corners of the world. Both Arya and Edward spoke four languages each. To expect them to belong to one country stood ridiculous to her mind.

"Sure, we give our blessing, and check," he announced, unnerved still. "I like the young man well enough. He looks decent."

Both Edward and Steven had left the couple to join a swimming gym class nearby where a stunning blonde jumped up and down shouting directions from the sides to the swimmers, who giggled lewdly as they followed her lead.

Edward looked delighted with the prospective brother-in-law, seeming to think the prospect delightful.

He darted looks towards his parents sitting on lounge chairs on the deck nearby to get the thumbs-up from his smiling mother, to turn and whisper something inside the man's ear beside him.

Steve got out, ran to them, kissed his future mother-in-law on both cheeks, hugged the father, and ran to inform his beloved Arya of her parents' approval.

"God bless you, son," Arya's father said, his voice breaking.

"Thank you, thank you. I promise never to disappoint you."

"You better think of a good proposal," Eddy told him. "She is very romantic, my sister."

"Yes, yes, what do you think?" Steve could not think straight.

"A balloon ride over the bay. There, you will tell her."

"Your parents know. I fear they will tell her before me."

"I shall go inform them of your plans. Go and arrange for a balloon ride for the two of you. Take a basket of champagne, an assortment of local cheeses, and maybe some grapes. You know, Steve. My sister remembers many lives and still harbours resentment towards her past-life husband's shabby wedding announcement, so watch it."

"The ring, would you go with me to pick a ring?" Steve asked panicked.

"Absolutely, let us run before mother spoils your plans." Eddy ran towards his parents sitting still by the poolside.

"Not a word mom to Arya, Steven wants to surprise her," he emphatically directed. "Not a word, from you, not a smile, a hint or anything."

"Fine, fine, I promise."

"Where is Arya?" Eddy asked.

"At the gym still," she informed him. "Does she have a clue to his intentions?"

"Not a clue," Eddy told his parents, "she was crying last night when she thought we were leaving in two days. She loves him. I have never seen her like that. You know Arya; she was never interested in any of the boys she met. She found our boys shallow, and selfish."

"Fine, then. See to it that she is safe with the proposal. We don't want an accident in that balloon ride," his father cautioned.

"I will arrange for the balloon myself, dad. Please, try to smile. It is not the end of the world. You need to be happy for her. I know, I know, it is too far from us, and we will miss her miserably. We have to think of their happiness. He is a class act, Steve. I like him very much." Edward was thrilled with the new brother.

It was hours before Arya surfaced, by then the men had purchased her ring, and smiled broadly her way mysteriously.

"What?" Arya asked checking her blouse.

"Nothing," Eddy responded and giggled like a boy.

"Mother, what is going on?"

Jezebel and her husband could scarcely look their daughter's way.

"You are all hiding something from me. Steve, what is it?" Arya asked.

"How should I know, Arya? Ask your father," Jezebel said.

Father giggled softly, winking towards the man who would soon marry his beloved daughter.

"You two are conspiring against me?" she said, happy that they got along well.

"Well, Steve has booked a balloon flight and a picnic for the two of you. We are all giggling because we know about your fear of height," Edward told his sister.

"Oh, no Steve," Arya paled. "I am acrophobic."

"I will be right there with you. It will be fun, no fear." Steve smiled softly to assure her.

And so the next morning, the entire family rode in the car towards the field from where the balloons flew.

Arya looked calm if clearly shaken. Her parents feared that she could freak out on Steve inside the balloon to ruin the surprise.

"Steve," Eddy said, "she could easily go bonkers up there on you. What would you do?"

"What does she usually do?" Steve needed information to remedy the dire eventuality.

"She usually has a full-fledged panic attack. You know, hyperventilation, sweaty palms, all that."

"I have a pill," Steve said. "Get me a paper sack from the shop."

"What is it for?" Eddy asked.

"For her to breathe into," Steve explained. "Don't worry, I know what to do. Just, please a paper sack; the type they package fruits in."

Edward ran toward the shop to fetch the paper sack that Steve asked for.

"How long a ride is it?" Arya asked him as he came back.

"Not long, Arya, relax. It is fun, don't think bad thoughts. Tell yourself it is going to be fun, and it will be. Do not go panicky on the man now."

She threw the empty Coca-Cola can on his head.

"I bet it is your idea of a date, you old bastard," she laughed.

"The fact that you are willing to brave height for him is a good sign indeed." Eddy taunted his sister.

They kissed the pair goodbye, and watched until the balloon rose in the sky.

"What a romantic way to propose a marriage." Jezebel beamed.

"I wish someone had taught us these things." Husband looked guilty. "We did not know these things were possible."

"Don't you worry, old man, you are the best with imaginative proposals and without them," Jezebel assured her husband.

Their son drove them in the hired car back to the hotel planning to return and await the couple on the ground.

"We need to celebrate this announcement," Eddy suggested. "What should we do, you think?"

"What if she does not accept?" Father fretted. "It could get sticky."

"That would be terribly embarrassing," Eddy said. "She would, surely. She speaks of nothing else. Knowing the self-control my sister is capable of, one never knows, though."

"We will make a plan in case she accepts," Jezebel suggested.

"Like, what do you think, dad?" Eddy could not think of anything.

"Like maybe dinner and champagne somewhere nice," his father offered.

"They are doing just that." Eddy despaired. "He bought caviar and pate de foie gras, cheeses, and all kinds of fancy stuff."

"What then?" Father despaired for a solution to celebrate. "Who would we invite, we don't know anyone here?"

"I don't know. I wish we were home; we would have given them a big party with all the family, and dancing, and joy. The family could use some of that stuff." Jezebel felt saddened by their isolation.

"That is out of the question, so soon after the death of both my parents. Not seemly. People will talk," the father reminded them.

"Yes, true," Jezebel agreed.

"Don't feel bad." He patted her hand. "It is normal for you to be happy for your only daughter."

"Thank you."

"Okay, you two. Enough loving," Eddy shrieked.

"Yes," his father agreed. "Going home is out of the question. How about if we all flew with Steve and spent a week in his hometown. There, we could give him a celebration, and invite all his friends and family."

"What a brilliant idea." Eddy grew distraught with nerves, "Dad, how about tonight? We need to do something soon, tonight, here, fast. I am already running late for their landing."

"Beside dinner, there is nothing we could do here. This is a resort, Eddy. What could we do?"

"Dad, the food here is free, and the drinks. We need to think of something creative to celebrate for them."

"A boat," Jezebel said as she watched a party of revellers in a boat, "and a band."

Eddy loved the idea.

"Where could we rent one?" he asked his parents.

"Find out. You, my son, are the most resourceful lad I know. So, use that ability to get us a boat to rent and fast. If not for tonight, then tomorrow night will do nicely," his father suggested.

"Steve knows a group of Americans he introduced us to. We could ask them to join us."

"What do we do about food and drinks?" Jezebel asked.

"Go talk to the chef inside the hotel. As all the invitees are from this club, they have to furnish food and drinks." Eddy ran towards the field to pick the couple back. "I am sure he would not mind. Seeing the vast amounts of food these people throw about, a few baskets for a party would be fine."

They arranged things with the headwaiter, and agreed on a set menu to be delivered to the boat on the docks by the hotel, hoping that their son could arrange for the boat.

They returned joyous with good news. The ride, Arya explained, was the most amazing event that had happened to her, ever. She had agreed to his proposal with absolute certainty, and had agreed to marry him in three months, in a Christmas wedding.

"Christmas Arya, in the cold, in three months, too fast," Jezebel disapproved vehemently. "Do not rush things, please. We need to take time with this. I am not ready to let go of my only daughter as fast as that. I need adjusting time." She broke down and cried bitterly.

"Oh, mom no, don't cry, my darling," Arya cried as she held her mother. "That is supposed to be good, my love."

"Don't ruin her engagement day," her husband whispered in her ear.

He ran to hug Steven, who had arrived with their son.

"Congratulations son, welcome to our family. I wish you both the best." His voice quivered, belying his obvious joy.

Steve bent down to hug Jezebel, understanding the tears.

"I will take care of her, Jezebel. You can visit and come stay with us any time."

"I have always wanted a brooding winter wonderland." Arya informed them.

"Would you be ready, though, in three months? I can't see the need for rushing this," the father needed to understand.

"Sure," Steve assured him. "We are having the simplest ceremony. We decided to invite fifty people each; the closest and dearest."

"Why can't you postpone the wedding until Easter time; the weather is better, as three extra months would give us enough time to prepare our own parties in our country for the family. We cannot let her go without a reception," Jezebel tried to convince them.

"No," Steve informed them, "only over the Christmas holidays could I get an extended leave. She wants a Caribbean honeymoon. That is the only way we could have a break. The islands are warm and beautiful around that time of year."

That clinched it. Her parents had always known of their daughter's wishes for that exotic honeymoon.

"Fine," she said, "Christmas it will be. We will be fine. Good luck. May the Lord bless you," Jezebel relented happily.

That evening, the entire world conspired to make their party an unforgettable event. Edward had arranged a band of young musicians to join them on the boat. He had ordered the cruiser decorated with rose petals strewn on the entire deck, and a garlanded arch under which the couple walked. These were Arya's favourite, pink roses, and white for Steve.

Upon seeing the efforts her brother exerted on organizing her engagement party, Arya surrendered to a fit of tears. She ran to him, hugged his neck and thanked him tenderly. Steve joined them in a group, bear hug.

"What a nice man he is," Jezebel told her husband.

"They make a beautiful couple," he told her proudly. "And our Eddy adores the man."

"Eddy has found a brother in Steven. They are so compatible the three of them," Jezebel stated.

The sun wore its best orange cloak just for Arya and the man who deserved her. It played games on the deck to entice the people who came to share her beloved's happiness. It danced on Arya's red hair, her eyes, her skin, making the woman look luminous with joy. The sea behaved as well lulling them softly inside her tender bosom. That, along the soft music from the violin, made for a magical atmosphere.

Soon, a constellation of stars exploded overhead, twinkling, twinkling away their love to Arya of the skies who had so suffered, so tolerated, to finally come out the other side unscarred, pure and triumphant.

The moon rose just for Arya that night. It rose right over the boat, as the woman danced her first dance with the man who would share her life and children.

"I love you," Steve said to her.

"I love you, Steven. I have waited for you for many years."

He kissed the side of her hair, as he glanced over to where her parents sat watching them.

"We will have a good life, no matter what happens," he promised.

"I know, I know," she nodded.

"How do you know?" Steve asked surprised at her answer.

"I know a great deal of things, Steve. I have always been intuitive."

"Fine then, tell me. How many children are we going to have?"

"We shall have two children. The first one shall be a girl, Claire, and the second one a boy, and his name shall be Daniel."

"Why only two children, Arya?" he wanted to know.

"Because that is what is written in the sky, Steve darling. We shall be good parents to these two people, raise them in our faith in the earth, tenderness, and fairness. Two is a good number, Steve."

"Why is that, darling?" he asked her.

"It just is," she smiled.

He encircled her within his arms, and squeezed, wanting to never let go.

"Let go, you are embarrassing me," she begged.

"I do not know if I am going to be able to wait three months," he said.

"We will be fine. Three months is not a long time. They will fly by. Maybe you could come over to my country to meet the family around Thanksgiving."

"Absolutely, consider it done." He kissed her hand gently.

With that, they danced the night away, drank champagne and roamed the stars and the sea, hope dancing over the waves for their future together.

Watching the couple Jezebel and her husband felt happy, secure that their Arya had found her mate, one she picked to find love and a new life on the new continent.

"It is a new life for Arya," he said. "I am happy for her."

"She is the daughter of Phoenicia, with roots that go back for centuries in the culture," her mother said, "I feel sad for the wrenching of roots. Her children will be mixed."

"Arya's miseries stem directly from this very attachment to land and lineage. It is the many memories, bad ones, as well as good ones, that had marred her life, making it impossible for her to live a simple life," her husband said to thrill her.

Jezebel jumped to hug him, kiss his face, to cry and cry.

"What happened to you? What have I said to deserve this?" he looked shocked by her abandon.

"You found it. You have found it. You are right. A wrenching of her roots is what she needs most. Our family seeped in an ongoing feud with a past of glories we could never let go. Arya is undoubtedly one of those leaders of our country that had somehow believed the country their property to never allow others in the nation rule. They have ruled the land for years, to die and return tortured by the obsessive need, greed, and attachment. The reason our daughter had chosen a foreigner, from the other side of the globe; with little respect to her blood, and the fallacy of its purity, its higher ranking, and sanctity, is because she has grown, grown. Can't you see it?" Jezebel explained.

"Not in so many details, but yes. It would do her good," he agreed.

"That proves that Arya is moving in growth. Attachment to things of the body is shattering. It can impede the divine's manifestations. She is finally out of that deep hole which had marred her lives, creating a false centre that destroyed any possibility of ever conducting a normal life. It is miraculous."

"What is?" she had lost him.

"You see, it is a known fact among the people who understood that all the world's populations grow in depth and spirit life after life, except the rulers of nations."

"Why is that?" he asked surprised. "That is horrible."

"They grow their false centres which become too hardened by greed and their memories of having ruled the people, never to be softened. Do you realize the work this child has done on herself so as to finally soften enough to let go of all that baggage and hardness. It is nothing short of miraculous." Jezebel was delighted at the discovery.

"Is Arya finally saved, you think?" he asked his wife.

"I don't know about being saved," Jezebel told him truthfully. "I only know that she is making progress towards salvation."

"Is this a good marriage?" he wanted to know.

"I don't believe so. I believe that this marriage is a pivotal step towards something better and bigger."

"This is awful. How could you say things like that? After all, we have just celebrated the woman's engagement."

"You asked my opinion. A successful marriage is one that is conducted on deeper, more serious grounds. It has to be divinely fated, minutely studied: on grounds of compatibility as well as depth of emotions. None of that is present here. The only thing I can see happening is the fact that Arya needs to learn a final lesson in spiritual surrendering, one she would get from this marriage so she could take the next step."

Disgusted, he got up, huffed, and left her.

About The Author

Born, Clemence Massaad, in the town of Rayak, Hosh Hala, of Lebanon's Bekaa valley, the author was raised in the town of Shekka, where her father relocated to start the Eternit Company. Their first house sitting by the majestic Mediterranean sea, furnished a space of silent meditating, managing to nurture a great deal of insightful seeking. She married her husband, Samir Musa, a Chemical Engineer, also from Lebanon, and together they moved to the United States, where she studied Psychology, and Journalism. The couple have three children, Indee, Abie and Sandra. Indee and Abie live in Texas, while Sandra, a student of Oxford Brooks, Oxford, of Great Britain, remains in England with her parents. Clemence Massaad Musa is the writer of "Lebanon, A Journey of Beauty," and "Chrysalis". "Arya," is the author's third book. The author is an avid reader of spiritual books, a sea lover, and a champion of humanity at large. Her lifelong dream is to see peace, not war, become the way forward for the planet. The couple live in the Great Windsor region, Berkshire, inside Templewood Forest, an idyllic setting and back-drop to seeking and writing. Their three children, and Celine, their first and only grand-child, are constant and cherished visitors to their home.

Printed in the United Kingdom
by Lightning Source UK Ltd.
114330UKS00002B/28-33